W9-DIV-934

LIVING
BACKWARDS

By Tracy Sweeney

Living Backwards by Tracy Sweeney. ISBN 978-1-62137-186-1.

Cover design by Elizabeth Jaeger.

Published 2013 by Virtualbookworm.com Publishing Inc., P.O. Box 9949, College Station, TX 77842, US. ©2013, Tracy Sweeney. All rights reserved. No part of this publication may be reproduced, stored in a retrieval system, or transmitted in any form or by any means, electronic, mechanical, recording or otherwise, without permission in writing from Tracy Sweeney.

Special Thanks

To my sister Lindsay – my first reader and my best friend. You made this possible.

To Carol – who scoured over every word with me. Eleventy billion times. You're magnificent. Just saying…

To my Mom – for being an inspiration. Because you can't have a little grace.

To Nina – I could never fully tell you how much your help and guidance has meant to me. Editor, therapist, superwoman, Meryl to my Albert. I love your hair.

To Sarine – you're ridiculously talented. I'm lucky to have you around to tell me when something stinks.

To my family – for being patient and understanding when my fingers were flying over the keys and my head was in the clouds.

To Gina, Kim and Nicole – the best cheerleaders and best friends ever.

To my Chicks and Hens, my Put Gals and all of the countless pre-readers who cheered me on along the way – I tip my pink sparkly flask to all of you. You're epic.

xoxo

Tracy

"I don't understand you," said Alice. "It's dreadfully confusing!"

"That's the effect of living backwards," the Queen said kindly: "it always makes one a little giddy at first—"

"Living backwards!" Alice repeated in great astonishment. "I never heard of such a thing!"

"...For instance, now," she went on, "...there's the King's Messenger. He's in prison now, being punished: and the trial doesn't even begin till next Wednesday: and of course the crime comes last of all."

"Suppose he never commits the crime?" said Alice.

"That would be all the better, wouldn't it?" the Queen said.

- *Through the Looking Glass* by Lewis Carroll

CHAPTER 1

Jillian

I learned an important life lesson at Carrie Picalow's slumber party when I was just ten-years-old: Horror movies are awesome…until it's time to go to sleep. Sure they're fun for two hours while you scream with your friends, but the following eight hours spent squeezing your eyes shut and attempting to fall asleep are torture. I made a vow to stay away from horror movies from there on out, but it never really worked. If I knew there was a scary movie on, I'd flip by the channel to get a peek. If I felt particularly brave, I'd stop and watch for a few minutes with my fingers partially covering my eyes. Even though I knew I shouldn't—even though I knew I'd be up all night staring at my closet convincing myself that there wasn't a scary little girl or a deranged clown inside—I'd watch. I couldn't stop myself. And just as I would have predicted, I'd spend the rest of the night huddled under my covers.

I got the same feeling every time I stared across the room at the computer on my desk. When I'd sit down and open up my browser, I wouldn't just check my email. I wouldn't check the weather or the local headlines either. No. Even though I knew I shouldn't—even though I knew it would only irritate me—I'd do something worse than watching a horror movie. I'd log onto Facebook.

Thanks to the so-called geniuses behind Facebook, suddenly people felt compelled to broadcast every thought, idea or mindless observation in their head on a minute-by-minute basis. But the worst part was that I couldn't look away. It probably wouldn't bother me as much if I actually knew any of the people complaining about having to go to work or needing their morning coffee. I didn't. Not really. My timeline was full of people whose names I knew—kids who went to my high school and lived in my town—but I wouldn't call them friends. Sure, I remembered that I had chemistry with that guy, and lived down the street from that girl, but I didn't hang out with them. Or anyone really. Now, over ten years later, I knew every detail of their lives.

Last week, Tyler Burroughs tagged our whole Reynolds High School class in his Twenty-Five Things About Me post. I couldn't understand why he thought I'd be interested. I hadn't seen Tyler in over a decade and I barely knew him then, so I could say without a doubt that I didn't care that he was still a terrible driver and almost lost his license twice. I didn't care that he went to Comic-Con and met Joss Whedon in the men's room. Unless Joss was whipping out

1

long lost *Buffy* footage, it didn't interest me. But for some reason, I kept coming back. Facebook had become the horror movie I was destined to watch every day of my life.

I blame my best friend Danielle who practically forced me into creating a profile. "Everyone is on Facebook, Jillian," she informed me. "Even my papa. Don't you want to be cooler than my papa?"

I couldn't argue with that logic so I gave in and joined the world of social networking. Now thanks to Danielle, I was able to view people I barely knew discuss high school parties I hadn't been invited to, dances I'd never attended and places I'd never been.

It really wasn't her fault. High school was different for Danielle. We went to the same school, but we didn't exactly run in the same circles back then. She was popular and outgoing, and I was...well...mute.

Looking back now, I didn't have a lot in common with *that* girl anymore. People change. And in my case, for the better, I think. I left the shy me back in the school library, eating lunch alone and chatting with the librarian because everything was different once I left Reynolds, Washington, for New York City.

It was during Summer Freshman Orientation at NYU that I ran into Danielle. Literally. I was walking through the quad daydreaming when I nearly plowed over what I thought was a small child. My backpack and papers went flying in the air, and I landed flat on my ass.

"Jillian Cross!" she exclaimed. "What are you doing here? How did I not know you were going to NYU?"

I winced from the pain in my behind and looked up into the pale blue eyes of Danielle Powers. Danielle was someone I had occasionally said hi to, but it was never much more than that. She was in my World Lit class senior year, she was exceptionally perky, and after bouncing off her, ridiculously sturdy for such a small little thing. With her button nose and short, stylish bob, she reminded me more of a cartoon character than an actual person.

"Danielle, wow," I stammered, suddenly feeling self-conscious. "I didn't know anyone else from Reynolds would be here."

"This is fantastic! Do you have a room assignment? We need to change it. You have to room with me and Megan."

Megan Dunn, Danielle's best friend, was practically an amazon—tall, beautiful and fierce with long, flowing blonde hair like the supermodels I envied as a kid. Megan was stunning, but she scared the living crap out of me.

Although every guy in our class would seem to lose control of their motor functions in her presence, Megan never seemed to care. She actually always looked like she wanted to kick someone's ass. Rooming with her sounded scary, but if I truly wanted a change of pace—a new life—I felt like I needed to say yes...and *then* make sure she didn't want to kick my ass.

There was something about our friendship from the beginning; we just clicked. I wished I had known that in high school because it felt like we were destined to be best friends. Danielle pushed me to break out of my shell and live instead of watching life pass me by. And Megan, not so fierce after all, could always see through my bullshit and set me straight. She became my rock.

So when we headed back to Washington after graduation, Megan found an apartment in Seattle near an Irish pub that serves amazing nachos. It was only a couple hours away from Reynolds so that was useful, too. Danielle worked long hours as the co-owner of an interior design business. Megan scored a position at one of the area's most prestigious art galleries, and I spent my days researching ways to remove stains from household furniture and water rings from wood tables for Homegrown Magazine.

Looking back, it was hard to imagine how I survived without them. Knocking Danielle over in the quad that day changed everything for me. I probably wouldn't have been on a first name basis with the school librarian if I had figured out how great they were a lot sooner. Although Judy was lovely and her book club friends were very nice, they were kind of geriatric and not a lot of fun on a Saturday night. I would have given up the pass on late fees in exchange for the memories Danielle and Megan had of high school parties, dates and proms.

It was Danielle's belief that I should make up for lost time. After insisting that I set up a Facebook account, she then decided that we actually needed to *see* these people in person. I nearly had a heart attack when she announced her plans for an informal high school reunion. I suddenly felt the need to retreat to the closest Reference Room for comfort.

"Jillian, I don't understand why you're so upset about this. You have us now," she reasoned. "And this is your chance to show all of the people who never got to know you how awesome you are. Plus, you'll get another peek at the Reconstruction of Sarah Spellman."

After going to a less-than-reputable surgeon for a breast augmentation, our former classmate's boobs were now crooked. We didn't run into her often— only every now and then—but when we did, I couldn't help but stare. The asymmetry was almost hypnotic. Like if you looked at them long enough, maybe they'd realign. That's what you get for buying a plastic surgery Groupon.

3

"As much as I'm just dying to see Sarah's bad boob job again, it's not enough to get me excited about a high school reunion."

"You can always bring Joan," she replied.

Danielle knew my weaknesses well. Joan was my beautiful, pink rhinestone flask, a gift she had given me for my twenty-first birthday. Joan was my savior. Danielle named her after she caught me talking to myself one night in the midst of a particularly rough evening with Captain Morgan. Like Joan of Arc, I had been hearing voices, too. My voices, however, were alcohol-induced and coming from a pink, sparkly inanimate object. *C'mon Jillian, you deserve a break. C'mon Jillian, you know you think he's cute. C'mon Jillian, you love this song. C'mon Jillian, it'll be fun.*

It had been one of those typical drunk college girl evenings where I threw myself at a guy in my Philosophy class, danced on a table, fell off said table, twisted my ankle and ended up getting carried back to our suite by some burnouts who reminded me of Beavis and Butthead. When Danielle came home, I was pouting while nursing my throbbing ankle.

"It's not my fault!" I cried, defensive under her condescending stare. "My good old buddy Joan wanted a shot at Mark Jensen. I mean have you seen that boy's—"

"Jillian, honey, I'm so glad that you're letting loose and enjoying yourself. Truly, I am," she began carefully. "But it's time to ease up on the cocktails once you start chatting with your flask. Talking flasks are not cool. Okay?"

But the truth of the matter was that I had more fun when Joan got me into trouble. I had spent so much of my time hiding in the library in high school. I wanted to go to parties and dance on tables and kiss cute boys. Joan helped transform me from the quiet girl who ate lunch in the library by herself to the charming and mildly-alcoholic woman I was today. And I liked that.

It had been Joan's idea to go to the party that night. *C'mon Jillian, you deserve a break.* It was Joan's idea to jump on top of Mark Jensen and shove my tongue down his throat. *C'mon Jillian, you know you think he's cute.* It was Joan's idea to dance on that table. *C'mon Jillian, you love this song.* And it was Joan's idea to tell Beavis that I'd go to Laser Zeppelin with him the next weekend. *C'mon Jillian, it'll be fun.* Unfortunately, in that case, Joan wasn't right.

But even now, years later, Joan still had my back. Uncomfortable work function to attend? Trusty flask in my purse. Stuffy interior design conference with Danielle? Flask in my purse. Football game with Megan? Flask in my purse. No, Joan didn't actually speak to me, but she always heard me when I needed her.

Sitting at my computer with a glass of wine by my side, I read through my timeline again. There was a message from Sarah Spellman in my inbox.

Danielle told me that you'll be at the little soiree on Saturday night. I completely forgot that you even went to high school with us. Isn't that crazy!? I always think of you as Danielle and Megan's roommate. I'm sure we'll have time to chat about good old Reynolds High on Saturday. Kisses.

God, I really hated Facebook.

CHAPTER 2

Jillian

I heard them entering my bedroom attempting to be quiet as soon as the door creaked open. It was a weak attempt because there wasn't much that was subtle about Megan or Danielle. I wanted to open my eyes and kick their asses for waking me up so early on a Saturday, but it felt as if someone had inserted a skewer right into my eye socket and stabbed my brain. The pain radiating from my eye throughout my entire skull was excruciating. My mouth was dry and my stomach was lurching. I quickly tried to remember what had taken place the night before and why someone would try to murder me in my sleep. Then I remembered the bottle of wine I opened to drown my Facebook sorrows. It seemed like a good idea at the time.

"Jillian, you little tramp," Megan, master of subtlety, shrieked. "You were cyber-stalking on Facebook last night!"

I slowly pried my eyes open and felt around my head searching for the skewer because I was still not convinced that something so yummy could inflict so much pain. It wasn't until I saw the empty bottle next to the computer screen that I finally could admit that I had the hangover of the century…or of the week. Whichever.

As if they weren't already loud enough, I heard Danielle squeal.

"Luke Chambers, Jillian? You were cyber-stalking Luke?" she asked incredulously. "Where the heck did *that* come from?"

I blanched. Where *did* that come from? I barely knew Luke Chambers. Definitely not a circle I ran in. In high school, Luke was all leather jackets and motorcycles—the embodiment of a modern day James Dean. He certainly wasn't known for hanging out in the library with quiet coeds and their elderly librarian buddies.

"I was not," I countered, sounding more like a guilty toddler than I'd like. "You're out of your mind. I probably saw his profile and got curious."

"I don't know, Jill," Megan added cautiously. "Looks like you sent him a Friend Request. I guess you weren't stalking. You were definitely fishing."

Immediately, I was pissed. I had been physically assaulted by a yummy yet dangerous bottle of chardonnay, woken up ridiculously early on my day off and then accused of some imaginary crush.

"Too bad Luke can't make it to the reunion tonight," Danielle offered. "He emailed me last week. He owns that bar downtown that his cousin used to run. His cousin moved back to Canada and Luke bought it. I guess it's busy and he can't take a night off. I'm glad he's doing well, though. He always seemed kind of lost in high school."

"Sorry, Jilly," Megan cooed. "Looks like you're going to have to set your sights elsewhere. Unless Luke has a talking flask, too. Maybe we can get your flask to convince his flask to come to the reunion."

"Okay, okay, you've had your fun," I finally shouted. "Now kindly remove your asses from my room."

"See. I told you she needs a boyfriend," Megan muttered under her breath. "So cranky."

"Actually, we just wanted to tell you we were running to the mall to get a few things for our outfits tonight," Danielle explained. "I'm not going to drag you along, but I'm going to ask that you wear what I buy you."

Danielle had also decided that it would be fun to dress like it was 1999. Seriously. I knew she wanted to get me into one of those ridiculously tight t-shirts and some low-rise jeans, but in reality, I wouldn't have been caught dead wearing something like that in 1999. But reality never stopped Danielle. She'd win, so why fight her? As long as I was spared from her version of retail therapy and could stay in bed, I was happy.

"Fine. I will comply with your wardrobe suggestions. But now, Posh," I motioned to Megan, "please take Scary over here and leave me and my hangover alone."

Unfortunately, though, after my roommates left the apartment in search of outdated attire for the reunion, I wished that they were back distracting me. Instead, I was left alone with a splitting headache and the certainty of my impending doom.

Once it was clear that my plan to sleep in late was ruined, I tried putting the reunion out of my head for a bit. I checked email, took like five Tylenol, cleaned the kitchen, called my only other high school friend Suzanne, and did my laundry. But after each task my eyes would automatically dart over to the computer. *A glance wouldn't hurt anyone, right?* Logging onto Facebook, I checked the timeline.

Sarah sent a virtual teddy bear to Tyler. *Who comes up with this stuff?*

Suzanne sent me a round of drinks. *Now that is thoughtful. Cheers, Suzanne.*

Luke Chambers accepted my Friend Request. *Well hello, Luke.*

I clicked on his profile. The tiny picture appeared larger and...beautiful. The shot was black and white. Luke wasn't looking directly at the camera. He was laughing, his cheeks pulled into a tight, open mouthed grin with deep creases in the corners of his eyes. He was stunning. It looked like he was behind the bar—his bar, I guessed. I didn't remember him looking like that in high school at all. I decided that I needed to make a trip to his bar soon, and if Luke looked anything like his picture in person, I might just request his assistance getting home.

Hearing the door to our apartment open, I quickly closed out of the page and logged off. I didn't need to give Danielle any more ammunition. I opened the door of my bedroom to find her in the living room with at least a dozen bags.

"Wow, Danielle! How long are we staying in 1999? This is just for the evening, right?"

"Your complaining is as bad as Megan's! I had to drop her off at Nate's because I couldn't stand it anymore. She can't concentrate on anything when he's back in town anyway. Can you both please try to enjoy yourselves tonight?"

Nate Barrett went to high school with us, as well. He was a starting linebacker for the Reynolds Rockets and an all-around good guy. After attending Florida State on a football scholarship, Nate was drafted by the Kansas City Chiefs in the fifth round. During their third preseason game, he tore his ACL and damaged his knee so severely that he was told that he'd never be one hundred percent again. When the Chiefs released him, Nate came home and got a position scouting for U-Dub.

No one knew at the time, but all throughout high school, Megan pined for Nate. After a few failed attempts at getting his attention, she opted to admire him from afar, although it was more like sulking about it from afar. While every boy in our class dreamed about dating Megan Dunn, Megan only dreamed of Nate. Unfortunately, Nate's first and only love was football. It wasn't until we ran into him at a football game a year ago that she worked up the courage to ask him out for coffee. They spent hours and hours talking, finally closing down the place and have been together ever since. She told me she was going to marry him after that first date at the coffee shop. Some people were lucky that way.

Naturally, his traveling put a strain on their relationship. He obviously couldn't scout from campus so she's on her own a lot. It worked well for me, though because I had a partner in crime. But I knew how much she missed him and how much he missed her, too. The money was good, though, and he enjoyed the work, but I knew that if something stable—something without travel—came up, he'd take it in a second. But those types of jobs weren't always easy to find. So, they made it work.

"How long is he home for?" I asked, rifling through the bags cluttering the couch.

"Two weeks," she replied. "It wouldn't be such a big deal if she had grown a pair and told him years ago how she felt. He wouldn't have accepted the job in the first place. He could've coached."

"This from the girl who found her soul mate at thirteen."

Danielle started dating Josh Fletcher in junior high. They never fought, they finished each other's sentences, and seemed to have a language of their own. I'd never admit this to Danielle, but seeing the two of them together made me a little jealous. Their relationship was perfect. Where he was laid back and calming, Danielle was vivacious and energetic—the perfect complement to each other. I knew that wasn't something everyone had.

I was still poking through the bags when Danielle's cell phone rang.

"This is Danielle…. Hey, Val."

I watched Danielle wince as she spoke to her obnoxious business partner. On prom night, Danielle and Josh found themselves sharing a limo with Valerie Cooper and my new Facebook buddy, Luke Chambers. On the way to the prom when the booze was flowing freely, Danielle shared with Val her dreams of running her own interior design firm. Val told Danielle how she'd be nearby at Columbia and suggested they team up to run the business together. She swore that it sounded like a good idea at the time and it was for a while. They spent the time early on researching and writing their business plan so that they could hit the ground running right after graduation. The business flourished teaming Danielle's flair for colors and patterns with Val's take-no-prisoners approach at running the company. Val was a fantastic salesperson and had wooed some high profile clients away from some of the larger design houses. The partnership was not without some major issues though.

"Yes…but Val…Val, we talked about this! No, I don't think you know what you're doing. He's a client! But tonight's the reunion…I swear…Val? Val?" Danielle turned to me with murderous look. "She hung up on me."

"I truly do not know how you can stand her," I replied while inspecting the t-shirts she bought.

I didn't know how dire the situation was until I heard her begin to sniffle. Danielle never cried—not even when I made her shop for knock-off pocketbooks.

"That's the point," she whimpered slumping onto the couch. "I can't do this anymore. I just want to walk away."

"*That* is not an option. I agree that Val is unbearable, but this company is all yours. It's your talent, your ideas, your blood, sweat and tears. You don't need her."

"You don't understand. I know I could run it myself. Maybe I didn't at first. It's just too late. Val's invested just as much money into the business as I have so she's just as much of an owner. She's just making really, really stupid decisions. Do you know where she is tonight?" I grimaced just imagining what was coming. I knew about Val's *dinner meetings.*

"She's visiting one of our largest clients at home tonight—a client whose wife happened to be lounging by a pool in Long Beach when I spoke to her this morning. Suddenly Val claims that Frederick needs to discuss a new project. New project, my ass."

"You need to talk to her," I reasoned, "before this gets out of hand."

"It's too late," she added. "We lost a huge client last week—right in the middle of the remodel."

"What!" I gasped.

"The client came home to Val and her husband finding creative uses for the antique dining room table I bought."

I was stunned. Sure, Val was inappropriate. She had no problem discussing her conquests in detail with anyone within earshot. I didn't shock easily, but Val had quite a resume. Even though Danielle had complained about Val's secret meetings with clients and buyers, none of us thought she would be stupid enough to risk the business.

"I obviously can't afford to buy her out," she continued. "And if I don't walk away now, I'm risking my reputation."

She looked so defeated that all I could think about was how much I wanted to strangle Val for making her feel this way.

11

"God, I'm so mad! We're supposed to be going out tonight and seeing all of these people we haven't talked to in ages, and I'm here crying over someone who's probably bent over the beautiful 18th century writing desk I found last week."

"Yeah…I didn't need that visual. You so owe me a drink tonight."

"Sorry. It really is beautiful, though. Mahogany."

"Danielle, my friend, I hereby swear on my beloved flask that I will not complain tonight. I will wear whatever ridiculous 1999 getup you'd like and I will dance until dawn with you," I replied slipping into best friend mode. "We will not let Val ruin our night, but tomorrow we put our heads together and figure a way out of this mess. Deal?" I asked extending my hand.

"Deal!" she exclaimed grabbing one of the bags on the couch and throwing it at me. "Now go and try this on. I wanna go live *La Vida Loca* or whatever it was we did back then. And let me know if the jeans fit. I think they'll make your butt look great. "

That was my Danielle. Worrying about my ass when it was hers that needed saving.

I grabbed the bag and pulled out a number of tight shirts in different colors and settled on one that didn't show off too much. Pulling out the jeans Danielle bought, I held them up against me in front of the mirror. With a hand on my desk, I bent over and attempted to pull the super-skinny jeans over my calves, but they just wouldn't budge. I tried again, jumping up and down to get the jeans up and over my rear end. Noticing I left my best buddy Joan on the desk, I leaned over and grabbed the flask, stuffing it into the back pocket. I bounced up one last time to secure them around my waist, but as I came back down, I clipped the edge of the desk and felt myself falling over.

It was one of those moments that happen in slow motion. I knew I was falling. I knew I couldn't stop it, and I just needed to brace myself for the impact. As my head hit the floor, I felt a sharp pain and then nothing but darkness.

CHAPTER 3

Jillian

B efore I opened my eyes, I was struck by two things: the scratchy fabric underneath my cheek did not feel like my pillow and my head was throbbing like hell. Neither one of those realizations was boding well for me. I didn't recall being drunk, but that didn't mean much.

I slowly rolled onto my back almost expecting my head to fall right the hell off. I blinked trying to get my eyes to adjust, but no matter how many times I blinked them, the scene in front of me still made no sense. There were a few possible explanations, but honestly, none of them were good.

The walls were purple. There was a small desk in the corner with a beat up old computer. A few CDs were stacked on the corner—Third Eye Blind, Korn, Lauryn Hill. The bookcase next to it was full of worn paperbacks. *Memoirs of a Geisha* sat on top. There was a messenger bag on the floor filled with textbooks. A few flyers were poking out from the inside. The alarm clock said it was midnight. I knew what station it would be set to.

This is so messed up.

I had to be dreaming and in this dream I was in my old bedroom back in Reynolds. Normally, I didn't have ridiculously bad headaches in my dreams, but it was the only explanation I was willing to accept. As I rubbed my head, trying to alleviate the dull ache, everything came flooding back. The reunion. The skinny jeans. My lack of coordination. The black out.

I hit my head. Hard.

There were two other possible options: I could either be dead or in a coma. If I was dead and this was heaven, someone had a lot of explaining to do. My old bedroom in my parents' house was not where I wanted to spend eternity. Suddenly I felt like I was in an episode of *Lost* because I didn't even know *when* this was. I needed to find a calendar.

I moved very slowly to get out of bed not knowing what the rules were when you were dreaming/dead/in a coma and waking up back in your parents' house. Maybe my legs wouldn't work right. I wasn't taking any chances.

13

On the corner of my desk was a calendar. It was one of those "Word of the Day" calendars and it was open to April 29, 1999. Less than a month to graduation. In June, I would be leaving for New York. The Word of the Day was *ephemeral*.

Ephemeral: 1. Beginning and ending in a day; existing only, or no longer than, a day; as, an ephemeral flower. 2. Short-lived; existing or continuing for a short time only.

It was clear to me that this was a message from my brilliant subconscious. I felt better instantly knowing that I was definitely dreaming. This visit was going to be short-lived, and I would wake up with a wicked headache tomorrow in my comfy little room back in Seattle.

Must remember to dig out that Korn CD, though. Forgot how good they were.

My curiosity got the better of me so I grabbed the messenger bag to inspect its contents. A number of vaguely familiar textbooks were inside: Spanish IV, trigonometry and chemistry. Someone should tell these kids that no one ever needs trig in real life. Proven fact. I'd vouch for it. One of the flyers fell to the ground.

Join the Senior Class on Thursday, May 20th for the Senior Prom and bid farewell to Reynolds High. Prom tickets on sale now in the cafeteria.

My mind suddenly flashed back to the prom posters littering the walls of Reynolds High. The prom committee chose Mariah Carey's *I Still Believe* for a prom song which I felt was pretty cheesy especially since Brenda K. Starr sang it better. But the prom song didn't really concern me. On prom night, I was not at the "I Still Believe" prom. I was at the dentist. Unfortunately, when you spend your entire high school career in the library or at home with your nose in a book, you don't meet many members of the opposite sex. So instead of sitting at home sulking because I was missing my prom, I decided to try and distract myself....by getting my teeth cleaned. My prom date gave me a spit bib instead of a corsage.

Thank you, Dr. Grayson, D.D.S. It was a magical evening.

I suddenly felt very sad looking at the flyer. Was this my subconscious' way of reminding me of how stupid I was in high school? Because I was pretty sure I knew this already.

While I was tempted to snoop around my room and visit with my seventeen-year-old self, I decided that I shouldn't prolong this trip. I should get back in bed, pull the covers over my eyes, forget that I knew what four-hundred thread-count felt like and go to sleep. As I climbed in, I felt a familiar jab in my side. I was still wearing the skinny jeans that got me into this mess.

14

Fishing into my back pocket, I found my good old buddy Joan. I gave her a quick shake and heard the wonderful sound of liquid sloshing around inside.

I slowly unscrewed the cap and took a sniff. Vodka. Normally I wouldn't drink it straight and would mix it with something else, but desperate times called for desperate measures. I took a gulp and felt the burn on my tongue and down my throat.

Much better.

The shot of vodka along with the trauma of waking up in my depressing seventeen-year-old life made me sleepy very quickly. I closed my eyes and bid farewell to *that* Jillian—the Jillian I left behind in Reynolds. Ephemeral. That's what she was. And I was glad.

I woke to the sound of my alarm. The radio was playing *Smooth* by Santana and Rob Thomas. The fabric under my cheek felt scratchy. I was wearing skinny jeans, and the walls were purple.

Shit.

There was no way that this could actually be happening. As nightmarish as this situation appeared to be, I was clearly not dreaming, but I refused to accept that a pair of retro jeans had killed me. I couldn't fathom that level of embarrassment. I'd also rather believe in a benevolent God that wouldn't banish us back to high school when we died. I was a pretty nice person overall. Maybe I tried returning an outfit once after I had already worn it, but I was a good person who deserved the wings, the harp and the flawless complexion in my afterlife. So if I wasn't dead, there had to be a logical explanation as to why I woke up in 1999. Actual time travel, while popular in a lot of movies, simply didn't exist. Ashton Kutcher can create his *Butterfly Effect* and Peggy Sue can decide whether she should get married, but in real life there was no *do over*. The possibility that I was in a coma was more likely, but still didn't explain the bump on the back of my head. It shouldn't still hurt. Regardless, I was back in time without the cool De Lorean.

Now maybe I've watched too much TV—well, I know I've watched too much TV—but I began to think about how complicated time travel movies were. There were tons of rules. If you change part of one person's future, it has a domino effect. Ashton Kutcher made one bad decision and—BAM—Amy Smart became a crack whore. This was serious business. There was no way of telling how or why I was here. I didn't want to screw up the future or become a crack whore so I needed to get my act together as soon as possible.

I glanced at the clock. It was already seven o'clock in the morning. I had been pacing for too long and now I needed to get ready for school. A new wave of panic washed over me as I realized that I had no idea when school started, where my locker was located, or what my first class was. I remembered nothing. Maybe I had blocked out my whole high school existence as a defense mechanism. Maybe all the booze I'd consumed had made me soft. Either way—I was screwed. Peggy Sue never had to worry about that stuff.

I dragged my ass to the bathroom and heard movement downstairs. My mom would most likely be working at the hospital already. It was probably my dad. I wondered if he would still be around when I left for school or if he had the early shift at the station. I was kind of curious to see him.

Walking into the bathroom, I noticed some of my parents' toiletries on the counter. I picked up my dad's aftershave and smiled. I wasn't far away in Seattle so I got to see them fairly often, but usually not for extended periods of time. The scent of his aftershave was always so calming. Part of me missed living here.

I formulated a plan while I got ready. I would head straight to the office when I got to school and ask to see my emergency card. I knew that every year we filled out a card so that Mrs. Jankowski, the school secretary, would know what class we were in if she ever needed to find us. It had our class schedule, locker number and if I wasn't mistaken, our locker combination. I crossed my fingers because that would be ideal. I was pretty sure my locker was on the first floor near Pruitt's bio lab, but I just didn't remember the specifics.

As I was trying to curl my hair without a much-needed roll brush, there was a knock on my door.

"Jill?" my dad called from the other side of the door. "I'm leaving."

I jumped from the seat in front of my vanity and darted across the room. When the door swung open, he jumped back. I was startled as well as I took in his appearance. His hair was jet black without the now familiar touches of gray. He clearly looked younger. The best part, however, was that he had a mustache—a freaking pornstache. I had totally forgotten his mustache phase. Why did I not find this funny ten years ago? I started to laugh and couldn't stop.

"Jill?" he said again confused. "What's going on? And why is your hair all...." He gestured wildly at my head. "You're just going to school, right?"

I managed to stop giggling. "Of course, Dad. Why? Do I have a choice?" Maybe school was optional. He looked at me strangely again.

"No, of course not. It's just that you looked kind of…fancy." He shifted from one foot to the other uncomfortably.

"Oh! No big deal, Dad. Just trying something new."

It's called brushing my hair before I leave the house and not pulling it into a messy bun. I'm not socially inept anymore.

He cleared his throat, uncomfortable again. "Well, okay then. I'm going to go so…I'll see you tonight."

With that, he turned and headed down the stairs. I noticed that he stopped and glanced back at me briefly before leaving. My dad was a pretty perceptive guy. Detectives interrogated people for a living, but I was sure he'd probably chalk my behavior up to just being a teenage girl.

I gathered up my messenger bag and looked at the Word of the Day for April 30th.

Redux: 1. brought back; 2. resurgent.

Well, that's a little obvious.

I headed downstairs and grabbed a Cinnamon Pop Tart from the kitchen. I jammed it into my mouth and headed outside.

Must remember to buy Cinnamon Pop Tarts after I dig the Korn CD out of my closet. Finding lots of hidden gems in 1999.

I saw the old Toyota I drove until it fell apart outside in my parking space. I called her The Red Baron. I had names for a lot of inanimate objects. I climbed inside, feeling sentimental. I loved this car. She wasn't slick. She wasn't fancy. She was a good old broad. But even the excitement of being able to drive my beloved car again couldn't lift my spirits. I put the key into the ignition and headed off to school with knots in my stomach.

As I pulled into the parking lot of Reynolds High, I noticed how small the school looked to me now. I spent four years at NYU. My dorm was the size of this entire school. I noticed some familiar faces milling around; people who I hadn't seen in years, but had been haunting my Facebook page. Tyler Burroughs was showing a group of kids a dent in his front fender. *Newsflash, Tyler, your driving doesn't get any better.* Sarah Spellman was walking into school with her arms crossed in front of her chest. *Oh Sarah, enjoy those perky boobs now because small and perky kicks big and wonky's ass any day.* Megan's black convertible was parked next to Erik McDougall's van. My heart sank. I wasn't friends with Megan or Danielle yet. I didn't even remember seeing much of Megan senior year. I couldn't imagine going into

17

school and pretending that they weren't two of the most important people in my life. But maybe I didn't have to. I was going to meet Danielle at orientation in little over a month. I wouldn't really be changing the future if I befriended her a few weeks early. It was practically just a matter of days.

Meg and I didn't have any classes together and I wasn't what you would call social; however, Danielle was in my World Lit class. I'd see her in class—whenever that was. I could say hi or maybe chat about the weather. As much as it sounded like I was getting ready to ask her to the prom, it was actually more important than prom. This had to work.

As I entered the main hallway, my nostrils were assaulted. The place smelled like teenagers—all full of sweat and angst. If I was sent back to my college days at NYU, at least I'd be able to handle the inescapable smell of the burning incense in the dorm. This was just plain nasty. Pushing my irritation aside, I took a deep breath and headed for the office. Mrs. Jankowski was sitting behind the desk looking just as irritated. Swell.

"Hi, Mrs. J," I squeaked. My palms were sweating and the day had barely even started.

"Jillian. Hello, how can I help you?" she asked with a wrinkled brow.

"Well, I was hoping to get a copy of my emergency card from you, please."

Polite. Concise. I'm doing all right.

"May I ask why you need that? It's a peculiar request."

She eyed me cautiously. It didn't occur to me that asking for a copy of my emergency card would sound weird, but now that I had actually said it out loud, it sounded really, really weird. There was no good reason why I should need her to make a copy for me, and because I obviously sucked at this, I never took the time to think of an excuse.

"Well, um, I've been taking a medication for…some dizziness that I've been experiencing."

I felt really proud of my ability to think on my feet because Mrs. Jankowski looked genuinely concerned.

"It's not a big deal," I continued. "I bumped my head because—you know me," I added rolling my eyes. "Super klutz. So, it makes me very forgetful, and I'm concerned I may forget my locker combo or my class schedule…" *Or what year it is.* I could see that she was buying my explanation so I trailed off, quitting while I was ahead. She walked around to the file cabinet behind her desk, searched for my card and headed to the copy machine.

"Here you go, dear, but please take care of yourself. We'd like you to make it to graduation in one piece." She handed me the paper with a smile.

"Thank you so much, Mrs. J."

I was a sweaty mess, but at least I could now find my locker and get the inevitable over with. Then as I turned the corner, I saw them. Danielle and Josh walking hand and hand. He stopped in front of a locker, spun her like a ballerina and kissed the top of her head. I had to catch myself from yelling "Josh, you nerd!" because, come on, who does that? But I held back, because I think if I randomly called a guy I'm not supposed to know a nerd, he'd be kind of pissed. Pretending not to know my friends was going to be harder than I thought. I had to talk to Danielle and fix this, so I needed to formulate a plan. Maybe I would see if she wanted to study together for…whatever we were studying. Then I would be my charming self and she would realize that I'm awesome and be my best friend.

I may need a more detailed plan.

Fortunately, I had some time to work on the execution because according to my class schedule, World Lit was after lunch. I had trig first period.

After a quick stop at my locker, I headed for Room 218. My plan for going to class was to arrive late after everyone was sitting down. Then I could just take the seat that was left. But as I peeked through the window, there were a number of open seats. It was three weeks to graduation and senioritis had invaded Reynolds High. After a sigh of defeat, I decided that if worse came to worse, I would stick with the head trauma story. It was completely believable because I was clumsy as hell.

"Ah, Jillian, so nice of you to join us today," Mrs. Jacob snapped from the blackboard. "Maybe you can help us find the reference angle in the example on the board."

I had no idea what a reference angle was and was fairly certain that I never actually did. I thought I was really good in trig, but I obviously didn't retain information well. I was under the impression that angles belonged in Geometry. Clearly math wasn't my strong suit.

"Um, no, that's okay," I responded casually. "I'm sure there's someone else that would be more qualified to do that. I'll just take my seat." She looked stunned for a moment, opening then closing her mouth. I thought maybe I'd gotten out of answering the question except I noticed her staring as I sat down in one of the empty seats.

"Jillian," she began. And I already knew what was coming. "Your seat is over there next to Valerie." She pointed across the room and my eyes met the bane of my best friend's existence.

Before I could think of an explanation as to why I was sitting in the wrong place, it hit me. I could fix this. I could make it so that Danielle and Val never go into business together. Maybe that was why I was here. It might be against the rules of time travel, but I doubt the laws of physics took Val Cooper into account.

"Jillian," Mrs. Jacob repeated.

"Oh, I'm sorry." I couldn't stop grinning. "Um, I bumped my head last night and could I…"

"Why don't you go see the nurse?" Wasting no time, I took off to start planning. With a note from the nurse, I managed to avoid classes for the morning. I was too nervous about having to set up my girl date with Danielle. It seemed silly since I had known her for over ten years, but it didn't change the fact that I was freaking out.

By noon, I was a wreck. I decided that I needed to get some air and get away from the high school smell for a bit. Following the walkway around the side of the school, I noticed a small space behind the gymnasium facing the woods. There were a few milk crates turned upside down to sit on and the ground was littered with cigarette butts. It looked like a giant ashtray. I sat down on one of the milk crates, bending my knees and leaning my back against the wall. I closed my eyes and tried to take deep breaths to calm myself down, but it wasn't working. I knew there was one thing that could help me relax, but it felt kind of wrong. It took me less than a second to decide I didn't care. I grabbed the flask from my back pocket, unscrewed the cap and took a quick sip. The familiar burn warmed me once again. Bending over, I rested my head on my knees, closed my eyes, and imagined a life where Danielle ran her own successful company. No inappropriate behavior to deal with. No lost clients. Her reputation intact. I was still visualizing how happy Danielle would be when I heard a strange noise.

Standing near the corner of the building, lighting a cigarette and looking at me with a curious expression was Luke Chambers.

CHAPTER 4

Luke

I woke to that annoying song by Santana playing on the radio. I must have knocked it on the floor while I slept because there was no way I would be listening to that crap. I grabbed my pillow and covered my head, attempting to drown out the noise. It didn't work and I knew that if I was late again I'd get stuck in detention, and I wasn't spending any more time at that school than was absolutely necessary. Since there was no use prolonging the inevitable, I slowly dragged myself out of bed and over to the bathroom.

Passing the calendar on the wall, I saw the date—April 30th. It was almost time.

22 Days

528 Hours

31,680 Minutes

And I would be gone.

It wasn't that my aunt and uncle weren't great. I'd always be grateful that Grace and Carter took me in. I just didn't belong here. I never would. I think Carter always understood that about me.

It didn't come as a big surprise that I decided not to go the college route. I was a decent student and wouldn't have had a problem getting into one of the local schools. It just wasn't in the cards for me. Carter had actually been the one who suggested I talk to his cousin Jonas about working in his bar after graduation. Jonas owned a pub in Seattle with his wife Maura. I always loved tagging along with Carter when he'd go into the city to visit. Even though the bar would have its share of sad and lonely old guys drowning their sorrows in scotch, I still always felt comfortable there. Maybe because I knew how those guys felt.

With Carter's blessing, I drove to Seattle to meet with Jonas. It had been an unseasonably warm and dry day so I jumped at the chance to ride my bike into the city. The wind against my face and the vibration of the pavement below made me feel more alive than I had felt in a long time.

It was just a matter of convincing Jonas that he should hire me. Every summer, he'd take on a college student to help out around the bar, but once school started he was usually left high and dry. I knew he needed someone on a permanent basis that he could depend on. I just needed him to accept that the person was me. I was a big risk and he would have to take a chance on me. At eighteen, I wouldn't even be able to man the bar for three more years, but I hoped that he would be willing to teach me the ins and outs of the business in the meantime.

One of the things I liked about Jonas was that he always shot from the hip. I didn't expect him to take it easy on me.

"Listen, Luke, you know I think you're a great kid and that underneath all the attitude is a hard worker," he began, "but I need to be sure you're going to take this seriously. You're family, but this is my livelihood. You can't screw this up."

"Jonas, man…" I replied quickly, attempting to calm him down.

"Don't 'Jonas, man' me. I mean it, Luke. The hours are long. The pay is shitty and you won't have much time off. In fact, I'd need you to start right after graduation. I need to know you're committed."

There was always a steady stream of bars opening and closing in Seattle, but Jonas' pub was successful and had been thriving for years. It was insane for me to pass up the opportunity even though he made it sound like a prison sentence. This was what I wanted. This was where I belonged.

"May 22nd is graduation. You can have me on the 23rd, man. You have my word." We shook on it. Jonas slapped me on the shoulder and smiled.

"May 23rd it is."

I just needed to survive the next twenty-two days and I could start over. Earning my way. Not having things given to me because I had become someone's obligation. I needed to do this on my own.

I heard the sounds of dishes clattering downstairs. Grace was most likely making a complicated breakfast like French crepes. She'd want to watch me eat them with wide eyes while waiting for my approval. Grace was writing a cookbook and I had become her unwilling guinea pig. While I wanted a simple bowl of Cheerios, Grace wanted to make me eggs benedict. And if it wasn't enough for me to eat the drippy eggs, I needed to let her know what I thought of her hollandaise sauce. I wanted to yell 'I don't give a damn about hollandaise sauce', but Grace would look so genuine and excited. So, I'd tell her it was creamy, but not too heavy, and I'd finish the plate. But for some reason, this morning I just couldn't deal. I wanted to get to school, do my time, and work on my bike later on. I didn't want to debate the merits of strawberry jam versus strawberry preserves.

Yes, they're different and it pisses me off that I know that. I wish I could climb out the window.

With a groan, I headed down the stairs and made my way to Grace's war zone. Her back was to me and her hair was falling out of the bun on the top of her head as she cleaned the dishes. A plate of Belgian waffles was placed at my seat along with fresh fruits and some whipped cream.

I wonder if she'd be willing to add "Bowl of Cheerios" to her cookbook. Then I could have a bowl of cereal for once like a normal person.

"Morning, Grace," I greeted with a yawn.

"Luke," she beamed. "I'm so glad you're here. I'm dying for you to try my vanilla waffles. Your uncle thought the vanilla flavoring was too strong, but I really think it's the perfect amount." And here it comes. "What do you think?" she asked looking at me with those wide eyes.

I wanted her book to be great, but I'll be honest, even if I started to choke on vanilla, I'd tell her that they were the best damn waffles I had ever eaten. Carter and Grace didn't have kids. I think that if they wanted kids they would've had them. It always bothered me that as wonderful as they were to me, having to raise a teenage boy with baggage was never in their master plan. I owed them a lot so if she wanted to hear that she made the best waffles I'd ever eaten, I'd tell her they were the best waffles I'd ever eaten. She deserved so much more.

"Grace, seriously," I began while still chewing. "These waffles are amazing." I wasn't lying. They were great. I had no idea how Carter knew whether there was or wasn't enough vanilla, but I wasn't dwelling. I couldn't have cereal, but I wouldn't be an idiot and complain. I'd eat my waffles like a man.

"I knew it!" she exclaimed triumphantly. "I'm keeping the recipe as is. Oh, and we're having osso bucco for dinner tonight. I'm adding the lemon zest this time to see if it gives it the kick it needs."

This would be the third time in as many weeks that we've had osso bucco for dinner. Find me another student at Reynolds High that knows what osso bucco is. I dare you.

"I think I'm going to be late tonight," I began apologetically.

"Late? Why?" She sounded so disappointed. God, I hated when that happened.

23

"I'm taking my bike to school today so Scanlon can take a look at it. I really need to find out what that sound is when I'm idling," I explained. "So I'll be spending some time in the shop after school."

I started taking Scanlon's auto shop class junior year and began rebuilding a '73 Honda CL 175. The parts were used and nothing was top-of-the-line, but it was mine and that was what mattered.

Scanlon was a good guy. He was probably the only teacher at the school who was worth listening to. He had a friend that could sometimes get parts cheap and seemed to enjoy working on the bike with me. I just hoped he could shed some light on the problem.

"You know I hate that bike, Luke. Why can't you just drive your car? That's why we got it." Yes, you bought the Lexus. I rebuilt my bike. It's mine.

"I don't know. Because it's nice out. Because school's almost over. Because I want to annoy you. Take your pick."

She shook her head and threw her dish towel at me.

"Fine," she sighed dramatically. "I suppose I can save you some and you can tell me what you think later. But don't be too late, okay?"

I gave her a quick kiss on the cheek, grabbed my beat-up rucksack, and headed for the door. Tossing the bag on my back, I jumped on my bike and heard the rattling sound again. I needed to get that figured out before I headed to Seattle. I probably won't have the time to screw around with my bike once I start working.

I was already in a bad mood when I pulled into the parking lot. The rattling seemed to have gotten worse at every stop. It sounded like it was the clutch side of the engine, but I wouldn't be able to take a look until later, and I knew it would bother me all day. While I parked my bike, I noticed Josh Fletcher waving me over. He was standing with his girlfriend and looking miserable.

"Hey, man," I greeted him.

I was lucky to have Josh for a lab partner considering some of the alternatives in our class. He knew what he was doing and never bailed on our assignments. He had a good head on his shoulders and never seemed to let shit bother him. If he did, he never let it show. But today he looked really stressed out.

"Luke, please tell me you still have your copy of the lab that's due today. I'm dying here."

"Yeah, I still have it. Why?"

"I love her, but Danielle here had to visit every limousine company in the Greater Seattle area before settling on the perfect one for the prom," he began, rolling his eyes. "I was trying to tweak a few things in our report while she talked for-*ev-er* with *every* sales rep at *every* place we visited." It was Danielle's turn to roll her eyes clearly not feeling very apologetic. "I must have left it in one of the thirteen places we went to."

"Jesus, Josh," Danielle chided, "reel it in a little, will ya?" Dismissing him, she turned to me. "So, Luke, I have the perfect limo booked. Have you got yours reserved yet? We have room in ours!"

"Prom's not really my thing," I replied. It was definitely not part of my Surviving-the-Next-Twenty-Two-Days Plan.

"Not your thing?" she asked incredulously. "But Luke, it's a rite of passage. How can a rite of passage not be your thing? Please tell me that you're at least going to the bonfire?!" She seemed truly upset now. I knew she meant well, but I was starting to feel as annoyed as Josh.

"Hate to disappoint, kid. Bonfires aren't my thing either. Don't worry about the lab, man," I added, speaking directly to Josh before she could argue with me anymore. "It's fine the way it is. We'll just turn in this one. I'll catch you later." I started walking away and turned back to nod a goodbye to Danielle.

"I'm not giving up on you, Luke!" she yelled as I walked off.

Awesome.

My day wasn't getting any better. Between Grace's culinary ambush, my messed up bike and now Danielle's sudden desire to adopt me as a pet project, I would've been better off staying in bed. Detention definitely sounded less painful.

The first two periods of the day were generally uneventful. Most of my teachers were reviewing for finals and the kids that decided to show up for class weren't interested. It seemed like a lot of people decided that today was a good day to stay home. I silently cursed myself for ignoring my instinct to stay in bed. The only thing keeping me sane was the knowledge that I had time to head over to the gym and have a cigarette after western civ.

As I sat in class, listening to that idiot Mrs. Dupont drone on about the Civil War, my mind wandered envisioning life in Seattle. I was picturing myself behind the bar, mixing one of those drinks with ridiculous names that girls order when they want to talk dirty without feeling guilty. My mood had greatly improved due to my fantasies of coeds and cocktails by the time the bell rang.

"Please pick up your papers at my desk on the way out," Dupont announced. I made my way to the front of the room slowly because I sat in the back of the class. "Ah, Mr. Chambers. Maybe if you spent less time staring out the window and more time researching your topic, you'd fare a little better."

She pursed her lips and arched her brow when she handed me the paper. Bitch hadn't liked me since I corrected her the first week of school. I looked down at the paper that seemed to have more red markings than black. And at the top was a larger red D. I knew I had hit my boiling point. I needed a cigarette. I needed out of this damn school.

I crumpled up the paper and threw it in the garbage on the way out the door. I heard Dupont calling my name, but I kept walking down the hall and out the front doors. It was cold and would probably start raining again soon, but I knew I had some time before it started again.

Originally when I was assigned a free period before lunch, I was irritated by the big gap in my day. But more and more frequently, I found myself needing to decompress. I was able to handle things better after sitting out behind the gym on one of the milk crates I had taken from the cafeteria. After a half hour, I wouldn't want to call Dupont an ignorant bitch for not knowing that Bay of Pigs wasn't Kennedy's idea. I wouldn't feel like kicking Mike Wakefield's ass for trying to paw some freshman up against the locker next to mine. I wouldn't focus on how many more days I had to suffer through until I left this town. It was enough to get me through the rest of the day.

Before I rounded the corner to the rear of the gym, I knew something felt off. I just couldn't figure out what it was. Turning the corner, I saw that for the first time all year, I wasn't alone. A girl was sitting on one of the milk crates. Her long brown hair was hiding her face as she bent over. In her hands, dangling between her legs was what looked like a flask. She looked more like someone who belonged at Jonas's pub than at a high school. The girl hadn't heard me coming and I was irritated because I just wanted some peace and quiet. Grabbing a cigarette from my pack, I cleared my throat not knowing how else I could get her attention and tell her to leave. She looked up, startled, and nearly knocked the wind out of me. It was Jillian Cross. Jillian Cross was sitting on my milk crate. Behind the gym. In my place. With a flask. And it was pink.

"Oh," she gasped climbing back up onto her feet. I watched her look from my cigarette to the butts scattered around at her feet. "I didn't know...I mean...I didn't expect anyone to come out here."

Logically, I realized that I had no issues with this girl. I didn't even know what her voice sounded like until just then. But as illogical as it was, I was really annoyed by her presence. It was just one more thing to add to my list of things that weren't going right today.

"Well," I snapped. "Now you know."

Her face, slightly pink from blushing, suddenly transformed. Straightening her back, she narrowed her eyes and glared at me.

"Well, you're a pretty big disappointment," she began as she walked past me. "What a waste!"

"What? Waste? What's your problem?" I sneered back. She didn't even know me. What the hell was she talking about?

"I could say the same thing," she replied with her hands on her hips. "My problem is that I've had a shitty day and you're acting like a jerk. So, while I have a lot of *problems* at the moment, the most irritating of them would be pretty boys who are far more attractive when they aren't speaking."

She turned to leave again as I stood there grasping at words and wondering what the hell just happened. I didn't want her here, but she made me feel like an ass.

"Hey," I called out to her. She stopped and turned around slowly, crossing her arms in front of her chest. It was only then that I noticed how tight her shirt actually was. Maybe having her around wouldn't be such a bad idea after all.

"I'm not...I don't usually..." I started stammering like an idiot. I needed to just spit it out. "I've had a shitty day, too."

She seemed to laugh to herself and shake her head. I was beginning to wonder if Jillian Cross was having some kind of a nervous breakdown considering the flask, the tight shirt and the inappropriate laughter.

"Don't worry about it," she replied softly shoving the flask into her back pocket. "But I'm pretty sure I have you beat in the shitty day department."

"You always carry a flask to school?" I asked, anxious to change the subject. She immediately stiffened and looked uncomfortable. "I'm just saying if someone catches you, it's your ass."

"Don't worry about my ass, Luke," she drawled leaning against the building. "Anyway, I keep Joan tucked away when I'm inside."

"Joan?"

She began to tell me this story about how she named her flask, and I didn't know whether it was kind of endearing or just plain weird. It was then that I decided that Jillian Cross was, in fact, having some kind of a breakdown. But before I could continue questioning her about the flask, I heard the bell ringing inside the building.

"Well, Luke, as heartwarming as this little chat of ours has been, I have to get to…some class," she announced, her voice trailing off. She pushed off the wall and began to walk away again.

"Hey," I repeated. I didn't know really what to say. Crazy or not, she was kind of amusing. "If you end up having another shitty day, there's always another seat here."

She gave me a small smile and walked away. I watched her make her way back to the main building, still reeling from the bizarre conversation. Suddenly, the desire to jump on my bike and leave school was overwhelming. The day was getting weirder and weirder, and I felt like I should just take off before it got worse. Taking a long drag from my cigarette, I repeated the words that I knew would get me through the rest of the day.

Twenty-two days.

CHAPTER 5

Jillian

M y head was still spinning as I walked back through the front doors of the school. I had tried unsuccessfully to calm my nerves and regroup before heading to see Danielle. The arrival of an obviously premenstrual Luke Chambers did nothing to ease the tension I was feeling. Luke was nothing at all like I had expected and I'd admit that I was more than a little disappointed. Just seeing him leaning against the brick wall with that ridiculous mess of hair, the worn motorcycle jacket and requisite bad boy cigarette caused my mouth to start watering. His attitude, however, left a lot to be desired. But despite his obvious annoyance, in the end he offered up an invitation to crash his hiding place again if I felt like it. Technically, I didn't need his invitation, but the sentiment was there. He was trying not to act like a jerk. I just didn't have the time or the energy to deal with him, so I decided I'd definitely stay away from his spot behind the gym from now on. I needed to focus on the task at hand. And my task was in Room 312 for World Lit.

Danielle could never get over the fact that we sat just a few seats away from each other in World Lit but never spoke. I didn't find it as hard to believe since I didn't speak to anyone in *any* of my classes. She was also bitter because she felt she would have done a lot better in the class with my help. I remembered Danielle being pretty chatty in class and getting detention fairly often so I wasn't sure my study guides would have really helped. Fortunately for me, all of Danielle's complaining made it easy for me to retain some memory of this class—that along with my love for the works that we covered. Finding my seat two desks in front of Danielle wouldn't be a problem. The problem was that my run-in with Luke didn't leave me much time to think up a good excuse to plan a study date with her.

It wasn't until I walked into the room and looked at the blackboard that everything fell into place. If things with Luke had gone smoother, I might have been fully convinced this was heaven. On the board was a quote: 'O, I am fortune's fool!'

We were reviewing Romeo and Juliet for the final exam. And we were obviously focusing on the scene after Tybalt's death where Romeo sees himself as a victim of fate instead of taking responsibility for his role in the deaths of both Mercutio and Tybalt. I knew the exchange from Act III very well having studied it in depth for a class on Shakespearian Literature in college. But even if I hadn't had the scenes from the play burned into my brain from the grueling papers I needed to write, I would know this scene by heart because of Danielle. I had watched Leonardo DiCaprio and Claire Danes in *Romeo + Juliet* probably two-hundred times. Danielle had a really, really unhealthy obsession with Leo. I didn't complain. It was common ground for us. I loved Shakespeare even if it was butchered. She loved Leo reciting…well, anything. She made such a spectacle of herself watching his movies. With *Romeo + Juliet*, she'd whisper Juliet's lines along with Claire Danes while gazing longingly at the television. The first time I saw her doing it, I couldn't help but make fun of her. I mean, she was swooning and sighing like a schoolgirl. But after she threatened to steal Joan and hide her from me, I decided that I would just need to get used to hearing both Claire and Danielle recite the lines together. Now I was finally beginning to see the payoff for all of the times that she yelled "Jillian, thou art a villain!" at me for not playing along.

Time seemed to move very slowly as I waited to speak to Danielle. At the end of class, Mr. Gilbert passed out a sheet of possible essay questions for the final. I hung back, pretending to study the sheet as I watched Danielle pack up her tote. As she passed my desk, I stood up quickly, bumping into her and causing her books to spill all over the floor.

"Oh my goodness!" I cried. "I'm so sorry!" I added, bending over to help clean up the mess. "I was just so distracted by how hard those essays look."

"Oh, no worries," Danielle replied in her usual airy tone. "And if you're worried about the final, I might as well call it quits!"

"Don't be silly," I said shaking my head. "I'm sure you'll be fine. I definitely need a refresher so I'm renting *Romeo + Juliet* tonight." I watched her eyes grow wide. "If you're going to study, you might as well have a little DiCaprio eye candy to keep you sane."

"Leo?" Danielle groaned. "Best movie ever, Jillian. If Leo starred in all of the Shakespeare adaptations, I swear I'd get an A in this class."

"Well," I began trying to sound unsure of myself, "You're welcome to drop by. I know it's a Friday night, but I figured I'd curl up with some popcorn and watch the movie." And now for the pièce de résistance. "Maybe make some Pad Thai."

"Pad Thai? You know how to make Pad Thai?" Thanks to my Food Network buddy, Alton Brown, yes I do. "I love Pad Thai," she added dazed and wide-eyed.

"Then it's settled," I replied. "Leo and Pad Thai at my place tonight."

"Oh no," she whined. "I have plans with Megan tonight, and I try very hard not to cancel on Megan. You do not want to see what she's like when you cancel on her."

I'd been there many times and completely agreed. Like the time I tried to cancel plans to go to the Giants game because Mark Jensen asked me to a study group he was hosting at his apartment. I assumed she'd understand. I mean, Mark Jensen...in his apartment...discussing The Philosophy of the Marquis de Sade. I thought it was a no-brainer. Megan disagreed, spending an entire evening schooling me on the fact that we choose "bros before hoes". Needless to say, I didn't attend the study session and went to the Giants game with my bro instead. However, this was an easy problem to fix.

"You could invite her along. Does she like Pad Thai?" I knew the answer already. She liked when I added in the peanuts.

"Are you sure?" she asked hesitantly. "I hate to impose, but I'll be honest, if you make Pad Thai and Megan finds out I didn't invite her, she'll never forgive me. You have to go to Tacoma to get even a subpar dish."

"It's really not a problem," I replied. "I need to run and pick up a few things after school. So why don't we say five?"

"Perfect! I love Girl's Night!" She responded bouncing on the balls of her feet. "I can bring the movie. I own it." With a small wave she turned and left, practically skipping out of class.

I was close to skipping myself. I had another hurdle to clear first, though. I knew Danielle and I would fall into an easy banter. That's how we were. Megan was going to be tougher. It had taken her some time to open up when we were at NYU. I didn't know what to expect since Danielle always said that Megan was a little grumpy in high school. I guess that's what happens when the guy you like decides he'd rather date a football.

I managed my way through last period gym by feigning an injury so that I didn't need to relive the horror of volleyball. I didn't feel the slightest ounce of guilt. Volleyball should be outlawed under the Geneva Convention. In what other sport do poor unsuspecting players get torturously and repeatedly beaned off the head with large balls? Gym was God's way of sticking it to the uncoordinated.

31

I made my way back to my car pleased that the day went so well. As I climbed into my car and started the ignition, I heard a large sputtering sound and looked across the parking lot to see Luke Chambers riding an old vintage motorcycle around the rear of the building near the auto shop. My mouth began watering again. Luke Chambers on a motorcycle. God, I wished he had never spoken. His attitude was such a major buzzkill, but he was still damn pretty to watch. I forced myself to stop ogling and headed to the supermarket. I knew my parents wouldn't have tofu, shrimp or some of the other ingredients I needed for Pad Thai. I had a lot of ground to cover and not a lot of time to do it in.

Pulling into the parking lot, I planned to run in quickly, grab a few ingredients and get home as soon as possible. I wanted to pilfer some beverages from the liquor cabinet, and I didn't want to get busted if my mom and dad were due home. Timing was everything.

Sprinting through the aisles, I was easily able to find the shrimp and the noodles that I needed. It was when I went to grab a package of tofu that I realized my problem. Normally, I marinated the tofu a day in advance, but since I had no time, I needed to tweak the recipe. But it had been so long since I had cooked it without the marinated tofu that I forgot which type I was supposed to get instead. Maybe it was finally the shock of everything around me, but I found myself frozen in the organic foods aisle staring at the packages in front of me in a full panic. I took a step back trying to search for a name brand that rang a bell when I stumbled over something—or actually, someone.

"Oh sorry," the tall man I nearly plowed over said. As I looked up, I noticed his sharp and distinguished features. He was wearing a tweed blazer with elbow patches. I wondered if they even manufactured blazers like that anymore.

"Oh no, I should apologize. I'm just having a minor meltdown," I replied with a half smile.

"Well, tofu can do that to you," he laughed.

"I'm not as insane as I look. I'm just planning on making Pad Thai for dinner and because I need to switch up the recipe, I can't remember if I need the dry tofu or the tofu in water and...." I stopped and realized I was babbling to a complete stranger. "Maybe I *am* as insane as I look."

"Well, if it's any consolation, my wife is an amazing cook and she uses the dry tofu," he added smiling.

"You're a life saver," I replied breathing a sigh of relief.

"Not a problem at all. My wife's writing a cookbook. I eat, sleep and breathe recipe ingredients. Tonight is osso bucco night." He seemed very excited and I was a little jealous. My mom wasn't the best cook around. She tried, but her flavoring was always pretty bland.

"Well, enjoy your osso bucco and thank you again," I replied with a small wave.

"Good luck with the Pad Thai."

I brought all of the items to the checkout and headed home. I needed to remember that although my situation was ridiculous, I need to refrain from assaulting people in the grocery story.

Back at Casa Cross, there were no cars in the driveway. I had yet to see my mom since she was already at the hospital when I got up this morning. I assumed she'd be home but no one was around. It was the perfect opportunity to raid the liquor cabinet that in my adolescence I never even imagined opening. In the den, I opened the bottom door to my mother's hutch and inhaled the intoxicating scent of commingled alcohols. *Come to mama.* But as I perused the selection, it became apparent that the bottles inhabiting the liquor cabinet must have been gifts from people who clearly did not like my parents: Seagram's VO, Midori, a couple random bottles of wine and my nemesis, Captain Morgan. I was desperate. *Captain, I'm willing to call a truce if you are.* I grabbed the brown bottle and headed to the kitchen as the phone rang.

"Hey, honey," my dad greeted.

"Dad, why aren't you home? And where's mom?" I asked, clutching the bottle to my chest.

"That's why I'm calling," he began. "She got stuck at the hospital because one of those yahoos called out sick. I'm gonna pick her up after my shift and head over to Capanelli's for dinner. You want to come along?"

I did a little dance in place. Capanelli's was in Tacoma. They'd be gone for hours.

"Oh Dad, I wish I could," I replied, sounding as disappointed as I could. "But I asked Danielle Powers and Megan Dunn to come by and study for our World Lit final."

"Don, who?" He snapped into the phone.

"Relax, Dad. Megan Dunn. Megan's a girl."

"Oh. Okay. Well, we'll miss you, but we'll try not to be late."

33

"No worries, Dad. You'll just be coming home to a bunch of giggling, obnoxious teenage girls. Take your time."

"In that case, we should probably go to a movie too!" he laughed.

It didn't surprise me that he wasn't concerned leaving me alone. I had never given him any reason to believe that I wasn't one-hundred-percent trustworthy. I felt a twinge of remorse as I realized this would be the first time I broke any of their rules. But it was only a twinge.

"Have fun, Dad. Don't do anything I wouldn't do."

"Have a nice night, honey."

Hanging up, I looked at the clock to see that it was almost five. I grabbed a large pan from the kitchen cabinet because I knew they wouldn't have a wok and began my preparations. Fortunately, part of my prep was to sample the rum to make sure it was suitable for my guests. I was a thorough hostess.

At five, the doorbell rang.

"Jillian!" Danielle beamed, embracing me in the doorway. "You know Megan." Meg walked through the door and gave me a half smile, her eyes narrow. I knew that look well. It was the look she gave Val every time we'd run into her. My best friend just gave me the Val Smile. This was not good.

"Hi Megan," I said, pretending I didn't know she was obviously unhappy to be there. "Come on in. I was just having a beverage." I raised the bottle of rum, and I thought I saw something spark in her eye, but it was probably her body's automatic response to its proximity to alcohol. She was partially to blame for my corruption in college, after all.

Handing them each a rum and coke, I began cooking.

"So Megan, you like Pad Thai?" I asked goading her into a discussion.

"It's all right," she shrugged. "There's a good place in Tacoma we go to."

"Please, Meg," Danielle interrupted rolling her eyes. "Spice and Rice is the worst. There's almost no taste to it! Jillian, I can't wait to see how you make it!" she added enthusiastically.

It didn't take long to pull all the ingredients together and serve up the noodles. Unfortunately, Megan's foul attitude was making me feel very uncomfortable. I needed to break the ice, but my idea was risky. Megan and I had bonded over a common enjoyable pastime: making fun of Danielle. It sounded mean, but Meg and I were a little dark and cynical. Danielle, on the other hand, was like an adult version of Pollyanna. How can you not make fun of a real live Disney character? But I needed to tread lightly.

"My parents are in Tacoma for the evening," I explained. "I think my dad wanted to avoid a house full of giggling teenage girls. But I'll level with you. I'm not braiding anyone's hair or playing Truth or Dare. In fact, I think we need to keep giggling to a minimum."

"I had no intention of braiding your hair," Danielle replied defensively. "But I brought my make-up case. You should totally be wearing darker colors. You're a winter."

"Sorry," I added. "Let me restate the ground rules. No giggling, braiding, truth or daring and no makeovers. Other than that, let's enjoy our girl's night!" I looked over to Meg and noticed that her scowl had morphed into a small, tight-lipped smile. I was making progress.

After finishing our dinner and wowing the girls with my culinary prowess, I suggested we bring our drinks upstairs and watch the movie in my room just in case my parents decided to come home early. It was mostly for my benefit. Since I had now reconciled with Captain Morgan, I felt that we should spend some quality time together. Danielle pounced on my bed, flopping against the pillows like a ragdoll.

"So, I booked a limo for the prom last night," she began with a dreamy look in her eyes. "I just can't wait. It's going to be the best night of our lives." It was amazing how we truly believed those things in high school. "And you, Megan, need to decide who you're going with," she added, shooting Megan a pointed look.

"It's just the prom, Danielle," Megan replied unimpressed.

"It's not just the prom, Danielle," she imitated. "It's The Prom, with capital letters. Right, Jillian?"

"Well, prom really isn't my thing," I replied cautiously. No use pretending. I was well aware that no one was going to ask me, and I was psyched that I'd get to relive that humiliation again. Really I was.

Danielle gave me a strange look. "You're the second person to say that. Wait!" she shouted.

"What?" I replied nervously.

"Do you see what I see, Meg?"

"See what?"

35

"Jillian." She motioned to me like I was the prize in some game show.

"Yes, I see Jillian. Are you already drunk?"

"Of course not. This is perfect!" She wasn't making any sense, even for a possibly drunk person.

"I agree. I'm pretty awesome," I replied confused. "But perfect? No."

"I meant for Luke Chambers!"

"Luke?" I replied incredulously.

"Yes, he said those exact words to me yesterday."

"He told you he was awesome?"

"No, silly. He doesn't think prom is his thing either. You should go together and be all anti-disestablishment together."

"That's not a real word, Danielle," Megan added.

"Yes, it is," she countered.

"*Irregardless*," I interrupted rolling my eyes. "I think we'd kill each other if we were forced to go to the prom together."

"Speaking of killing each other," Megan interrupted with a look that screamed she had a good story to tell. I was just grateful for the diversion. "Major girl fight in the cafeteria today. Did you hear that Mike Wakefield asked both Karen Larson and that freshman Jen to the prom? Instead of kicking his ass like they should have, they started scratching and pulling at each other's hair. Karen's extensions came out. It was amazing!"

I snorted. "I don't understand the lure of Wakefield. He's a mouth breather."

"A what?" Danielle asked.

"You know…someone who doesn't breathe through their nose so they always sound like an obscene phone caller when you talk to them." I was startled by the belly laugh that escaped from Megan.

"She's right! He sounds like he's run a marathon every time he talks to me," she mused. "And sometimes he gets this gross spittle in the corner of his mouth."

"I know!" I squealed. "I was paired up with him for a project once and I spent the whole time trying not to look at him because the spittle on his lips made

36

me gag." While it didn't last long, I got a small smile out of her, and it wasn't the one that looked like she smelled something bad. *Fess up, Meg. You like me. I rock.*

"Getting back to Jillian," Danielle began. "I think you and Luke would look so good together. He's a winter, too." I needed a new diversion.

"Danielle, what did you mean when you said that Meg needed to decide who she was going with? Is there a waiting list?"

"She's had five different offers," Danielle explained. "Three of which are pretty decent, but she has yet to answer any of them."

I was fairly certain that I knew why Megan hadn't accepted any of the offers. I just needed her to confirm it. I couldn't let the opportunity to ask about Nate pass by.

"Is it because you're waiting on someone else?"

"No, no," Danielle answered for her. "She's just stubborn and likes to torture me. So, you need to pick one, Meg. I say you should go with Grant. He's always been very sweet and he'll look great in a tux."

Meg was either extremely uncomfortable or found the laces on her Reeboks fascinating. I think my buddy Captain was working his magic on her, as well. *Tell the truth.*

"I'm right, aren't I?" I added. "Who is it?" Danielle's head shot up and she furrowed her brows.

"Megan Dunn, are you seriously holding out on me?" Danielle chimed in.

"It's nothing," she replied, picking at the soles of her sneakers.

"It's not nothing, Megan, if that's the reason you clam up every time I mention the freaking prom."

Megan took a deep breath before looking up, clearly not wanting to discuss this with us.

"Who?" Danielle asked softly. "Why can't you tell me?"

"Because it's embarrassing, all right? He doesn't even acknowledge my existence! I've tried everything and he doesn't even glance my way. I feel so stupid."

37

"Maybe you're just going about it wrong," I offered letting the alcohol do the talking.

"Jillian, I don't need any advice on how to land a date," she snapped. I had to remind myself to tread lightly.

"Is it Kurt?" Danielle asked still trying to pry the truth from her.

"No," she sighed burying her head in her hands. "It's Nate Barrett." Her response sounded muffled, but we heard her loud and clear.

"Nate ?" Danielle gasped.

"Yes, I-love-nothing-but-football Nate. I'm-too-busy-to-think-about-girls Nate. I-don't-even-notice-when-Megan-is-wearing-a-see-through-top Nate," she muttered.

"Wait a second," I added. "Maybe that really isn't the way to get his attention."

"Jillian, I've tried talking to him and he's still completely uninterested."

"Have you tried talking to him about football," Danielle asked. "I told Josh that I was into Weezer even though I only really liked the lead singer's glasses. It still worked like a charm."

"I think Nate would figure it out if Megan was faking her way through a conversation about football. You don't know anything about the game, do you?" I asked, knowing full well that Megan won the football pool at the bar in our neighborhood almost every year. The girl was a football encyclopedia.

"I love football. I just don't want him to see me as one of his buddies."

"Guys dig girls who like sports. We just need to grab his attention."

I hadn't really planned to get involved in altering another aspect of the past, but if Megan and Nate would eventually meet and fall in love, I wasn't technically changing anything. Just speeding it up a bit. I didn't have a plan in place yet, though. I had to think quickly. "Meg, I'm not calling you a stalker or anything, so don't get mad, but do you happen to know Nate's schedule?" You're totally lying if you say you don't know the schedule of the boy you like. Every girl does; it's a fact. Meg began to blush. Of course she did.

"He has western civ, gym, trig and chem in the morning. I think he has third lunch, then auto shop and Spanish." The plan was forming quickly thanks to an image in my head of Megan Fox in Transformers. I was sure that Megan wouldn't mind this Megan stealing one of her moves.

"I hereby decree that Operation Nate will commence at 0800 hours on Monday. Are you with me?" I asked putting my hand out. Danielle quickly put hers on top of mine. Megan looked like she was going to throw up, but slowly put hers on top of Danielle's. "That's what I'm talking about!"

I began filling them in on my plan until we all started to yawn. We hadn't even watched the movie, but I felt that the study date was a tremendous success. I convinced the girls to spend the night with very little effort. Even though I was the one drinking most of the rum, I didn't want to take any chances. Once I heard their steady breaths from the blankets on the floor, I padded over to my desk to take one last pull from the bottle. On my desk sat the calendar and its Word of the Day. I pulled off April 30th to reveal the word for the May 1st.

Ineluctable: 1. incapable of being evaded; 2. inescapable: an ineluctable destiny.

Tomorrow's word seemed appropriate for Meg considering our plans. I already knew *my* destiny. I knew what the future had in store. There wasn't anything here for me. I needed to focus on Meg and Danielle, and make things right for them. That was my destiny.

CHAPTER 6

Luke

"**L**uke," Scanlon called from the doorway of the teacher's lounge. He was sipping from a mug that said "Mechanics Do it Better" which was kind of inappropriate. "The parts for your bike arrived this morning. Swing by after school and we can get started."

On Friday, after running some diagnostics, he figured out that there was more going on with my bike than I thought. We had to rebuild the clutch. Fortunately, his buddy who worked with vintage cycles could get the parts pretty quickly.

Instead of feeling relieved, though, I was pretty irritated. Mrs. Dupont had finally cornered me and sentenced me to detention all week in her Dungeon of Misinformation. Torturing me was probably going to be the highlight of her week.

"I can't after school, Mr. S," I explained. "I have detention with Dupont all week."

"Three weeks to graduation, Luke," he replied with a disapproving tone, "and you're spending one of them in detention. Was it really worth it?" I know he didn't really want me to answer that question. While it may have been stupid to storm off like I did, I still thought her grading sucked. And Scanlon knew that Dupont and I didn't have the best relationship. I was sure he'd heard her complain about me as well. I could see her ranting about "that Chambers kid" who thought he knew everything. I may not know everything, but I was pretty sure I knew more than she did.

I shrugged my shoulders because while it may not have been worth it to lose time in the shop, given the chance, I'd probably do it again.

"Well," he began, rocking slowly back and forth on the balls of his feet, "I have a class during second lunch that's mostly seniors. I'm sure they wouldn't mind learning a thing or two about vintage cycles. Isn't that your lunch period?" he asked with a raised brow.

"Yes, it is," I replied, my smile broadening. "I actually have a free period, then lunch."

"I'm monitoring the cafeteria for first lunch so I can't meet you any earlier, but come by during your lunch break and we can get started," he offered patting me on the back.

"Thanks, Mr. S," I replied as I turned to leave.

"And Luke," he called back to me with a smirk, "lay off Mrs. Dupont, okay?" I nodded grudgingly. Scanlon had been good to me and if that was all he asked in return, I could try to silently put up with her ignorance for just a little longer.

As I made my way back to my locker, I noticed Mike Wakefield trying to molest another unsuspecting victim next to my locker. His back was to me and he was practically leaning on top of the poor girl. I'd never understand what girls saw in the guy. I wanted to bring in a stun gun and zap him in the nuts to keep him away. As I got closer, instead of being assaulted by the cooing and baby-talk that I normally had to endure, I heard a voice laced with venom.

"Let me get this straight," the girl sneered. "I'm supposed to be flattered that you've never found me attractive before, and now suddenly you think I'm hot? Do I have that right?"

"Don't get upset, baby," he replied. "Maybe I didn't notice you then, but you sure have my attention now." I could see his hand sliding up and down her arm.

"Let me make this abundantly clear, Mike," she snapped. "I am not, in any way, interested, and if you don't take your hands off me, I will kick you square in the balls."

Smart girl.

"Jillian, come on."

I turned quickly because if he was touching her, and she didn't want him to, I'd gladly take the opportunity I'd been waiting for to pummel him. As I grabbed his shoulder to pull him away, true to her warning, Jillian brought her knee up forcefully right into his nuts. Mike immediately doubled over into a drooling mess on the tile floor.

"Bitch!" he howled cupping his junk as he rolled around on the ground. I winced, shifting uncomfortably.

"Expect company today, Chambers," she said as she breezed past me. "It's been another shitty day."

I watched as she walked down the stairs and through the front door leaving me speechless while Mike rolled around on the floor in agony. It wasn't often that someone surprised me, but I was standing there staring at the door like an idiot, totally caught off guard. Whatever it was that had gotten into her was kind of hot in a crazy-girl kind of way.

I looked down at Mike who was still swearing and groaning as he crawled onto his knees. I held out a hand to help him up, but as he regained his balance, I pulled him up to me by the collar of his flannel.

"Don't you ever let me catch you bothering her again," I growled into his ear. "You hear me?"

He pulled away, brushing the dirt from the floor off his clothes.

"You can have her," he sneered.

And I don't know what it was. Maybe it was the fact that he was acting like an asshole. Maybe it was because I had spent the last eight months watching him grope Karen Larson's boobs against my locker. Maybe it was just because of Jillian. Whatever the reason, I drew back and punched him, sending him careening backwards into the lockers on the other side of the hall. I turned around to leave as I saw Karen run from the other end of the hall to help him. As I walked down the stairs, I wondered if he'd tell her why I punched him. If he were smart, he'd keep his mouth shut then he could keep on grabbing her boobs and I could avoid more detention. Regardless, I couldn't find it in myself to feel sorry. He deserved it.

I didn't wait until I was behind the gym to grab a cigarette. I couldn't wait because my knuckles were starting to feel sore now that the adrenaline had faded. It was a small price to pay. Punching Wakefield felt good. I could scratch that off of my list of things I wanted to do before I graduated. I guess I should thank Jillian for that.

When I rounded the corner, she was sitting on one of the milk crates with her head against the wall. The sparkly, pink, sad excuse for a flask was at her lips.

"If you're crashing my party, Cross," I began boldly. "You better come prepared to share." She narrowed her eyes at me, as if she were sizing me up before raising her arm and offering me the flask. I looked at it for a moment. If I hadn't just punched Wakefield, I wouldn't have been able to justify drinking from a pink flask, but I needed something to numb the throbbing. I took a quick pull.

"Vodka? Really?"

"Maybe you should get your own if you don't like it," she responded sarcastically.

"See, that's where we differ," I replied. "I'm not crazy enough to bring my flask to school or to give it a name."

"I'm sure we differ in lots of ways, Luke," she shot back, clearly not offended.

"Yeah, I'm not Wakefield's type."

"That was just the icing on the cake of my day. I volunteered to help a friend with boy problems," she explained rolling her eyes. "I shouldn't say 'volunteer' since it was *my* brilliant idea."

"So what's the problem then?" She was going to have to spell this one out for me.

"Well, you have a few drinks. You get a brilliant idea," she began slowly, taking another sip. "You sober up and realize that your idea may not be as fool proof as you may have initially believed."

"I don't get that about girls—the need to play matchmaker," I responded grabbing the flask from her again.

"I'm not playing matchmaker," she countered. "They would have figured it out in their own time. I'm sure of that. I'm just helping them along. It's my approach that I'm just not so sure of." She looked down at her watch and groaned. "Time to put the plan in motion. Wish me luck."

"Sounds like you'll need it," I replied as she gathered herself up from the milk crate. "Later," I added with a smirk as I watched her leave. I was beginning to enjoy watching her walk away a little too much. I couldn't really blame Mike for taking a sudden interest in her.

"Your turn to bring the refreshments," she called back grinning. Apparently intending to turn my afternoon breaks into a pot luck.

I finished my cigarette and tossed it with the dozens of other butts on the ground. I walked through the parking lot to grab my bike and drove it around the back of the building where Scanlon's shop was. After parking it in one of the open bays, I made my way over to Mr. S.

"Luke. Great, you're here," he greeted me. "Listen up, people. We're going to learn a little bit about motorcycle repair today while I help Mr. Chambers here rebuild the clutch on his bike. Last year, Luke started to rebuild a 1973 Honda CL 175, a beautiful bike. He's been experiencing some problems with the clutch so we're going to remove the whole assembly and install a new one."

He grabbed the box of parts on the table in front of him, carried them over to the bay with my bike, and immediately went to work taking it apart as the class looked on.

"Now Luke, we need to make sure the shifter shaft arm is aligned correctly," he began while handing me a pivot bolt. "The arm should point directly to the center of the clutch and the ball bearing lifter mechanism will ride on the shifter arm. So—"

"Excuse me, Mr. Scanlon?" We all looked up at the voice that interrupted him. It was Jillian. "I'm sorry to interrupt, but there's something wrong with my car and I can't figure it out. I was told you might be able to help."

Jillian hadn't mentioned anything about car trouble, and I had just left her twenty minutes ago. If she had said something, I could've looked at it.

"Sure, sure, Miss..."

"Cross. Jillian," she replied. I didn't think she even realized I was in the class and for some reason it irritated me that she hadn't made eye contact yet.

"Okay, Jillian, can you pull it into the bay over there," he asked pointing to the middle doorway. As she pulled the car in, I noticed the white smoke coming out of the exhaust pipe.

"So, what seems to be the problem?"

"Jillian!" I turned and noticed Megan Dunn running over. "Jeez, can you trust me and not go running off when I'm trying to help you?" she fumed.

"I'm sorry, Megan," Jillian replied sounding exasperated. "I'm sure you think you know what the problem is, but I'd like a professional opinion."

Megan turned to Mr. Scanlon, her arms crossed in front of her chest and her head held high.

"It's a blown head gasket," she stated matter-of-factly. "The engine is overheating. It miss-fires and the check engine light comes on. And she's always adding coolant to the radiator." She turned to Jillian. "He needs to do a cooling system pressure test for you to see if there's a leak in the system."

"Can you please let Mr. Scanlon decide what's best to do?" she countered.

"Actually, Jillian, your friend here is right. Let me grab the kit." Jillian watched him walk over to his tool cabinet. As she scanned the room, she noticed me standing by the door, gave me a small smile and winked. Then it started making sense. This was part of whatever scheme she was talking about.

45

Under any other circumstance, I would've been pissed that she was taking up time I could be using to fix my bike, but I was finding the show amusing. As I looked around the room, it appeared that the other guys in class were too. Maybe too much.

"Here we are," Scanlon began when he returned with the small black case.

"Mr. Scanlon, may I?" Megan asked holding out her hand towards the case.

"Oh, it's a little complicated, Miss…"

"Megan Dunn. And I've used one before. I need to prove to my friend that I know what I'm talking about."

"Well, let me help you," he replied tentatively. Megan pulled open the hood stretching up tall, and looking down onto the engine. I don't think there was a person in the room other than Scanlon that was looking inside the hood. All eyes were on Megan's tight tank top and small jean skirt. I, on the other hand, found my eyes drifting over to the small brunette standing back and watching the scene unfold with a satisfied smirk.

When Megan bent over the hood to attach the pump, brushing her hair off her shoulders, I watched Nate Barrett and a few of his football buddies suck in their breaths.

"Could you hold this for me?" she asked Nate, reaching out to hand him one of the parts. He had to move closer in order to reach, but he seemed frozen in place. One of his friends gave him a quick shove forward which snapped him out of his trance. It was when she bent over again, pointing out the different parts of the engine that the entire room heard a very distinct groan emanate from his chest.

I guess I know who the poor schmuck is now.

"Sorry," he replied nervously clearing his throat. "I've got a dry throat."

Is that what they call it these days?

I hadn't noticed that Jillian had slowly backed up next to me. I couldn't stop fidgeting, turning the pivot bolt around in my hand.

"And *that* is how it's done," she whispered enjoying her opportunity to gloat.

"Pleased with your handiwork?" I asked, teasing her.

"If I do say so myself," she answered smugly.

"How'd you know you had a blown head gasket?"

"I didn't," she began wide-eyed like a kid telling a secret. "Megan figured it out. I was going to yank out The Baron's spark plugs or something, but she took a look in the hood and told me what was wrong. She's the real deal over there."

"The Red Baron?" I asked confused.

"My car," she explained as if it were obvious.

"Naturally," I replied shaking my head. "Why wouldn't a girl who names her flask name her car too? What was I thinking?"

"Don't be a buzzkill, Luke," she scolded. "I just made a love connection. Show some respect."

"I'll give you this much," I offered, "there are a lot of guys that are going to be sitting uncomfortably for the rest of the day after seeing her bending over the hood like that."

"Oh, really now?" she asked, one brow shooting up.

"She's not my type, Cross," I replied quickly without thinking. I thought I had a type, but lately I wasn't so sure. At any rate, I wasn't about to discuss "my type" with Jillian especially since I was staring at her ass less than a half hour ago. "Shouldn't you be in class somewhere?"

"I have World Lit but Danielle Powers told Gilbert that I was having female problems," she whispered scrunching up her nose. "It's cliché but it totally works."

"Speaking of Danielle," she continued. "You better watch out for her. It's her mission to get your ass to the prom." My heart started to race. I dropped the pivot bolt and it went rolling across the floor.

"She told you that?" I groaned. I was really hoping that Danielle had moved onto another project.

"You could say that. She claims she's found you the perfect girl, but if you're nice to me, I may be able to get her off your back."

"The girl is insane," I fumed. "I barely know her and she's killing me."

"Danielle's pretty intense," she agreed with a nod.

"So who's she going to spring on me?"

47

"Don't worry about it," she replied waving her hand. "I can get her off your back, but I have a favor to ask." Now it was my turn to quirk an eyebrow.

"Go on," I said with caution.

"As you duly noted earlier today," she began, "my beverage options are very limited. I'm assuming since you have your own flask that you have access to a wider selection..." She trailed off waiting for me to offer her some insight.

"I may have the means to purchase items occasionally," I offered not giving her any details.

"That's what I thought," she replied smugly. "I want one, too."

"You're extorting me?" I asked incredulously. "I get you a fake ID and you get your friend to chill out?"

"I don't like thinking about it as extortion," she replied innocently. "I'd like to think you'd want to help a friend procure some libations."

The last thing in the world I wanted was for Danielle Powers to guilt trip me into taking one of her chipper little friends to the prom. No way. I needed Seth to touch up the ink on one of my tattoos anyway so taking Jillian to see him would be killing two birds with one stone. I just wasn't sure I wanted to drive all the way to Tacoma with Jillian. She was funny in small doses, but stuck in a car for an hour is entirely different. However, the alternative was, by far, much worse.

"There's a guy I know in Tacoma who can help you out," I sighed. "I was planning to make a trip to see him soon anyway. When I go, I guess you can tag along."

"Great. How's Saturday?" She didn't waste any time, but obviously noticed my surprise. "I don't want to impose..."

"No, no. Saturday's fine."

"Awesome!" she replied grinning. "We'll chat about the details later. I should get back to Miss Grease Monkey and make sure that Nate will, in fact, have a *hard* time sitting for the rest of the day."

She turned and walked back over to Megan, Nate and Scanlon. Scanlon had added some engine block sealant while Megan explained the process to Barrett's friends. When Jillian slid into the driver's seat and started the engine, I looked back at the tail pipe and noticed the white smoke was gone. After a few minutes, Jillian and Megan were gone too leaving the atmosphere tense and uncomfortable. Maybe her planned had worked.

48

When the bell rang, I was relieved to head to chemistry because I still needed to talk to Josh about his girlfriend and why she was trying to torture me. When I got to the lab, he was already hunched over in his seat listening to his Discman. I nudged him on the shoulder.

"Hey, man," he replied, removing his headphones and placing them on the lab table.

"We need to talk," I began. "You have to explain to Danielle that I don't want her searching for prom dates for me anymore. I'm not going so it's a waste of time." I didn't want to sound like an asshole, but her type of crazy just wasn't funny.

"Oh, you heard about that?" he asked looking slightly uncomfortable.

"Yeah. It's crazy."

"She's not that bad," Josh countered. "I think she's actually pretty funny."

"What? Who are you talking about?"

"Jillian," he explained giving me a strange look. "Who are *you* talking about?"

I knew I was just staring at him with my mouth open, but I was physically unable to close it. He had to be joking.

"Danielle wants me to take Jillian…to the prom?" Definitely a turn of events I wasn't expecting.

"Wait, I thought that's what you were upset about. She's pretty cool. I picked Danielle up at her place on Saturday and the girl had us rolling on the floor. She's hysterical. You could do a lot worse, Luke."

But Jillian knew Danielle wanted me to ask her to the prom and had just agreed to get Danielle off my back. She didn't want me to ask her, and for some reason, that really pissed me off.

"Earth to Luke." I jumped when Josh began waving a hand in front of my face.

"Sorry, man. I was…I didn't know she…Does Jillian know this? I mean, is Danielle harassing her, too?" I was stammering like an ass again.

"Relax," he replied stuffing his Discman into his backpack. "But, seriously, you should consider it. Once Danielle sets her mind on something, it's damn near impossible to change it…which is why I'll be wearing a top hat to the prom."

"You'll be what?"

"She watched some Ginger Rogers and Fred Astaire movie the other day. I'm going to look like an idiot, but if it makes her happy…" He looked at me like I knew what he meant. But I didn't. You wouldn't catch me in a top hat. Ever. Poor Bastard.

"Whatever you say, man," I replied as Mrs. Quimby called for the class' attention. Josh began taking notes, but I couldn't concentrate on the review. I kept replaying my conversation with Jillian over and over. We had only forged our strange friendship a couple days ago, but it seemed like Jillian was everywhere I turned and it was messing with me. I sat for the rest of the class with a weird feeling in the pit of my stomach. I could only imagine that if I went to the prom with Jillian she'd probably name the limo or insist on flashing her flask in one of those cheesy prom pictures. As funny as that might be, my Nineteen-Day-Plan to survive until graduation absolutely did not involve going to the prom or naming limousines.

After class, I had a few minutes before I needed to report to Mrs. Dupont's Dungeon of Misinformation. I walked back to Scanlon's shop to pick up my bike and drive it to the student parking lot. Scanlon would need to lock up, and I had no idea how long Dupont intended to torture me. As I pulled my bike into a spot in front, I looked across the emptying lot. I noticed Jillian, Megan, Josh and Danielle leaning against Jillian's crappy car. It looked like Jillian was telling them about shop class. With exaggerated motions, she lifted the hood, fluffed her hair and bent over looking inside. It gave me an amazing view of her ass and I bit back a groan. Danielle and Josh were cracking up at the show she was putting on. She sauntered over to Josh, pretending to hand him something and began batting her eyelashes and rubbing his arm. Megan, clearly fed up with being the butt of the joke, threw her coat at Jillian. I continued watching as Jillian put the coat on and began parading around the car fluffing her hair and swaying her hips.

"I'll kick your ass, Jillian Cross," I heard Megan yell as she took off after her. Jillian let out a scream and hopped into her car locking the doors. She gave Megan a big grin and started the ignition. With a small wave, she drove off leaving Josh and Danielle doubled over laughing.

Even though I was headed to Dupont's room for an afternoon of grueling detention, even though my knuckles were throbbing, even though I wanted to be on my way out of school instead of in, I laughed all the way there.

CHAPTER 7

Jillian

The next couple of days went by in a blur. I had been thrilled with the outcome of our visit to auto shop, and I was still feeling really superior for rocking Phase One. Nate seemed genuinely impressed with Megan's knowledge of car engines. He also seemed impressed with her other *attributes* as well. If all went well, Phase Two would bring him to his knees. I didn't want to rush it, though. To maximize the impact of the next phase, I wanted to give him a few days to stew thinking of Megan, her short skirt and many talents. It was the strangest foreplay I'd ever seen, but who was I to question? I was the one who hadn't had a decent date in months.

In the meantime, I faked my way through my classes, made up elaborate reasons to excuse myself from volleyball and hung out behind the gym with Luke. On Tuesday, he provided refreshments and I only managed two sips of Jack before I found myself giggling like a school girl. Well, I guess I *was* technically a school girl. On Wednesday, he told me Green Day sucked, and I tried unsuccessfully to convince him that Billie Joe Armstrong was the voice of a generation. He scoffed at me and claimed he was going to introduce me to "real music". On Thursday, he handed me a jewel case with a blank CD inside, offering to enlighten me with a few songs from a "new" band called The White Stripes. He had downloaded the EP from Napster and seemed really impressed with himself. More importantly, he also brought Southern Comfort. I already knew the songs so I appreciated the booze much more.

On Friday morning as I was curling my hair, I began humming an annoying song that played incessantly on the radio in 2011.

I wonder what you're doing now, Ke$ha.

It sucked having a song stuck in my head that I couldn't even listen to. Just another awesome thing about time travel the movies don't seem to cover. I felt like I should be taking advantage of the more lucrative aspects of being sent back in time. If I were smart, I'd forget all about Megan and Danielle and go invent Facebook. Fortunately for them, I still believed Facebook was the portal to hell and didn't want to be held responsible for unleashing that crap.

Looking at my reflection in the mirror, I ran the new tube of red gloss across my lips and blotted them with a tissue. I felt much better. *That* Jillian had no make-up so I made an emergency trip to the pharmacy after school for supplies. I couldn't resist picking up a teen magazine with a virginal Britney Spears on the cover looking up at the camera with wide, innocent eyes.

You don't fool me, Brit Brit. I know everything.

After taking one last peek in the mirror, I grabbed my messenger bag from the floor and looked at the calendar on my desk. Today's word was *myopic*.

Myopic: Lack of discernment or long-range perspective in thinking or planning.

Well, they can't all be winners.

I barreled down the stairs and into the kitchen to find a plate of burnt toast on the table.

"Morning, mom," I sang, shaking my head. "I see you've been cooking again and I use the term 'cooking' loosely."

"Have your fun, Jill," she replied frowning and narrowing her eyes. "When you're in New York this summer and you need to make your own breakfast, you'll miss your good old mom."

I do miss you, mom. Never your cooking though.

"Oh," she added. "Suzanne Santin called last night. I forgot to tell you. She wanted to know if you were sick."

I gasped and felt my stomach tie into knots. I was a terrible friend. In the midst of all of the chaos caused by finding myself in another decade, I had neglected to keep up with one of the positive aspects of my old high school life. I had blown off Suzanne all week. Back in high school, I used to meet Suzanne in the library every morning. For me, it was a good place to hide so that I could avoid any awkward socializing before the bell for homeroom rang. For Suzanne, it was an opportunity to spend some time with her boyfriend (now husband) Connor who was a library monitor. I began to panic thinking that she'd be angry that I hadn't called her to explain. Suzanne was a great friend and although I didn't get to see her as often as I'd like, she was still very important to me. I had some backtracking to do.

"I have to get going, mom," I managed to reply. "Are you working tonight?"

"Sorry, honey, but I'm on second shift for the next two weeks to cover Marta's vacation," she said sadly. "Maybe you can pop by the hospital for dinner one night. I'm sure I can get one of the other techs to cover for a bit."

"Sounds good," I replied absently. "Gotta run. I need to catch up to Suzanne."

I sprinted out the door with a piece of burnt toast between my lips. I knew it was silly to worry that Suzanne would be angry. She was so easy-going. I just felt really guilty for forgetting about her in my attempt to woo Megan and Danielle.

When I walked into the library, the familiar smell of old books immediately calmed my nerves. It felt like home. Suzanne was sitting at a long table by the window, peering into her textbook. Her long, dark hair was pulled into a bun on the top of her head.

"Suze, I'm so sorry I've been MIA!" I said a little louder than was socially acceptable.

"Jillian! You had me worried. I heard Val say that you freaked out in trig and when I didn't see you for a few days, I got nervous."

"I'm so sorry, really. I've been a little out of it, but I'm doing much better." Her expression softened and I knew we were cool. I still felt like a jerk, though. "So how are you?"

"Well, I got my prom dress," she beamed. "Connor is still complaining about having to wear a tux, but he knows I'll beat him silly if he doesn't relent soon."

"I'm sure he'll be amazingly handsome," I added smiling. I suddenly wished I could tell her what was going on, but I barely believed it myself.

"So what about you?" she asked hesitantly. "Can I convince you to come with us? You know Connor would love to have a hot babe on each arm." I chuckled just imagining it. Yes, Connor would love that.

"Did I hear my name?" he asked walking up behind us and placing a kiss on the top of Suzanne's head. On his t-shirt was some anime girl with big boobs. To this day, his office at home is full of those stupid comic books. I didn't get it at all.

"Hey, Connor. I was just telling Suzanne that I appreciate the offer to be your second prom date, but I think I'm sitting this one out," I replied with an apologetic smile. I briefly thought of Danielle's mission to get me and Luke to go to the prom together. I might have even agreed if I didn't already know he goes with Val. Even though he's too good for her.

"Well, think about it, Jillian," he replied. "There's enough of me to go around." With a sweep of his arm, he mockingly bowed in front of us.

"You could help me out with something, though," I added. "Something that doesn't involve dancing and public humiliation."

"Of course, name it."

"I need to find statistics on this year's NFL Scouting Combine," I asked.

"Football? Um, why?" he asked clearly taken aback.

"It's actually for a friend. I'm helping her with a project." Suzanne and Connor were gaping at me. As far as they knew, I had no knowledge or interest in football. I didn't start following it until college, and it wasn't until I got to know Nate that I truly understood the ins and outs of the game.

"Well, I think we have *Pro Football Weekly's Draft Preview*. I'm sure that will have the stats for you. Let me check and I can drop it by your locker later." I thanked him profusely before he set off to dig through the periodicals. I planned to start filling Suzanne in on Operation Nate, but my mind strayed to the spot behind the gym, to Jack Daniels and to The White Stripes.

"Suze, can you keep a secret?" I asked quietly.

"Always," she replied leaning in closely. I scanned the room to make sure no one was listening.

"Well, lately during my free period and lunch, I've been hanging out behind the gym." Before I could finish and let her know about the bizarre friendship I'd formed with Luke, I was interrupted by the sound of a door creaking open. I looked up and saw Luke himself walking towards the front desk. After he dropped a large book into the book depository, he turned and our eyes met. He smirked and winked at me before breezing out of the library without a word.

"Um, Jillian, what was that all about?" Suzanne asked with eyes as large as saucers.

"Ah," I stammered. "I'll catch up with you tomorrow morning. I have to run."

I tried to walk and not sprint out the door. I honestly didn't know what possessed me to follow him. I just knew that his smile did bad things to my girl parts. When I pushed through the double doors to the third floor hallway, I found him pulling books from his locker. I kept my eyes trained ahead and tried to act as casually as possible. I wasn't very successful. He turned around slowly just as I was passing him, leaning his back against the locker.

"Behaving yourself, Cross, or were you just looking for new places to stash booze?" he asked with a sarcastic smile.

"You wound me, Luke," I retorted with my hand covering my heart, "I take my Reference Rooms very seriously. And just what were you doing with that monstrosity in there? What was that? *War and Peace?* "

"If you had been paying any attention in shop on Monday instead of orchestrating a peep show," he began coolly, "you'd have noticed that Scanlon was fixing my bike before the class was so rudely derailed. The book was a reference guide."

I suddenly felt sheepish. I hadn't considered that barging into class the way we did would actually interrupt something important. What made it worse was that it was something important to Luke. It was two weeks to graduation, and I guess I figured everyone was just goofing off. Maybe I just wasn't thinking at all.

"Don't worry about it," he added pushing off the locker. He towered over me and I could smell the smoke on his jacket and a hint of mint on his breath. "Having a front row seat to the show made up for it."

"I thought you said she wasn't your type," I replied softer than I would have liked, feeling a twinge of jealousy.

"I wasn't talking about Megan," he added, before turning and leaving me standing there feeling twitchy and awkward. I didn't exactly know what he meant, but I was pretty damn sure that Luke was flirting with me. While I had obviously been hoping for some kind of response when I bolted out of the library after him, it nevertheless rendered me speechless. I had a Master's Degree in English Literature. I was a walking dictionary and knew the difference between *effect* and *affect*. I didn't do speechless. I had to get a hold of myself.

"Bye, Luke," I called to him as he walked away. "I hope you're not too lonely without me today." With that he stopped, staring at me suspiciously before stalking back to where I was standing. I was beginning to enjoy baiting him.

"And why's that?" he asked cautiously, arching an eyebrow.

"Phase Two commences at lunch today," I answered lightly, pretending that I hadn't noticed the change in his demeanor. "I'll be in the cafeteria with the law abiding students today. Since you were such a fan of the first performance, I'll save you a front row seat just in case."

It was juvenile, but I wanted to be the one to walk away first. I wanted to leave *him* standing in the hallway looking twitchy and awkward. I wanted him to miss me when I wasn't around. After a few steps I turned back, waving over my shoulder while I tried not to giggle like an idiot. I knew he watched me walk down the hall. I could feel his eyes on me and the charge that ran through my body was like nothing I had ever felt before. Yes, I definitely enjoyed baiting him.

My heart was hammering in my chest after that brief exchange with Luke, but I needed to focus on Phase Two so I tried to push the thoughts of him away even though I still felt the crazy energy coursing through me. When I reached my locker, I found Connor trying unsuccessfully to jam a magazine through one of the slots.

"Are you defiling that poor innocent periodical on my account?" I teased.

"What are friends for?" he retorted, handing me the crumpled up magazine. "And here's *Pro Football Weekly's Draft Preview.* Maybe you'll tell me one of these days why you *really* needed this." He gave me a playful punch in the arm and turned to leave.

"Promise," I called to him with a smile.

During my first few classes, I scoured the Combine statistics and took notes on running times instead of reviewing for finals. It was a good draft in 1999 with a lot of talented players. I had all of the information I needed when I met Megan at her locker. I showed her my notes and gave her my opinions based on the player's actual performances in present day. When we walked into lunch, I was confident that Megan was ready to knock his socks off. A part of me was disappointed that I wouldn't be hanging behind the gym for Happy Hour with Luke. I hadn't even realized how much I looked forward to that part of the day, but Operation Nate was important. It was why I was here.

Looking across the cafeteria, I spotted Danielle and Josh at one of the tables. They were sharing a chair, and if it were anybody else I'd say they were about to fall off, but that kind of thing worked for them. I, however, would have landed flat on my ass. Josh had clearly done what I had asked and convinced Nate to sit at their table. What stopped me in my tracks was the sight of the familiar leather jacket in the seat across from Nate. My heart started to race and I felt my cheeks burn. I guess he didn't need me to reserve a seat for him after all.

"It's showtime," I said to Meg under my breath. "Knock'im dead."

I followed Megan's lead as she walked over to the table and dropped her books on top with a thud. Pulling out the chair next to Luke, she slid down into it with a sigh.

"Problems, Megan?" Danielle asked on cue.

"Oh, I've just been trying to narrow down my picks for the Fantasy Football Draft and I'm torn between a few players," she began in a dismissive tone.

Nate seemed to shift forward a bit. If I hadn't been watching for it, I might have missed it. I pulled up a chair at the head of the table so that I could watch Megan and witness Nate's reactions as well. My eyes met Luke's briefly before I looked away. I had to stay focused. This was about Megan.

"Which players?" Josh asked as if it was the most natural thing in the world to be discussing Fantasy Football with her.

"Well, the Redskins just signed Champ Bailey from Georgia and he ran a 4.4 40 at the Combine. He was All-Southeastern Conference and All-American cornerback. It's such a risk picking a rookie, but I think he can be amazing." She tapped her finger against her lip as she studied the page of statistics in front of her. Champ Bailey was a machine. He was a great pick. He was with the Broncos now, and he kicked our butts every time we played against him.

Nate was watching the exchange closely, and I noticed him looking uncomfortable. I wondered if he thought Megan had just memorized some words to impress him. It really wasn't the case. While she may not have had enough knowledge back then to successfully maneuver through a Fantasy Football draft, Megan understood the game better than any other girl I knew. Her dad had season tickets to the Seahawks and during the away games, Meg would watch with him, yelling profanities at the TV when Kitna would throw an interception. While Megan would never normally swear in front of her parents, on Sunday afternoons there was an unspoken understanding that calling Kitna an asshole in front of her dad was completely acceptable. Technically, Megan didn't need my help or those statistics, but I knew she would definitely get his attention by picking out some of the shining stars of that draft.

"If I can get Brett Favre, I'll definitely take him for QB, but have you seen Peyton Manning's arm? And the guy can audible his way out of any formation. He's got nerves of steel," she added shaking her head from side to side.

"Take Bailey if you can get him," Nate interjected. He played absently with the straw in his drink and didn't make direct eye contact. "He's an amazing corner. One of the best rookies I've ever seen."

I was actually stunned that he chimed in so soon. She hadn't even gotten to the bit about Ricky Williams or Edgerrin James.

"You think?" she replied playing it cool.

"Yeah. And I'd go right for Manning," he added finally meeting her gaze.

"Really? Even if Favre is available? I mean he's *Brett Favre*."

"Yeah, but he's getting old. How many years do you really think he has left?" *If he only knew.* "Manning was bred to play the game. I have some tapes of him playing with Tennessee. The guy is unreal. I can bring them in for you…I mean, if you're interested."

"I'd love to see them, but maybe you should send them to Kitna if he's as good as you say. He might learn something," she replied sarcastically.

"Now, now," he countered holding this hands up in mock surrender. "He's not that bad."

"Right," Megan added rolling her eyes.

"He has his merits," Nate voice grew a little louder.

"When he holds onto the ball," she answered with equal intensity.

I watched them volley back and forth. Meg was completely straying from the script, leaning over the table as she argued that the Seahawks should have drafted more defensive backs. Nate felt that they needed to build up the secondary. They were moving closer and closer, and I honestly didn't know if he wanted to throw her down on the table and kiss her or kill her. Even I, who was used to how explosive they could be, was feeling uncomfortable watching the highly charged exchange. I felt like I should interrupt and get them back on track, but I never got involved when they squabbled like this because they usually ended up naked very shortly after.

"Please," I heard Megan sneer. "I could run circles around your ass. I've seen how fast you are."

Somehow the topic of conversation had switched from the speed of Megan's Fantasy picks to whether or not Megan could beat Nate in the forty-meter.

"You're joking, right?" he asked incredulously.

"I don't joke," she replied dryly. "Try me."

"Fine," he replied smirking at her. "After school at the track." He got up from his side of the table and slowly walked over to her. "You better be ready to show me what you got," he added, his voice husky and low.

"Plan on it," she added standing up and gathering her books. "Danielle? Jillian?" she called beckoning us as she turned to leave. I looked back at the table as we followed her out of the cafeteria. Luke had been laughing with Josh and his smile almost caused me to lose my footing. As he turned to face us, our eyes met again. His smile faded as he watched me with an intensity that made my cheeks burn again. I wished that I knew what he was thinking at that moment. His expression was so strange.

After exiting the cafe, Megan held it together until she managed to scramble into the nearest restroom to jump up and down with excitement. I was thrilled that things had gone so well. It was classic Nate and Megan foreplay. I wouldn't be surprised if she tackled him right on the field in front of the entire track team after school.

"This is a cause for celebration," I announced pulling Joan from my back pocket. "To Megan and Nate," I began, raising the sparkling flask for my toast. "May all your ups and downs be under the covers." Megan batted my arm, but I managed to take a swig and hand it over to Danielle.

"Here's to the top," Danielle added raising the flask. "Here's to the middle. Let's hope after school, Meg gets a little." She took a swig, winced and handed it to Megan.

"I'm pretty sure it's not 'little', girls," she teased grabbing the flask. "And I'm gonna smoke him after school regardless."

"Now, you realize that he's going to get all hot and sweaty?" I asked. "It might be a little distracting."

"Trust me, Jillian," she replied with a sinister smile. "You haven't seen distracting yet." She tipped the flask back, finishing it off.

"This is going to be awesome," Danielle began. "We'll meet at the track after school so Megan can show Nate what she's got," she added with a hip shake.

I shoved Joan into my messenger bag so that I could remember to refill her at home. As we walked back out to the hallway, I noticed that I had a few minutes before I needed to be in World Lit. It was just enough time to take a peek behind the gym. He would probably need his daily nic fix.

"I'll catch up with you guys," I said nonchalantly. "I forgot something in my locker."

I knew if I rushed, I could make it there with a few minutes to spare. I told myself that it was more to hear his take on the scene in the cafeteria than for any other reason. I rushed through the sea of students quickly, but in my haste

I found myself colliding with a frazzled freshman. As I hit the ground, my bag opened, spilling the contents all over the floor. I watched in horror as my flask went skidding down the hall finally bouncing off of Mrs. Jacobs' shoe. She picked it up, inspected it and slowly looked over at me as I sat on the floor frozen.

"Jillian Cross," she began sternly. "In my classroom. Now." My heart was in my throat. I had never gotten in trouble before. And this was big trouble.

"I don't know what has gotten into you, Jillian," she began, glaring at me from behind her desk. "Your behavior has been strange, and now you're bringing alcohol to school?" She shook it testing to see if there was anything inside. I suddenly was extremely grateful that Megan was a flask-hog and finished up the rest of the vodka. "It's empty," she stated.

"Yes, I swear. I just brought it as a joke," I replied trying to rein in my panic.

"I'm really disappointed in you, Jillian. You should know better. Report to detention today. And I'm confiscating the flask."

The blood drained from my face and I felt the tears well up in my eyes. No. No. She couldn't take it.

"Mrs. Jacob, I understand what I did was wrong," I implored. "I promise I will never bring it back to school again. If you could just give it back to me—"

"Jillian, it's not appropriate for a seventeen-year-old girl to be carrying around a flask even if it's just a joke, so no, you're not getting it back," she replied. "Detention is in Mrs. Dupont's room today," she added dismissing me. I watched her drop Joan into the top drawer of her desk, turning the key to lock it once it was closed.

I could barely see through the moisture in my eyes as I left the room. It was so stupid to have taken it out inside the school. Well, it was stupid bringing it to school in the first place, but I needed it and now it was gone and I had no safety net. I was barreling back down the hall to hide in the restroom when I felt a tug on my arm.

"Jillian," Luke asked, his brows furrowed, "what's going on?"

I really didn't want to be in the hallway when the waterworks started, but when I looked up at him, the flood gates opened and I began to cry.

"I fell and my bag opened and Joan…" I was so angry and upset that I couldn't get the words straight. "You were right. I shouldn't have brought it here. Now I've got detention, and I don't even know what people *do* in detention."

"It isn't all that bad," he replied, his face softening. "You do your homework. You sit quietly. You act sorry and then you go home."

"It's not just that. She confiscated my flask. It was a gift and it meant a lot to me. I know you think I'm stupid, but it's important."

"Listen. Yeah, I think naming your flask is a little ridiculous, but I never said I thought you were stupid," he said looking at me intently again. "Come on. You need to get to class." He placed his hand on my shoulder to steer me back down the hall.

"So I'll see you after school with the rest of the burnouts," he said, chuckling. "This time it's my turn to save *you* a seat." He moved a strand of hair away from my face. It was wet from my embarrassing breakdown.

"Hey," he added, his voice soft and low, "smile."

It seemed so cliché. Like the part of the movie when the cute boy tells the sad girl that everything is going to be all right and suddenly it is. He told me to smile and I did. But once he went off to class and I was left to fester, I began to panic. I was going to Tacoma tomorrow with Luke, and I'd be doing it without my liquid courage. That was unacceptable.

By the time the bell for dismissal rang, I felt like I was going to be sick. As I entered Mrs. Dupont's classroom, I balked at how stereotypical the group in front of me was. There was a guy dressed in all black, carving something into the wood of his chair with a Swiss Army Knife. No one seemed to be paying attention to him. When he caught me staring, he leered at me. Apparently I was interrupting.

There was a guy and girl I recognized as juniors making out in the back of the classroom. She was sitting on one of the desks while he leaned over her, standing in between her legs. I think he was trying to vacuum her face off. I felt like I should pelt them with prophylactics and maybe some anti-bac soap.

Cody Adams was sitting front and center. He was the guy who tried to sell brownies and muffins laced with marijuana in the Senior Bake Sale. He thought it would be funny to get the whole class "baked at the Bake Sale." But the brownies tasted so bad, everyone that bought them started throwing up all over the place. It was just like that scene in *Stand By Me* except everyone got the munchies afterward. I'd had an aversion to baked goods ever since. *Thanks for that, Cody.*

Luke was sitting by the windows, watching me survey the room. He quirked his head calling me over, as if I was going to sit any place else.

"It's a freak show in here," I whispered leaning in close.

"Yeah," he agreed. "I heard there's a girl that talks to her flask."

"Har, har," I retorted. "You never told me why you were here anyway."

"Pissed off Dupont last week," he replied dismissively as he fidgeted with his pen. I noticed scabs on his knuckles.

"What happened to your hand?"

"Nothing," he answered quickly. "Just from fixing my bike." I thought there might be more to the story, but it was clear that Luke was not interested in telling me.

"So tomorrow," I began. "Are we still going to Tacoma?"

"Do I have a choice?" he replied smirking. I was suddenly struck with a terrifying thought.

"We're not going on your bike, are we?" There was no way I could handle riding on the back of Luke's bike with my arms wrapped around his waist. Just smelling his smoky, minty goodness now was making me light-headed.

"Would that be a problem?" he asked clearly mocking me.

"Well, yes," I stammered. "It's just that…well…it would be…I mean, I…"

"Relax," he said, interrupting my meltdown. "I have a car."

"Oh. Right. Good," I babbled ridiculously. "Not that the bike isn't good. Just not in this instance."

"So aside from replenishing your stash, we need to get you a new nameless flask," he added while doodling on his notebook.

"I don't want another flask. I want my flask," I pouted. "It has sentimental value." He got that same funny look on his face that I noticed in the cafeteria. I was about to ask him what was wrong when Mrs. Dupont walked in and instructed us to take out our homework and work silently. I tried to concentrate on my trig study sheet, but it was really distracting sitting next to Luke. He, however, didn't seem to have the same problem as he worked on some chemistry report.

Ten minutes before detention was over, I heard something hit the floor next to me. Looking at the ground, there was a balled up piece of paper. I looked at Luke and he made a slight motion for me to pick it up. *Luke Chambers is passing me a note? Is he going to ask me to go steady and drive to Inspiration Point, too?*

I grabbed the note off the floor and slowly flattened it out. Mrs. Dupont looked up, but I carried on as if I were arranging the papers on my desk. Inside I saw what Luke's messy handwriting looked like. The note read:

Don't ask any questions. When it happens, do what she says and don't act suspicious.

I was about to ask him if Cody had offered him some baked goods when I noticed he was up at Mrs. Dupont's desk asking to go to the restroom. How was I supposed to avoid acting suspicious when I had no idea what he was talking about?

Luke had been gone for about five minutes when the deafening sound of the fire alarm ripped through the school. *He wouldn't. Would he?*

Mrs. Dupont seemed to lose her hard edge and nervously ushered us out of the building and over by the football field. From where I was standing, I saw Megan and Nate running on the track. Meg was wearing a tight t-shirt and sweat pants while Nate had on loose track shorts and a tank top. I couldn't believe I was missing all of the action. I couldn't see Luke anywhere.

Since it was already three-thirty, Mrs. Dupont dismissed our motley little group so I headed to the track, confused by what had happened. I found Danielle and Josh sitting on the bleachers.

"It's the badass herself," Josh greeted, his arm slung around Danielle's shoulder.

"That's me," I mused sarcastically. "So fill me in." I looked out at the field. Meg had somehow removed her sweats and was now running in her sports bra and bike shorts. Nate was shirtless.

"It's like some bizarre mating ritual," Danielle began in a low voice. "They won't stop doing laps, and they're slowly stripping off all of their clothes. One more lap and we may have to call the cops."

"So, is someone winning?" I asked leaning against the railing.

"I don't think there'll be any losers here," Josh laughed.

"So, you got an early reprieve," Danielle added. "We heard the alarm. Someone try to blow up the chem lab?"

"I'm not sure what happened. I think Luke might have done it, but I don't know where he went."

"Why would you think Luke had anything to do with it?" she asked curiously.

"He passed me the most ridiculous note. I swear he watches too many spy movies because it was way too cryptic."

"Wait," she interrupted with a raised brow. "You were passing notes with Luke Chambers in detention?"

"Well, not really," I argued. "Just one note." I felt silly justifying it, but I didn't want Danielle thinking something was going on when it wasn't. Val would be asking him to the prom any day now, and I didn't want Danielle to get her hopes up that Luke and I would end up together. It just wasn't meant to happen.

"There he is," Danielle said motioning to the bottom of the bleachers. I watched him as he climbed up the stairs two at a time and stopped next to me.

"Well hello, Luke," Danielle greeted. I could tell she thought he had come because of me, and she was feeling smug. Clearly, he had wanted to see Nate and Megan's showdown.

"You know, detention was going to be over in another ten minutes," I teased. "You didn't have to go to such extreme measures to spring us."

He flashed me a mischievous smile, dug into his coat pocket and tossed my sparkly pink flask into my hands.

I was shocked, almost speechless. "What? How?" Luke shrugged.

"I went back after everyone was gone. She left her desk unlocked. Scored a cool lighter," he replied, casually twirling a black lighter with red flames around his fingers.

I couldn't believe it. He had pulled the fire alarm and evacuated the school to get my flask back. No one had ever done anything like that for me before. Overcome with emotion, I threw my arms around his neck and hugged him tightly. However, once I felt him up against me, I realized what a mistake I had made. I was grateful, but I didn't want him thinking I was throwing myself at him…even though I kind of was. Obviously surprised, Luke seemed to struggle with what to do with his hands for a moment before I felt them settle lightly on my hips. It felt really nice—too nice. I needed to keep it casual so I pulled away quickly.

"Sorry," I began trying to sound light and breezy, "I didn't mean to attack you. I just can't believe you did this."

"All in a day's work, Cross," he replied sarcastically. Something told me he was trying to keep it light and breezy too, but that strange expression was back on his face. "I'm taking off," he finally added. "Meet me here tomorrow at noon?"

"Absolutely," I replied watching him slowly walk back down the steps, lighting a cigarette once he reached the bottom. I looked down at Danielle after Luke had left.

"I can't believe you don't see it," she said in a serious tone.

"Is this about prom again?" I whined. I had just gotten Joan back. I didn't want to fight about prom right now.

"No. Not prom, Jillian," she shook her head and looked away. "Wow. You really don't."

There was one thing I did know—things were the way they should be. I was standing next to Danielle and Josh in the bleachers, watching Megan and Nate running neck-and-neck around the track. Just as she would pull ahead, Nate would bow his head and push forward catching up. I think in the battle of distractions, Megan's sports bra was winning.

I thought about how I had only been back in high school for a week, and I had made so much progress despite my minor setback with Joan today. I thought about the black and white picture of Luke on Facebook and the boy I had come to know. It would sting too much witnessing Val asking him to the prom knowing that she would most likely attack him on prom night. It shouldn't bother me, but it really did. I thought about *That* Jillian and what she would be doing right now instead.

The lines were getting blurred and it was getting harder and harder to differentiate between the things I should change and the things I shouldn't. No matter which way I looked at it though, I couldn't shake the feeling.

Luke should not go to the prom with Val.

CHAPTER 8

Lake

Something didn't seem right. I was alone behind the gym, which was weird because that never happened anymore. She was always with me. And for the first time in a long time, I felt restless instead of relaxed. The wooded area behind the school was replaced with a field of flowers growing in small patches. The sweet scent reminded me of whatever kind of perfume she wore.

Where the hell is she?

I stood up to leave and suddenly saw her leaning against the wall, watching me. She was wearing the red lipstick that had been driving me insane all week. It matched the little shirt she wore and it was already making me feel that uncomfortable tightening in my chest. She had a funny smirk on her face, and I was just about to ask her where the hell she'd been when she spoke.

"I can prove that you're full of shit, you know," she said looking cocky and smug.

"Oh, really?" I challenged, watching her red lips.

"Really," she responded walking towards me, dragging her finger along the wall as she moved. I twisted and leaned my shoulder against the building, waiting for her to explain. She stopped, leaning in to face me. I could feel the heat from her breath as she spoke.

"You tease me for naming my flask. You tease me for naming my car. But I'm willing to bet there's something that *you've* named," she added as her eyes darted below to the zipper on my jeans. She looked back into my eyes, daring me to respond. My heart started to race, and I choked out a cough.

Jillian was talking about my dick.

While I was more than willing to discuss this topic with her at great length, I was taken aback by the direction of the conversation, so to speak.

"All guys do, don't they?" she asked arching an eyebrow.

"Only the douchebags," I retorted trying to appear unaffected.

"I could help you," she offered, looking up at me from under her long lashes.

"What are you talking about?" I managed to ask. I was starting to breathe heavy.

"Think of a name. I'm good at it," she added as her tongue quickly wet her lips. "Naming things, I mean. But there are a few things I need to know." I knew there'd be no turning back if I answered her. I knew I shouldn't engage her, but I wanted her too much.

"Like what?"

"Well, there are things I need to know in order to think of the perfect name. Take my flask, for example. I know how it looks," she began as she ran her hand down my arm and positioned herself in front of me. "It looks….enticing. I know how it feels," she continued, resting the palms of both hands on my chest. "It feels hard and rough."

I was working so hard to regulate my breathing, but I could hear myself practically panting. "I know how it tastes," she whispered in my ear before slowly lowering herself so that she rested on her knees in front of me. "It tastes…delicious."

My as-yet-unnamed dick was already reacting to her presence. While this wasn't something I expected from Jillian, I couldn't deny the fact that the sight of her on her knees in front of me was un-freaking-believable. But this couldn't happen.

"Jillian…" I warned.

"If you don't want my help, just say so, Luke," she interrupted. Without breaking eye contact, she reached for the button on my jeans. It slowly popped open and her eyes moved from mine to the open fabric in front of her. I held my breath as she reached for the zipper, but before she was able to grab it, I heard a snicker. I panicked looking around wildly and saw Nate and Megan sitting in director's chairs by the path leading to the parking lot.

What the hell?

"I'm telling you, Nate," Megan began as she gestured wildly. "Her form's all wrong. I mean, look at that. She'll never last long kneeling that way."

"Meg, Meg," Nate countered. "While I respect your opinion, you have no idea what you're talking about. Does it look like my man Luke is complaining? Who cares about form?"

I can't believe this shit.

"What the hell are you two doing here?" I barked. Jillian just stared up at me with wide eyes. *Just please don't move. I will make them go away. I promise.*

"We're just trying to help you, Luke," Megan explained. "You don't have to get all worked up." She snickered again. "Well, I guess it's too late for that."

"Nice," Nate added raising his palm for a high five.

"Out! Both of you!" I demanded pointing down the path the chairs were blocking. Jillian didn't need any coaching. We were doing just fine on our own.

"Chill out, man. You have your work cut out for you there, Jillian. He really needs to learn to *release* these bottled up feelings," Nate added, his shoulders shaking as he giggled like an asshole.

"Oooh!" Megan squealed. "Another good one. Let's get out of here. I can tell when we're not appreciated." I glanced down at Jillian, trying to gauge her reaction. She seemed amused, and I was filled with relief that she didn't go storming off. When I looked back up again, Megan, Nate and the chairs were all gone.

"Finally," I sighed smiling at the beautiful girl before me. "Where were we?"

"I believe I was discarding these," she replied finally dragging the zipper of my jeans slowly down. They pooled on the ground at my feet leaving me in my boxer briefs. I should have felt the chill in the air, but I didn't.

I heard a gasp and moved to yank my pants back up, but Jillian was kneeling on them. My eyes darted around to locate the source of the interruption and found Danielle and Josh leaning against a tree behind us.

"Jillian, don't you dare!" she scolded. "Josh, do you believe what you're seeing?"

"I think it's pretty clear what we're seeing," he replied with a lazy smirk. He seemed distracted by the music playing on his headphones.

"That's not what I mean, Josh," she replied exasperated. "I mean it, Jillian. Get up now! I will not let you go down on Luke while the ground is littered with trash. You're going to ruin those cute jeans. Jesus, Luke, this place is a mess!"

"So help me God, Fletcher," I growled. "If you don't get your girlfriend out of here right now, I will kick your indie-music-loving ass."

"Honey, I think you're pissing Luke off," he said a little too calmly for my taste. Damn right I was pissed. This was all so inappropriate.

"Fine, Luke," she sneered. "But if her clothes are ruined, I'm holding you responsible." They turned up the path, arm-in-arm and disappeared.

"Jillian, I'm not going to be able to handle it if anymore of your friends interrupt us again," I managed in a strained voice.

"I'm not easily distracted, Luke," she replied. "I think I was working on 'touch', right?" She was torturing me, wanting me to ask for it.

"Oh God, yes," I panted, closing my eyes. I was positive that I would spontaneously combust if she didn't touch me soon.

Taking deep breaths, I peered down and watched as Jillian reached out—almost in slow motion—and as soon as she made contact with my erection, I squeezed my eyes shut and shuddered violently. As I cursed through the jolt of pleasure running through me, I awoke startled.

I wasn't in the woods behind the gym.

I wasn't with Jillian.

I was in my bed, sweaty and sticky with my dick in my hand. I hadn't had a wet dream since I was fifteen, and it was goddamn humiliating.

I dragged myself into the bathroom to clean up while trying to imagine how I was going to look her in the eye without seeing her on her knees. I splashed cold water on my face and stared into the mirror at my flushed reflection. I had only really known her for less than a week and she was driving me crazy. The hardest part—well, *one* of the hardest parts—was that I just couldn't read her. She'd go toe-to-toe with me, not backing down. She wasn't afraid to disagree with me or say something that sounded crazy. Actually, most everything she said sounded kind of crazy. But I never felt like she was trying to impress me. She just...was. But even in our bantering, there was a line we never crossed. She never said or did anything blatant. She seemed interested, but I definitely felt her holding back. I wondered if there was someone else she talked about flasks with and stupidly wanted to pummel the faceless asshole. I didn't have time for this kind of distraction. This girl had become a real problem. Now I had another reason to dread going to school.

I'd at least have the morning to shake off my dream before I'd see her, and I still had a car ride to Tacoma to deal with tomorrow. That was a whole other problem. By then, though, Dream Jillian would hopefully be a hazy memory. It was kind of bittersweet, though. I knew I couldn't have a normal conversation with her if the memory was crisp, but part of me didn't really want to let the dream go yet.

I sampled Grace's apple-something coffee cake because she added sour cream this time and, apparently, that was a big deal. She was distracted revising a recipe for dinner Sunday night for veal saltimbocca so I didn't get the usual third degree. She was muttering something about butter, garlic and gruyere, which I thought might be a cheese. Giving her a quick kiss on the cheek, I flew out the door, passing my bike in the driveway and hopping into the Lexus instead.

When I got to school, instead of dealing with Wakefield at my locker, Val Cooper was passing by instead.

"Luke! Where have you been hiding yourself these days?"

It was pretty well-known around school that Val liked to have a good time. She had a great body and wanted everyone to know it. Most of the guys at school would kill to go out with her. And while she had a nice rack, she was crazy as hell. I indulged her when she cornered me, but I wasn't interested in half the school's sloppy seconds.

"What's up, Val?"

"What's up? You tell me," she purred. "Will I be seeing you at the bonfire next week?"

"Don't know yet," I replied casually. I wasn't going to make the same mistake I'd made with Danielle. I was done talking about the stupid bonfire.

"You have to let me know then," she added resting her hand on the arm of my jacket. "I'd like to see more of you." She smiled, waiting for me to respond, clearly impressed by her double entendre. Unfortunately, I wasn't. It sounded like bad porn dialogue to me, and no one watches porn for the dialogue.

"You'll be the first to know," I replied before heading to the library. If she didn't come on so goddamn strong, she'd be all right.

Once I got into the library, I dropped the repair manual into the return bin. Connor Hentschel was sitting behind the librarian's desk staring at something across the room. I turned to see what had him so distracted and saw that it was Jillian. It had only been a few days since I had pummeled Wakefield, my knuckles were still scabbed over, and I was already imagining pounding my sore fist into Connor's face. I wasn't sure when I started making it a habit of kicking people's asses over some girl who wasn't mine. That wasn't okay. But fortunately when I glanced back at her table, I realized that she had been sitting with Connor's girlfriend, Suzanne. I felt like an ass.

I really wasn't ready to deal with her yet, and I was pissed at myself so I kept walking and decided I'd play it off like I hadn't noticed her. That brilliant idea lasted about thirty seconds because as I walked by, my curiosity got the better of me and I looked up. She was staring right at me. I smiled and in a panic—I don't know where it came from—but I winked. I walked straight to the door and the moment I made it back into the hall, I wanted to bash my head against the wall. Who the hell winks? Well, me, apparently.

I was pulling books out of my locker, feeling like an idiot, when I heard the door behind me. I knew it was her. When I turned around, I saw her walking my way, staring straight ahead, and I was sure she was ignoring me because I was the biggest douchebag on the planet—a douchebag who winks. I had no choice. I had to test the waters.

When we spoke, I noticed right away that there was something different about our conversation this time. While we fell into our regular back-and-forth and I teased her about her liquid lunches, it took every ounce of my self-control not to focus on her lips. I tried to keep the conversation light, but it wasn't working. When I mentioned interrupting Scanlon's class, her cheeks flamed, and it made it even harder not to stare. I commented on how much I enjoyed the performance, but she thought I was talking about Megan. While I wouldn't deny that I noticed Megan's legs, it wasn't what I remembered most about that day. I only remembered Jillian.

I went on with my day, but no matter how hard I tried to put her out of my head, I couldn't. When I finally made it back to my locker, I was about to grab a smoke out back when I saw Danielle heading in my direction.

"Luke!" she called from down the hall. "Wait up!" Pretending I didn't hear her, I continued on, but sure enough began to hear the clattering of heels behind me.

"Luke! Slow down!" she shouted from behind me. "Jeez!"

"Hey kid," I replied casually. "Did you need me?"

"Enough is enough, Luke," she began seriously. "You have to go to the prom." I needed to take Dream Luke's advice and tell Josh that I'd kick his ass if he didn't keep his girlfriend away from me.

"Why is that?" I replied indulging her.

"Because years from now when you've moved on from your rebel-without-a-cause phase, you'll be reminiscing with friends and someone will tell a funny story about how they spiked the punch at prom and they'll be like 'What was your prom like, Luke?' and you'll be all 'I didn't go. It wasn't my thing' and they'll be like 'What the hell does that mean, Luke? It's the freaking prom' and you'll feel stupid, and I don't want you to feel stupid, Luke." Once she finished, she took a deep breath, and I stood there speechless.

"C'mon. Walk with me," she quickly added. "We'll discuss how you're going to ask her."

I thought that maybe if I stayed really still she'd just go away. Wasn't that how you treated predators in the wild? But she was still standing there, smiling and waiting for me to follow. The girl was exhausting. Her prom plans were inconsequential anyway. Jillian didn't want to go to the prom with me so it didn't matter. Why would I go through the trouble of asking her only to be turned down?

I didn't feel like arguing with Danielle, so I walked with her to the cafeteria. She was detailing some complicated plan that involved notes in Jillian's locker when we got there. I wasn't really listening, but the parts that managed to sink in were damn near comical. I don't write poetry. Before I needed to comment on her asinine plan, I spotted Josh sitting at a table with Nate Barrett.

"Luke," he greeted. "What are you doing here? I didn't even know you had this lunch."

"I usually eat earlier, but I got tied up today," I began, not wanting to admit why I had come. Danielle slid into the same seat Josh was in, which didn't make sense because there were chairs everywhere.

"Well, grab a seat," he replied. "Nate was just telling me about the training program they have at FSU."

"So you're headed to Florida?" I asked pulling out the chair across from Nate.

"Looks like it," he replied with a sigh. He didn't seem overly enthusiastic. "My dad's an alum. It's always been a dream of his for me to go there, and they have an amazing football program."

"My mom got kind of crazy when I started applying, too," Josh added rolling his eyes. "She didn't want me to move away. She didn't want me pre-law. She didn't want me on the east coast. She had *lots* of opinions."

"So what did you do?" Nate asked.

"Well," he replied looking at Danielle. "I'm pre-law at Fordham next year while my little lady here is at NYU." Danielle leaned in and kissed the Poor Bastard's nose. Nate still looked deep in thought.

73

"Where did you want to go?" I asked.

"Florida's awesome, really," he began shifting uncomfortably in his chair.

"But…" I interrupted trying to get him to talk.

"Well, my granddad was a big college football fan. I would watch the games with him on Saturday afternoons, and I knew all the fight songs. But it was when I watched that movie *Rudy* that I started thinking about Notre Dame."

I suddenly felt very sorry for him. He just looked so damn sad. As much as I hated disappointing Grace and Carter, I didn't think I could make that big of a concession for them. Honestly, they would never have put me in that position.

"Did you apply?" Danielle asked.

"Yeah," he replied, staring down at the straw in his drink. "I didn't tell my dad, but I had to at least know if I'd get in."

"So?" she coaxed.

"Yeah, I got in. But it doesn't matter," he replied brushing it off. "FSU has a great program, and who wouldn't want to spend four years in Florida instead of South Bend? What the hell do they do out there anyway?"

"Florida does sound fantastic," Danielle agreed.

"I don't want to pry, Nate," Josh added hesitantly, "but I think you're making a big mistake. Especially if Notre Dame is your dream school."

"You need to talk to your old man," I added. I barely knew Nate, but I couldn't stop myself from chiming in. If I had the opportunity to go to Notre Dame, I sure as hell wouldn't let anything get in my way.

He was about to respond when Megan collapsed into the chair next to me looking pissed. I looked up and saw Jillian standing at the head of the table. She avoided eye contact with me, and it made me uneasy again.

When Danielle asked Megan why she was pouting, she launched into a crazy explanation involving Fantasy Football and the draft. Right away I recognized the look on Nate's face. It was the same one I saw when Megan bent over the hood of Jillian's car in Scanlon's class. He had it bad. It was when Nate started to challenge Megan to some kind of a race after school that Josh leaned over to me.

"Twenty says she gets his pants around his ankles before prom," he whispered so Danielle couldn't hear. The prom was in less than a week. Despite the angry sex that was brewing between the two, I'd give them a little more time.

"You got it. I'll give them until graduation," I countered extending my hand.

Before I knew it, Megan was strutting out of the cafeteria with Danielle and Jillian in tow. Nate's eyes were trained on her as she left.

"One of you jackasses could have stopped me before I stuck my foot in my mouth," he complained.

"And interrupt that?" Josh replied with a smirk. "You're going down, Chambers," he whispered.

It was pretty funny seeing Nate so flustered. Jillian had been right. It wasn't something I would've wanted to miss. I turned back to the door of the cafeteria and caught sight of her. She had been watching me, and I didn't look away when our eyes met even though I knew I should. I wondered if I was as transparent as Nate.

Looking at my watch, I realized I had a few minutes before I needed to be in class so I headed out back for a quick smoke. I sunk down on the milk crate and leaned back finally feeling calm. Despite Danielle's intensity, I liked hanging out with Josh and Nate. I could almost envision us all in Danielle's "perfect" limo heading to the prom. Jillian would naturally be passing around her flask because we wouldn't be able to make it through the evening without a few shots. Megan and Nate would probably be arm wrestling or whatever it was they'd do to get off. Josh, the Poor Bastard, would be wearing his top hat. And Danielle would be loving it because I had finally caved.

But, again, it didn't matter. Jillian didn't want me to ask her. I almost wished she had never brought it up.

Heading to chemistry, I noticed a commotion in the hallway. Jillian was dashing towards me. She looked like she was about to cry. I grabbed her arm as she passed by me, and noticed her eyes were welling up and her face was flushed. If Wakefield was bothering her again I'd kill him. Her lip started to quiver, and I began envisioning all of the gruesome things I could do to him to make him pay.

She started to stammer through her tears. It was at least a relief that Wakefield wasn't harassing her again, but I couldn't understand what her flask had to do with anything. When she explained that Mrs. Jacobs confiscated it, and she was given detention, I realized why she had been all worked up. Detention wasn't a big deal, and we could get another flask if that's what she needed.

She stopped crying, but her eyes were still red and a few pieces of her hair hung loosely around her face. I hated seeing her this way. Without thinking first, I tucked a strand of hair behind her ear, and she smiled, blinking up at me through wet lashes. I was probably grinning back at her like an idiot, but I didn't care.

I made a point to get to Mrs. Dupont's for detention early. I wanted to be in the room before she got there so she wouldn't get too freaked out. You never knew who was going to show up. I scanned the class and saw Lester carving up the desk again. Anne-Marie and Jon were about to screw on a desk in the back, and Cody was zoned out as usual. Pretty mild crowd.

When Jillian arrived, she peered into the room with wide eyes. Anne-Marie picked that moment to moan behind me. Jon had his hand up her shirt. When Jillian looked my way, I motioned her over. She was damn lucky that flask was empty or her parents would have been getting a really unpleasant phone call from Mrs. Jacobs, and she'd be getting a three-day suspension.

I was relieved when Mrs. Dupont arrived and told us to take out our homework. I needed to distract myself or I wouldn't be able to stand up without physically declaring that I had been thinking about Jillian all day. I grabbed my chemistry report and read the same paragraph three times. To someone watching, it might have looked like I was engrossed in the most interesting thing I'd ever read, while in reality I was thinking about the drawer in Mrs. Jacobs' room where she kept confiscated lighters and cigarettes. I had lost many packs and a few lighters to that drawer. She kept it locked and always had the keys on her. If I could swipe the keys, I would be able to grab the flask. I just needed to do it without throwing any suspicion on Jillian.

I considered going to her class and pretending that I needed help with trig, but I didn't know how I could get her to leave me alone with the keys. And honestly, the idea of doing extra work in trig was really unappealing. I needed to get her out of the building.

The plan came to me pretty quickly. I was taking a really big chance, but once I fleshed out the idea, I knew I was going to do it. I ripped out a sheet from my notebook and scribbled a quick note to Jillian because I needed her to leave with everyone else. As silly as it sounded, she needed an alibi. I crumpled up the paper and dropped it on the floor between us. When I motioned for her to pick it up, she looked at me like I had two heads. I didn't want to stick around and answer questions, and I definitely didn't want to lose my nerve so I marched up to Mrs. Dupont and asked to use the john. She shot me a look that told me she'd rather say no, but agreed to let me leave.

I needed to move fast so I jogged right over to the gym locker rooms. I knew there'd be team practices and people milling around that might see me, but it was the only way to avoid suspicion. If an alarm was pulled in the building, it would obviously incriminate me. With all of the practices and people using the weight room, they'd never be able to narrow it down. I just needed to move fast.

I was surprised to find the hallway outside of the locker room empty. Looking from side to side, I quickly grabbed the fire alarm on the wall and pulled the handle down. I'd be lying if I said I hadn't always wanted to do this. Once the deafening sound rang out, I bolted back down the hall through the school. I watched around the corner as a frazzled Dupont ushered the detention class out of the building.

I quietly crept into Mrs. Jacobs' empty room, closing the door behind me. If worse came to worse, I could probably pick the lock. But as I had hoped when I inspected her desk, I found the she left quickly without locking her drawers. Inside the top drawer was the jackpot of illegal items: cigarettes, bongs, matches, rubbers, some cool lighters and one pink sparkly flask named Joan. While I was tempted to empty the contents into my rucksack, I tried to focus and grabbed the flask. But I couldn't resist snagging a black lighter with red and orange flames. I deserved a little reward.

I checked the hallway, making sure no one was around and walked calmly out of the school through the side door on the opposite side of the gym. When I ran into Mrs. Dupont over by the track, she was alone.

"Mr. Chambers," she said eying me suspiciously. "Where have you been?"

"I heard the fire alarm when I was in the john," I replied casually. "I was busy."

Her scowl softened slightly.

"I dismissed the class, Mr. Chambers," she sneered. "I trust that you'll be able to keep your temper in check going forward so I won't have you in detention next week, as well."

"Of course, Mrs. Dupont," I replied remembering Scanlon's plea for me to be nice. I turned and left before I changed my mind. I needed to find Jillian.

As I passed the track, I saw a half-dressed Megan running along with a shirtless Nate. *Jesus, I'm going to lose that goddamn bet.* I scanned the stands and saw Jillian leaning against the railing talking to Josh and Danielle. I was suddenly really nervous. The gravity of what I had done hit me. I pulled a fire alarm for her. I evacuated a school. I should just serenade her like John-Freaking-Cusack while I'm at it. I slowly climbed the stairs feeling their eyes on me as I got closer.

"Luke," Danielle greeted with that smug little smirk. She could see right through me and it pissed me off. I wasn't about to give her the satisfaction so I remained as casual as possible.

"You know, detention was going to be over in another ten minutes," Jillian teased. "You didn't have to go to such extreme measures to spring us."

I couldn't help but smile. She had no idea what I had done. I dug into my pocket and threw the flask over at her. She stared at it stunned before looking up at me wildly.

"I went back after everyone was gone. She left her desk unlocked. Scored a cool lighter," I replied, impressed with my ability to act like the whole thing was no big deal. I had managed to remain composed until she threw her arms around my neck and pressed herself against me. My body immediately reacted remembering Dream Jillian.

I was terrified to move and found myself frozen in place with no idea of what to do. Taking a breath, I pushed the memory of the dream out of my head and settled my hands softly on her hips. Keeping it casual.

"Sorry," she began nervously, "I didn't mean to attack you. I just can't believe you did this."

"All in a day's work, Cross," I replied trying to hide my discomfort. I knew I was screwed if I had to spend the day with her alone tomorrow. We had an hour ride to Tacoma and an hour back home. It was going to be a disaster. "I'm taking off," I said knowing I just needed to leave and clear my head. "Meet me here tomorrow at noon?"

"Absolutely," she said as I turned and walked back down the steps.

Away from the chaos of school, I started to obsess over how crazy my life had gotten. A little over a week ago, I had daydreamed of coeds and body shots and the start of my new life. Last Friday, I was consumed with the need to forge my own path—earning instead of taking. Friday afternoon, I heard her voice for the first time and thought she was ridiculous. On Monday, my knuckles throbbed because I laid into Wakefield for screwing with her. On Tuesday, she wore a really tight pair of jeans and I saw the slightest hint of crisp, white lacy panties when she bent over on the milk crate. On Wednesday, she tried to tell me that Green Day embodied the social conscience of our generation when all I could think of was their song about jerking off. On Thursday, when I told her about getting a job at Jonas's, she made me promise to teach her how to mix dirty drinks when she came home for break. On Friday, I pulled a goddamn fire alarm so that I could swipe her flask from Jacobs' desk. And all I can think about is Jillian with her red lips and shirt.

When I woke up the next morning, I felt hung over from the lack of sleep. My eyes burned, my body ached and I knew I was going to need a few extra minutes in the shower to remedy one particular problem.

After an extra long shower and two helpings of Grace's pesto scrambled eggs, I felt refreshed. I climbed into the Lexus and drove to school wondering what craziness she was going to unleash on me today. As I turned into the lot, my heart stopped and my dick hardened again. Leaning against her car looking hot as all hell was Jillian wearing a tight red shirt and smiling at me with shiny red lips.

This was a horrible idea.

CHAPTER 9

Jillian

When I heard the Cher song coming from my alarm radio my stomach immediately lurched. It wasn't because I had anything against Cher or because I seriously loathe techno music, it was because I was an idiot. Blinded by my desire for a decent cocktail, I was practically forcing Luke to take me to Tacoma to get a fake ID. At the time, it seemed like one of the best ideas I'd ever had. In retrospect, I was definitely not thinking it through. In my defense, I never would have predicted the events of the previous day. From getting caught with Joan at school to Luke's decision to pull the fire alarm, that one day was more action-packed than my previous four years at Reynolds High combined.

As I lay in bed last night thinking about Luke and everything that happened, I became more aware of the shift in our dynamic. Could he have actually been flirting with me in the hall yesterday morning? Did I really catch him staring at me in the cafe? Did he notice my blush when he tucked the strand of hair behind my ear? I was twenty-nine-years old, and I was swooning over a boy pulling a fire alarm. It was wrong on so many levels.

I dragged myself out of bed and looked for my non-existent iPhone for the eighth day in a row. I missed my apps and instant iPod access. I was naked without it. When I got back to 2011, I was never taking it out of my pocket again.

If I get back to 2011.

I had attempted over the past few days to push that idea out of my head, but it would inevitably sneak back in. I was trying hard not to interfere with the natural course of events, knowing that at some point I would need to deal with the repercussions. While it was tempting to send Britney Spears an anonymous tip to avoid any backup dancers that reeked of desperation and weed, I knew better. I would only allow myself to speed along these minor events that were destined to happen anyway, not change things altogether. That was a time travel no-no. But then the uncertainty would creep in. What if I were stuck here reliving my whole existence all over again? If I were staying, shouldn't I be given a chance to do what I want? *Or who I want?* If you're given a chance to do things over, shouldn't you take advantage?

It had only been a week, and I wasn't ready to accept that I could be sentenced to relive the last decade over again. I needed to have faith that I was here for a purpose, and once Danielle was free from Val and once Nate had discovered how happy he was with Megan, I'd be sent back to my old life. That would mean that Luke Chambers would have to be off limits.

I had to put on my big girl pants and get ready for the trip to Tacoma. Swoon-worthy or not, I couldn't allow myself to think of Luke that way anymore. I would behave, and I wouldn't bait him anymore.

I walked over to my closet secure in the notion that I would act like the nice little girl that I was back in high school. Scanning the contents, nothing seemed appealing. Then my eyes fell on that tight, red shirt Danielle bought me for the reunion. It couldn't hurt to look good. As long as I didn't encourage him, looking good was not a crime. In fact, I was sure there were several states that would outlaw some of the other fashion disasters in this closet. It was really the only option. And if I was going to wear the red top, I would need to wear the skinny jeans, too. Danielle bought them to wear together and who was I to question her fashion sense?

I had a lot of time to kill so I flipped on the radio and listened to a local Top 40 Countdown. I was really enjoying the blast from the past until the DJ played a song from a "new" group called Smashmouth. I groaned when I realized I had to endure listening to *All Star*. Why was it that more than ten years later, this song was still in every commercial and movie in existence? I swear Mr. Smashmouth must be rolling in royalties. I turned off the radio unable to stomach hearing them "get their game on" again. Before heading downstairs, I tore off Myopic and looked at the Word of the Day.

Cognizance: awareness, realization, or knowledge. I am cognizant of the fact that my old wardrobe sucks.

I was happy to find that my parents weren't home, but were out running errands. I didn't want to risk answering questions about where I was going or who I was going with. I didn't think they'd be thrilled with either response. Honestly, neither was I.

I was about to walk out the front door when I heard the phone ring.

"Hello," I answered, twirling the long cord of the wall phone around my finger. I think my parents bought their first cordless phone two years ago. They weren't particularly high tech people.

"You'll never guess who's going out on a date tonight," the voice exclaimed without an introduction.

"Well, hello, Danielle," I replied facetiously. "I'm fine. How are you?"

"Did you hear me, Jillian?" she retorted. "This is huge!"

I really wanted to invent the 'That's what she said' joke, but I didn't. "So, Nate grew a pair and asked her out? That *is* good news, Danielle." I gave myself a mental pat on the back. "So, where's he taking her?'

"There's some early preview of that new *Star Wars* movie," she began with obvious distaste in her tone. "I guess Meg was really into *Star Wars* when she was younger. Who knew?"

Unfortunately, I knew only too well. I had to listen to her dissect and criticize almost every scene in those disastrous prequels. Although she denied it, I'm pretty sure she wrote a letter of protest to George Lucas regarding the casting of Hayden Christiansen. I remember her clearly saying that he was only capable of two things, scowling and pouting, and that Vader would never pout.

"So I'm heading to her place to help pick out an outfit for the evening. Are you still doing chores for your folks today?" she asked. I could tell she was practically giving me the puppy-dog eyes through the phone.

"Huh? Oh, yes," I stammered, almost forgetting that I had already created a cover for myself. "Tell her to make him hold the popcorn. Only good things can come from having to reach into his lap and then pop something into her mouth. Oh! And make her wear a skirt. They'll be sitting side by side and her legs will brush up against his from time to time."

"Jillian!" she exclaimed. "You are so bad! I'll call you as soon as I hear how this next phase goes."

"Wish her luck for me!" I hung up the phone and smiled, secure in the feeling that things were finally falling into place for her.

I pulled into the school's parking lot early, feeling strange in the empty space. I found myself tapping my fingers against the steering wheel, feeling pretty twitchy. If I had to wait long, I knew my nerves would get the best of me. I hopped out of the car to stretch a bit and to release some of the pent up energy coursing through me. I took yoga. Well, I went to one class once, but I remembered the breathing exercises. Leaning my back against the car, I closed my eyes and started thinking positive thoughts.

I will not smell Luke's minty goodness.

I will not imagine touching his hair.

I will not watch his lips when he talks.

I'm in control.

I'm the boss of me.

We are just pals.

I opened my eyes when I heard the faint rumbling of an approaching car. When the car turned out to be a silver Lexus I relaxed, realizing that it couldn't be Luke. But then it turned into the parking lot.

No. Really?

He pulled up alongside my car and rolled down the window. He looked different in the car. Still hot, obviously. Still wearing his leather jacket and still sporting the hair that's just asking for me to grab at it. But he looked older. And in my case, that wasn't really a bad thing.

"A Lexus?" I asked, not hiding my surprise.

"My aunt…" he began, rolling his eyes before shrugging it off. "Are you going to get in or what?"

"Well, when you put it that way," I replied sarcastically, grabbing the handle of the car door. When I climbed inside I was immediately jarred. The shocked expression on my face must have been evident.

"What's wrong now?" he asked as he navigated the car out of the lot.

"You smoke," I replied.

"And…"

"Your car smells like…lemons," I added, stunned. I knew grown men who couldn't keep their cars clean to save their lives. I once dated a guy whose car looked like a coffee cup graveyard. Luke smoked and his car smelled like citrus.

I looked over at him, gaping, and he seemed to be blushing.

"My aunt…" he trailed off again. "She doesn't like that I smoke."

The contradictions in this boy were staggering. Thinking back to the picture I painted of him in my head, I thought he was such a rebel. Now, I didn't know how I'd describe him. He dressed the part, got detention and smoked like a fiend. But he returned his library books, rescued my flask and kept his car lemony fresh because his auntie liked it that way. It had happened again. I had been in the car with him for less than five minutes, and I was speechless.

"So, did I mention that Seth's shop is a tattoo parlor?" he asked, snapping me out of my trance.

"Tattoo parlor? And he dabbles in illegal documents?"

"Seth's an artist," he explained. "His designs are amazing. He has this uncle that works for some software company in Seattle. He's in charge of updating some graphics program that he thought Seth would really like because he's good at this stuff. So he gets Seth a version of this Photoshop thing and you can do anything with it. You can screw around and take someone's head and put it onto someone else's body. You should've seen what he did with the picture of his ex."

"So he Photoshops IDs?" Was it really that easy back then? Nowadays, ten-year-olds could use Photoshop. God, 1999 was such a simpler time.

"Yeah, so you'll need to think of a name for your ID. Shouldn't be a problem, especially for you," he teased, flashing me a smile.

"That's tough," I replied, playing along. "I usually only name inanimate objects. So what did you choose? Probably something that makes all the girls swoon, right?"

My plan not to bait him was already thrown out the window.

"I make you swoon? Is that what you're saying?" he asked, knocking the cocky right out of me.

In our struggle to maintain the upper hand, I knew I needed to recover quickly, but my uneasiness clearly gave me away. He was chuckling, amused that he managed to get me flustered.

"Yes, as a matter of fact," I began, suppressing my grin. "Since we're going to a tattoo parlor and I find you so swoon-worthy, I'm thinking of getting your initials tattooed on my hip. Right about here," I added, pulling the corner of my jeans down to expose my hipbone. I looked up, satisfied to witness Luke focusing on my exposed skin. It was then that I noticed that the car was drifting across the center lane. I screamed, pointing at the road as we drove down the dotted center line.

"Christ," he growled, yanking the steering wheel to the right. "Can you try and keep your clothes on while I'm driving!"

Our easy banter had suddenly been replaced with unbearable tension. Not only had I sworn to myself that I wouldn't bait him, I took things too far, and now I needed to fall on my sword and apologize. But how the hell do you apologize to your platonic teenage guy-friend for inappropriately pulling down your pants?

"Don't be mad. I was just kidding around."

"I'm not mad," he sighed. His face showed no real signs of anger, but his body language told a different story. He gripped the steering wheel tightly with his right hand and leaned his head towards the window on his left. I think if he could have put a football field between us, he would. We had another twenty minute ride to Tacoma, and I wouldn't be able to take this kind of tension the rest of the way.

"So," I began, attempting to break the ice, "you said you needed to see Seth for something. Are you getting a tattoo?"

"I already have a tattoo," he replied, still looking straight ahead. "Two, actually."

This information was not helping me keep my hormones in check. Now I wanted to know where they were and if I could touch them.

"You have two tattoos?" I asked trying to remain composed even as my voice started to crack. "Where?"

"Now, it wouldn't be any fun if I just told you," he replied, his wide grin returning.

"Are you embarrassed?" I was eager to tease him again, to lighten the mood. "Luke, do you have a tramp stamp?"

"No, I don't have a tramp stamp," he shot back, mimicking me.

"No cute little butterfly on the small of your back?"

"Oh, you're gonna get it," he murmured, shaking his head.

"Relax, Luke," I added offhandedly. "I know you're not that type of girl."

"What about you, Cross?" he countered. "What type of girl are you?

Luke had an uncanny ability to turn things around on me in the blink of an eye. Did he want to know what type of girl *That* Jillian was or me? I wanted to say something snarky and be done with it, but my mind started racing. I didn't even know how to answer the question.

If you asked Danielle and Megan what I was like, they would tell you that I liked to have fun, I cursed like a sailor and I was very particular. They'd also tell you they loved teasing me about my inability to stay in a relationship for a long period of time because of this. If you asked the last guy I dated, Jeremy, he'd tell you that I had a problem "connecting" with him. He was definitely the chick in that relationship. Then there was Jay, owner of that collection of used styrofoam coffee cups. When Danielle started plugging her nose because my coat smelled funny after riding in his car, I knew it wasn't going to work. Jay told me I was just looking for an excuse to bail. Maybe I was.

I'd agree that my string of short-term relationships didn't make for an impressive resume. I'd admit that I didn't let my guard down often, but I didn't want to believe I was intentionally shutting people out. I started to wonder if there was any truth to what they had said about me. I wanted to keep it light with Luke, but I suddenly felt pretty dark.

"I don't know, Luke," I sighed. "While some may say I'm emotionally unavailable, I like to say I'm just selective with the company I choose to keep."

"Emotionally unavailable?" he asked arching his eyebrow. "That's pretty deep, Cross. You're depressing the shit out of me, you know that?"

"Relax," I replied, reaching for the knob on the car radio. He was right. I'd depressed myself, and I just didn't want to talk about it anymore.

"Oh, am I boring you, unavailable one?" he questioned sarcastically.

"Is it 'that time of the month', Luke?" I clutched my chest, feigning sympathy. "Midol works wonders for those pesky mood swings."

"You're a pain in the ass, Cross. Play your music. Don't let me interrupt," he added, signaling to the radio with a sweep of his hand.

"Thank you," I replied dramatically. "Jeez."

We listened quietly while I tried unsuccessfully to shake the funny feeling I had left over from his question. When he pulled into the parking lot of Ink Credible Art, I was relieved that we had reached our destination.

I followed Luke up the rickety steps into the small building. Inside, the walls were lined with squares each showcasing a variety of Seth's available artwork. There were flowers, butterflies, fairies and wild animals, tribal bands and zodiac signs. I couldn't understand how anyone could choose something so permanent and meaningful. It wasn't like buying a pair of murderously skinny jeans. It became a part of who you were.

"Luke, man, back so soon?" I turned towards the voice and saw a massive, California redwood-sized man standing behind the counter. His arms were completely covered with designs that seemed to flow together seamlessly.

"Seth, hey, this is my friend, Jillian," Luke began, motioning to me. "She's having an identity problem."

Ain't that the truth.

I reached out to shake his hand without thinking. It didn't occur to me that seventeen-year-old girls probably didn't shake hands. I know I looked like a complete idiot, but there really wasn't any turning back. Seth looked at me suspiciously, grasping my hand to shake it anyway.

So far, batting a thousand.

"I figured while we were here, you could add that artwork we talked about," Luke proposed, reaching into his pocket and extracting a folded up piece of paper.

"So you decided to add the flames?" Seth asked eagerly. "I knew you would. It'll enhance it, trust me. Let me go find Dice. He can help Miss Jillian here and we can discuss ink."

He disappeared into the back room, and I turned to face Luke who was inspecting the artwork on the wall.

"You're getting work done today? You could have mentioned that at some point," I remarked, feeling slightly irritated.

"I could have," he responded casually. He was acting strangely, and I hoped he wasn't still mad about my little stunt in the car.

Seth returned with another giant hulk of a man, this one with long, scraggly hair and only a few scattered tattoos on his massive arms. He introduced himself as Seth's brother Dice, and this time I resisted the urge to shake anyone's hand.

"Why don't you come out back with me so we can get started while Seth gets Luke set up," he suggested, motioning me over to the door in the back of the studio. I looked over to Luke who was already showing Seth the crumpled up paper from his pocket. He didn't seem alarmed by Dice's suggestion, so as uncomfortable as I was, I followed him into the back office.

Can you get killed by a crazy stranger when you're a possibly comatose time traveler? I wasn't sure how this works.

"So," he began, taking a seat in front of a massive computer system, "you want some identification? Drinking's bad for you, you know," he commented with a wink.

"Yeah, well, not drinking's worse," I retorted, annoyed that Luke sent me off alone with the giant, creepy tattoo guy.

"So how'd a moody bastard like Chambers land a sweet little thing like you?" he asked, glancing over his shoulder and smiling.

"He *is* a moody bastard, isn't he?" I laughed. "No, Luke and I aren't together. He's just helping me out."

"Well, isn't that lucky for me," he added, turning back to the screen. He was creepy, but seemed harmless. I watched as he pulled up a photo of a Washington State license on the screen. With a few brush strokes, he removed the name, date of birth, height and weight. I oohed and aahed where I felt necessary, and pretended I didn't see the art department at work do this stuff on a daily basis.

"So, what did you say your name was again?" he asked, raising an eyebrow.

Once I started thinking of names, I knew I had to pay homage to the patron saint of time travel. I just needed to tweak it a bit.

"Marcy," I replied. "Marcy McFly."

"Alright, Marcy McFly," he repeated, chuckling as he typed. "Go on over to that chair in the corner, and let's take some photos."

Looking behind me, I noticed a small chair placed in front of a blue backdrop. Taking a seat I suddenly felt the urge to check my hair in a mirror. I never took a good license picture.

"All right, say 'Moody Bastard'," Dice instructed from behind the tripod.

"Moody Bastard," I repeated with a smile. After the flash, Dice grabbed the clunky camera and attached it to a dock on his PC. I glanced over at the desk as I listened to the whirling sound of the computer downloading the pictures. Along with his lamination equipment, I saw a beautiful hard covered copy of *The Book of Kells* on his desk. My great grandparents were from Ireland, so I recognized the book immediately. I used to flip through the pages as a little girl, admiring the beautiful Celtic knot designs.

"You're researching Celtic knots," I remarked, opening the book.

"You know them?" he asked, grabbing the tiny photograph from the printer.

89

"I've always loved them. My grandmother always wore Celtic jewelry." My mom still had most of it in her jewelry box at home; silver brooches adorned with colored stones looping in a fluid, continuous pattern. I always thought she looked regal when she wore one.

"Take a look at the pages I have jammed in the back."

I found a few sheets of thin tracing paper inserted into the back cover. Each sheet was covered with beautiful, curvy designs. Luke had raved about Seth's ability, but it was clear that Dice was pretty good, as well. One page was filled with traditional Celtic knots, each with its own significance. To help identify it, he marked the meaning underneath each drawing. He drew a beautiful trinity and wrote "Spirit, Mind, Body" beneath the sketch. There was an interwoven knot with no discernible beginning and end. The word "Eternity" was written below. Finally, there was a horizontal loopy knot with "Strength" written below the design. Each of the three had similar variations to choose from.

When I flipped to the next page, I noticed the designs became more detailed and intricate. Each knot morphed into an animal shape—an eagle, a fox, a horse, and butterfly, all beautifully designed with the loops and spirals. The last page had different types of shapes, and I noticed immediately that the majority of the shapes were crosses.

Each cross varied slightly, and seemed to have different meanings. One had the word "Transition" written below, while another represented balance. There were crosses for hope and temperance. And then, on the very last row of the page, was a cross for navigation. "To find your way home" it said below.

Reading the words, feeling as lost as I did, the design resonated with me. It wasn't just a matter of finding my way back to where I came from, I needed to find where I went wrong—who I was and where I was headed.

Something had been stirring in me since the conversation we had in the car. As much as I wanted to think that I was better than *That* Jillian, I was still making the same mistakes. Still living life on the sidelines.

"Dice," I called out, swallowing back the tears, "how long would it take to get this done?"

His eyes widened when he saw that I was pointing to one of his designs.

"You want a tattoo? One of mine?" he asked incredulously. "I'm assuming you're eighteen?"

"You have the ID in front of you that says so," I replied, smiling. "How long would it take? I don't want to hold Luke up."

"Well, he's obviously not concerned about holding you up because if Seth is gonna work on those flames they were discussing, you'll have more than enough time."

It was impulsive, but it just felt right. "Let's go for it," I said firmly.

"Very cool!" he replied. "I'm almost done laminating, so we can get you set up in just a few."

I watched as he ran a small folder through the lamination machine. When it slid through to the other side, he opened it up and removed the ID. He shook it quickly, cooling it down, and inspected it. "Perfect...Ms. McFly."

He handed me the warm plastic, and I placed his money on the desk. I looked at the picture on the plastic card. She wasn't *That* Jillian anymore, but she wasn't what she could be either.

"Let's get you set up at my station," he added, clapping his hands together and heading for the door.

I was lost in thought when I walked back into the studio, completely unprepared for the sight before me. Luke was sitting on something that looked like a massage chair...shirtless. Seth, perched upon the stool next to him, was dragging the tattoo gun along Luke's bicep. I could only see part of his back through the spaces in the chair, but even from across the room, I could make out the defined lines in his arms. They had always been hidden by his bulky leather jacket. I had no idea that Luke was so ripped. I wanted to lick him. I never had a tattoo fetish before, but seeing Luke shirtless with the outline of some ink on his arm made me lightheaded.

I walked slowly over to him, staring at his arm. If I looked him in the eye, I knew my eyes would wander to his chest. I wondered what it would feel like to touch him, and I felt my breath catch again. I was practically standing next to them, and Luke had yet to notice I'd entered the room. He seemed very focused, staring straight ahead. I was sure the tattoo gun wasn't particularly comfortable, but I didn't see him wince either. It gave me a moment to study his arm.

I don't know what I was expecting. After hearing all the talk of flames, I guess I was expecting bright reds and oranges, maybe something menacing like a skull, but I should have known better. Luke wouldn't just get any tattoo. Luke's tattoo would be simple...and hot. All in black, a tribal phoenix with two large wide wings raising high up on each side, graced his upper arm. Seth was adding what looked like three small flames on each side below the bird.

The phoenix rising from the ashes.

91

"All right, sweet thing," Dice called over to me from his station, "let's get this show on the road."

I prayed that Luke wouldn't ask why I hadn't announced myself sooner. Would he know I had just spent the last five minutes panting and ogling him? I might have spontaneously ovulated.

"Hop on," Dice added, motioning to the chair, and dropping it into a reclined position. Luke was visibly alarmed when he saw Dice prepping his station.

"Wait, what the hell are you doing?" he barked. His indignation irritated me. I wasn't a child.

"This *is* a tattoo parlor, Luke," I replied casually, laying down on the flat surface. "I'm getting a tattoo."

"Okay," Dice began. "Where is this bad boy going?"

"I was thinking about my hip. On the left side." I pointed as if he couldn't figure it out himself. I wanted to be thorough. We went to NYU with a girl who asked for a hip tattoo, and it ended up in the middle of her stomach. Granted, she was dumb as a stump, but I wasn't taking any chances.

"Jillian, I don't think you've thought this through," Luke warned through gritted teeth.

"Luke," Seth warned, "you're moving around too much, man. I'm almost done, but you have to stay still."

"How much longer?" he asked, his voice sounding strained.

"Ten minutes tops." I didn't know what he had planned—if he was intending to force me to leave or something.

"Hey Dice," Luke called, motioning him to Seth's station with a slight tilt of his head. Dice leaned in as I heard them speaking in hushed tones. I was able to hear something about ten minutes but not much else.

"No problem," Dice replied, "I still need to make the transfer." He disappeared into the office again, leaving me by myself at the station.

"Um, hello," I objected. "I *am* still here you know."

"Calm down, Jillian," Luke responded in a tired voice. "He's just going to make a transfer. It's like a temporary tattoo that he'll use as a guide."

"Oh," I replied. I was a bit surprised that he had given up so easily. I had visions of him throwing me over his shoulder caveman-style and dragging me into the car. Although that kind of sounded fun. If he wasn't telling Dice that we were leaving, it made me wonder what that conversation was all about.

"So what are you getting? Not my initials, I presume," he asked sarcastically. Although he was joking now, there was still a strange tone in his voice.

"I told you I was," I joked through the uneasiness. "I'll just have to get your middle initial out of you." He was quiet for a few moments, and I wondered if I had pushed too far again. I had been so good at reading him, and today I seemed to be saying all the wrong things.

"Robert," he finally offered. "After my grandfather." I hadn't expected a reply. Everything was tense again, and I couldn't understand why.

"Alrighty." I heard Dice from behind me and exhaled a sigh of relief. I didn't think I could continue a conversation about branding myself with Luke's initials anymore. Even though it was a joke, it didn't seem funny now.

"I'm going to have you unbutton the top button of your jeans and scoot them down so your hip bones are exposed. Then I'm going to tuck this towel into your jeans so I don't get any ink on your pants." I took a deep breath and followed his instructions, feeling self-conscious. Teasing Luke in the car was one thing. Unzipping my jeans and exposing myself to perfect strangers was another.

"Okay," he continued, leaning over me, "I'm going to apply the transfer."

As he went to work, I found that I was afraid to look over at Luke. I didn't want to see his look of disapproval and chicken out.

"Take a look," he added once he was done. It was only about the size of a silver dollar. The cross had four equal sides, each pointing in a different direction. Just like a compass.

"Are you comfortable?" he asked as he applied some ointment to the area. I nodded, but wouldn't have exactly described myself as comfortable.

I saw a flash of something out of the corner of my eye and craned my neck to see what it was. Luke had pulled up a stool and was positioned on the opposite side of me. His shirt was still off and there was a large white bandage on his upper arm. I could smell his Lukeness.

"Grab my hand," he instructed firmly, extending his hand out to me. I looked back at Dice, and he already had the tattoo gun in his hand. I could feel my heart pounding in my ears as I squeezed his hand tightly.

93

"Okay, Jillian," Dice began, "Take regular breaths. We don't want anyone passing out."

Luke leaned his head down close to mine. I took a deep breath, waiting for that minty smell to fill my nostrils.

"The first few minutes are the worst," he explained, looking at me intensely. "Focus on me and it'll pass quickly. Your body gets used to the feeling, and it's not as bad."

I heard the buzzing sound begin, and Dice leaned over my hips once again. When the needle hit my skin, I was jarred by the stinging sensation. I started to feel panicky and my face suddenly felt hot.

"You're fine," Luke said inches from my face, staring into my eyes again. "It's a normal reaction. Breathe."

I slowly nodded, staring back at him, using his face as a focal point. He began applying some pressure and rubbing small circles into the palm of my hand, mimicking the harsh spirals of the tattoo gun. I was beyond any words and beyond feeling ashamed. I knew that I just needed to focus on him to get through the discomfort of the needle on my skin. It was as if we were frozen together, unable to look away.

"How are you doing?" he finally asked, his voice sounding breathy.

"I think I'm okay," I replied softly. "It hurts, but it's bearable."

"What am I gonna do with you?" he asked, smiling and shaking his head.

Anything you want.

Luke distracted me by talking about the other tattoo on his shoulder blade. I all but forgot what was going on when he pivoted in the stool to give me a view of his back. On his left shoulder, opposite the phoenix, were two Chinese symbols.

So very lickable.

"They're the symbols for strength," he explained with a tight smile. They could have been the Chinese symbols for "bite here". I didn't care. I was imagining my hands running up and down his back, my nails scraping across his smooth skin. He'd taste salty.

"All right," Dice began, standing up from his crouched position. "What do you think?"

I propped myself up on my elbows and looked down at my hipbone. My skin was red and swollen, but in the midst of the puffiness was a beautiful and elegant cross.

"Beautiful," I replied, still stunned.

"Yeah," I heard Luke agree softly beside me.

"I'm going to bandage it up now," Dice explained. "You'll need to put some ointment on it regularly. All the information you need is on this sheet," he added, extending a paper to me. Luke grabbed it and began reading it over. I realized when I glanced his way that my hand was still wrapped around his. I didn't want to be the first to pull away, but I also didn't want to look like a fool if he was trying to figure out an escape route.

"Thank you," I said in a low voice, glancing down at our hands. The fact that they were still clasped together seemed to finally register with him. He slowly removed his hand from mine, shoving it into his pocket and holding my aftercare instructions in the other.

"Let's get you up," Dice began, helping me into a sitting position. My hip was burning. I wished I had worn softer pants. Or none at all.

I watched as Luke walked back to Seth's station and put his shirt back on. The muscles in his back stretched as he lifted the light cotton over his head. I didn't even get to fully appreciate my proximity to his half-nakedness. My timing was impeccable.

He walked up to the front desk where Seth was sitting, fishing into his back pocket and extracting his wallet. Then it hit me. I had no idea how much my tattoo cost me, and I only had enough to cover the cost of the ID. I wasn't used to thinking before I bought things. I used credit cards and spent more money than I made like the rest of the free world. But at seventeen, I didn't have any plastic at all.

"Um, Luke," I motioned over to him nervously. Noticing my worried expression, he walked quickly back to me.

"What's wrong? Is it hurting?" he asked frowning, his brows creased.

"No, no, um, how much does something like this usually cost?" I asked, pointing to the gauze on my hip. I felt my face grow red.

"Cash flow problems, Cross?"

"I wasn't planning…If you could cover me, I'll pay you back," I stammered uncomfortably. He looked at me for a minute and then laughed to himself.

"I'm sure you will," he replied as he turned to walk back to Seth's desk. I was so focused on Luke that I didn't hear Dice approach.

"I guess I *am* out of luck," he began as he cleaned up his station. "But if this thing you've got going on with Chambers doesn't work out, I'd like a shot," he added with a wink.

"I told you…" I argued, but he quickly cut me off.

"I know what you told me, but I also know what I see." Before I could protest any further, Luke was standing next to me, putting his coat back on.

"Ready?" he asked.

"Yeah," I replied, hopping off the chair. I felt him place his hand on the small of my back as we walked out of the studio.

"Dice was getting pretty cozy in there with you," he remarked as we walked to the car.

"I don't think I need to worry too much about it since he seems to think that we're a thing," I added, motioning between the two of us.

"What did he say?" he asked, his brow creased again. I remembered Dice's words and began to laugh.

"He wanted to know how a 'moody bastard' like you landed a wonderful, witty, intelligent, and kickass girl like me," I teased.

"Oh, that's what he said?"

"Well, I may be exaggerating a little. He at least got the moody bastard part right, though," I replied. "I can't say I'd disagree."

I felt a rumble in my stomach and looked at my watch. I couldn't believe how long we were in the studio. We'd missed lunch and it was almost time for dinner.

"Is the wonderful, witty and kickass girl late for a date?" he asked coolly.

"You forgot intelligent, and no, I don't have a date, but I'm a little hungry."

"So let me get this straight," he began. "I drive you to Tacoma so we could get an ID. Then I pay for a tattoo on the hip you like to flash around. And now I have to feed you? Is that right?"

"Most guys would consider this a win, Luke," I retorted. "You were half naked. I had my pants down, and you didn't even need to buy me dinner first."

"Pain in the ass," he grumbled.

"Come on. I may not have enough for my little cross, but I can swing a couple burgers. I owe you that much," I said, laughing. I wasn't going to give him any time to protest. I was really hungry and licking Luke was probably a bad idea.

As we walked along the sidewalk heading towards The Greasy Spoon, we passed the multiplex, and I was reminded of Nate and Meg.

"Oh, I forgot to tell you," I exclaimed, causing him to jump. He seemed to have been a million miles away. "Nate and Megan are having their first date tonight. I am the official doctor of love," I bragged.

"Well, let's hope your patients can keep it in their pants for a few days," he added dryly. "Josh bet me that Barrett would nail your pal before prom, and I hate to lose."

"Oh, damn," I began without thinking. "You're so gonna lose. She practically attacked him on their first date."

My eyes grew wide when I realized what I had said.

"Wait. What? They already had sex?" he exclaimed. "I thought tonight was their first date. Goddamn it," he fumed.

"No, wait," I stammered. "I meant she already had sex with him on their first date...in her dream last week." Luke arched his brow and looked at me suspiciously. I began to panic. "I just misspoke," I added. "I'm just saying that...I don't know...Megan's easy?"

As soon as the words left my mouth, Luke doubled over laughing. I, however, was horrified. She would murder me if she ever knew what I said. It was true, though. Not that she was easy—that she had sex with Nate on their first date. I found Nate wearing Megan's robe in our kitchen the next morning, which strangely was the start of a tradition for us. Nate and I were early risers, so we'd watch trashy tabloid shows on the DVR and make fun of people from *Jersey Shore* while we waited for everyone to wake up.

"So, they haven't?" Luke asked.

"No, but you're probably going to lose," I added. "Megan and Nate are...explosive. I just know."

"Because you're the love doctor," he added facetiously.

"Precisely."

It was unseasonably dry, so when we got to the diner, I suggested that we grab the food and bring it to the picnic tables in the park. It also kept things undate-like and casual. I ordered two hamburger plates at the take-out window and attempted to pay for them before Luke hip-checked me out of the way. He paid for both meals and carried them to the park across the street while I grumbled behind him.

I climbed onto one of the picnic tables, sitting cross-legged, and wasted no time biting right into the juicy burger. Luke stood there for a moment, his styrofoam container in hand, watching me.

"What? Do I have ketchup on me?" I asked, feeling self-conscious under his gaze. "Tell me."

"No, but you sure look hungry," he stated, looking at the burger I was mauling.

"I'm a man's man, Luke," I replied without any shame. "I don't pull that girly shit. Are you gonna hop up here and eat, or what?"

He climbed up and sat down with his feet on the bench below. After unpacking his meal, he bit into the burger and groaned. *So not fair. I do not want to be jealous of a fast food meal.*

We ate in silence for a few minutes before Luke began to speak.

"So, are we gonna talk about the elephant in the room?" he asked plainly.

Elephant? We had a whole damn herd.

"What do you mean?" I had no idea what he was talking about, but he had me feeling very anxious. Did I say that thing about being jealous of the burger out loud?

"Well, I brought you to Tacoma as part of a deal," he began, a hint of a smile playing on his lips. "Do you remember our deal?"

I didn't like this. I couldn't read his expression.

"Of course," I replied nervously. "I told you that you wouldn't have to worry about Danielle setting you up for the prom."

"And?" he asked, sounding cocky.

"And you haven't had to ask anyone, right?" I suddenly wished I was back at the studio with a needle on my skin. It was more comfortable.

"Well, your friend Danielle told me a lot about this mystery girl and she seemed pretty convinced that we'd have a good time together," he explained. "She has my interest piqued."

Danielle had told me that she'd stop bothering me about the prom. Maybe she found someone else for Luke to ask. Maybe it was Val.

"Oh, so are you going to ask someone now?" I could actually feel the lump in my throat. He stared at me for a moment and laughed quietly.

"Why didn't you just tell me?" he asked, looking at me curiously.

I felt sick. *He knew.*

I had no idea what to say. We couldn't go to the prom together. It was too risky, but there was no way I could sit around and let him go with Val either. This whole situation was more complicated than I could handle. My mind was racing, and I couldn't seem to pull together a cohesive thought.

"Danielle is crazy. I didn't want her...she can be persuasive and you might feel...God, this is awkward," I stammered, burying my head in my hands.

"Well, you *do* owe me now since I've bankrolled your day of rebellion. I need Danielle off my back, and it's not going to happen unless we go to this thing. So, what do you think?"

"About going to the prom?" I gasped. "With you?"

"Well, that's what I figured," he replied, trying not to laugh.

"Yeah. I mean, yes. That'd be cool." I know I sounded breathless, but it was happening all so fast.

"But if we're going to do this, we need to make sure that we give her the prom experience that she's looking for," he added with a glint in his eye.

"What do you have planned?" I asked suspiciously.

"You'll see," he replied, flashing me that smile I loved.

I knew the right thing to do was to tell him I was washing my hair that night or in my case, going to the dentist, but I just couldn't. I wanted to go. I even wanted to wear a fancy dress and uncomfortable shoes. I wanted to dance to that awful Mariah Carey song. I wanted to dance with him.

"So, we're going to the prom." It sounded halfway between a question and a statement. It didn't matter. It really wasn't a question anymore.

99

"Looks that way," he replied. I got the sense that he was as surprised as I was.

We walked back to the car, discussing how we thought Danielle would react to the news. We both agreed that spontaneous combustion was possible. I would have to make sure there wasn't anything breakable around when I let her know.

A different type of tension settled upon us on the ride home. While we had joked and laughed about Danielle on the walk back to the car, it seemed that once we sat down next to each other, all joking seemed to have stopped. There were uncomfortable attempts at small talk. We discussed the finals that I had yet to study for, and how I really didn't want to go to the bonfire, but Danielle was practically forcing me. I was almost expecting him to start talking about the weather. It was *that* lame. I hadn't really helped the conversation along. When he spoke, I couldn't bring myself to look at him. When I did, I'd focus on the spot on his jaw, right below his ear. I had added it to my list of Places on Luke I Wanted to Lick. Then, when he shifted gears, I focused on his hands and how good it felt when he touched me back at the studio. I imagined placing my hand on top of his, stroking the rough skin. Before long, I imagined sucking his fingers into my mouth and had to physically shake the thoughts out of my head. I probably looked like I had Tourette's Syndrome. So instead of gawking at his lickable jaw and suckable fingers, I stared straight ahead just to be safe.

It was already dark when we pulled into the school parking lot. I was anxious to get out of the car and get as far away from him as possible. I needed space to clear my head and preferably a really cold shower. Luke broke the heavy silence first. His voice sounded unsteady.

"If you have any questions about the tattoo, call me. I've done the whole aftercare thing before." While the offer clearly blurred the lines of our friendship, he said it with such ease that it made me believe that he was just trying to be nice.

Without a warning he leaned over me, reaching his right arm across the front seat to open the glove box. While he rifled around inside, I tried unsuccessfully to push myself as far back into the seat as possible. It didn't help because I could already feel the perspiration gathering on my neck and chest. After what seemed like an eternity, he pulled out a pen and paper and began writing down what I assumed to be his phone number. He handed me the paper, still leaning towards my side of the car. His close proximity was making it hard for me to breathe. I was convinced that he affected my respiratory system. I had probably already caused a fracture in the space/time continuum by agreeing to go to the prom with him. If he continued to lean over me, I couldn't be held responsible for my actions. Wanting Luke as much as I did could end up bringing on the apocalypse. I needed to get out of there.

As I grabbed the door handle to leave, I reminded myself that I was supposed to be keeping things light and airy. It was hard to act airy, though, when I was drenched in perspiration. Not only had he shut down my respiratory system, Luke had somehow commanded every single pore in my body to explode. I just needed to hang on a little while longer. I'd be securely in my car in less than a minute.

"Well, thank you for accompanying me on my day of rebellion," I joked, terrified that he could tell I had been turned into a human puddle. "My parents are probably wondering where the hell I went."

I grabbed the handle and breathed a sigh of relief when I stepped out of the car. The air cooled my skin, and I felt the tension lift immediately. It was as though I had been under a spell in the car and had just woken up. Turning around to say goodbye, I heard Luke call over to me and the car door slam.

"You forgot this." He jogged over to my car with the aftercare instructions in his hands.

"Thanks," I replied nervously, grabbing the sheet from him. As quickly as it had lifted, I felt surrounded by that tension once again. Luke didn't make any effort to leave. He jammed his hands into his pockets and slowly leaned a shoulder against my car.

Is it possible to want to step away and move closer to a person at the same time?

"Is it hurting?" he asked, motioning to my hip. His voice sounded low and rough. I wanted his lips. I wanted him to back away. I couldn't be trusted anymore. I'd already broken the rules.

"Not too much," I replied, looking away. I couldn't handle the way he was looking at me. He seemed so focused and unashamed. I found myself once again wondering what he was thinking. I thought I felt uncomfortable in the car when I needed to stare straight ahead. This was unbearable.

"I can't believe you got a tattoo," he laughed, shaking his head.

"Me either," I replied, instinctively looking down at my bandaged hip. When I looked back up, it wasn't my tattoo he was looking at. I had been on enough first dates to recognize what was going on. From the awkward way he was leaning against the car to the intense look in his eye, I was fairly certain that Luke Chambers was staring at my lips, and that he wanted to kiss me. To say I wasn't prepared for this was an understatement. This hadn't even been a date. You couldn't kiss someone goodnight if you weren't on a date! There were dating laws to abide by. Could you be on a date without actually knowing it?

I suddenly thought of Marty McFly and the picture he had in his pocket of his brother and sister. Every time Marty screwed up, someone's head in the picture would fade away—ceasing to exist. I didn't have a magic photograph to look at, but I knew I was sucking at Time Travel 101. Every fiber of my being wanted Luke to kiss me, but I could end up with a whole bunch of theoretically headless people in my life if I messed this up.

"I have to go," I blurted out nervously.

I couldn't look at him. My pulse was racing and my voice was shaky. I wasn't hiding my nerves very well. For someone who was allegedly closed off, I wasn't doing a good job at shutting out how much I wanted to stay.

I turned and grabbed my door handle and felt a soft tug on my arm. His hand felt warm against my skin. I couldn't focus on anything else. He didn't say anything right away when I turned back to face him.

"What's wrong with you?" he finally asked, searching my face again.

"Nothing," I lied, pulling away slowly. "It's just been a long day."

I pulled the car door open and climbed in quickly. Fumbling for my keys, I started the car and rolled down the window. Luke was still standing next to my car, his hands back in his pockets and his head tilted down.

"Thank you for today," I said, hoping he understood I wasn't talking about the ID.

"Anytime, Cross," he replied. His smile was tight-lipped and forced.

As I drove off, I watched him in the rear view mirror, standing in the middle of the empty school parking lot. I hoped that leaving him standing there was the right thing to do.

When I walked into my room I collapsed on my bed, feeling emotionally spent. Too much had gone on and I needed to regroup. As I leaned back to relax, I noticed the glint of pink rhinestones out of the corner of my eye. There, on my desk, was Joan. The same Joan who I never left the house without. The same Joan who made living in the past bearable. The same Joan who I thought I needed in order to survive the car ride with Luke. Joan sat on my desk at home all day and I hadn't even realized it.

No matter how hard I tried to remain detached, Luke was turning my world upside down. While I could easily say that my behavior was due to my circumstances, I knew better. It wasn't where I was or what year it was. It wasn't what I was drinking or what I was wearing. It was who I was with.

102

There was one thing I was becoming more aware of when it came to me and Luke. There was no turning back.

CHAPTER 10

Luke

In the sixth grade, Becky Peterson let me grab her boobs on the beat-up couch in her parents' basement. The place smelled like mold and mothballs, but for me it was easily one of the greatest afternoons of my life.

During a pep rally freshman year, Laura Nichols pulled me under the bleachers and my dick out of my pants with the skilled precision of a junior who had clocked her fair share of time on her knees. It was the best "Welcome to High School" I could have ever imagined.

Sophomore year while I was visiting Jonas in Seattle, his new waitress Dana asked me to bring some boxes out to the storage room. When I found her waiting for me, undressed and uninhibited, I wanted to write a thank you note to Carter for sending me to Seattle in the first place. It would have been inappropriate, but if he had seen Dana, he would have understood why.

I didn't have a Little Black Book. I didn't have a long list of conquests. Now, thanks to Jillian Cross, I didn't have any balls either. When did I become the guy who couldn't kiss the girl?

Raking my hands over my face, I stared up at the ceiling. I couldn't drag myself out of bed. I just replayed the scene in my head over and over trying to figure out where I went wrong. I had never been with anyone as difficult as Jillian. She'd continually draw me in only to back off at the last minute. I was getting seriously pissed off. And she had the nerve to call *me* moody. She'd be moody too if she had to deal with this mountain of mixed signals I was buried under. The worst part was that when it came down to it, as easy as it was with Becky, Laura, Dana or any of the other girls I'd been with, I never wanted them the way I wanted Jillian. And that pissed me off the most.

Looking at my alarm clock, I groaned realizing that I'd have to get up soon. At least it was Sunday, and I wouldn't need to worry about dealing with Jillian until tomorrow. Today I needed to focus on finals and stop dissecting everything that she said while we were in Tacoma. *What kind of word is 'swoon-worthy' anyway?*

I swung my legs over the side of the bed and sat there, scrunching up fibers of the shaggy carpet with my toes. The scent of cinnamon filled the air, and I knew Grace was downstairs cooking. For once, her third degree was going to be a welcomed distraction.

I found her dicing chicken on the butcher block, and had to check the clock again. It was ten o'clock in the morning, right?

"Grace, please tell me that chicken isn't part of whatever you're making for breakfast." If she said yes, this would be the morning I finally poured myself a bowl of Cheerios.

"Don't be silly," she replied with an eye roll. "There are cinnamon rolls warming in the oven. I'm making chicken salad for your uncle. Well, I *was* making chicken salad for your uncle. He's stuck at the hospital because of some disaster training, and I was going to bring him lunch, but my editor is going to call me back around one and I need to put some finishing touches on this section of the book before I go over it with her. There's just no way I'll be able to make it to the hospital in time," she rambled, dicing harder and harder with her frustration.

I opened the oven and the smell of cinnamon filled the air once again. I was starving. Grabbing one off of the cooking sheet, I winced at the burn on my fingers, the sticky residue covering them in the process.

"I can bring it to him if you want," I offered, biting off a chunk.

"Are you really talking to me with a mouthful of food?" she asked, cocking her brow.

"It's not my fault that you're a culinary genius, Grace," I replied innocently. "I just get carried away."

I heard her mutter something about being fresh under her breath, and I couldn't help but chuckle.

"Jonas called," she said suddenly. "He wanted to know when you're bringing your things by. I told him that I assumed you'd be moving into the apartment on Sunday." She didn't look up, but there was a wistful tone in her voice. "I can't believe this is your last Sunday here."

It occurred to me that I hadn't thought of my countdown in days. Now suddenly, I was leaving in a week. Something felt off though.

"He said to call him at the bar when you can," she added.

"Don't worry about Carter. I'll stop by the hospital this afternoon," I offered, needing to change the subject. I just didn't want to think about Seattle anymore, and I'd probably need a study break by then anyway.

After inhaling three of Grace's gooey cinnamon rolls, I headed back upstairs to go over the review sheet that Mrs. Jacobs handed out for the trig final. I quickly found that I couldn't concentrate on trig because I'd associate Mrs. Jacobs with Joan. Then I would get pissed that I was calling Jillian's flask by name—like I was as crazy as she was. Her brand of crazy *was* probably contagious.

Frustrated, I tried moving on to chemistry, but was once again reminded of my conversation with Josh about the prom and the report I reread ten times in detention as I plotted Joan's rescue. I threw the book across the room when I found myself calling the stupid thing Joan again.

It was twelve-thirty and I hadn't accomplished much, but I figured some fresh air might help clear my mind. Grabbing the brown bag Grace left in the refrigerator and my coat, I headed off to see Carter.

I tried to ignore the stares of the young girls at the front desk as I walked to the switchboard to request that Carter be paged. I paced the lobby distracted, pushing the thoughts of tattoos and pale skin out of my mind. He seemed to be taking forever, and I grew increasingly uncomfortable listening to giggling behind me. Frustrated by my inability to get an ounce of peace and quiet, I moved out of the lobby and began wandering the corridor. A fire alarm mocked me from its spot next to me on the wall. There was just no escaping her.

The chime of the elevator snapped me out of my haze. When the doors opened, I almost dropped Carter's lunch on the floor in front of me. Jillian stepped out of the elevator wearing the most sinfully tight black top I'd ever seen. The corners of her mouth turned up when she saw me.

"Luke," she greeted me. The tension from the prior day seemed to be a memory.

"What are you doing here, Cros⌐?" I asked, unable to hold back my grin. "Trying to score some rubbing alcohol? I thought we got you an ID so you wouldn't have to resort to this."

As she shifted her weight onto one foot, a sliver of skin along the waist of her jeans grabbed my attention.

"I may be an emotionally unavailable, future alcoholic, Luke, but I *do* have my standards," she retorted, crossing her arms in front of her chest.

Oh, God, not that. Do not look at her boobs. Do not look at her boobs.

"I was having lunch with my mom," she added as my eyes naturally flashed to her boobs. "She's an x-ray tech."

Hearing someone call my name, I was shaken from my breast-induced trance. From the look on his face, it was apparent that Carter had caught me red-handed.

"Hey," he said, looking at Jillian. "Pad Thai!"

"Hey, osso bucco!" she replied, smiling.

"*Hey*...you two know each other?" I asked suspiciously. My heart was hammering in my chest. What the hell was going on?

"Yes, we met at the grocery store last week when I stopped off to get some things for Grace," he explained. "I'm Carter Chambers, Luke's uncle."

"Jillian Cross," she began, extending her hand to him. "Luke and I go to school together." I watched as Carter's eyes darted curiously from Jillian's to mine.

"Carter's a head shrinker," I explained. "Comes in handy when I meet people who act a little...off."

"You're funny, Luke," she replied, rolling her eyes.

"Well, it's nice running into you again, Jillian," Carter added, looking more at me than at her. Wonderful. I was staring at her boobs and now he wants answers. "So how did that Pad Thai turn out?"

"You were right," she laughed. "I definitely needed the dry tofu. My friends are practically promising me their first borns to make it again."

"I was telling my wife about our meeting and apparently I was supposed to recommend a certain brand. I wish I could remember..." He trailed off as I looked dumbfounded at the two of them as they talked like old friends. "Why don't you walk back to the office with us and I can call her. She's probably prepping for veal saltimbocca night," he added.

Jillian pivoted on her heel with her fists planted on her hips, full of righteous indignation.

"God, Luke! How can you hang your head and sulk all day when you have this glorious woman at home cooking you osso bucco and veal saltimbocca?" she fumed.

"And scones," Carter the traitor added. Jillian's eyes grew wide. She reached up and shoved me.

"Scones!" she exclaimed. "And veal saltimbocca is my favorite. That's it. I'm officially adopting Auntie Grace as my own. You do not appreciate her."

Carter was enjoying Jillian's outburst just a little too much as he practically doubled over laughing.

"You know, Jillian," he began. "Tonight is actually a sort of goodbye dinner for Luke. It'll be our last big Sunday dinner together."

"Oh right," she replied understanding. "Seattle."

His eyes flashed over to mine again. "Oh, he's told you," he said, clearly surprised. It was like he couldn't believe that I talked to a girl. *Trust me, Carter. I've talked to girls before. If you need to see my resume, we'll discuss it later.*

"Yes, I'm sure hearts will be breaking all over Reynolds when Luke rolls out of town next week." She glanced over at me with a playful spark in her eyes as she joked with him.

"You should come by for dinner, Jillian," Carter suggested.

Wait. What? He was acting like we invited strange girls over to the house for family dinners all the time. If this was his idea of a going away gift, it wasn't cool.

"Grace would welcome the chance to tell you everything you'd ever want to know about Pad Thai. Plus, how can you pass up your favorite dish? Right, Luke?"

I had never been at such a loss for words in my life. If I agreed, then I'd be subjected to a night of terror as Grace and Carter started mentally planning our wedding. If I said no, I'd look like a dick.

"Luke?" Both Carter and Jillian were staring at me. This was a disaster.

"Right," I replied. Maybe if I pissed her off, she'd decline. "Come by for dinner, Jillian," I offered, exaggerating the angelic charm in my tone. "It'll be swell."

She narrowed her eyes at me and turned back to Carter.

"I would love to come to Luke's goodbye dinner. I wouldn't miss it for the world."

"Excellent! Why don't you come by around five-thirty? I'm sure Luke can give you directions," he added, winking at me. Maybe I'd inherited winking from him.

"I'm assuming this," he added, pointing at the brown paper sack, "is my chicken salad." Grabbing the bag, he glanced at his watch. "I have to get back to my meeting, but I will see *you* tonight, Jillian."

He waved, walking off with his lunch in hand, already unwrapping the sandwich before he turned the corner.

"So, you're really coming by for dinner tonight?" I mean, she couldn't be serious. You're supposed to avoid situations like this, not embrace them.

"Why? You don't want me to come over and meet the family?" she teased. I rolled my eyes at how blasé she was acting. It was as if we hadn't had the most uncomfortable car ride in the history of car rides less than twenty-four hours ago.

"I just hope you know what you're getting yourself into."

"Are there some strange Chambers family rituals I need to know about?" she asked skeptically.

"So you really didn't get what was going on there just now?"

"Apparently not. I thought I got invited to dinner by a charming gentleman with a rather socially inept nephew."

"Carter thinks you're my girlfriend or at least he suspects you are." *Now if that doesn't scare her away, nothing will.*

"Why would he think that?" she asked, furrowing her eyebrows. *Because he caught me staring at your boobs and blushing like a schoolgirl.*

"I don't know, Jillian, but trust me he does. So, you're really subjecting yourself to a meet-the-parents dinner," I explained, proud that I was pulling this out of my ass so quickly. "I'll tell Carter that you forgot you had something to do at home. He'll get over it."

"No, Luke," she replied firmly. "I'm not going to cancel on your uncle. It was very sweet of him to invite me. Just relax," she added as the corners of her lips turned upward again. "I won't start talking china patterns with your auntie yet."

"It's just Grace. Her name is Grace," I corrected. *Auntie, my ass.*

"So, how do I get to Casa Chambers?" she asked, flashing me a shit-eating grin. I'm glad she found this funny. I was going to have to show her how funny it could be.

After giving Jillian directions, I high-tailed it out of the hospital and back home. I needed to finish studying for finals. I hadn't begun to pack anything and now I had to get ready for our impromptu dinner guest. Just what I needed. Was she completely oblivious? I know I hadn't imagined the tension between us yesterday, and today she was acting as if none of it happened. I was so distracted that I spent the afternoon staring at the ceiling instead of tackling any of the things I needed to do.

By five, I was ready to murder Carter for trying to ruin my life. Grace was fluttering around the kitchen frantically like we were expecting Martha Stewart for dinner. She was even wearing a dress.

"Luke," she exclaimed, looking up, "why haven't you changed?"

"Change? Why?" I asked, looking down at my gray t-shirt and jeans.

"Luke, come on," she replied shaking her head. "Go put on a nice shirt. You're having a guest for dinner."

"No," I corrected. "*You're* having a guest for dinner. I have no part in this."

"Don't be difficult," she sighed as she set the plates on the table.

This was all Jillian's fault. She didn't seem concerned that Carter thought we were together. She didn't think the car ride home was the most uncomfortable hour of her life, and she didn't see that it was just weird for her to come over. She was assaulting my dreams every night and taunting me with her tight shirts every day. She was driving me insane, and I was done. It was time to take control of this situation.

"Grace, I'm sure Jillian isn't concerned with my wardrobe choices," I replied, trying to appeal to her rational side. She seemed to think about it for a minute before a soft smile brightened her face.

"All right. You win. Here," she added, handing me a long loaf of bread. "Can you slice the bread for me?"

I grabbed the cutting board and started slicing away until the chime of the doorbell broke the silence. *Okay, Jillian, let's see if you still think this is a good idea.*

I opened the door to find her standing in the entryway wearing the black shirt from earlier and holding what looked like a cheesecake with strawberries on top.

"I made dessert," she announced as she handed me the plate. It was time to show her who she was dealing with.

"Strawberries. Just what I've been craving lately." I pulled a large, juicy berry off the top of the cake, closed my eyes and took a sloppy bite. I darted my tongue out to collect the juices dripping along the corners of my mouth. When I opened my eyes, I felt the rush of victory. Jillian's lips were parted and her eyes were trained on my mouth. *That's right. I'm not the only one with a wandering eye.*

"Luke," I turned to see that Grace had entered the room. "Are you eating the dessert that Jillian brought already?"

"Jillian was just giving me a taste," I replied, smirking at the expression on Jillian's face. "Weren't you, Jill?"

It was almost unfair. If she hadn't been torturing me, I'd feel bad because the pain in the ass actually looked speechless.

"Jillian," I began, swinging my free arm around her shoulder. I felt her body tense up under the weight of my arm, and gave her a squeeze for good measure. "This is my Aunt Grace."

"It's so nice to meet you," Grace beamed as she extended her hand. "Carter tells me we share a common passion." Jillian's eyes grew wide and darted over to me. "I can't wait to hear all about your Pad Thai recipe." I felt her relax a bit and square her shoulders.

This was fun.

"Oh, yes," she agreed hesitantly. "I love Pad Thai. It's one of my favorite dishes. Thank you for having me," she added in a shaky voice. I hadn't even gotten started yet.

"It's our pleasure, really," Grace replied, moving behind me to close the door.

"Yes," I added, whispering in Jillian's ear. "It's my pleasure." I heard her breath hitch.

"Now, I'll leave Luke to show you around. I have some veal to attend to." Grace left the room, and I anticipated the wrath of Jillian.

"What the hell was that?" she hissed as she yanked my arm off her shoulder.

"I was going to ask you the same thing," I replied, feigning concern. "You seemed like you were struggling with something back there. Should I open a window? You're a little pale."

She eyed me suspiciously. I could see the wheels spinning as she tried to figure out my angle.

"Just give me the damn tour, Luke," she began as she narrowed her eyes.

"So impatient," I said, shaking my head. "Dying to get a look at my bedroom, I see." I headed towards the stairs, suppressing a grin as I heard her grumble behind me.

"Are you taking me to your bedroom?" she hissed again.

"Do you always demand to be taken to the host's bedroom when you're invited for dinner?" I could tell I was really pissing her off, yet she continued to follow me. This was a lot easier than I expected.

"You knew what I meant, Luke," she sneered.

I rounded the corner at the top of staircase on my way to my room, but as I walked inside, it occurred to me that there was a major flaw in this part of my plan. The real Jillian would be in the room where Dream Jillian had been visiting me every night for the past week. I wasn't prepared to have my worlds collide, but now it was too late to turn back. She was already leaning against the door jamb studying the layout.

"Luke Chambers makes his bed and there's nary a sock on the floor. You're pretty good at keeping the living quarters neat and tidy," she commented with a small laugh.

"I'm pretty good at a lot of things," I replied smugly. Ignoring my response, she walked slowly into the room while gazing at the pictures on the wall before stopping at my desk.

"I meant to ask you yesterday," she began cautiously. "What's the story behind the phoenix?"

"It's not very interesting," I replied, trying not to sound like I was brushing her off.

"It obviously means something to you," she added, looking at me intently. "So it's definitely worth hearing, but if you'd rather not talk about it, I understand."

The last thing I wanted to do was talk about any depressing shit so I managed a small smile, but didn't elaborate on it. She continued on with her inspection of my things, flipping through the stacks of CDs I had organized next to my computer.

"Did you download all of this from Napster?" she asked, examining the jewel cases.

"Most of it."

"You have dial-up, right?" she added with a smirk.

"What else would I have?" I replied, baffled by the direction of the conversation.

"Must have taken a long time," she mused. "Just don't upload your music unless you plan on spending some time in the pokey. You're just too pretty to go to prison, Luke."

"What are you talking about?" I meant the pretty part, but I didn't know what her problem was with Napster either.

"Just trust me," she replied. "It doesn't end well."

"And you know this…how?" I asked, not even attempting to hide my sarcasm.

"Just trying to offer some advice," she added, picking up a case. "Lots of hard rock here." I decided against cracking any jokes about being rock hard. Hit too close to home.

"I don't see any Britney," she teased. "Bet she has a tramp stamp, too."

"She'll be in rehab in six months." For some reason, Jillian found this hysterical.

"She's dating the kid from N'Sync, you know?"

"Did the crystal ball tell you that, too?"

"I have people, Luke," she said with another laugh.

"Are these real people, Jillian, or the ones you hear in your head?" I asked sarcastically. "What else do the voices tell you?"

"That Meg White isn't Jack's sister. She's his ex wife. Hey, do you really like Limp Bizkit or did you just download this accidentally? Because if you meant it, you just lost some serious cool points."

It became apparent that somewhere along the line, I lost control of this conversation, and I wasn't going to let that shit happen again. She was facing me while she leaned back against my desk. Holding a CD in her hand, she continued reading the list of songs I'd recorded. I walked towards her, stopping only inches from where she stood. Her neck was tilted slightly and I was distracted by the smooth, pale skin. I had never left a mark on a girl before. Hickeys were an amateur's calling card, but something about Jillian brought out the caveman in me. I couldn't stop thinking about my lips on her neck.

Moving closer, I reached behind her to grab a CD on the desk, leaning completely over her in the process. I heard a small gasp as she angled back further, fighting to create some distance between us. I stood back up and handed the CD to her, noticing that her face was flushed. The maneuver was worth it even though my dick was now making its own "hard as a rock" jokes.

"You'll like this one," I said smirking, as I handed her the CD. It had some Buckcherry and Staind on it. "They're pretty good."

I didn't step back, standing closer than I would have under normal circumstances. The blush had yet to dissolve from her cheeks. As happy as I was to finally have an effect on her, it was working a little too well, and I was having flashbacks of the night before when she ran before I could kiss her. Now here she was in my bedroom, beautiful and blushing, staring at me with those deep brown eyes.

"Jillian," I said softly. She leaned towards me slightly, and I noticed that she seemed to be having a hard time breathing again. I tried regulating my own breath because I'd be damned if I let her get the best of me this time.

"Yes." Her response was barely audible. It was more of a sigh than a word.

"You're sitting on my Chili Peppers CD."

As soon as the words left my mouth, Jillian's body jerked back. I didn't even attempt to mask the smirk on my face, wanting her to know that whatever act she was putting on hadn't fooled me. She was as into this as I was. I was sure of that now. I just couldn't figure out if it was another guy or something else that was holding her back.

I expected some type of snide comment or remark, even another shove. Instead, we seemed to be locked in some type of sick staring contest where neither one of us wanted to be the first to look away. It was probably only thirty seconds, but seemed so much longer. I only looked away when I heard Grace calling my name.

"Are you still upstairs, Luke?" she yelled from the downstairs landing. "Dinner's almost ready."

"Can't keep *auntie* waiting," I said softly before walking to the door. I was already halfway down the stairs before I heard her footsteps following.

Grace was carrying a large plate of veal into the dining room as Carter finished setting the table. I heard Jillian walk up behind me. *I'm not done with you yet.*

"Sorry we took so long," I announced. "Jillian really wanted to see my bedroom." I stumbled forward as she shoved me in the back. Feisty.

"So glad you could make it, Jillian," Carter greeted her. "Have a seat."

She pulled out a chair and made herself comfortable. I took the seat next to her as Grace returned with a pitcher of lemonade.

"So Jillian, Carter tells me that your Pad Thai was a success. What else do you enjoy making?" Grace asked enthusiastically.

"Well," she replied. "I took a class on making sushi. I don't get to do it often, but it's a lot of fun."

"How often do you get to...*do it*?" I asked before taking a bite and slowly pulling the fork out of my mouth.

"Not nearly enough," she sneered, glaring at me.

"Well then, I have a great recipe for California Rolls for you to try," Grace added, oblivious to the game I was playing.

"So tell me, Jillian," Carter chimed in, "where are you headed in the fall?"

"NYU. I'm actually leaving in a few weeks. There's a writing workshop that I'm taking part in so I'm staying after the Summer Freshman Orientation. I'm majoring in Journalism so it's a good head start for me."

That news surprised me. I hadn't realized that she was leaving before the end of the summer. I was going to Seattle on Sunday so I shouldn't really care. I wouldn't be around either, although if she was in Reynolds, she'd only be a few hours away.

"NYU?" Carter sounded surprised and his eyes darted over to me. He needed to seriously stop that shit. "That's a long way off."

"Some of my friends are going too so I won't be all alone out there."

"I'm sure your parents will be anxious for you to come home to visit," Grace added with a warm smile.

"I'll miss it here." Her voice seemed far off. "But I'm excited about New York. I wish I had a little more time, though."

"That reminds me, Luke," Grace interrupted. "Did you call Jonas to make arrangements for the move?"

"I'll call him tomorrow," I replied quickly. I couldn't focus on Seattle with Jillian sitting at the table. It was too much.

As they continued questioning Jillian about her living arrangements and class schedule, I found myself getting more and more irritated by all of the New York talk. I couldn't believe that it hadn't come up just once that she was going to be leaving for the summer.

When Grace brought out Jillian's cheesecake, I decided to distract myself by torturing her a little more. While Carter and Grace discussed the merits of fruit toppings versus whipped cream, I seized my opportunity. Taking another hearty bite of the strawberry, I once again let the juice drip along the corner of my mouth. I took another quick bite and sucked at the spot where I had just bitten in, extracting the juice from it. When I looked up, Jillian was darting her tongue out towards the corner of her own mouth even though she hadn't even taken a bite herself.

"God, Jillian, these berries taste delicious. Sweet and juicy," I groaned. I thought I heard a moan, but I wasn't sure. She caught me watching her and squared her shoulders, playing it off like she hadn't been staring at my lips.

"So," she began once she regained her composure, "are you really going to wear a tux or will you be showing up at my doorstep with your leather jacket on?"

Crap.

I heard the gasp from Grace first. "Luke! Are you taking Jillian to the prom?"

"It's not a big deal," I explained. "Jillian has this friend…"

"Oh my goodness!" she exclaimed, ignoring me entirely. "Jillian, you need to let me know what color you're wearing so that Luke can get you a corsage. Oh, and Luke, we'll need to make sure your tie matches, as well."

"What?! What do you mean *we*?"

"Well, I'm coming with you to get measured," she replied firmly. *Um, no you're not.*

"Grace, I think I have this under control," I cautioned.

"I think he's perfectly capable, Grace," Carter added while laughing.

"I really think he may need my help, especially if he needs to choose a color—"

"Actually," Jillian interrupted. "I haven't decided on a color, so he can probably hold off on getting the tie done tomorrow."

"Oh," Grace added, clearly disappointed. "Well, I guess you can go on your own if they're only measuring you. Do you have it narrowed down, Jillian? Maybe I could help?"

Grace was nothing if not genuine, but I needed to intervene before this got out of control. Jillian was staring down at her empty plate uncomfortably. I decided that she had enough torture for the evening.

"Actually, I promised I'd help Jillian with a final paper she's working on. We should probably get started. I don't want to put it off much longer." Not catching on, Jillian looked at me curiously.

"What's it on, Jillian?" Carter asked. She froze for a minute, and I was about to spout off some bullshit before she beat me to it.

"Um, it's on…Joan of Arc," she managed to reply. "I love…Joan."

"Oh, Joan of Arc," he replied, as he raised his brows. "She was a remarkable girl."

"Yeah," I replied looking at Jillian. She was.

"Well, it was a pleasure meeting you," Grace added. "And I'd love to see you all dressed up on Thursday. Maybe you could stop by here on the way?"

"Of course," she agreed. "I mean, if that's okay with Luke."

"That's fine," I quickly replied because we needed to make our escape as soon as possible. "Let's get out of here fast before she offers to take you dress shopping," I whispered to her.

Jillian said her goodbyes and headed toward the front door.

"We're going this way," I corrected her as I walked through the kitchen.

"That was a great save in there, Chambers," she added. "You probably should've warned me to keep my mouth shut about the prom, though."

"No big deal," I said as I opened the door to the garage. I grabbed my extra helmet and tossed it at her. She caught it and stared at it wide-eyed.

"What are you doing?" she asked, panicking as I fastened mine on.

"We're leaving," I replied.

"On your bike?"

It was nice to see her drop the bravado for a change. "What is it with you and my bike?"

Swinging my leg over the seat, I sat down and looked over at her. She was still staring at it like she'd never seen a bike before.

"You gonna hop on?" With a final look of determination, she strapped on the helmet and stood before me nervously.

"Um, I don't…I've never done this," she stammered.

"Put your left hand on my shoulder and swing your right leg over so you're straddling the bike." *Or me, whichever you like.*

I braced myself for the impact and the assault on my senses. I knew I'd have to contend with the weight of her hand on my shoulder, the smell of perfume surrounding me, and the heat from her body as she struggled to get comfortable. I wanted it.

"Hang on," I added, adjusting to the feeling of her body molded against mine. She placed her hands lightly on my hips. I knew once we took off, her grip would tighten and I would lose my mind, but I wanted this. I wanted to feel her wrapped around me.

I hopped up to kick-start the bike and felt the familiar rumble. Jillian tensed up behind me. I knew where I was taking her. I just didn't know if it was the right call.

"Remember," I called over the roar of the engine, "hold on tight."

Just as I suspected, as I took off out of the garage, Jillian let out a small yelp and wrapped her arms tightly around my waist. My need for the girl made me dizzy.

"Where are we going?" she yelled from behind me.

Tracy Sweeney

"You wanted to know about my tattoo," I replied. "I'm gonna show you."

I headed for the cliffs and prepared to tell her what I hadn't spoken about in almost five years.

CHAPTER 11

Luke

I could find my way to the cliffs blindfolded. Coming here with Carter as often as I had, I knew the landmarks as if they were in my own backyard. With Jillian trailing behind me, I ducked under the bushes in the corner of the parking lot and walked along the trail towards the hollowed out tree I'd passed many times. In silence, we followed the path as it twisted and turned before slowly giving way to a clearing, hidden away from the highway not two miles from here.

No matter when I came here, alone or with Carter, it was always completely undisturbed, free from discarded bottles of Ole English and cigarette butts. Maybe there were others who chucked their trash off the ledge and sent it plummeting into the ocean below. Maybe we weren't the only ones who came here. But it felt that way.

Once the path opened to the rocky ledge, I heard a gasp from behind me. "We haven't been walking very long," she marveled. "I couldn't even hear the waves from where we parked."

"I know. It's crazy," I replied, looking up at the sky. It wasn't dark enough yet. "It's completely silent. That's one of things I love about this place."

"I don't understand, though. What does this have to do with your tattoo?" she asked. She sounded so sincere. It seemed like such a crime to dampen the mood, but she had asked so I'd tell.

"It has a lot to do with Carter. I didn't always live with them...Grace and Carter," I began slowly. "I moved here when I was thirteen. Before that I lived in a small suburb a few hours outside of Boston with my parents. My dad is...*was*...Carter's brother."

I glanced over to gauge her reaction. She sat down cross-legged on a small patch of grass by the rocky ledge with her gaze fixed on me. Our conversations were usually pretty light, and I didn't know if she had any idea what she was getting into by asking the questions she had. She seemed anxious to hear the rest so I sat down next to her and took a deep breath before continuing.

"My parents probably shouldn't have gotten married. I'm obviously not an expert on marriage so I'm not judging anyone, but they really weren't…right," I began, struggling to find the words. It had been so long since I had spoken about them to anyone aside from Carter. It wasn't easy to say certain things out loud, even this many years later.

"They started dating when they were in high school. Young and stupid. It wasn't long before she got knocked up, and they were forced to get married. It's not easy being told at eighteen that any chance you had of getting out of your small, nothing town was gone. They had a baby to think about now….responsibility. They had to make sacrifices that neither one of them wanted to make.

"In the beginning, I think they held it together for me. They hid a lot of things or maybe when you're a kid, you just don't see it." The memories flashed like snapshots in my head—the broken glass, my mother crying, a knock at the door.

"I think they always fought, but were able to hide it when they weren't so screwed up. By the time I was ten or eleven, there was a pattern to their fights. During the week, they seemed to stay out of each other's way. He was a carpenter and he worked long hours. For as long as I can remember, he'd come home, sit down in his recliner, turn on the news and watch TV with a cold beer. Every night except for Friday because on Friday, he'd trade in the beer for something a little stronger, usually vodka tonic," I recalled, remembering what became his weekend staple.

"By eleven, the yelling would have woken me up. They'd fight over the stupidest things. 'You left your socks on the floor', 'You forgot to pick up the dry cleaning', 'You didn't say *Bless You* when I sneezed'. It's the same ridiculous shit other people deal with, but at that point, I don't even think they *liked* each other anymore so the same ridiculous shit became this continuous epic battle.

"And my mother…God, my mother. She loved throwing things. I got pretty good at figuring out what she was throwing," I added, looking over at her. "If I could hear the pieces scatter for a long period of time, it was a platter or maybe a serving bowl. If the crash was sharp and quick, it was probably just a saucer or a mug. She was all about equality," I mused darkly. "As long as it was breakable and could possibly hit my dad, she'd throw it.

"Then on Monday, like we were in the Twilight Zone, everything would go back to normal like nothing ever happened. He'd go off to work, come home, watch TV and have his beer. But on Friday, the cycle would begin again.

"I started to find bottles stashed around the house. The first time it happened, something had rolled under the couch. I don't remember what...but I reached under and felt glass. When I pulled it out, I saw that it was an empty bottle of whiskey. And it's funny. I assumed that it was my dad's," I laughed sadly. "It didn't occur to me at the time that my dad was pretty open about his vodka.

"I found a few more over the next few months, stuffed into the garbage cans out back and in the recycle bin. Then one day I came home from school early, and my mom was sitting in the kitchen. She was crying and nursing a glass of the whiskey I'd been finding hidden around the house. When she saw me, she scrambled to hide it, but it was too late. I don't know if she started drinking because of the fighting, or if she was just better at hiding it than he was. Either way, they were both pretty messed up and the fighting just kept getting worse."

I watched as she absently pulled at the blades of grass in front of her, taking in everything I said.

"Have you ever had to go around the house and make sure all the windows were closed because you didn't want your parents to broadcast your shitty life to the whole neighborhood?" I asked. "It was a nightly ritual in my house.

"So I was almost thirteen, I think, when I decided that I had enough. Every weekend we'd go through the same cycle of vodka and whiskey, fighting and screaming, broken platters and broken saucers. You'd think they'd run out of the shit. Then one night after I was pretty sure I heard a whole set of glasses shatter against the wall, I stormed down the stairs just ready to end this shit. And for the rest of my life, I'll remember the look on their faces while they listened to their twelve-year-old kid tell them to cut the shit and get their act together," I winced, remembering their pained expressions. "Just humiliated.

"After that, they were on their best behavior. At least that's how it appeared. Even weekends weren't that bad. There were fights here and there, but dishes were staying in the cabinet and I figured that was a decent start.

"So one night a month or so later, my mom told me that they were going to a party at her co-worker's house. She asked her friend Trina to stay with me while they were going to be out. She was nice enough not to say that she was babysitting me," I laughed softly. "God, I was so pissed, too.

"I was half asleep when the phone rang and Trina was still downstairs watching *Melrose Place* or one of those stupid shows. She was always loud so I could hear what she was saying to the person on the phone. 'How long ago did they leave?', 'Was it bad?', 'Who started yelling first?' I knew right away that they had gotten into it at the party...'"

I trailed off thinking of how defeated I felt, knowing that I'd have to listen to the sounds of breaking glass all night. I thought about packing up and leaving. I even started planning where I'd go.

"And then Trina said to the person on the other end that my parents should have already been home and all I could imagine was that they pulled over on the side of the road and started beating the shit out of each other because to me, that was the next step."

I remembered the panic on her face when I walked into the living room. They had left over an hour and a half earlier, and her co-worker lived only fifteen minutes away.

"When the doorbell rang, I knew. I didn't need to listen to what the police said. I didn't need to hear where the car went off the road, or how they thought it happened. I knew. They held their shit together for me, but you can only hold back the inevitable for just so long. You can't stop it. The only saving grace was that I didn't need to witness their last blow up."

"So, what happened?" she asked softly. I hadn't realized I had stopped talking.

"They drove off the embankment and the car flipped over. She died instantly. He died at the hospital the next day. Never woke up."

Jillian's eyes were glassy and her lips were drawn down. I don't know what I expected, telling her the story. Great job, Chambers. Such a people person. Now I wished I could just take it all back. All of it.

"God, Luke," she said sadly.

"I turned out just fine," I added, not needing any pity.

"I know," she replied. "Them, I mean. They wanted to do what was best for you, but the best thing would have been to split up. They seem so...misguided."

"They were alcoholic, Jillian," I corrected her solemnly. "Let's not romanticize it."

"I'm not. I'm just looking at it from their point of view. Sometimes the very best intentions have disastrous results."

As much as I would have liked to have agreed with her, I couldn't. They were selfish and destructive. They ruined each other and almost took me down in the process. I wasn't going to argue with her though. She didn't need to know how bitter I was.

"Carter and Grace flew out that night and took care of all of the arrangements. I spent all day in my room, not wanting to walk around the house. It was too quiet. When they asked me to move to Washington, I actually wanted to leave so much I didn't fight it.

"At the airport, Carter tried telling me about my new room and what the schools were like. I wasn't the most talkative kid at the time, though. They tried so goddamn hard," I recounted painfully. "I wasn't trying to be a dick, but I'd spent the last three years watching my parents slowly commit suicide. I had a hard time having a normal conversation after everything that had gone on.

"My first night here, Carter told me he wanted to go for a drive, and I just wanted to shut the door to my room and drown everything out. Carter's persuasive, though, and he managed to talk me into going. He grabbed a long, thin black bag and hauled it into the car before we took off. He didn't force conversation or try to say anything life-altering or profound. We drove in silence, but it didn't feel awkward either.

"And he brought me here. When he got out of his car, he grabbed the bag and told me to follow him through the path. The whole time I was thinking *why the hell are we hiking in the middle of the night.*"

I laughed remembering how pissed I'd been. "When we got to the clearing, he opened up the bag and started assembling a telescope and I didn't know what to say. My parents had been dead for less than a week, and he wanted to show me the moon? I probably looked at him like he was an asshole. He obviously could tell how irritated I was so he didn't ask me if I wanted to use it; he just started looking into it himself.

"He had been staring up at the sky for a while before he mentioned that he and my dad would go to the park with my grandfather to look at the stars when they were kids. My grandfather taught them all about the location of the constellations and the mythology behind each of them. I just wanted him to get to the point, but he was going on and on about how he and my dad would pretend they were Perseus, sent off to kill Medusa. I had no clue at the time what he was trying to tell me, how he wanted me to see who my dad was before he broke.

"Then he told me about a smaller constellation called the Phoenix. You can't even see it from where we are. It's only really visible during the winter in the southern hemisphere. The Phoenix builds a nest, lights it on fire and throws itself into the flames. Then, it's reborn from the ashes. When Carter was done telling the story, he looked at me with the saddest expression on his face, and I couldn't believe how much older he looked. He said, 'I'm not going to ask you to forgive him, and I'm not going to ask you to understand. But you don't have to let this break you. You can rise above this'.

"I felt like the biggest dick. Here he is mourning his older brother, taking in his kid, and I was acting like a spoiled brat," I explained, feeling guilty and embarrassed.

"You were a kid, Luke," she added. "A kid who had to deal with a lot of adult problems."

"Maybe. I don't think I fully appreciated Carter until then, though. His message was loud and clear. I didn't need to go up in flames. I could survive this.

"So it became a regular thing for us. If one of us had a tough day, we'd grab the black bag with the telescope in it and just catch the other's eye. We usually didn't need to say much. He'd grab the keys to the car and I'd follow. If we were in the mood to talk about what was going on, we would, but more often than not, we'd just look through the telescope or look out at the water.

"Right after my eighteenth birthday in April, I told Carter that I was getting a tattoo. He wasn't thrilled, but he didn't try to talk me out of it either. When I was leaving to go to Seth's, Carter grabbed his keys and started walking towards the door. He told me that if I was going to get a tattoo, he was coming with me."

"He went *with* you?" she gasped.

"I couldn't talk him out of it! I just stood there for a minute, trying to picture Carter in his Brooks Brothers button down and corduroys hanging out in a tattoo parlor. But he wouldn't back down.

"So when we got to Seth's, I showed Carter the picture of the phoenix, and I was actually kind of glad that he was there. Until I heard him asking your buddy Dice about some drawing on the wall. Before I knew it, Carter is sitting at Dice's station getting a tattoo on his shoulder blade."

"What!" she exclaimed. "Uncle Carter has a tattoo! Of what?"

"The Chinese symbol for family," I replied.

"Luke," she sighed. "That's really beautiful. You're very lucky to have them."

"I know…That's one of the reasons why I'm going to Seattle."

"I don't get it," she replied, furrowing her brow, looking cute as hell.

"One day about a year ago, I snuck out to buy some cigarettes. I'm sure they thought I was asleep. I overheard Carter on the phone with the bank talking about some kind of college account for me. I heard him asking the person when I'd get access to the money."

"Then why aren't you going?" she asked, confused.

"Jillian, come on. Just how much more am I expected to take from them? If they wanted kids, they would have had them. Now they've been saddled down with a kid for the last five years. They both put a lot on hold because of me; Grace's cookbook and Carter's career. I'm sure he would have worked more if I wasn't around. I've been a huge interruption in their lives. There's no way I'd let them pay for college."

"Luke, that's a horrible reason not to go to college. Please tell me that's not why," she demanded. "If you felt that college wasn't right for you, well, that's different. I know lots of people…" She trailed off, suddenly looking frustrated, but I wasn't going to let her complete her thought.

"I can't take the money from them, and they wouldn't let me turn it down," I explained. "Anyway, I have the bar now."

Even as I said the words, they sounded hollow to me. I had been so focused on Seattle for so long, but hadn't managed to get myself packed or ready. The move really hadn't been a priority lately—because of her. Now I just didn't want to think. I didn't want to wonder what was going to happen if I left, or what would have happened if I stayed. I needed to stop obsessing and just change the subject.

Jillian was staring blankly up at the sky when I turned to face her.

"You know, your cross is up there, too," I began, pleased that I had found an escape from the current direction of our talk. "The Northern Cross."

"Really? Where?" she asked, craning her neck up. I leaned back on my elbows and she followed me as we both stared up at the lights in the sky.

"See the group of stars right over there in the shape of a cross?" I asked, pointing above our heads. "We can see it in the summer and fall."

"The phoenix and the cross are both constellations?" she asked, looking amused.

"Yeah, just never in the same sky at the same time." The smile quickly left her face.

127

"I guess the timing is off, huh?" she added softly. I got the impression that we weren't talking about stars anymore. I just couldn't understand why. She was so hard to read. Before I had a chance to question her, though, she pushed herself up off her elbows and glanced at her watch.

"My parents are going to kill me if I don't get home soon."

When I looked at my own watch, I felt guilty for keeping her out so late the night before finals. I knew she was right and we needed to get back, but I still didn't want to go. Something was off, though. There was a sadness in her voice that wasn't there a minute ago, and I just wished she'd talk to me.

The walk back to my bike was quiet, as I wondered what had gotten into her so suddenly. I climbed on and offered her my hand, bracing myself for the warmth of her body as she settled in behind me. For the fifteen minute ride back to my house, I could enjoy the feeling of Jillian wrapped around me and not worry about the frustration that it would inevitably bring.

Pulling up to the house, I told her to hold onto my shoulders as she stepped off the bike. As soon as she was gone, I started thinking of reasons to call her back. I decided then and there that I'd do whatever it took to get her back on my bike again soon. I needed to feel her like that again…all the time.

I took off my helmet and hung it from the handlebar. I turned around as Jillian unclasped hers and slowly shook her hair out. It was a mess of curls and snarls, twisted and knotted from the blowing wind. She leaned against the bike with her hair flowing wild and something in me snapped. Without over-thinking it, I walked to her, ignoring the way she eyed me suspiciously and took her face in my hands.

Don't tell me to stop, Jillian. I don't want to play this game anymore.

My breath was shaky and my mind was reeling, but I could only see her lips. As soon as I leaned in and pressed against them, I breathed her in and parted mine. She didn't pull away, but she wasn't responding either.

"Let me kiss you," I pleaded softly, grazing her lips again while my forehead rested against hers. She released a breath and slowly nudged my mouth with hers. Her lips were soft and warm and everything I wanted and not enough.

"Jillian," I breathed out softly. *It doesn't have to be this difficult.*

It only took the slightest move from her for me to respond. When her defenses crumbled, I lost all sense of reason. I didn't worry about scaring her away. I didn't give her the opportunity to run. I didn't even give her a chance to tell me she wanted me, too. I just didn't think at all because kissing Jillian felt better than anything I had ever felt before.

I threaded my fingers into the tangle of snarls and curls in her hair, drawing her as close to me as I could get. All of the pent up frustration from the past two weeks came crashing down, and I couldn't control myself anymore. When I felt her hands settle on my forearms, grasping tightly, I wound my fingers deeper in her hair, tilting her head to the side. And when the kiss deepened, I fought back every impulse in my body that screamed for me to lay her down on the seat of my bike and show her how she had ruined me.

It was when she let out an inadvertent groan that I felt her stiffen before pulling away completely. Her eyes were wild, her skin was flushed and she was beautiful and dangerous, panting in front of me. I couldn't understand why she was making this so goddamn difficult.

"Jillian," I began, attempting a pre-emptive strike on any excuse she was going to give me. Why couldn't she see how right this was? "We need to—"

"Luke..." she interrupted, squeezing her eyes shut and shaking her head. "I just...It's not that I don't...I wish you knew how hard this is for me."

"You're making it hard," I replied, reaching out for her.

"I have to go," she choked out, hurrying over to her car. This was all new to me. I had never had a girl run away from me—nevermind one that did it every time I came close to touching her. I assumed that Jillian wasn't the most experienced girl in the world, but it was getting ridiculous. How many times did she expect me to chase her?

"I'll talk to you tomorrow, Luke," she added with a sad smile before climbing into the car. I stood there dumbfounded as she drove down the gravel path that led to the highway.

What the hell just happened?

I watched as her car disappeared, leaving me standing there alone...again.

No.

No.

I wasn't doing this again.

We were going to talk about this tomorrow.

No more veiled comments. No more games.

We were going to figure this out because this...whatever *this* was...whatever we were....*this* was right.

Tracy Sweeney

No more running. No more hiding.

Screw this shit.

CHAPTER 12

Jillian

On Monday morning, I was leaning against Megan's convertible, trying with little luck to listen to her rehash her date with Nate. I vaguely remembered her mentioning an argument over the origin of the onion ring and a competition that involved the winner eating the most disgusting food combination. (Nate won with pickles and pistachio ice cream.)

"And then we were walking out of the theater and I was saying that this bullshit they're selling about The Force being some normal biological response not only spoils the original mystique, but insults the intelligence of true fans," she raved. "I was like 'New Hope, my ass.' Then he stopped dead in his tracks, and I thought he was actually going to defend the stupid movie because, for the love of Christ, he can't agree with a thing I say. Instead, he just looks at me with this dead serious expression and says 'Go to the prom with me.' I agreed and we went to the arcade at the mall and played Tekken. I kicked his ass!" she added triumphantly.

"How romantic, Megan," Danielle replied, clearly not understanding the dynamic she'd come to know very well in the years ahead. "Sounded like a disaster there for awhile."

"Disaster?" Megan spat back. "Are you kidding? Were you even listening? Not a disaster at all. He has an original Millennium Falcon, Danielle! We went back to his house and—"

"...he let you play with his rocket ship?" she asked sarcastically. It was probably true.

"Screw you, Danielle. Back me up, Jillian."

I heard Megan call my name, but I wasn't sure what the question was. Were we really discussing *Star Wars* action figures when my life was falling apart around me? Every thought that ran through my head would bring me back to Luke. Everywhere I looked and everything I did brought him to mind. I was even seeing him in my sleep. I had tried so hard to keep my feelings at bay, but after everything that happened over the weekend, it was impossible.

Everything I thought I knew had been turned around in just two days. And the scariest part was that just one of the things that happened would have chipped away at my resolve. From holding my hand at Seth's, to taunting me with his strawberry lips at dinner, then telling me his secrets by the cliffs and breaking me down when he kissed me. I was in uncharted territory and I was lost.

I replayed that kiss in my head a million times, maybe more. I'd kissed my fair share of toads over the years. There were the timid, tight-lipped kissers and the overly-ambitious slobberers. There were sweet kisses and ones I'd rather forget, but *nothing* came close to what I felt when Luke kissed me. It wasn't like in the movies when you'd see fireworks, or in romance novels when you'd feel an electrical charge. No. Everything was quiet and still, like the eye of the storm. We were in our own world…until I heard myself groan like an animal.

I couldn't deny that I wanted him. God, did I want him, but giving into that feeling scared the living shit out of me. I didn't have a spirit guide or a cool sidekick telling me what to do, and I could screw some serious shit up if I wasn't careful. So, I ran away like a…well a teenage girl, and Luke probably hated me. Hell, *I* hated me.

"Earth to Jillian!" Danielle interrupted, waving a hand in front of my face. I turned to respond just in time to witness Luke's bike pull into the lot. He looked straight at me and while he didn't look angry, his expression seemed serious, and it was unnerving.

"Sorry to cut the chat short, ladies," I stammered. "But I promised I'd quiz Suzanne before her Spanish final this morning so I have to head to the library. Catch you later?" I hurried into the building without waiting for a response and made a bee-line into the safety of the Reference Room. I threw myself into the seat next to Suzanne, burying my head in my hands.

"Problems this morning, Jill?" she asked gingerly.

"You have no idea," I mumbled through my folded arms.

"Wanna talk about it?" *Did I?* If I didn't say something to someone I was going to go explode.

"Let's pretend for a moment that I studied for finals," I whispered louder than I probably should have. "Let's pretend that I wasn't riding around on the back of a motorcycle last night or that I wasn't meeting his family and seeing his room and smelling his smell. Let's pretend that I'm not in so ridiculously over my head that I can't even see straight anymore. Can I please pretend, Suzanne? Because I am seriously losing it."

"Shit, Jill," she replied wide-eyed. "What's going on with you?"

"Luke," I replied, dropping my head back down on the desk.

"Luke Chambers? When did this happen?!"

"He's taking me to the prom," I added, raising my head for a moment before returning it to my hiding place.

"And this is a bad thing?"

"Yes, Suzanne, this is a very, very, very bad thing," I replied, still agitated.

"You're going to have to spell this one out for me because I'm not getting why going to the prom with Luke is a bad thing," she added, sounding concerned. I couldn't blame her. I sounded like a raving lunatic. Hell, I *was* a raving lunatic. I was changing the past, for Christ's sake, so Luke being a "bad thing" was the understatement of the year…and possibly the next decade.

"Suzanne," I began, trying unsuccessfully to rein in my overwhelming panic. "It's bad because Luke and I are just not supposed…we're just not…" I collapsed back down on the table defeated. I had been reduced to a stuttering idiot. Years of schooling and studying the English language had been obliterated by a motorcycle-riding bad boy with messy hair. If he bottled this shit, he could rule the world.

"Jillian, before you hurt yourself, can I give you a piece of advice?" she offered gently. "You may think you know what's best, but I'd hate to see you pass up on something that might actually be good. He clearly has some kind of effect on you," she surmised, motioning to my body sprawled across the library table. "You just don't want to be one of those people years from now who looks back on high school and says 'I wish I had'." she added. "Regret sucks. You don't get a 'do over'."

Stunned, I stared at her just waiting for Ashton Kutcher to jump out from behind the stacks to tell me that I was being *Punk'd*. When he didn't show up, I just laughed at the irony of the situation. While her comment about changing the past was quite obviously wrong, she was right about one thing. Regret sucks. I just wished there was some way of knowing whether I was doing the right thing or not.

"Thanks, Suze," I replied, grabbing her in a bear hug. "You always know just what to say."

"Anytime," she began with a mischievous grin. "So, are you going to be able to concentrate today or are you still 'smelling his smell'? What's that all about?"

I shoved her arm, laughing. "Don't judge me, Suzanne, unless you've been there."

"Fine, fine. So are you going to go find him and sniff him some more?"

"You're hysterical. Really. Have you always been this funny?" I asked sarcastically. I mean, really, apparently my life needed to fall apart for Suzanne to perfect her standup routine.

"Seriously," she urged.

"I think I need some time to decompress, but yes, I'm going to go and sniff him some more," I answered with a smile.

"That's my girl!" she replied, raising her hand for a high-five.

"All right. I've amused you enough for one morning. I'm off," I quipped as I picked up my books.

"See you at the bonfire tomorrow?" she asked, raising a brow. My body stiffened again. The bonfire. *Shit.*

"Yes," I replied. "Danielle's forcing me, so I'll see you there."

I walked to my trig final feeling uneasy. It could have been the fact that I still had no idea what a reference angle was or that I was still hiding from Luke. It was likely a combination of both along with the impending forced fun of the school-sponsored bonfire. Instead of obsessing, I decided to focus on a new high school experience. I was about to fail my first test.

Shuffling into Mrs. Jacobs' classroom, I noticed Val filing her nails and checking her iridescent gloss in her compact mirror. It looked to me like she had just eaten a glazed donut. Probably not her intention. I couldn't help but laugh at how desperate she was.

As Mrs. Jacobs placed a copy of the test on each desk, I held my breath, offering up a prayer to God, Michael J. Fox, the guys from *The Big Bang Theory* and anyone else who could get me through this mess. Turning it over, I immediately recognized a few problems that we worked on in class, but the majority of the test looked like gibberish. If I was lucky I'd manage a D and then use my fake head injury as an excuse for failing. I could always explain that I knew for a fact that trig was useless in my future life. It was worth a try.

While trig was a disaster, my next two finals weren't quite as bad. After taking Spanish all throughout high school and college, I was able to fake my way through that final with a lot more ease. Although at one point I think I wrote that I was turned on by the lesson instead of that I *understood* the lesson. That might have actually worked to my advantage though because Señor Gustavson was a bit of a pervert. Maybe I'd get extra credit.

World Lit was a breeze because I knew the material inside and out. I had to stop myself from quoting passages from other works and drawing comparisons to authors I studied in college, though. It was difficult to maneuver, but in the end I think I did fairly well.

I was exhausted after taking three tests in quick succession. My thoughts briefly flickered to Luke as I wondered where he was and what he was doing. I knew we'd need to discuss the shift in our relationship soon, but I was still struggling with the possible ramifications so I walked swiftly through the hall, hoping we didn't cross paths. I still had to tackle two finals so a little study time in the library would do me some good. The added bonus being that it was also a great place to hide. As I jogged around the corner towards the double doors, I felt a hand grasp my elbow.

"I think we need to walk in this direction," he whispered in my ear, turning my body completely around to walk back down the stairs.

"What are you doing?"

"You've avoided me long enough," he replied matter-of-factly, steering me towards the pathway to the gym.

"You can let go now," I added, rolling my eyes and motioning to his grip on my arm.

"So you can find another reason to run off?" he asked. "I think I like my way better."

"I'm not running off," I sneered childishly.

"Oh?" he replied. "So you weren't going to spend the day hiding in the library?"

"I wasn't hiding," I lied. "I was studying. There are finals today in case you hadn't noticed."

Incensed, I wrestled my arm away. Everything he was saying was true, but he was still pissing me off. I stormed around the corner behind the gym, probably looking like a toddler having a tantrum. "Was that really necessary?" I fumed, folding my arms across my chest.

"It wouldn't have been if you didn't have a habit of taking off when we needed to talk," he replied darkly, stalking towards me.

"My life is really complicated right now, Luke," I added, trying to offer an explanation. "I wish you could understand."

"I told you already, you're the one making this hard," he responded, closing the distance between us. I wondered if he chose those words intentionally, but then chided myself for having my mind in the gutter. "You know that, right?" he added as he ran the tips of his fingers softly down my arm.

Startled, I took a step back, colliding with the brick wall behind me. He held one arm up against the building and leaned over me slowly.

"I will hold you down if that's what I need to do to get you to talk to me." His voice was low and rough, causing me to shiver.

God, that's hot.

The intensity of his stare and the positioning of our bodies clearly affected my ability to function. In an attempt to escape his gaze, I forced myself to look away, but my eyes stalled and focused on the lips that had been haunting me all day. He was only inches away and I wanted to laugh because I knew Suzanne would ask me if I was smelling his smell.

I don't want to smell his smell. I want to taste his lips.

Before I could second-guess myself or think about the consequences, I launched myself at him, wrapping my arms around his neck and pulling his bottom lip between mine. His surprise was apparent as I felt him stiffen for just a moment before quickly recovering. He wasted little time, raising his hands to twist into my hair. My hands settled on his waist, instinctively pulling him closer. As he pinned me against the wall, his warm lips tugged at mine. I gasped as I felt his right hand move down from my hair, dragging along the side of my torso before wrapping around my thigh and hiking it over his hip. He ground himself against me, and I suddenly couldn't remember why I had been holding back for so long.

Everything about him was enveloping me. I had always been a level-headed girl. Sure, I let my flask make a few decisions for me here and there, but overall, I thought things through before acting. But at that moment, I didn't care how old I was or where I came from. I didn't care about Peggy Sue or the goddamn space/time continuum. You could have told me that I had a photo album full of headless friends and family. Nothing at that moment mattered but us.

"What are you doing to me?" he panted softly, pulling away to catch his breath. *What am I doing to him? Is he serious?*

"Luke," I sighed, feeling dizzy and breathless. "I'm not sure if this is a good idea. We should talk…"

I was saying the words but I didn't mean them. His hips were flush against mine while my leg was still hitched up around his back. We were both gasping and panting, and I was suggesting we have a cordial talk about the fact that I was an insane visitor from the future who was probably ruining his life. The absurdity of the situation was not lost on me.

"I think we can talk later," he replied, dipping his head down and nipping at my lips again.

I was about to argue when I heard the distinct sound of giggling off in the distance. My eyes shot open to witness the blood drain from Luke's face and a look of panic set in.

"The hell," he growled under his breath. With my thigh still strategically perched on his hip, he began to swivel around, looking from side to side for the source of the interruption. The motion caused my head to loll back against the wall, and I thanked God for that one yoga class I took because I wanted to spend all day standing just like that.

When I managed to pry my eyes back open, I saw Anne-Marie and Jon, the juniors who gave us the peep show in detention, stumbling through the trees to our right. Her shirt was off and his hands were already clawing at her zipper. I was mentally chastising them for lacking the class to screw somewhere halfway decent before I looked around me and remembered that I was wrapped around a boy in a dirty, woodsy area behind a high school gymnasium. I was a trollop too now. Solidarity, sister.

"You have got to be kidding me," Luke exclaimed, releasing my leg and pushing off the building. I groaned as he moved away, silently cursing the horny, pubescent assholes for interrupting.

"Oops," Anne-Marie giggled, covering her mouth. "Honey, I think our spot is taken today."

"Your spot!" Luke raged. "*Your* spot? How often are you bringing your girlfriend out to 'your spot', Jon?"

"Settle down, Chambers," he replied casually as Anne-Marie pulled her tank top back on. "And you two were just studying back here, right?"

"I'm just saying that it would have been nice to know if I needed disinfectant every time I came back here for a smoke," he continued, eyes ablaze. Before

137

he could go on raging like a maniac, I grabbed him by the arm and pulled him away.

"We were just leaving," I added, smiling apologetically at them. When we rounded the corner, it was his turn to wrestle his arm free.

"It doesn't bother you that they've been screwing back there the whole time? We're there every day!"

"You're being so dramatic, Luke," I replied, teasing him. "School is over. Time to give up the fortress. Pass the torch, so to speak."

"That's not the point," he replied, still irritable. "Not to mention," he added, his scowl lifting into a mischievous smile, "they interrupted."

Moving closer, he reached out, threading his fingers through my hair. "So that may have been the best talk we've ever had."

"At least top ten," I replied, lost in the feeling of his fingers tugging on the long strands. "Listen Luke, I meant it when I said my life is kind of complicated right now."

"As long as you're not hiding in remote areas of the school instead of talking to me, we'll figure it out."

"We still need to talk," I began carefully. "But I'd like to have this discussion somewhere else." There was just no way I would be able to think clearly after the "discussion" we just had.

"Tonight then," he suggested, letting his fingertips glide gently across my cheek. "I'll come by and pick you up?"

"That's not the best idea, unless you want to be subjected to Henry Cross' version of meet-the-parents and, trust me, he will not be as pleasant as Grace and Carter were. Why don't I just meet you somewhere?" I offered.

"How about the lot by the cliffs," he replied. "Six o'clock?"

"Sure. Six o'clock," I repeated, trying to appear calm and confident when I was anything but.

I wasn't even sure what I was going to say to him. Before Luke, I never had to tell someone how much I wanted them or how much I needed them. No one had ever made me feel the way he did. He honestly scared me to death. But since there was no way of knowing if I'd ever get back to my life in 2011, if I was stuck in 1999, I wanted to be stuck with him.

"I have to meet Josh to work on some problems for our chem final," he said, looking at his watch. "I'll see you tonight?"

His eyes burned through me, and I wondered if he planned on kissing me again. Instead, he grasped my hand tightly and rubbed a small circle into my palm with his thumb. After a quick squeeze, he released it and walked back into the building without another word.

I stood frozen in place, watching him as he left. Well, I watched certain parts of him as he left. *Why hadn't I watched him leave more often?*

I knew it would be impossible to concentrate on finals when I had just been minutes away from tearing Luke's clothes off behind the school gym. Instead of studying like the good girl I once was, I was ogling Luke's ass and wondering if he wore boxer briefs or rolled commando.

I spent the rest of the day extremely distracted, but somehow managed to tackle my last two final exams. Driving home with my stomach full of butterflies, I counted down the hours until I could see him again. I found myself envisioning Luke in a tuxedo at the prom, and wearing his cap and gown. I saw myself riding on the back of his bike again, and laying side by side in the grassy clearing by the ocean's edge, looking at the stars. My thoughts shifted to the future, wondering what it would be like to have the man in the black and white photo standing behind the bar and smiling that smile at me.

When I walked into my living room a short time later, I was startled to find my mother home, sitting on the couch, and my father pacing the room furiously. The sound of the door closing caught their attention and their stern faces turned to me. I winced as I noticed the empty bottle of Captain Morgan on the coffee table. I forgot that I shoved that under my bed.

Fantastic.

"Sit down, Jillian," my father began in a scarily calm voice. I could tell he was upset, but I had never really gotten into trouble before so I wasn't sure how angry he really was. I decided it was best to comply.

"What...how...I can't believe...."

Okay. He's super mad.

"Henry," my mother interrupted, sending my father a look that said she would continue the interrogation. I had to say, for a police officer, he was rather ineffective.

"Jillian," she began. "Can you explain to me why I found an empty bottle of rum underneath my seventeen-year-old daughter's bed? Is this the same bottle that's been missing from our liquor cabinet?"

I stared blankly at my mom. Offering to run to the store and replace it probably wasn't what she was looking for.

"Mom, Dad, I'm sorry, I was...curious and when I tried it...it just tasted horrible. I can't believe people actually drink that stuff! I, for one, was disgusted so I just...poured the whole thing down the drain," I blurted out. I felt my body inadvertently shudder. I would never waste alcohol.

"Do you really think....are we supposed to..." my father continued fuming until my mother shot him another cautioning glare. Thank God the crime rate was low in Reynolds, and he didn't need to do this often. He might hurt himself.

"Let me get this straight," my mother added doubtfully. "You took a sip, hated it and decided to rid the house of alcohol by pouring the remainder down the drain?"

"Yes?" I replied, wavering. I'd admit this wasn't the best excuse I probably could have come up with, but it had been a rough day.

"Nice try, Jillian," she replied. "Go to your room. You're grounded."

There was a part of me that was a little excited to be grounded for the first time. It was a rite of passage that I never experienced. However, when I remembered that I was supposed to meet Luke at the cliffs, my heart plummeted. While I had planned to put on my best disgruntled teenager act, I didn't really need to pretend. I stormed upstairs and into my bedroom. The phone rang as soon as I closed the door.

"Hello," I answered in a huff.

"Hey, Jillian! Great news!"

"Danielle, this isn't a good time," I began, dragging the corded phone across the room to my desk.

"This is a fantastic time because I found you a fantastic prom dress," she replied triumphantly. I was suddenly having *déjà vu* as I thought back to the day I hit my head two weeks ago because of her damned skinny jeans. A prom dress from Danielle could possibly kill me.

"Aren't you going to ask me what it looks like?"

I knew better than to disagree or debate her. She had picked out some of the most fabulous items of clothing I'd ever owned. I was pretty sure that the prom dress would be incredible, ridiculously over-priced and probably dangerous.

"Sure. Yes. Of course," I replied. I really didn't have time for chatting. I needed to find the aftercare instructions for my tattoo where Luke wrote his phone number.

"It's black with silver trim and it's just the most adorable thing you will ever see," she gushed.

"It sounds great," I added, preoccupied with my search. "Listen, my parents found that bottle of rum I swiped when I made the Pad Thai and I'm in a lot of trouble. Maybe we can discuss this tomorrow?"

"Oh no!" she muttered. "What are you going to do?"

"Throw myself at their mercy? I don't know. I already tried lying and it didn't go very well. I'm going to hang up before they remember I have a phone in here and take it away," I explained finally spying the rumpled up paper jammed underneath one of my textbooks. I knocked my Word of the Day calendar over in the process. Today's word had been *misconstrue*.

Misconstrue: 1. to misunderstand the meaning of; 2. take in a wrong sense; 3. misinterpret.

Thinking of my current predicament, I wanted to toss the whole calendar across the room. I needed to call Luke and explain before he got the wrong idea and assumed I was hiding again.

"Well, good luck," she replied sympathetically. "I'll bring the dress to school tomorrow. I have to get going anyway. Meg found a dress, too, and I'm trying to convince her that heels with six-inch clear platforms are only for strippers and prostitutes. Chat later!" she added before hanging up.

My stomach again did a flip flop as I stared at the phone knowing I had to call and cancel on Luke. It was already five, so I needed to call soon to catch him. I took a deep, calming breath and began punching in the numbers.

"Hello." The sound of Grace Chambers's voice immediately put a smile on my face, despite my nerves.

"Hello...Grace," I stammered. "This is Jillian. May I speak to Luke, please?"

"Oh, hello, Jillian," she greeted cheerfully. "So nice to hear from you. Luke had plans this evening so he isn't home right now. I'll tell him you called, though."

How the hell did we survive without cellphones?

"Oh, thank you, I was supposed to meet up with him later, but I'm...well, I won't be able to make it," I explained, suddenly embarrassed that I'd been grounded.

"Oh no," she replied. "I'll make sure to tell him. I'll see you Thursday night, though?"

"Yes, of course," I added. "I actually just spoke to my friend Danielle who has apparently found the perfect dress for me. I haven't seen it yet, but from what I hear, it's black with some silver in it. The silver has me a bit concerned. I'm just praying I don't look like the prom date from the future."

"I'm sure you'll look beautiful," she said kindly.

"Thank you, Grace, and please apologize to Luke for me," I added.

"Of course," she replied before disconnecting.

I stared at the phone again, feeling uneasy. Glancing at my watch I knew in an hour Luke could be sitting at the cliff waiting for me. If he didn't head home first, he was going to think I stood him up. I just hoped he'd understand.

That night in my dream, I found myself walking through the front door of a bar.

Behind the dark wooden counter stood the bartender. I watched his back muscles flex beneath his crisp oxford shirt as he twisted his towel around a glass, then returned it to the drying rack.

"What do I need to do to get some service around here?" my dream-self asked, settling down on one of the barstools. I crossed my legs, allowing my skirt to fall away from my upper thigh. The bartender turned around, his brown hair askew and his smile crooked as his gaze rested on my legs.

"I'm fairly certain you've been served quite well," he replied with an evil smirk.

"That may be true," my dream-self quipped, enjoying the banter.

"But since today is a special day," he added, coming out from behind the bar. "I may be able to help you."

"Today's a special day?" I asked, teasing him. "Remind me again?"

"I think I reminded you last night," he replied, whispering in my ear, "and this morning before work and again in the shower."

"I think I may need you to refresh my memory," I murmured as his lips swept across my neck. I grabbed the back of his head and held his mouth against my neck as he devoured me. Dragging his tongue along my collarbone, he nipped and teased before descending on my lips, leaving me breathless and wanting.

"Happy Anniversary, baby," he said softly, grabbing my hand and spinning the rings on my finger.

"Happy Anniversary," I replied.

When I woke up, I could almost smell the beer, mint and Luke.

Arriving at school, my eyes immediately scanned the lot looking for him. I was struck by how in a day I had gone from skulking around the halls dodging him, to nervously fidgeting as I waited for his arrival. With Senior Week activities officially beginning, the parking lot was buzzing with excitement. Luke hadn't arrived yet so I wasn't able to share in the merriment. We were only in school for a few hours for an assembly so I needed to find him as soon as I could. I didn't want to risk waiting until later in the day. I could easily see him skipping out on the assembly, and I couldn't imagine him going to a school-sponsored bonfire.

I decided to be bold and head over to his locker, and explain myself before he got the wrong impression. There was no use in hiding how I felt anymore. I think I had made my feelings abundantly clear when I attacked him behind the gym. I needed him to know that I wanted him as much as he seemed to want me, probably more. I just hoped that Grace was able to convey my regret for not being able to see him and do some damage control. I didn't have a great track record, and I knew I would think the worst if I were in his place.

Turning the corner, heading towards his row of lockers, I froze, panic-stricken by the sight before me. Luke's back was facing me as he leaned against his locker door. Facing him in all her spandex glory, was Val.

For weeks now, I waited for Val to ask Luke to the prom, knowing that seeing them together would hurt like hell. When he asked me to go instead, I thought that maybe I'd dodged a bullet even if going with him was risky. But nothing prepared me for the pain I felt seeing him leaning into her as she twirled a lock of her over-permed, over-styled hair around her skanky, little finger. I wanted to kill her.

I slowly inched my way down the hall so that I could hear what she was saying while trying to remain undetected.

"So have you thought at all about what we talked about the other day?" she asked, chewing on her bottom lip.

"Oh right," he replied. "The bonfire. Yeah."

"Really?" she exclaimed with a bounce, jiggling her partially-covered boobs in his face. I had always assumed it took years for Val to become the tramp I'd come to know so well. In reality, she'd always been one. "That's fantastic! I'm so glad we'll get to spend some time together. It's been too long."

I felt like someone punched me in the stomach. Luke was going to the bonfire with Val.

I barreled through the doors and down the stairs, desperately trying to hold back the tears that were threatening to fall. I couldn't function. I couldn't be here. I couldn't deal with the idea of Luke and Val. I knew it was possible that he would assume I blew him off, and I was prepared to explain myself, but I never imagined that he would have given up on me so easily. The pain was so overwhelming—so acute—if I didn't know better, I would swear I needed medical attention. But I knew better. I knew why it hurt so much. I knew why I had never felt this way before, not with anyone else.

When I reached my car I could barely see the door. I blindly reached for the handle, blinking back tears. As I pulled out of the parking lot, I passed his bike and tears began to fall. I waited too long and I blew it.

I was in love with him and I was too late.

CHAPTER 13

Jillian

D uring our first year as roommates, Danielle and Megan introduced me to many new and interesting experiences. I didn't know what beer pong was. I'd never cut a class. I never stayed out all night or watched the sun come up. I never had a boy in my bed. Hell, I couldn't even play "I Never" because I had never done *anything*. So, I relished each new experience feeling as though I was finally an active participant in life instead of a spectator watching from the sidelines.

One thing I was not pleased about was Megan's insistence that I learn to love horror movies. She argued that it was a perfect activity for a first date that had some potential. If the date was going well, there was the opportunity to grab his hand or snuggle into his side when the action became too intense. If the date was a disaster, you could ask to leave because it was too hard to watch. So it was before a date with a cute guy from our dorm that Megan suggested we scope out *Final Destination*. If I was able to make it through the movie, I could suggest it for our date. While in theory any movie that involved the decapitation of Seann William Scott scored points with me, I still watched the majority of it with my hands covering my face.

Megan continued to force me into watching similar films. I never took a liking to the genre, but that one movie stuck with me. So now, sitting on my bed, my face red and splotchy, I was reminded of the premise. You can't cheat fate. Luke and Val weren't together in the future, this I knew, but it was clear to me that fate wanted them together now. Who was I to fight fate?

I found it ironic that after almost three weeks of running around in circles, the day I decided to throw caution to the wind and follow my heart, fate kicked me in the proverbial balls. Fate is kind of an asshole. I may have really wanted to be angry at Luke, and I certainly wanted to kill Val, but when it came down to it, there really wasn't anyone to blame. Luke wasn't meant for me and it hurt.

While I tried to come to terms with the fact that he was off somewhere probably getting mauled by Val, I knew there was no way that I was going to the bonfire to witness it. After having him so close and then losing him, the sight of them together would be too much for me to handle. The prospect of sitting on my bed and sulking didn't appeal to me either. If I were back in

2011, Danielle, Megan and I would buy some obscure and ridiculously expensive bottle of chardonnay, order too much Chinese food from the cute little restaurant around the corner and watch reruns of Project Runway. We'd eat, drink and make fun of the designers until one of us (usually me) passed out or fell asleep. But I didn't want chardonnay or Chinese food. And I obviously couldn't watch Heidi and Tim Gunn either. I needed a distraction.

It took less than a minute to decide what I was going to do and where I was going to go. Hopping off the bed, I grabbed the keys from my desk and scowled at the Word of the Day.

Candescence: 1. The state of being white hot; 2. incandescence.

Oh yes, I'm just on fire these days.

I jogged down the stairs and began rifling through the storage closet in the back porch. Once I found an old duffle bag to use, I stuffed the old scratchy wool blanket my dad used for camping inside. I couldn't find the kerosene lamp I knew we once had so I settled for one of the hundreds of Mag Lights we had lying around. It was one of the perks of living with a cop. I also needed reading material. While *That* Jillian would have nursed her heartbreak by flipping through the worn pages of *Sense and Sensibility*, I'd rather poke my eye out. I had already lost the boy. I didn't need to be reminded that like Marianne Dashwood, my Willoughby was at the bonfire with Miss Grey. Only in my version, Miss Grey had a bad perm, big boobs and a knack for defiling antiques. So instead of torturing myself, I decided to bypass the reading material.

Fortunately, both of my parents were working so I wouldn't need to hold a press conference, lying about where I was headed. Throwing the duffle into my car, I climbed in and retraced the route I had driven with Luke just a few days before. After taking a few wrong turns, I soon drove past the small parking area where we left his bike on Sunday night before traipsing into the woods. As I pulled into the lot, it occurred to me that there was a major flaw in my plan. Although I had my dad's trusty Mag Light, the idea of walking by myself along the dark path was not very appealing. In fact, it was a really bad idea. I could come across wild animals, serial killers or giant spiders. It was the alternative that kept me going. I'd rather chance an encounter with a serial killer—possibly even a giant spider—than head to the bonfire.

I grabbed my bag from the front seat and jumped out, prepared to take on any spiders or serial killers head-on. On an intellectual level, I knew it had taken twenty minutes or so to walk from the parking lot to the ledge; however, alone at night, I was convinced I had been walking for hours and I'd never find my way back.

By the time I reached the end of the path, my fingers were sore from gripping the handle of my bag and my nerves were shot. At least in the open and away from the canopy of trees, the ledge was bathed in moonlight. I'd be able to look out for spiders.

Glancing up, I was overwhelmed by the beauty of the night sky with its scattered stars and constellations. My chest tightened as I located the Northern Cross. Pulling the scratchy, wool blanket from the duffle, I laid it out on the grass. It might not have been the most comfortable place in the world, but it was a hell of a lot better than pouting at home or watching Val and Luke at the bonfire.

As I began reflecting on the events of the past few weeks, I was reminded of what Suzanne had said to me in the library the day before. "You don't get a do-over." What about a do-over for your do-over? Where do you start when you're allowed to rewrite your history?

I always thought I was a fairly happy person. I had great friends who loved me and a decent job. It didn't bother me that I wasn't in a relationship. Over the years, I had gotten used to being the fifth wheel in our little group. Now, surrounded by teenagers preparing to embark on the greatest adventure of their lives, I found myself feeling sad and wistful. Would I have done it differently? Seventeen-year-old Jillian might be slightly disappointed in how things turned out for her. *That* Jillian wanted to travel the world and write a novel, learning about new languages and new places. It was what I had meant to do, but I needed a stable job. When the position at the magazine opened up, I knew I had to take it—even if it meant that I was tied to a desk and not touring the globe. I hadn't ever really given it a lot of thought. Not really what *That* Jillian had dreamed about on her graduation day.

And while I had never gotten hung up on the fact that I was nearly thirty and still single, I would be lying if I claimed I didn't want someone to share my life. Knowing that I could feel the way I did with Luke made me hopeful, but it was bittersweet. I wondered who he belonged to in the future and what she was like. I wondered if he was as happy as he appeared in that photo. I wondered if I spent all my time in vain trying not to alter my life when now I had to live with the knowledge that I loved someone and he was out there somewhere…with someone else. If I were forced to relive my entire life, would I be able to move on? I didn't have any answers, and dwelling on it wasn't going to dull the ache in my chest.

I shot up when I heard a rumbling off in the distance. Pointing the flashlight in the direction of the noise, I squinted, attempting to see if anyone or anything was coming. I suddenly wished I had brought something more formidable with me to fight off the spiders and serial killers. There'd be no quick getaway for me on foot.

147

When nothing appeared, I reluctantly focused my attention back on the starry sky until I heard the unmistakable sound of branches snapping. Whatever was in the woods was heading my way and moving fast. My heart raced as I began to curse myself for being so goddamn stupid. I had no way to defend myself except for a few things I learned during the one self-defense class I took with Meg. To be fair, I did not quit this class. We were asked not to come back after Meg broke the instructor's nose. Nevertheless, I was pretty defenseless.

Raising the Mag Light over my head, I prepared for whatever was heading my way. Despite any bravado I had somehow mustered, I let out a scream as a figure appeared in the pathway.

"Damn it, Jillian. Are you out of your mind?" Luke fumed, his eyes wild. I was startled by his hostility as he came striding over to me.

"You're up here all by yourself with nothing but a...a flashlight to protect yourself!" he roared, grabbing it from my hand.

Confused, I ignored his tirade. "Luke, why are you...why aren't you at the bonfire?"

This didn't make sense. I heard him agree to go with Val and now he was here yelling at me about flashlights.

"Maybe you should be telling me why you *weren't* at the bonfire," he retorted, exasperated and annoyed.

"How did you know I wasn't there?"

"Because I was," he replied as if it was just common sense. "Danielle told me you were going together."

"Why?"

"I have no idea why you'd want to go with her," he quipped, straight-faced.

"I mean why were you looking for me?" I was shivering and couldn't stop fidgeting with my hands as I tried to hide that fact that they had started to shake.

"Because I thought that we could go for a ride or something."

He suddenly looked shy and unsure, the complete opposite of the picture of quiet confidence he was yesterday.

"When your car wasn't at your house, I figured I'd check a few places. I didn't think you'd be stupid enough to come up here all by yourself in the middle of the night."

"I saw Val ask you to the bonfire," I added, ignoring him again, feeling jealous and stupid.

"Val? Seriously? I can't believe you thought….Jillian, there's no way I would go anywhere with Val," he scoffed. His face softened and he looked uncomfortable again.

"You told her no?" I couldn't get past this.

"I told her I was going," he explained, "but I wasn't going there for her." His eyes smoldered as he looked up at me. "I don't want *her*."

We had been slowly moving towards each other, but with his admission I froze. I wanted to believe it was me he wanted, but I was very good at hearing what I wanted to hear. As I stood there shaking and staring at this beautiful boy in the moonlight, I wanted so badly to ask him to clarify what he was saying. I needed to hear it.

"I don't understand," I murmured, my heart racing.

"It's not her I want." He seemed to laugh at himself. "There's this emotionally unavailable, future alcoholic I've had my eye on."

I wanted so much to tell him that I wasn't like that anymore. If he only knew how much he'd changed me...without even trying. I'd never be the same and it scared me to death.

Everything had been so carefully planned from encouraging Megan to pursue Nate to getting him to ask her to the prom, and then keeping Val away from Danielle. Not this. Not Luke. I thought he was kind of crazy and wonderful. He made me feel seventeen again, and I wasn't sure I ever felt seventeen. At seventeen, I was in a book club with an elderly librarian, for Christ's sake. I couldn't trust myself around him anymore. The rational part of my brain was telling me to retreat because I was probably about to do something I might regret, but he was smiling and I couldn't stop looking at his lips.

I'm so not leaving.

"She sounds like a pain in the ass. I didn't know you had a thing for the crazies," I replied nervously. Sarcasm was like a second language to me. I couldn't be straight with him even though I knew he'd see through it.

"Not crazy," he insisted. "She's just been difficult to figure out. That whole emotionally unavailable thing. But I think I understand now."

His head was down, but when he looked up—all deep eyes and eyelashes—he was smiling that smile again.

"You understand?"

"Yeah. You see, she thinks too goddamn much. So I made a decision," he announced, moving in closer and running the back of his knuckles up and down my arm.

"A...decision?" My inability to communicate coherently had apparently kicked in again while his confidence had clearly returned.

"I'm not going to wait for her to figure out her shit anymore. I'm not letting her avoid *this* anymore," he added, staring me down. "Because I know she wants me too."

As he leaned toward me, I lifted my head up to meet his gaze. He was challenging me to run again, knowing this time I wouldn't. I was frozen.

RIP Jillian's brain cells.

"Luke...." I sighed as my eyes shifted down again to his mouth. True to his word, while I was trying to figure out how to respond, he placed his hands on my cheeks, making it impossible for me to look away. Before I could even acknowledge what was happening, his mouth was on mine, and I was swept away once again by the sensation of his soft, warm lips. The familiar scent of mint along with the faintest hint of his Marlboros washed over me.

What started out soft and gentle quickly turned desperate and needy. We were pulling and pushing, and I was on autopilot. Jillian's brain had left the building. It was a familiar feeling—the buzz that pushes you to sing an obnoxious and overplayed karaoke song with your girlfriends, or that gives you the courage to dance with the hot guy sitting at the bar. It's a happy buzz that makes you feel like you're invincible and no one can touch you. I've spent a lot of time feeling this buzz. Now I stood at the edge of the world, in the eye of the storm, with this beautiful and frightening boy. I was sober, but I felt it. I was pretty sure that I was drunk on Luke, but I knew that didn't make any sense.

"I told you I wasn't waiting for you to figure this out anymore," he whispered. "I want *you*, Jillian. No one else."

"I don't know what I'm doing," I managed to reply, but I didn't mean it the way he thought I did.

"Me either." But he meant something else too. "I can't stop thinking about you."

Grabbing me by the waist, he pulled me down onto the blanket. I knew I could list a hundred good reasons why I should turn around and leave, but I was always excellent at justifying my questionable decisions. So, in that moment, I decided not to think about consequences and focus on how his hands felt in my hair and how my legs felt wrapped around his torso. In that moment, I was seventeen and I was with Luke. It was exactly where I was supposed to be. I didn't want to stop that feeling and not thinking felt really good.

I was sure he didn't realize how huge this was for me. I wanted to stay here with him. I didn't want to go back there and be who I was. He made my brain functions cease and my body do strange things.

Impulsively, I grabbed at the hem of his shirt, yanking it off him and dropping it to the ground. The initial shock on his face gave way to something darker as I rested my palms against his bare skin, feeling the rapid rise and fall of his chest.

"You have no idea how crazy you make me," he whispered in a low, raspy voice.

"I think you're wrong," I replied, raising my arms and locking them behind his neck. I threaded my fingers through the back of his hair, using the opportunity to pull myself even closer.

There was no struggle for dominance, no awkward posturing. I let go, giving myself over and allowing Luke to set the pace. His hands were everywhere, grabbing, kneading and feeling so good. I laughed as my discarded shirt was sent sailing off into the darkness.

A sudden look of uncertainty passed over his face. I knew what he was thinking. Everything was moving so fast and he was worried that I was getting carried away. I was supposed to be a naïve seventeen-year-old who shouldn't be rolling around in the dark with a boy. But *That* Jillian wouldn't have been here with him in the first place. *That* Jillian would be at home reading Jane Austen and popping microwave popcorn. *That* Jillian hated Facebook because it reminded her that she never took any chances. *That* Jillian would definitely be peeing her pants right now.

"Luke, don't think so goddamn much," I said softly, mirroring his words from earlier. And because he still needed the encouragement and because I'd been dying to do it since that first day behind the school, I grabbed his crazy, unruly hair and pulled his lips roughly down to mine. He moaned against my mouth, and it was the sexiest thing I had ever heard in my entire life. I wanted to hear

151

it as many times as I could, and vowed to pull every last beautiful hair out of his head in order to hear it again and again and again. Everything about him set my body on fire. My dad always wanted me to keep a fire extinguisher in the car. I wished I'd listened.

His left hand began making a continuous circuit from my ankle to my knee, then up my thigh and back down again, rubbing and kneading. I wanted to say "Bring it, Luke", but I was an impatient, squirming mess. I wanted more.

Emboldened, I tugged at his zipper and was startled when he suddenly pulled away.

"Jillian, we should slow down," he mumbled, panting. I was literally speechless. *He* was telling *me* to settle down? Really? *Sorry Luke, I don't feel like behaving tonight.*

I wasn't expecting him to put up much of a fight. He was an eighteen-year-old boy after all. He wouldn't need much convincing. Once my hands were back in his groan-inducing hair, my lips by his ear, skin against skin, there wasn't any question.

Even though I wasn't really a teenager, even though I had been down this road before—just differently—nothing felt familiar. I should have taken some comfort in the fact that I was supposed to know what I was doing. I should have felt like I had the upper hand. I should have had a little more control over my body. But I didn't. I was shaking and quivering like I was about to jump off the ledge into the ocean below. I had never felt so bare, and it had nothing to do with the shirt and pants that had been discarded, lost somewhere in the night. No one had ever made me feel the way Luke did, and what scared me the most was that I was pretty sure no one else ever would.

So I held on tight to him, to us, and tried not to think of the implications of the decision I had made. I focused instead on the way he felt, the way we moved, the way we were together, so I could commit it all to memory. Because any boy that came before him didn't matter. And if all of this ended tomorrow and I was sent spiraling back to my old life, no other boy would ever matter again. Just him. Just us.

It turned out that being with Luke wasn't like being caught in the eye of the storm at all. He was like a tsunami and I was ready, willing, to be pulled under with him. But I wondered—half-dazed—as I finally let go, now that I was truly here with him, would I ever be able to drag myself back to the shore?

CHAPTER 14

Luke

T here weren't a lot of things that shocked me. If you paid attention, you could anticipate almost anything. It didn't surprise me that someone invented a pill to help old guys get it up. I wasn't shocked when Alicia Silverstone turned out to be a terrible Batgirl. And while the whole world was brought to their knees when the President's intern was caught on hers, I wasn't exactly blown away. All in all, I saw shit coming. I guess I *used* to see shit coming. Until now.

I didn't see this. *Her.* Invading my space, my mind, my everything. I didn't even recognize myself anymore. I wasn't the guy who went to bonfires with drunken assholes. At least I hadn't been. Until now.

I was there for her. Once I found her, I knew I could convince her to leave. She didn't like those types of things anymore than I did. And I had a better idea. I wanted her on my bike again. I wanted to feel her wiggle onto the seat and press herself up against my back. I wanted to feel her lips, her hands, her breath. I just *wanted*. The memory of our ride on Sunday was still fresh in my mind, and I needed more. We needed to finish what we started.

Leaving my bike in the lot, I made my way through the crowd, trying to avoid talking to anyone. The air smelled of pot, beer and puke—a definite sign of amateur night.

When I spotted Danielle, I moved a little faster, rushing past the couples mauling each other in the sand. She was sitting on a blanket with Fletcher, drinking some kind of pink wine cooler. I never understood how girls could stand that shit.

"Well, hello there Luke," she said, smirking. "Fancy meeting you here at the bonfire. Wouldn't think that this was your 'thing'."

"Yeah, you didn't mention you'd be here," he added, grinning up at me like an idiot. He knew.

"Unless you're looking for someone," she added. "Are you, Luke? Looking for someone?"

"You're hysterical. Are you done?"

"Oooh! So serious," she replied. "And before you ask, she's not here yet...which is surprising considering it *is* getting late." Danielle furrowed her brow as she checked the time on her watch.

"She was supposed to meet you here though, right?"

"Yeah, but she had to help her folks with something. Maybe she got caught up?"

"You sticking around?" Josh asked, still smiling, still an asshole.

"Nah. I'm taking off," I replied, turning to go. "Catch you later."

As I headed off past the half-naked girls in the sand and the half-baked kids on the dunes, I heard Danielle's voice off in the distance.

"Tell Jillian I said hi, Luke."

I pretended I didn't hear her. I pretended that I wasn't about to hop on my bike and ride straight over to her house. I pretended I wasn't insane. I had never even gone to her house before—never met her dad, who incidentally carried a gun. I wanted to see her, but I really didn't want to make small talk with her dad when I had spent the better part of the night thinking of his only daughter laid out across the seat of my bike. He interrogated people for a living. If Josh and Danielle could see through me, her dad would probably know exactly what I was thinking before I even said a word. Yeah, I was obviously insane.

Despite coming to the conclusion that I had lost all sense of reason, I flew across town, making it to Jillian's place in no time. When I rounded the corner onto her street, instead of seeing her crappy car in front of the house, her driveway was empty.

My frustration peaked because it shouldn't have been this hard to find her. Reynolds wasn't a big town. We had more than one traffic light, but less than a dozen. Where the hell was she?

Frustrated and annoyed, I headed back home. There was no way I would let Danielle and Josh see me back at the bonfire so that wasn't an option. Clearly, it just wasn't my night. We'd have to pick up where we left off some other night, but soon. I was sick of playing games.

As I passed the parking lot near the cliff, I slowed my bike down, noticing a glint of metal through the trees. As I got closer, I saw it. There, in the far corner almost hidden from the main road, was her car. A sudden burst of adrenaline flooded my system. She had to be out of her mind to go traipsing through the woods by herself at night. It was reckless and stupid. Yet why was I surprised?

Parking my bike next to her car, I bolted down the path quickly, grateful that the route was familiar even without a light. When I finally entered the clearing, I found her standing there, eyes wide and panicked, raising a goddamn flashlight over her head. Was she planning to club me to death?

I had spent the whole night trying to plan what I wanted to say. I wanted to tell her to cut this shit out. I wanted to tell her I was done playing games. Then I saw her eyes, deep brown and wild, and everything I planned to say seemed stupid and trivial because nothing would ever be enough. How do you tell the girl you only really met three weeks ago that there had never been anyone that made you feel the way she did? How do you tell her that you hadn't returned Jonas' phone calls or that you couldn't imagine going to Seattle now? How do you tell her that you were going with her to New York? How do you say all of that without freaking her out? Because honestly, I was freaking out myself.

You couldn't. *I* couldn't.

But she looked so conflicted. I didn't want to hear that she didn't want this. I didn't want to hear that she didn't want us. I needed her to want me the way I wanted her. My entire life had been turned upside down in just a few weeks because of this crazy girl who carried a pink flask and wanted me to find depth in Green Day.

It only took the slightest touch and we were flying. And it was so good. *We* were so good. It wasn't part of the plan, but I didn't care because the plan had just gotten infinitely better.

Sometimes even when you pay attention to what's going on around you, you can't even imagine what's going to happen next.

"You're a million miles away," she said into my ear as we lay wrapped up in each other, looking up at the sky. I didn't even know how long it had been since I had last spoken. I felt like I was in a fog. The vision of her moving underneath me replayed in my mind over and over while I struggled to find the words to tell her how I felt. It shouldn't have been like this and I needed to…God…apologize for letting everything get so out of hand. It shouldn't have been like this. She deserved better and I screwed up.

"I was just thinking," I muttered, my brain unable to pull together the right words. I needed something profound, something to let her know that she wasn't just any girl. She was *the* girl. "Are you okay?"

"I'm fine," she whispered softly. "A little chilly." She pulled the corner of the blanket up under her chin and burrowed into my chest. I felt her warm breath on my skin as she inhaled.

"Do you want to leave?" I asked, because I didn't know what the protocol was in situations like this. The Danas and Lauras of the world were used to screwing in offices and under bleachers. They wouldn't have had a problem with where we were, but this was Jillian, and she was special. My mind was racing and I couldn't focus on anything.

I should have stopped this.

She didn't even have the common sense to be pissed off about it. I always thought girls wanted their first time to be on a cloud surrounded by flowers and candles and shit. Not like this—wrapped in a scratchy, wool blanket with a Mag Lite. The guilt was overwhelming. I never had a problem talking to her before and now when it mattered the most, I couldn't find the words. All I could think about was that for the rest of her life, she'd wince remembering the scratch of the blanket and the chill in the air because the guy she chose to have sex with didn't have the decency to tell her to hang on and take her someplace nice.

"Um, yeah, I probably should get back," she stammered, tucking the blanket under her arms and sitting up. Everything was coming out wrong, and it sounded like I was trying to get rid of her. I felt my heartbeat accelerate and was thrown into a panic again, desperate to think of something to say other than "don't go".

"I...um...don't know where my shirt went," she added shyly.

That's right. Not only do I lack skills, I lack class, as well.

I grabbed my boxers, pulling them on quickly, before popping up to search for her clothes. At least it would give me time to think so I wouldn't need to stall.

When I saw the bright white of her blouse a few feet away, I walked slowly over to it. I knew I needed to get it together, but I couldn't stop thinking of how she looked, how she felt, what we did. I wanted all of her, all the time. But before I could have her, we needed to talk. I needed her to know that this wasn't a passing thing for me despite how reckless I'd acted. But I had lost my mastery of the English language. I threw my head back, defeated, staring up at the star-filled sky.

Is this what the phoenix feels like when it's about to burn?

Grabbing the shirt, I walked back to her. She had found her jeans, but was still wrapped in the blanket looking as uncomfortable as I felt. I passed her the shirt feeling like I was in one of those movies where the audience starts yelling at the guy to stop acting like such a tool, but I had no idea how to fix this mess.

She wasn't making it easy for me. Every time I looked at her, I lost my focus. She kept running her fingers through her tangled hair, and her skin seemed to glow in the moonlight. I stared at her with her tousled hair and her red, swollen lips. She was the most beautiful thing I'd ever seen.

"You're beautiful," I said out loud, sounding low and raspy and awkward. She smiled, looking down at her fingers. I waited for her to say something, watching as she shifted from one foot to the other.

Help me fix this, Jillian.

"I should get home," she said breaking the silence.

"Yeah," I replied. "Sure."

I wanted to ask her why she chose this place—why she was here. I wanted to know if she would even want me to go with her to New York. There was so much I wanted to say, but instead I just began walking toward the path to the parking area.

"I'll follow you home," I told her.

"You don't have to—"

"Hey," I said, stopping her mid-sentence. This had to stop. I couldn't deal with her telling me that I didn't need to follow her home. It made me feel even more like the selfish bastard I always knew I was.

I reached out to touch her cheek because I just needed to feel her again. Searching her eyes, I found that conflicted look on her face again—a look that I clearly put there. I brushed my lips against hers, testing the waters, not even knowing how to kiss her anymore. When she exhaled her warm breath against my mouth, that was all the encouragement I needed. I'd be lying if I said my dick wasn't pleading with me to throw her down and show her how good I could make her feel, but I needed her to understand what I was failing miserably at saying. I couldn't even say the words myself. It didn't make sense. You don't fall in love with someone in three weeks. Not in real life. But shit. She was everything.

So I didn't listen to my dick. I didn't jam my tongue down her throat or wrap my fingers around her hair. Christ, I wanted to. I kissed her softly again, then pulled back to look into her eyes.

"I'm following you home," I added firmly.

157

Pushing back the desire to pin her against the car, I kissed her again—soft, slow, rated PG. She broke away first, her smile tight on her face, not really reaching her eyes and I knew she was still in her head. I just needed to get the hell out of there before she decided I was an idiot and never spoke to me again. I turned away, slapping the hood of her car twice as I passed by heading to my bike. She was supposed to be on the bike with me. Not alone in her car. Everything was all wrong.

I followed close behind her, killing the engine a few houses down from hers. I didn't need to alert the entire neighborhood that I was there. She jumped out of the car, gave me a nervous wave and practically ran into the house. If there had been a wall near me, I would've slammed my head against it. Twice.

I flew back home, breaking every traffic law imaginable and dragged my ass up to my room, avoiding any possible conversation with Grace or Carter. I could only imagine how that would go:

"How was your night, Luke?" Carter would ask.

"Oh, it was great. I had sex with Jillian outside by the cliffs. What did you do?"

"Grace made lobster bisque. We saved you some."

"Thanks, Carter, I had been hoping to have dinner with Jillian, but since I'm a douche, that didn't pan out."

"That's too bad, Luke. Do you need to talk? I'll grab the telescope."

"No, Carter. I can never go to the cliffs again because of said sex and douchbaggery. Ruined. Forever."

The end.

I stared at my alarm clock from the spot on the bed that I had occupied since I got home. It was one in the morning—three hours since I followed Jillian home without saying anything to her at all. As if I hadn't screwed things up enough already. I had to make it right, and as terrifying as the idea was, there was only one thing to do.

I was no amateur at sneaking out of the house undetected, but in my Jillian-induced haze, I went barreling down the stairs to the kitchen where I had dropped my jacket and keys earlier. Carter was sitting at the kitchen table reading *Newsweek* with a glass of milk.

"Shit," I exclaimed startled by his presence, "What're you doing up?"

"I could ask you the same question," he replied raising his eyebrow and glancing at the kitchen clock.

"I was going to check something…with my bike," I stammered nervously.

"Your bike?" he asked with a smile.

"Yeah, it's making that weird noise again, and I figured I'd go take a quick look. I couldn't sleep," I explained.

"Right," he added smirking. "You realize her father is a detective, right?"

"What? What are you talking about?" I replied stumbling over my words, wondering how the hell he knew where I was going.

"Take your car," he added as he picked up his milk and walked toward the stairs. "It's quieter."

I stood in the middle of the kitchen—stunned—as he started up the stairs, stopping suddenly.

"And Luke, if you get caught, Grace'll kill you." He turned and continued walking up the stairs, humming quietly to himself.

Shaking off the crazy conversation, I bolted from the house before Carter came to his senses and told me to get my ass back upstairs. For the second time in the same night, I was headed to Jillian's house with no idea what I was going to do or say.

I parked the car a few houses down and around the corner. If I could make this right, I couldn't risk her dad finding me skulking around his house at one-thirty in the morning. My heart started racing as I passed the neighboring houses. I heard some tiny dog yapping and hauled ass into the darkness of her backyard.

I had no idea where her bedroom was. There seemed to be two possible options, one room with white patterned curtains and one with a purple color. I felt edgy. I needed a cigarette, and I couldn't believe that I was actually considering throwing a rock at her window like Richie-Freaking-Cunningham.

I looked around the driveway for some pebbles because I wasn't going to be the asshole that breaks her window with a rock. I had a few in my hand when I glanced up and noticed a light on in the purple room. I saw some movement behind the curtain and decided to just go for it, and launched the pebble into the air. Instead of hitting the window, it ricocheted off the roof and into the neighbor's yard. Yappy Dog started to bark, and I was seriously beginning to think throwing a large rock in his direction would take the edge off.

On the second attempt, the pebble bounced off the glass with a clink. I waited for her to appear behind the curtain or for her dad to show up with a gun. I honestly didn't know which one would be scarier because there was really no hiding how you felt after you showed up outside a girl's window at one-thirty in the morning. This was it.

For the third attempt, I threw two pebbles together and the sound they made reverberated sharply. The curtain moved first and my heart seemed to beat in my throat. Slowly, it pulled back to reveal Jillian wearing a pink tank top with her hair in a ponytail. Even from down here, I could tell she was shocked. She struggled to pull the window open and when she leaned over, all I could see was the top of her boobs pressed against the sill. So much for my concentration.

"What are you doing?" she whispered harshly. "My parents are in the next room."

"I need to talk to you," I whispered back.

I watched as she took a deep breath, as if to calculate whether she should come down and talk to me or tell me to go to hell. She sighed, dropping the curtain and disappeared back into the room. I thought how awful it would be if she had just climbed back into bed and wasn't on her way downstairs. I waited and held my breath.

When the door swung open, she was there wearing tiny boxer shorts, showing off her long legs. It was the ponytail that did me in, though. I'd never seen her hair up. Seeing the slope of her neck reminded me of that night in my room when I wanted nothing more than to mark her, keeping everyone else away.

"Are you crazy?" she rasped with her hands on her hips. "My father owns a gun! More than one, actually."

As she continued raving about how easy it would've been for me to get caught and how unhappy her father would be, I took the few quick steps over to her and did what I should've done in the first place.

I didn't wait for her to stop talking, and I didn't ask for permission. Wrapping my hand around the back of her head, right below that ponytail, I pulled her to me. Startled, she tensed up, but then dropped her shoulders and rested her palms flat on my chest, slowly responding as I kissed her, taking from me and giving back. I poured every bit of what I was feeling into each motion. It was soft, slow and hot as hell. While I wanted to pick her up and wrap her around me, I held back. I'd do things right.

"I never would have wanted it to be like that for you," I said breathlessly, resting my forehead against hers. "You deserved—"

160

Better. Everything. More than I probably can give you.

"Luke, stop," she interrupted, leaning into my chest. "I don't regret anything. I'm a big girl." I groaned as she pressed her body up against mine. I could feel every curve—every part of her. How was I supposed to concentrate?

"You don't understand what you do to me," I tried to reply, but it came out in a raspy whisper. "I don't want to lose this."

I can't lose this.

"I'm right here," she added as she burrowed into the groove in my neck. "And here...here's where I want to be."

I had no idea how we got here or what cosmic event led her behind the gym that day, but I wasn't going to argue because I never considered myself particularly lucky. And suddenly I was. She was with me now, and I wasn't going to screw this up.

"Well, I'm glad we finally agree on something."

"You really should agree with me more often. I'm usually right," she teased, ghosting her lips across my jaw. "Even about Green Day."

"I didn't say you were wrong," I replied. I wanted to sound defensive, but it was difficult with Jillian's mouth on my neck.

"But you didn't agree with me, either."

"I said they weren't the voice of our generation," I retorted half-heartedly, pulling her hips closer to me, trying to maintain my composure, "not that they weren't any good."

"They're amazing," she countered, sounding breathless.

"Yeah, right up there with The Beatles." I buried my head in the crook of her neck, and ran my tongue along the sensitive skin.

"You're a snob," she replied, letting out a small groan and grabbing at my hair.

"And you have bad taste."

"Clearly," she shot back pulling away and smirking.

"Oh, really? Well fortunately for me, *you* taste fantastic."

Grabbing her by the waist, I spun her around, pinning her against the car. I was running my hand down her thigh, about to grind into her so I could feel that friction again when I heard her gasp, just not in the way I wanted.

"My parents," she exclaimed, pushing me so that I stumbled backward. She was staring at the upstairs window. The light was on in the second bedroom.

"You should go," I groaned, pissed that we were interrupted. As I reached out to pull her back toward me, I heard the creaking of the screen door.

"Jill?" her father called from the porch.

"Shit," I hissed, ducking around the front of the car.

"Oh, dad, hey," she stammered, wrapping her arms around her chest.

"What the heck are you doing out here in the middle of the night?" he asked scanning the yard. Her dad was a smart guy. I was so screwed.

"Oh well, I…thought I heard the engine running. I was worried that I left the keys in the ignition so I came out to check."

"You thought you left the car running? All this time?" he asked incredulously.

"Crazy, right?" she continued, gaining some confidence, "You wouldn't want it to…overheat," she added, dragging out the last word. "Or for something to…explode. So I figured I'd come outside and take care of it."

I was starting to sweat listening to her mess with me right in front of her dad.

"I think you should just get inside, Jill," he replied looking at her strangely. I heard her snicker as she bounced up the steps. After she walked through the doorway, her dad stayed on the porch staring into the darkness.

"Explode?" he muttered to himself, shaking his head before following her into the house.

Relieved to have dodged a bullet…literally, I headed back to my car. I hadn't made it past Yappy Dog's house when I started feeling pissed again that I hadn't been able to really say goodbye or to make her gasp the way I wanted. She'd be getting ready for the prom all day, and I wouldn't see her until it was time to go. We wouldn't have much time alone if Danielle was involved.

I spun around, walking backwards as I looked up at the purple curtains. Once the light went out, the curtain pulled back. Jillian stood in her window, smirking. She fanned her fingers out, wiggling them as she waved. It was nice to see that she had enjoyed herself, even if it was at my expense. At least things were good. We were good. And after we talked about New York, we'd be great.

The next day, I stood in front of the mirror, clasping the rental bowtie around my neck. I refused to wear one of those bands around my waist. I didn't care what Grace said about the way it was supposed to look. It was ridiculous. I would bet my left nut that Josh would be wearing one, though. If the Poor Bastard showed up in a top hat, he only had himself to blame. His girlfriend was out of her mind.

While things had fallen into place for me and Jillian, it didn't change the fact that Danielle's meddling was torture. But I had planned to pay her back. She wanted the perfect prom experience. I was going to give it to her.

Truthfully, I really never imagined myself going to the prom. The prom was for kids in John Hughes movies and on *Dawson's Creek*. But there I was, wearing a tux, a gray bowtie and shiny black shoes. There were flowers downstairs for Jillian and a limo waiting for us at Danielle's house. Grace was making canapés and bruschetta. I'd be willing to bet that Carter was sitting at the table trying to figure out how to use the camcorder.

I ran a hand through my hair. Grace would give me a hard time about that too, but I nearly choked when I saw the tub of gel she left on my bureau. Luke Chambers does not gel his hair. Not even for Jillian.

Tonight wasn't about the tux or the shoes, though. And it definitely wasn't about my hair. I was finally calling Jonas tomorrow to let him know that he needed to find someone else to help out over the summer. Tomorrow I'd start looking for a job in New York. I was sure I'd be able to find something near her campus. It wouldn't be as good as the job Jonas was offering, but we'd be together and we'd figure shit out.

But tonight I wouldn't think about Jonas. Tonight I'd forget that proms reminded me of bad made-for-TV movies, and I'd dance with Jillian, holding her close, remembering what she looked like in the moonlight. Tonight I'd ride in the limo with her friends, and laugh at the ridiculousness of Josh and Danielle. Tonight I'd tell her that I couldn't leave, not when we were just getting started. Tonight I'd say the words that had been playing in my head over and over because you don't throw rocks at windows and move across the country without saying those words.

This time when I headed to Jillian's house, I knew exactly what I was going to say.

Tracy Sweeney

CHAPTER 15

Jillian

When I was a little girl, I used to dream of what it would be like to sneak out after dark to meet a boy. I pictured him waiting by the streetlight around the corner. I never really saw his face, but I envisioned him leaning against the pole, his legs casually crossed at the ankle.

I devised complicated plans. If my parents were in the living room, I would open my window, climb onto the roof and like the inner gymnast I believed I could be, would grab a hold of the edge and catapult myself safely onto the driveway pavement below. If they were in the kitchen, I would crawl on my stomach, like a cat, across the living room floor until I reached the door. I would ever so carefully open the door and slide out through the tiniest crack I could manage. If I was feeling really adventurous, I'd try to shimmy down a drainage pipe, but even in my daydreams, I imagined that I'd find myself in the emergency room.

All of the careful planning was in vain, though. I never once snuck out of my parents' house. One time, Suzanne and I skipped last period and went back to her house to watch TRL. It was new and interesting. We hadn't figured out that Carson Daly was lame yet. Afterwards, I was so overcome with guilt that my parents found me in their bedroom that night, sleepwalking where I proceeded to admit to them that I skipped school and listened to the devil's music. They were so amused by my Footloosian admission that I didn't even get punished.

So when I heard a clinking sound at my window, the last thing I expected to see was the cute boy, waiting for me in the moonlight. Especially the cute boy who freaked out after sort of deflowering me earlier in the evening.

For a brief moment, I flashed back to those plans I made years ago and wondered if I really could have catapulted off the roof. But in this daydream, instead of running into his arms, I'd clock him. Not only had I dealt with his embarrassing post-coital meltdown, but now he was risking the wrath of Henry Cross by pelting my window with debris. I couldn't begin to imagine what the hell he had to say when I couldn't get a coherent thought out of him just a few hours earlier. Was it worth risking my second grounding ever for him to look at me with that pained "oh-I-screwed-up-and-shouldn't-have-had-sex-with-you" look? I considered hopping back into bed and pretending none of it ever happened, but this was Luke. He might not be the kind of guy that would stand under my window with a boom box, but I couldn't imagine him leaving until I talked to him either.

I had spent the last three weeks over-thinking and analyzing everything— trying to keep him at bay. When I finally let my guard down, I channeled my inner teenage trollop and ended up attacking him. When I messed up, I did it right.

So while I waited for Luke to tell me how sorry he was for stealing away my virtue, I verbally kicked his ass. But as I was describing just how unpleasant I would make his life if I was grounded again, he charged over to me.

Instead of telling me that he had made a huge mistake or engaging in another round of tortuously awkward dialogue, he was honest, sweet and just...genuine. I may not have had as many boyfriends as Megan, but I dated enough to know that was rare.

That night as I lay in bed all I could see was the image of Luke, walking backwards down the street, staring up at my window with a devilish smirk. It took hours before I finally fell asleep and when I did, it was restless and fitful.

It was already mid-morning when I woke up with a vague recollection of the dream that had haunted me all night.

I'm lying on my bed, curled up and clutching a pillow. The comforter is littered with balled up tissues. I'm devastated. The pain in my chest is staggering. I hear a rustling in the doorway and I look up. It's Danielle. Her arms are crossed and her brow is furrowed. She slowly crosses the room and sits down, careful not to disturb the pile of tissues I've accumulated.

"Do you want to talk about it?" she asks, brushing aside a dampened piece of hair.

I look at her, wondering how I can explain the gaping hole in my chest. I can't, so I say nothing.

"Let's get you cleaned up," she adds as she grabs a waste basket and starts throwing the tissues inside. I take a deep breath, knowing I need to get up, but I can barely move. I stare at the comforter, wanting nothing more than to lie back down and disappear.

I could almost feel the ache in my chest as I recalled the scene from my dream. What bothered me the most was that the comforter wasn't purple. It was white like my bedroom in Seattle.

Because I had slept in, I didn't have the luxury of lounging around in bed. I had already vetoed Danielle's suggestion that we spend the day primping. Having trained Danielle years ago on the ways of Jillian Cross, she knew not to drag me shopping or force me into some ridiculous get-up. She knew my style and she'd usually buy something appropriate. I always held veto power and she normally respected that. When Danielle-Circa-1999 was informed that I wouldn't be spending the day having little rhinestones applied to my toenails, she was not pleased. I met her halfway though, and allowed her to come by at noon for lunch, and we could paint our own nails like normal people. Her visit was kind of unavoidable anyway since I had yet to see the dress she picked out for me.

Always punctual, at noon Danielle was standing on my doorstep, holding a black garment bag. Her eyes were shining with excitement as she bounced on the balls of her toes.

"I cannot wait for you to see this dress," she beamed walking into the living room. "I listened to everything you said. No pastels, no gloves, no satin, no lace, no plunging necklines. I did, however, break one rule."

"Which rule?"

"The one about the bows," she replied, wincing as she prepared for my inevitable meltdown.

"Bows?!" I exclaimed. "There are *bows* on the dress? For the love of all that's holy, do I look like someone who should be wearing a dress with bows?!"

My mind began racing as I mentally tore through my closet in search of a less offending option.

"Just hear me out, Jillian," she cautioned. "When we saw this dress, we just knew—"

"Knew that I wanted to look like a Christmas present?" I asked, irritated that this Danielle was not yet schooled like my Danielle was. Now I was going to look like an idiot, going to a prom I wanted no part of.

"Why don't you just—"

"Stay home? Okay. Great idea." Maybe Dr. Grayson still had an appointment available for a cleaning. Or maybe a root canal. That might be less painful.

I turned to tell her that I was just going to wear whatever I found in my closet. But as I turned around, instead of glaring at Danielle, I found myself staring at the black dress that was hanging from her hand. Dangling on the hanger by spaghetti straps was the most beautiful dress I had ever seen. The bodice was

167

plain black, but gave way to a full length tulle skirt with tiny silver bows affixed to it. It was understated. It was elegant. It was perfect.

"Danielle," I gasped. "You're—"

"Amazing? Fantastic? Unbelievable? Yes. I am," she replied, looking smug and satisfied.

"There are silver strappy shoes in the bag," she added. "Low heel."

"I'm an ass. I shouldn't have barked at you," I replied sheepishly. I should have known better than to question her. She knew me inside out even when we first met in college. Of course, she'd find me the perfect dress...and the perfect date.

"I just want you to have fun tonight. And look how well you and Luke get along!" she mused. "Did he get a hold of you last night?"

I froze at the mention of last night, images of the cliff and his subsequent trip to play Romeo underneath my bedroom window flashed through my mind. Yeah, he got a hold of me all right.

"What do you mean?" I asked, looking away so that the blush on my face wouldn't give me away.

"He came by the bonfire acting all...well, like Luke, and wanted to know where you were. I figured he stormed off to find you."

"Yeah," I stammered, remembering how he marched over to me raving that I wasn't at the bonfire and by the cliffs alone. "He...wanted to know what time to pick me up."

"Oh," she replied, furrowing her brow. "Well, did you tell him you needed to be at my house by six?"

"Yeah, but I think Grace wants to see us first."

"Who's Grace?"

"Luke's aunt."

"And you're on first name basis with Aunt Grace...how?" she inquired suspiciously, cocking her right eyebrow.

"I had...Luke invited me...well, technically Carter invited me to dinner last week," I explained, averting my gaze again.

"Carter?" she asked, the arch in her brow rising higher.

"His uncle," I added meekly, hoping that she'd just drop it. Danielle was my best friend. I never kept any secrets from her. Ever. But for some reason, I just didn't want to talk about Luke, last night or any of its implications yet.

"Well, well, well," she sang. "That's interesting. You hadn't mentioned dinner with the Chambers family before, Jillian. Is this a common occurrence for you?"

"Relax, Danielle," I replied coolly. "It wasn't a big deal. His uncle works at the hospital with my mom. I ran into them. His uncle thought I was Luke's girlfriend or something so he invited me over."

"Whoa, whoa, whoa, whoa. Hold on," she interrupted, palms facing out dramatically. "Why did Uncle Carter think you were Luke's girlfriend if he had never met you before?"

That was a good question. Luke never answered that one. Either way, I was digging myself deeper having this conversation.

"I don't know, Danielle. It was stupid, and I was just giving Luke a hard time so I accepted the invitation," I answered defensively.

"But why—"

"Danielle, honestly, I think we have more pressing issues to discuss."

I had to end this conversation and there was one sure-fire way to stop Danielle from cross-examining me. Unfortunately, it was a miserable idea, but in this instance, I needed to take one for the team.

"You know," I began. "I was thinking that a few rhinestones would look fantastic on my toes."

Danielle popped up on the balls of her feet, clapping. "I'll call the salon now!"

I spent the next hour in white trash hell as an over-processed blonde attached shiny rhinestones to my toenails. Even in my high school do-over, I'd have a humiliating experience to recall. At least I'd match Joan.

After a quick lunch, I convinced Danielle to head home. I didn't need a team of stylists to get me to a high school prom. I could curl my own hair and apply my own makeup. Well, I was never really good at the make-up thing, but I'd figure it out.

By five o'clock, my bravado had faded and my stomach was in knots. The nervous energy had turned me into a twitching mess. After nearly burning my forehead on the dime store curling iron that I apparently never used, I stubbed my toe when one of the rhinestones got caught on the area rug.

Maybe I *did* need a team of stylists.

I did a quick twirl in front of the mirror, grabbed my purse and shoved Joan inside. She, of course, was empty since I had barely used her in two weeks. Then I stuffed a few things into my duffle so that I could spend the night at Danielle's house. Before heading for the door, I glanced at my calendar. The Word of the Day was *terminus*.

Terminus: 1. the end or extremity of anything; 2. the point toward which anything tends; goal or end.

It will be the terminus of me if I didn't calm down.

I hobbled down the stairs in my amazing dress, looking the part, but feeling utterly terrified.

"Oh my goodness!" my mother squealed. "Henry, come in here and see Jillian," she called into the kitchen. "Oh, honey, you look so beautiful. You're just going to knock this boy's socks off."

Yes, and he may pin me after prom, mom. God, I was better off not dating in high school if this is what I was missing.

"Thanks, mom," I replied instead.

"Do you have a coat or something to wear with that, Jill?" my dad asked as he entered the room. He motioned uncomfortably towards my bare shoulders. "You might want to…cover up a bit."

"Henry!" my mother exclaimed. "She looks beautiful! You look beautiful," she reiterated turning towards me. "Oh! I almost forgot. Let me look for that Polaroid." She scurried into the back hall and was rummaging through the closet when the doorbell rang.

I was going to throw up.

Taking a deep breath, I walked to the door, swinging it open. I hadn't put a lot of thought into how Luke would look. I knew he'd wear a tux and he'd naturally look amazing. I just hadn't really visualized it. It was hard to reconcile the guy with the leather jacket and motorcycle wearing a tuxedo and bowtie. So when I opened the door to find Luke standing on my doorstep dressed in black and holding a clear plastic case with what appeared to be an orchid inside, I immediately felt all the blood in my body flood my face.

He stepped forward across the doorway, reaching his hand up and running his thumb along my cheek.

"Beautiful," he whispered softly.

"Found it!" I heard my mom exclaim from inside. She turned around, finally noticing Luke in the doorway. "Oh my goodness! Where are my manners? Please come in. I'm Jillian's mother, but you can call me Lucy," she beamed extending her hand. I cringed, knowing how uncomfortable Luke probably felt and how awkward the ensuing conversation was going to be.

"Hello, Mrs. Cross, it's nice to meet you," he replied, grasping her hand. "I'm Luke Chambers."

I was pretty sure that spittle had accumulated in the corners of my mouth because I had yet to close it. I stared in awe at the pleasant exchange between my mother and Luke who seemed more like a chess club member than a motorcycle-driving tough guy. Who was this boy?

"This is for you," he said opening up the clear case. He pulled out the white and purple orchid, carefully sliding the cloth-covered elastic around my wrist.

"I need to get a picture of this," my mother squealed. "Luke, can you pretend you're putting the corsage on her wrist again?"

"Of course," he replied looking up at me through his lashes. He tilted his head towards my mother, breaking our gaze at the last minute before the flash of the Polaroid blinded me.

"Okay, why don't we just get a few shots over by the fireplace?" she suggested, shaking the damp photo in the air. "Jillian, you stand in front of Luke."

"Mom, please," I ground out through gritted teeth.

"Oh, come on, Jillian," Luke added smoothly, "You don't want something to remember this by?"

I stared in disbelief as he smirked at me. I was about to tell him he had already given me a lot to remember him by before he grabbed my hand and led me over to the fireplace. He stopped in front of it and spun me around so that my back was pressed against his chest. Resting his hands softly on my waist, he squeezed my hips lightly, in a way that wasn't noticeable to anyone else but me. I felt my face flame once again as I recalled the last time he touched me that way.

"How is this, Mrs. Cross?" he asked innocently.

171

"I told you, Luke, call me Lucy," she admonished.

"Sorry," he corrected himself with a grin. "Lucy."

"That's much better," she replied pointing the clunky camera at us. "Say 'cheese'."

"Root canal," I sang at the same time Luke parroted his response.

"You're going to hurt my feelings," he whispered softly in my ear. "I thought you liked it when I touched you like this."

"Okay, just one more," my mom added as she finished shaking the shit out of the picture she had just taken. "And say 'cheese' this time, Jillian. Try to look enthusiastic."

"Now, I know for a fact that you can be enthusiastic," he whispered again. My eyes widened just as the flash went off.

"Perfect," my mother exclaimed.

"So, Luke," my father began, walking towards us with his hands in his pockets. "You drive a Lexus."

"Yes, sir," he replied.

"A little fancy for a high school kid," he added, staring out at the silver car in the driveway.

"Dad," I warned him, knowing he was just seconds away from embarrassing me.

"Actually Mr. Cross, my uncle did some research and found it did well in crash tests. Since he works at the hospital and sees so many accidents, he wanted me to get the safest car possible," he explained fluidly.

My dad nodded silently.

"Got a big backseat there, Luke?" he asked as he narrowed his eyes.

"Dad!" I exclaimed.

"What, Jill? I just want to know if he spends a lot of his time in his backseat. Do you, Luke?"

"Oh my God!" I fumed, grabbing Luke by the arm. "We're leaving."

"Have fun tonight, kids," my mom called after us as I rushed towards the door. Before I slammed it shut, I saw the bulb flash one last time.

Luke opened the door to the car for me and I climbed in, my fists still clenched. He settled into the driver's seat and glanced over at me.

"Was your dad asking me if I was planning on having sex with you in the backseat of my car?"

"Yes. Yes, I think he was. And we will never speak of it again," I replied unable to look him in the eye.

"Great way to start off the evening," he muttered, pulling out of the driveway. "I'll try to make the stop at my house a little less painful."

"Your aunt could be knitting baby blankets for us and it wouldn't be as uncomfortable as that was."

"Was that your attempt at lightening the mood?"

"Speaking of light. Joan really needs a refill. Can we stop off and grab something…anything? She hates going to a party empty-handed."

"I haven't seen that thing in a while. I thought you might be on the wagon."

"Wagons are overrated," I replied. "I hope you brought one too because I don't want poor Joan to be dateless on prom night."

"Sorry. I don't think my flask is mature enough to date." He was staring straight ahead, but I could see the smile playing on his lips. I couldn't resist teasing him a little.

"I didn't know you were such a prude, Luke."

"I think you know I'm not, Jillian," he said, turning toward me. The sweet smile that I had just witnessed was gone, replaced by something darker. We weren't joking around anymore. I had been trying to keep it light, but he was messing with my ability to think straight.

"I still might need convincing," I added, my voice sounding shaky as I tried to sound more confident than I was. I wasn't pulling it off.

"While I'd love to convince you," he replied, pulling up the gravel path to his house. "I'm pretty sure that my uncle has a camcorder aimed out the window so he can catch the whole prom experience on film. I'd rather he not witness what I want to do to you right now."

My mouth fell open. I could hear myself breathing heavy, and I sounded like I was making an obscene phone call. It had been hard enough trying to keep myself composed before Luke mentioned…doing things. Now, I wasn't in any shape to make small talk with Carter and Grace—not while I was daydreaming about doing salacious things with their nephew. Luke was enjoying my reaction a little too much. He smirked, arching his eyebrow again as he turned to get out of the car, and came around the side to open my door. I hoped the fresh air would help my breathing problem.

He led me up the path to his house, and when he opened the door, both Grace and Carter came rushing into the living room. Carter hadn't been perched at the window waiting for us, but he did, in fact, have a camcorder trained on us as we entered the house. *Awesome.*

"Oh, Jillian!" Grace gasped, clasping her hands under her chin. "You're breathtaking."

Auntie Grace is officially my new favorite person.

"You look lovely, Jillian," Carter added as he looked through the lens.

Luke wrapped his arm around my waist, squeezing tightly. I was momentarily taken aback by such an open gesture. It would have surprised me if he had done something like that in front of our friends, but it astounded me that he was doing it in front of his family. I was both a little excited and nervous at the same time.

"I made canapés," Grace announced happily gripping a tray with both hands. "These are ginger orange chicken, Jillian," she explained raising the tray for me. "It's a new recipe."

I grabbed one of the round baguettes and took a bite of pure bliss. I couldn't stop the moan that resonated from deep in my chest.

"Grace, that right there is a little slice of heaven," I replied. I turned to Luke planning to ask if he had tried the yummy goodness, but when I looked at him, his eyes were focused on my mouth and his breathing was shallow.

Looks like it's payback time.

"Could I have another, Grace?" I asked sweetly.

"Absolutely," she beamed. "I'm so happy you like them. I'm not a big fan of last minute additions, but I think I need to include this in the book."

I grabbed another baguette and turned to Luke.

"Have you tasted this, Luke?" I asked, using the same innocent tone he employed with my mother. I slowly took a bite, running my tongue along my lips and groaning. "I just can't get enough."

I heard the low rumble coming from Luke as he shot me a warning glance.

"The sauce is a little sticky," I added licking my fingers. "But it tastes so good!"

"We're going now," he announced hastily as he cupped his hand around my elbow and turned me toward the door.

"Oh, just one picture before you go," Grace pleaded fumbling with a camera.

Luke sighed loudly, turning us back to face his aunt. Again, he gripped my waist tightly, and I tried to smile, but I was feeling so overwhelmed. Grace snapped the picture, temporarily blinding us again. Before she could say anything else, Luke marched us out the door.

"Luke," Carter called behind us. "Remember our talk."

He closed his eyes, inhaling deeply. "You're trying to kill me, right?" he muttered, closing the door swiftly.

"What was that all about?"

"Let's just say that your dad wasn't the only one that wanted to discuss the birds and the bees with me today," he explained reluctantly.

"Well clearly neither of them got the memo that I'm not into prom night clichés. I took care of all that business before prom," I deadpanned.

He doubled over, laughing. "Jesus Christ. You never say what I think you're going to say," he said, shaking his head.

"Well, someone's got to keep you on your toes," I replied with a smirk.

"That you do," he added softly.

As soon as we turned onto Danielle's street, I saw the white limousine that Danielle rented parked in front of her house. She and Josh were standing on her front lawn. Her mouth seemed to be moving a mile a minute and I knew already that she was in overdrive. I really needed a drink.

"Shit!" I exclaimed. "Joan is empty and Danielle, well Danielle looks like *that*," I added pointing her way. "I'll never survive!"

"Relax," he replied calmly. "What kind of prom date would I be if I didn't try to ply my girl with liquor?"

He reached into the backseat (or my dad's supposed Den of Fornication) and pulled out a bottle of Goldschläger. It was kind of "high school" and well, gross, but when in Rome.

He must have picked up on my puzzled expression.

"Girls like that stuff, trust me," he replied. I nearly fainted watching him arch and turn next to me as he proceeded to funnel the clear liquid into Joan. I bet she was thirsty.

With Joan filled, we each took a pull. I had forgotten how wretched Goldschläger was. At least it would dull the pain of prom.

Since there wasn't any reason to delay the inevitable, we made our way over to see what was causing the commotion. Danielle was still very animated, her hands motioning out by her sides. The focus of her tirade seemed to be Josh.

"Poor Bastard," Luke muttered as we approached. "Add a cane and he'd look like Mr. Peanut."

Luke was right. Poor Josh was wearing a basic tuxedo, but had a top hat in his hand. I couldn't imagine what possessed her to make him wear that. Danielle, despite whatever caused her hysteria, looked amazing. Years later she would say that the sapphire dress was a monstrosity, but it really was impossible for Danielle to look bad. Her dress had a beaded corset top and a full length skirt. The dark blue color made her skin appear to shimmer. She was stunning.

I had obviously seen the prom pictures of Danielle and Josh under the pink and silver balloon arch. Danielle bitched and moaned about the atrocious colors and how they clashed. I always felt a little sad and wistful when she complained. I wasn't there at the prom, so I didn't have a strong opinion either way. I guess I would now.

"Josh, how does one accidentally lose a cane?" We heard Danielle ask as we approached.

"I don't know, Danielle," Josh replied sarcastically. "Canes are in high demand on prom night. Maybe someone took it."

"Well, we're going back to the tux shop and getting another one."

"Danielle, honey," I interrupted, causing her to jump. She hadn't even noticed we'd arrived.

"Oh, Jillian!" she sighed grabbing my hands and taking in my dress. "The dress looks lovely on you!"

"Thank you. You look amazing, too," I replied carefully. "I couldn't help but overhear the conversation you were just having with Josh."

"Can you believe it?!" she fumed.

"I think we need to let the cane go, Danielle," I added cautiously.

"But—"

"No. I think we need to move along. For everyone's sake. Where are Megan and Nate anyway?" I asked looking around.

"She said they were running late," she replied, just as Nate's car rounded the corner. He stepped out, shooting us a wide grin as he opened the door for Megan. Unlike Josh and Danielle, whose photos I had seen a million times, this was the first time I would actually see Megan and Nate together at the prom. Megan originally went with Grant Peters and ended up giving him a bloody nose. He spent prom night in the ER and Megan spent the evening icing her hand. Hopefully, he would think twice before trying to cop a feel on some other unsuspecting girl.

When Megan stepped out of the car, I swore it reminded me of one of those scenes from *Baywatch* when Pamela Anderson and Yasmine Bleeth would run in slow motion across the beach. She stepped out slowly, a leg peeking out from the high slit in her purple fitted dress. I fought back a chuckle when she finally stood outside of the car. When I first saw a picture of Megan's dress, it was during a girls' night that consisted of too much wine and not enough verbal filtering. I burst out laughing because the big flouncy sleeves and ruched fabric reminded me of a mariachi singer. After that night, I learned to keep some of my musings to myself.

Nate leaned in, whispering something in her ear as they linked arms. Whatever it was that he said caused a blush to spread across her face. I could count on one hand the number of times I saw Megan Dunn blush. This was a very interesting development. As they approached, I noticed that the buttons on Nate's shirt looked funny. I tried not to stare, but it was hard not to. He buttoned his shirt wrong.

"Pay up, man," I heard Josh say as he leaned toward Luke.

"Damn it," he cursed reaching into his back pocket for his wallet. He pulled out a twenty and slapped it onto Josh's awaiting palm.

"What's that all about?" I asked.

177

"You seriously don't know?" he asked, his brow arched again. "Mr. & Mrs. Obvious over there were too covert for you?"

I stared at him, narrowing my eyes.

"The bet, Jillian. I lost the bet," he explained motioning to Megan and Nate.

"Oh. OH!" I exclaimed, inspecting Megan for any telltale signs. She seemed to be properly buttoned and zippered. "Sorry, Luke," I added, rubbing his back. "I told you so."

He leaned into me, so that I felt his weight against my arm. The heat from his body led me to forget what we were talking about altogether until I heard someone clear their throat.

"Sorry to interrupt," Megan said smirking at me. "Just wanted to tell you that you looked very nice, Jillian."

Was she taunting me? Really?

"You too, Meg," I replied sweetly. "Oh and Nate, love the statement you're making with the tux shirt. That I-just-screwed-my-girlfriend-in-the-limo look is all the rage."

"Burn!" Josh exclaimed raising his palm for a high five. I slapped his palm giggling, but was met with Megan's furious glare when I looked up. While I should have been terrified, I knew better. Girlfriend was probably dying to kiss and tell.

"Oh get over it, Meg," I added. "It's all in good fun."

"We really should get going, though," Danielle said checking her watch.

"Okay, everybody," Mrs. Powers announced walking over to the limo. "Group shot before you leave."

"I think Jillian should go in the middle because she balances the blue and purple of our dresses on either side," Danielle explained to Megan, who rolled her eyes, and took her place by my side. Then each of us stood in front of our respective dates, smiling for the camera. After the flash, Danielle popped up and scurried over to the limo door.

"Chop-chop, people," she called out clapping her hands and motioning into the car. "I've been dreaming of my prom since I was a little girl. We need to get there early so that I can give the DJ the list of songs that need to be played and the order in which to play them."

"Be right back," Luke added, jogging over to his car. I climbed in and wasted no time grabbing Joan from my purse. If Danielle was this amped up now, it was going to be a long night.

When we were all settled, Luke slipped into the limo, covertly pulling out the bottle of Goldschläger from his jacket. Josh grabbed some glasses from the bar as Luke poured shots for the others. I unapologetically sipped from Joan in the interim, watching the others interact. Megan was attempting to convince Nate that the Macarena was sexy when done by the right person. Josh had his drink in one hand and held onto his top hat with the other. Danielle and Luke seemed to be having some kind of silent conversation. She had a pretty smug expression on her face, and Luke looked entirely too annoyed. He must have sensed I was watching because he turned suddenly and looked across the seat at me. A slow, sexy smile spread across his face when he caught me staring. I recognized that smile right away; it was just in black and white the last time I saw it.

Mine now.

A few minutes later, we pulled up to the Reynolds High School gymnasium for the I Still Believe (Brenda K. Starr Sang it Better) Prom because nothing said romance like the smell of jock straps and gym socks. I was feeling pretty good. After a couple weeks "on the wagon" as Luke put it, I welcomed the tingly feeling the Goldschläger provided.

The first thing I noticed as we walked through the gym doors was the balloon arch. It was silver and white, not pink and silver.

Oh shit.

"Thank God they listened to me," Danielle sighed staring up at the arch.

"Who?" I asked slightly dazed.

"Oh, the prom committee," she replied nonchalantly.

"But you weren't on the prom committee," I replied because I knew for a fact that arch was supposed to be pink, and Danielle had no part in planning the color scheme.

"No, but I just got so excited about all of us going to prom together. I wanted to make sure everything was perfect so I kind of imposed my will on the committee girls," she explained. I stared at her, stunned. I'd been on the receiving end of her powers of persuasion. I could only imagine what she put those poor girls through. There were probably tears involved.

"What did you say to them?" I asked.

179

"They have no concept of design and color," she added. "They were going to use pink balloons, Jillian. Pink! Hello, clashing color! Someday, dear Jillian, people will pay a great deal of money to have me design for them. Reynolds High should be happy they got me on the cheap."

Danielle led us over to the area for prom photos explaining that we needed to get the necessities out of the way before we were allowed to have fun. While we waited in line, she bounced over to the DJ to make his life miserable. I focused on the balloon arch overhead, wondering what else had changed and if it was a bad thing.

I was still pondering the implications of Danielle's actions when Luke slid his hand into mine. He was staring at me with the softest, sweetest smile. It was such a small gesture, holding my hand. Not something people even think about anymore, really. But with that small gesture, everything seemed to change. Our unspoken words hung in the air between us, causing the atmosphere to feel heavy and charged.

In front of the jungle of silver and white balloons, Luke stood behind me once again, but this time when we faced the camera, there wasn't any teasing. This time when he rested his hands on my hips, he pulled me in closer to his chest. This time when I felt his breath on my neck, I leaned my head towards his. This time was different, and we both knew it.

He led me over to the table where Megan and Nate were seated, pulling out a chair for me to sit down in. Danielle skittered over to us grabbing my hand before I could sit.

"Let's go, ladies!" she exclaimed. "My good friend DJ Dan has promised me some *Genie in a Bottle* and I need my girls for that."

I glared at Luke silently imploring him to intervene. He shrugged his shoulders and smiled, leaving me to fend for myself. Danielle proceeded to drag me roughly onto the dance floor as Meg gladly followed.

As if on cue or more likely by threat, Christina Aguilera began playing as soon as we hit the floor. Megan grabbed Danielle by the hips and began doing that ridiculous grinding thing girls do to get the attention of every guy in the room.

Sorry, Danielle, love you, but I will not grind on anything but Luke from here on out. Non-negotiable.

So while the girls hypnotized the whole room with their hip swiveling, I danced alone next to them and kept my rear end to myself. DJ Dan, master of the mic that he was, clumsily segued from rubbing us the right way to Lonestar's *Amazed*. Turning to head back to the table, I collided, mid-step, into Luke's chest.

"Dance with me," he said. I think I nodded, but I was too busy freaking out over how I was going to dance with him. I wasn't sure if we were going to attempt the G-rated version, his hands on my waist and mine on his shoulders. Or the PG version, wrapping my arms around his neck and moving our bodies closer together. Then there was the scarier R-rated version the kids seemed to be so fond of that involved grinding and undulating. I really didn't think I could pull that off. At least not sober.

I could feel the sense of panic flood my body. As if he knew what I was thinking, Luke grabbed my right hand and pulled it in close to his chest. I placed my left on his shoulder and felt the electric current in the air once again. As soon as we began to sway, I wrestled my hand from his grip and placed it on his shoulder. I slowly drew him closer as my arms met behind his neck. It suddenly didn't feel very PG as he moved his hands from my waist and clasped them at the small of my back.

From this position, I couldn't see Luke's face anymore, but could feel the rough fabric of his tuxedo jacket against my cheek. I never liked this song. I wasn't into sappy music or bands with names like Lonestar, but at that moment, they could have been playing Megan's Macarena and it wouldn't have been anything less than perfect.

I didn't lift my head from his shoulder when the music ended. I didn't want that feeling to go away, but Luke pulled back so I withdrew my arms from behind his neck, saddened that we'd lose that connection. But instead of releasing me from his grasp, he held me for a beat longer and stared into my eyes. I felt like I could be reduced to ashes under his gaze.

"You really do look beautiful tonight," he whispered. "But the evening would be significantly better if I had you to myself."

I was so used to snarky comebacks and comedic banter that I didn't know how to deal with just being straight with him. The fire in his eyes was unsettling and honestly terrifying.

"I wish we were alone too," I replied. He grabbed my hand, walking us back to the table with the others.

"Think we can sneak out later for a bit without anyone noticing?" he asked flashing that wicked smile.

"I think that can be arranged," I replied because honestly he could have asked me to follow him anywhere and I would have.

Facing the table, I watched Nate hand Josh a twenty dollar bill. The look of satisfaction on Josh's face and scowl on Nate's was reminiscent of the exchange between Luke and Josh earlier.

"What's that about?" I asked eyeing Josh's hand suspiciously. His eyes grew wide for a moment before he seemed to settle down.

"He just owed me some money," he replied. I knew Josh well. He wasn't a good liar, and he was definitely lying now. Before I could investigate further, Megan cleared her throat.

"Nate has some exciting news," she announced.

"Way to sound like his mom, Meg," Danielle muttered. She narrowed her eyes before turning back to Nate.

"While I appreciate the fanfare, it's hardly a big deal," he added looking a little uncomfortable with the attention.

"It's a huge deal, Nate," she replied, leaning closer and rubbing his back. He smiled at her, pushing a lock of hair behind her ear.

"My dad's going with me to check out Notre Dame this weekend," he announced. I had fortunately put my drink down because if I hadn't, I would have choked. Nate never toured the campus. It was still a sore subject with him. You couldn't even mention "fighting" and "Irish" in the same sentence without getting him upset.

"I told my dad that I paid the deposit to hold my spot. He's keeping an open mind. I think he's a little upset that I don't want to go to his school, but I think he understands how much I want to be in South Bend," he explained.

"Nate, man. That's great news," Luke replied.

"You were right," he said to Luke. "It sucked having to tell him, but I'm glad I did. And what about you?" he asked enthusiastically. "Meg tells me you're heading to Seattle on Sunday. It's your cousin's bar, right?"

"Second cousin," he answered curtly. I noticed he was bouncing his knee, as well. I really didn't feel like talking about Sunday either, but I didn't leave for New York for another couple weeks. If Luke wanted to see me, I wouldn't mind making the trip to Seattle to visit a few times before I left. It wasn't something I particularly wanted to think about tonight, though.

"That's a sweet deal, man," Nate added. "And if the Tom-Cruise-in-Cocktail thing doesn't work out, you can try Tom-Cruise-in-Risky-Business. You've got U-Dub right there," he suggested. We all looked at him in disbelief.

"What?" he asked staring back at our gaping mouths.

"Are you seriously suggesting that Luke run a prostitution ring?" Danielle asked, clearly repulsed.

"What? No! I meant go back to school and study business or something. Didn't he do some entrepreneurial shit? Jeesh."

"Well, thanks for the advice, Nate," Luke replied, trying to restrain his laughter. "I'll keep it in mind."

He leaned over to me, and I felt his lips and warm breath close to my ears.

"I have a small task to take care of," he whispered, his eyes darting towards Danielle. "I'll be back in a few. Tell them I needed a cigarette, okay? Oh, and don't drink the punch."

With that he disappeared into the crowd heading toward the front of the gym.

Don't drink the punch? Oh God. What did he do?

I anxiously scanned the room, checking for anything abnormal. I was about to chalk it up to Luke acting dramatic when I saw Mrs. Jacob and Mr. Gilbert...dancing...the R-rated way. Then, Sarah Spellman hopped up on one of the tables and began dropping it like it was hot. And this was before we even knew that was what it was called. Tyler Burroughs had just yanked off his bowtie and was swinging it around over his head, air spanking, hooting and hollering. I needed eyeball bleach. STAT.

And that skank Val was sitting on some older guy's lap, grinding and leaning her back against his chest.

Someone should get singles to stuff in her cleavage.

"Jesus Christ!" I exclaimed. "This prom is turning into Sodom and Gomorrah."

"Oh my God!" Danielle cried. "What the hell is going on?!"

"And what the hell is Val doing?" Josh asked.

"Stop looking at her, Josh. You might catch something," Danielle replied cupping her hand over his eyes. "I can't believe this is happening. They're all wasted."

We watched in horror as Karen Larson staggered up onto the stage.

183

"Hey, Class of 1999," she squealed into the mic, adding a drunk girl "woo" to punctuate her enthusiasm. "So, I'm supposed to announce your Prom King and Queen, but I thought I'd take the opportunity to tell each and every one of you just how important you have been to me. And I would like to share this with you…via song."

Karen bowed her head dramatically and then like a gift from the Gods of Comedy, she began to sing.

Shania Twain.

From This Moment.

And I died.

When she wrapped up, she punctuated her outpouring of affection with yet another "woo" before grabbing the envelope from the DJ.

Luke slid into the seat next to me slightly out of breath.

"Yeah. Definitely don't drink the fruit punch," he whispered across the table to everyone.

"You did this?!" Danielle exclaimed, motioning around the room. "I can't believe you, Luke!"

"I was just giving you the perfect prom experience, Danielle. You said I shouldn't forgo a rite of passage. Spiking the punch is one of those things," he explained, smirking.

Danielle's murderous glare was interrupted by the commotion caused by Karen's near tumble off the stage.

"Whoops! The nominees for Prom King and Queen were Kimberly Rock and Paul Martin; Gina Walters and Scott Montgomery; Sarah Spellman and Tyler Burroughs and Karen Larson and Erik McDougall." She gave a "woo" and a pump of the fist when she read her own name.

"And the winning couple is…" she began as she tore open the envelope. "Danielle Powers and Josh Fletcher?"

Her confounded expression was dwarfed by Danielle's deafening screech. She hopped up, jumping and clapping, knocking her chair over.

"And *that* is how it's done," he said into my ear.

"No way!" I whispered incredulously.

"Well, if I'm going to go to the prom, I'm making this the best made-for-TV movie possible," he explained. "And in the movie, the cool guy always stuffs the ballot box."

"You are unbelievable," I replied, shaking my head.

"Why don't we sneak out while the Prom Queen is otherwise engaged?" he suggested, motioning to the stage where Danielle was clutching her scepter and Josh was replacing his top hat with a crown.

Grabbing my hand, he pulled me out the side door into the cool night air. I didn't know where we were headed until he began walking a route that had become very familiar. When we reached the back of the gym, it was so dark that I couldn't see the milk crates or the discarded cigarette butts littering the ground. It didn't even look like the same place, but maybe it was because we were so different now.

"You certainly know how to woo a girl, Luke. Taking your date behind the gymnasium on prom night."

"Is that an invitation, Cross?" he asked smirking again.

"Settle down, Romeo, I'd like to have a respectable evening."

"I think I've behaved rather well considering what I'd rather be doing," he added as he backed me up against the brick wall. "Now this seems strangely familiar, like I've done this before.

"So tell me," he asked, trapping me inside his arms, "How do you feel about going to graduation on the back of a bike?"

"I think I feel really good about that," I replied softly.

He leaned forward, threading both hands into the hair at my neck and kissed me, strongly, soundly. I ran my hands slowly up his arms, across his shoulders and finally into his delicious groan-inducing hair. He groaned into my mouth as I twisted the unruly waves around my fingers.

"You feel it too, right?" he whispered breathlessly against my lips. "It's not just me."

I couldn't say for sure what he was talking about because I felt so much when I was with him. I felt teenage nerves when I was about to see him and very adult passion when he touched me. I felt a connection I'd never felt with anyone...ever. But at that moment, I just feared his move to Seattle on Sunday.

"I don't want to lose this," I replied honestly.

I heard the muffled intro to *I Still Believe* begin to play inside the gym.

"We should probably go inside," I said, making no attempt to move.

"We should," he agreed, not moving either. "But I don't want to."

"But we should," I reiterated unconvincingly. "It's the prom song. We should dance to it, right?"

"We can dance here," he replied, grabbing me by the hands, placing them around his shoulders and wrapping his arms around my waist. I sighed, reveling in the feeling of his body pressed against mine. I craned my neck up towards his face and the intensity in his eyes nearly made my knees buckle. Our lips were pressed together once again, moving against and along each other. With a tilt of his head, he deepened the kiss, soft, slow and sensual. I felt myself getting lost in him—in what we had become.

"You ruined all my plans, you know?" he said, laughing wistfully. I didn't really know what he meant, and I hoped he was planning to elaborate. "If you told me three weeks ago...I mean that first day you basically told me to screw," he paused, not really making much sense. His brow wrinkled as if he was battling with what he wanted to say.

"I know this is crazy but I don't care that this thing between us has only been going on for a few weeks. I don't. I know what I want," he said softly. "And I only want you."

I had spent the last ten years searching in vain for a man that had an ounce of the passion that Luke already possessed at eighteen. I knew that being with him was risky, but there really wasn't any turning back now. How could I ever return to my old life when I knew I could feel this way?

"I never knew it could be like this," I replied, aware that he couldn't possibly have any idea what I actually meant. I wished that I could explain that I had given up on the idea of finding love. I never thought it was in the cards for me. Before I could think straight, he kissed me again, frantic and passionate, solidifying for me exactly how intense our connection was.

"I wish we had more time," I choked out breathlessly.

"I wanted to talk to you about that," he began, pulling back slightly so that he could look into my eyes. "I'm...I'm not going to Seattle."

"Excuse me?" I asked, immediately feeling the heat in my face.

I must have heard him wrong.

"I can't go," he continued, shaking his head. "Not now."

He was staying.

"But what about Jonas?"

"I'm calling Jonas," he replied, coolly. "I'm telling him I'm going to New York. With you."

"With me? You're going *with* me?" I exclaimed.

"There has to be a million bars near NYU. I'm sure I won't have any problem finding something for the time being."

I felt sick. Seeing the wrong color balloon arch at the prom was a little scary. Nate talking about going to Notre Dame made me extremely nervous. But Luke giving up the opportunity to own Jonas's bar was just plain lunacy. I felt dizzy as my mind played over and over the possible scenarios. In each one, I saw Luke working at someone else's bar for minimum wage instead of owning his own. I couldn't let him do that.

"I see that look on your face and I understand why you're freaking out, but Jillian, there are people who spend their whole lives looking for what we have. I'm not throwing that away. I couldn't live with myself."

"What if you enrolled in NYU with me?" I offered, trying desperately to fix this.

"Listen, don't worry about it, really. It's going to be fine. I'm going to start making some calls tomorrow to find a job. I don't want you worrying. We're going to be great," he said, rubbing the pad of his thumb along my cheekbone.

At that moment, I knew what I needed to do. Luke would already have been packed for Seattle if I hadn't come into his life. He'd go on to buy Jonas's bar and live the kind of life that makes your smile reach your eyes. The kindest, smartest thing I could do now would be to leave before I screwed up his future even more than I already had, no matter how wonderful being with him might make my own. If I left, he'd go to Seattle, he'd buy the bar, he'd smile that smile. I loved him too much to steal that from him.

While I'd like to think he'd still be happy in the future if we stayed together, we'd be gambling with a future he wasn't even aware existed. At least I *knew* he was happy in the future without me. I wanted so much to stay. There was just no way I could be sure that things would end well for Luke if I did. I didn't have a lot of time to think about alternatives. Maybe if I did, I could think of a better plan, one that wouldn't break my heart into a million pieces.

"Let's talk about this later," I began, my voice slightly quivering. "We should get back inside."

He knew I was holding back, but he didn't push me. I knew he wouldn't give up, either. He was leaving me no choice.

When we reentered the gym, I excused myself and headed straight for the punch bowl. Grabbing the ladle, I poured a generous amount into my cup and downed the fruity red liquid in one quick gulp. My throat burned and I was glad.

"Jillian!" I spun around and saw Suzanne racing towards me. "Don't drink that! Someone spiked it."

I refilled the cup, raised it high to toast my train wreck of a life and drained it again.

"It's my lucky night, then," I replied, feeling the dull, woozy feeling settle in.

"Jillian, what's going on with you? Is it Luke?" she asked, her tone full of sympathy and concern.

"I screwed up, Suze. I. Screwed. Up. And now there are pictures without heads everywhere," I railed. "I just love him too much."

"God, Jillian, why don't I get you a seat," she offered nervously.

"I'm fine, Suze. I'm fine. You're a good friend. You send me virtual drinks," I muttered before stumbling back to the table on shaky legs.

"Jesus Christ, Jillian!" Megan exclaimed as I collapsed into my seat.

"What the hell did you do?" Luke exclaimed, rushing over to me.

"What I had to," I answered, my own voice sounding funny in my head. "I don't want to."

"It's almost eleven o'clock, guys. We should get her back to Danielle's house before this gets ugly," Josh suggested.

"Oh Joshy," I mused, "how many times over the years have you come to my rescue?"

"Jesus. I'll go find the driver," Danielle announced as Luke and Nate held me up on either side.

I embraced the cool air on my skin. I felt like I was burning up inside. They settled me into the limo as the world began to spin. I searched for Luke's face. It was distant and distorted.

"I'm sorry," I choked out and then let the darkness in.

CHAPTER 16

Jillian

I could practically feel the rain battering the roof of my car. This was an angry rain.

As I drove frantically through the busy streets, the harsh lights of the city reflected off the giant puddles that the surprise storm had created on the pavement. I focused on the clock on my dashboard and nervously laid on the horn.

Looking up at the street sign, blurred by the rain, I knew this was the turn I needed to make. I jerked the wheel roughly, pulling into the darkened parking lot. I didn't care that my umbrella was at home. I didn't care that there wasn't a hood on my jacket. I didn't care that the rain would turn my hair into a wet, frizzy mess.

I stumbled out of the car, running up the steps of the building behind a clearly smarter person holding an umbrella. I dashed into the elevator and up to the twenty-seventh floor. Panting and shivering, I rang the doorbell then knocked impatiently.

When the door cracked open, I was blinded by the glare inside. It got brighter...brighter...and suddenly...

...Painful.

I slowly forced an eye open. Oh, God. The spins. It was light out and I still had the spins. I hadn't had the spins since college after that vodka/grape juice incident when I forgot to add the grape juice.

Close your eyes. Deep breaths.

"Whoever's messing with the curtains," I began, "please take your torture devices elsewhere. You won't break me."

"Jillian, sweetie, you should at least get up to take a Tylenol and drink some water," I heard Danielle say.

Bits and pieces of the previous night came flooding back and I was reminded why my brain was currently trying to force itself out of my skull. Luke was following me to New York. Well, he *wanted* to follow me to New York, but I wasn't going to let that happen.

"Honey, there was absinthe in that punch. You need Tylenol. Maybe a whole bottle of it," she explained. "Luke feels awful."

"Not as awful as I do," I muttered, throwing a pillow over my head.

I heard the deafening sound of the bottle of Tylenol shaking near the bed. Each tiny capsule sent a jolt of pain through my skull. Doesn't that defeat the purpose, Tylenol?

"Drink," she commanded, bumping my arm with a bottle of water.

I opened an eye once again, assaulted by the bright lights and pastel coloring of Danielle's bedroom. Megan was curled up in a sleeping bag on the floor, arms splayed over her head with her mouth hanging open. If I had a cellphone, I would absolutely snap a picture and assign it to her number or maybe upload it to Facebook. That was what Facebook was for, right?

"Why does Meg get to sleep?" I whined, seeing three water bottles in front of me instead of one. I chose the middle one. I was a professional.

"Because Meg didn't willingly poison herself last night. Care to explain?" she asked.

"It was the prom. I got drunk. That's what you do," I deflected.

"I don't know what Luke was thinking," she added. "Absinthe is no joke. Did you know he had it stashed behind the gym? I'm sorry that I made you go with him. It's all my fault."

I pried my other eye open, focusing on Danielle clothed in her flannel Joe Boxer pjs and still wearing the cheap rhinestone tiara on her head. Her fault? I couldn't let her think that. This was all me.

"Danielle, I'm a grown woman," I replied.

"Sure, Jillian. We're all grown women. Pretty soon we can vote," she deadpanned.

"You know what I mean," I sneered, trying to recover from my slip. I was definitely not on my A-game. "I'm just saying that I could have said no if I wanted to."

I could have said no to a lot of things.

"And hey," I added. "If I hadn't gone with Luke, you wouldn't have that nifty crown. Not that it wasn't deserved."

She furrowed her brow as her hand drifted to the crown on her head.

"Oh, yeah," I replied, pulling the blankets over me. "That would be his handy work. Ballot-box subterfuge."

"Well, that was kind of decent of him," she muttered.

"Yeah, he's a decent guy," I answered sarcastically. "Listen, I need you to close the blinds so I can get up. I have some calls to make today, so I should probably get home after I become violently sick in your bathroom. Are you going to be around later? I may need to chat with you if I don't succumb to alcohol poisoning."

"Of course," she replied, closing the curtains and restoring order to my synapses. "Something wrong? Other than the violently sick part."

Only everything.

"No, no. I have to figure some things out and I'll let you know." I slowly swung my legs off the bed and felt the thumping in my head immediately. I really needed a steak and cheese sub from Supremes. That always cured my hangovers. I wondered if they delivered to Reynolds. It was a long way from Seattle, but I'd tip well.

I shuffled into the bathroom while the scraping sound of my feet against the carpet assaulted my ears. I just wanted to rewind the whole evening and pretend it didn't happen. My stomach apparently agreed as I emptied its contents into the bowl.

Everything hurt. My stomach, my head, my feet. And then there was the gaping hole in my chest. Oh, Dr. Grayson, how wrong I was about you. I should have been getting a fluoride treatment instead of attending the disastrous prom.

When I was as cleaned up as I could possibly get under the circumstances, I returned to Danielle's room to find her lounging on the floor with Megan, both still in their pajamas.

"Danielle, are you getting dressed now?" I asked, feeling annoyed.

"No, why?"

"Um, because I don't have a ride home," I replied, wanting to add a "duh" at the end.

"Oh, that," she replied. "Luke and Nate crashed at Josh's last night. When I called Josh this morning, Luke was still there. He said he'd drive you home so that I could rest up. Being Prom Queen is very tiring, Jillian."

"Luke is coming here? Why? Why can't you drive me home?" I exclaimed, considering the state of my appearance.

"Why can't you drive me home, *Your Highness*," she corrected.

"I'm not above beating you with that scepter, Danielle. Don't tempt me," I warned.

"So touchy," Megan added. "Maybe Luke has something that could make our little Jillian a little less grouchy."

Oh, we are so not going there.

"Megan!" Danielle squealed. "She barely knows him! Although, Jillian, you could do worse. I have a feeling about him."

"Does Josh know about these feelings, Danielle?" I replied sarcastically.

"Har, har. I'm just saying be nice to him," she suggested with a sly smile. "He made me Prom Queen. And he should be here any minute."

Flustered, I grabbed my overnight bag and attempted to pull myself together. I was tempted to check my hair in the mirror, but I didn't think I'd get away with it. The girls barely moved from their spots on the floor, unaware of my inner meltdown. I was about to beg Danielle to reconsider when the doorbell rang. I wasn't ready to see him yet.

"Despite the fact that you have pawned me off on someone I 'barely know', I will talk to you girls later," I managed as I slid my sunglasses on.

My stomach lurched as I took to the stairs. Just to be safe, I said a quick prayer that I wouldn't throw up in his car before opening the door.

Oh sunlight, why do you hate me?

When the hysterical blindness passed, and I was able to actually see Luke, he didn't seem particularly happy to see me.

"Hey," I said, utilizing my stellar vocabulary.

"Hey yourself," he replied, shoving his hands into his pockets. An image flashed in my mind of Luke standing by his car the first night I thought he was going to kiss me. He shoved his hands roughly into his pockets just like that and later told me it was the only way to stop himself from touching me. I could feel my cheeks flame just from the thought that he might be trying to restrain himself again. I had to stop thinking this way. It was only going to make it harder.

I followed him down the walkway and climbed into his car, breathing in the lemony scent. I wanted to commit everything to memory. I didn't have much time left, and memories would be all I'd have.

"So, do you want to talk about last night?" he asked, inserting the key into the ignition.

"Last night is a little hazy for me," I replied with an awkward laugh. I honestly didn't know if he was referring to my Amy Winehouse impersonation or his plan to follow me across the country. Neither topped my list of great conversation topics.

"That's the problem," he replied sounding irritated. "I told you not to drink the punch."

"It was stupid. Something else to add to the list of stupid things I've done."

"So," he added with an uncertain voice, "it didn't have anything to do with what we talked about last night?"

It has everything to do with what we talked about last night.

The words crashed into me like waves.

You feel it too, right? It's not just me.

I never knew it could be like this.

Danielle told me that in high school Luke was lost, but once he settled in with Jonas he found his place. This time around, *I* found him and *I* didn't want to lose this. Sitting here with my pounding headache, my aching feet and my upset stomach was still infinitely better than my best days before because I was with him. There was no one telling me what the right choice was, though, and I needed help.

"I just have a lot on my mind," I replied with a weak smile.

He pulled up along the curb in front of my house, throwing the car into park. I didn't want to turn and face him. I'd want to touch him, and I felt so damn transparent.

"So, I'll pick you up at eleven?"

"What's at eleven?" I asked, wondering if I had committed to something in a less than coherent moment last night.

"Graduation?" he replied with a laugh.

"Oh, right. On the back of your bike." I couldn't fight back the smile on my face as I imagined myself pressed against him, my graduation gown trailing open behind me.

"Well, we could always slide into the back of my car instead, but I think your father's already onto me," he teased.

"No, the bike is good."

"So," he began, shifting closer to me as he leaned across the console. I was drawn toward him even though I knew I should just get out. "Eleven o'clock?" he added, his lips grazing, but not quite reaching, mine.

"Eleven o'clock," I replied, finding it hard to catch my breath. As soon as I finished speaking, he closed the distance between us, taking my lip between his. He slowly pulled it into his mouth, his tongue darting out to meet mine softly. He leaned into me, pushing me backwards so that my back made contact with the door. As I let the hands on his shoulder snake around the back of his neck, I couldn't help but wonder if this was the last time I'd feel him this way. Even though I knew it was wrong to let it continue in light of my decision, I kissed him back and reveled in the feeling of his hands all over me. I always knew we had an expiration date, but now faced with the reality, I was so conflicted. I couldn't fathom a life without him, but I couldn't bear a life where I ruined him. There was too much at stake. I just wasn't prepared to gamble with his future.

I had been over it in my mind a dozen times since he told me his plans. I could see us in New York living happily in a beat-up studio apartment with lousy heating. We'd make love in front of a space heater instead of a fireplace. I'd stay up late studying, waiting for his shift at the local bar to end and fall asleep in his arms. We'd sleep late on the weekends, both exhausted from our schedules. We'd watch bad reality television and argue over whether there was any entertainment value in watching a bunch of people starve on an island and argue all the time. We'd love each other.

But it wouldn't always be that way. I'd graduate and get a job. There'd be no way of telling if he'd ever be able to manage a bar somewhere, nevermind own one. Could he be happy bartending forever, no college degree to fall-back on? And did I even know where I'd end up? Knowing what I know now, would I settle for writing household tips instead of writing something of my own? Whichever path I chose, I'd have to work hard to get ahead, and he wouldn't have his own career keeping him equally occupied. Bills would need to be paid and even though the teenage me would have wanted to believe that love conquered all, in the real world love could get complicated when bills piled up. He'd resent me. I'd resent me. We'd break each other, and he would have given it all up for nothing.

I wouldn't do it. I wouldn't risk it. It would hurt him. Hell, I was hurting myself. But I'd rather die a million times over than be responsible for destroying his future happiness. If someone could just *prove* to me that my being with Luke would make his life better, no power on earth could keep me from staying with him and never letting him go. But it didn't work that way, did it? He was only eighteen now. How could I possibly be certain that what we have means the same for him at eighteen as it does for me at twenty-nine? I knew what was out there and what I was losing. He had no idea. What kind of a monster would I be if I removed that choice for him?

That left me with two options: either hurt him now—a little bit—before we were any deeper into this thing, or be selfish and take what made me happier than I'd ever been in my life, regardless of the fact that I might be stealing his chance at happiness down the line. I hated myself, but there was no other way. So as he kissed me in his lemony-scented car, I tried to burn every sound, every touch, everything into my memory. I needed that even if it was unfair and selfish. When he began trailing his mouth down my neck and I began to squirm in my seat, I pulled away, gasping. It had to stop. I needed to let go.

"I really need to get inside," I added nervously. "My dad is probably looking for his binoculars right now."

"If your dad was watching, I'm pretty sure I'd be dead already after that," he replied in a breathy voice.

"Let's not test the theory, okay?" I forced a smile as I stepped out of the car. Danielle's words were on autoplay in my head.

I'm so glad he's doing well.

I'm so glad he's doing well.

I'm so glad he's doing well.

197

I wouldn't let him be my Amy Smart and the mere thought of being the Ashton Kutcher in any situation was revolting.

I waved back at the car as I opened the door and my heart broke. I could see him so clearly, ducking his head so that he could watch me through the passenger side window. His smile was warm and genuine, but not mine anymore.

My eyes were stinging by the time I closed the door. I didn't know how I was going to pull this off. It would involve stretching the truth…a lot. I stepped into the kitchen and saw my mom staring curiously at the cabinets.

"You know that staring at them will not make the food magically appear on the table, right?" I asked tentatively.

"Jillian! Baby, how was the prom?" she squealed. "Luke is so handsome!"

"It was good, mom. What're you doing?"

"I'm just pulling a few things together for you to bring to school. You'll need something to eat your Ramen noodles on," she teased.

"God, I hate Ramen."

"Give it a month. Tastes great at midnight," she replied. I wouldn't call it great, but I had been known to snack on it when I was too lazy to head out for a quick bite. It was actually a college dorm pre-requisite.

"I'll keep that in mind. Have you seen my admission packet around here by any chance? I think dad had it to fill out the financial aid forms," I asked. The knot in my stomach grew tighter as I envisioned the impending phone call.

"I think he left it on the coffee table," she replied pulling a hot plate from one of the cabinets. That was going in the trash immediately. I started a small fire in our room the first week on campus. Megan almost evicted me.

Scanning the living room, I found the packet lying on the table as she had said, waiting for me to either do the right thing or screw everything up royally. I pulled out the handbook, flipping to the directory, and grabbed the phone. I had survived my first day of school conversation with Mrs. Jankowski, I was sure I could handle this. I was, after all, a time travel pro now.

"Student Life," the chipper voice answered.

"Hello, my name is Jillian Cross."

"Hello, Jillian. I'm Helena. How can I help you?"

"Well, I'm currently enrolled in Professor Monroe's Summer Writing Workshop, so I'm scheduled to move into the dorms on June 12th, but I was wondering if it was too late to apply for earlier Summer Housing."

"The deadline to apply for Session I housing was in April," she explained, "but you're already registered because your workshop starts before the second session begins."

"So what does that mean?" She laughed at my apparent confusion.

"It means you can move in when the students enrolled for Session I move in. Those classes begin a week from Monday."

"Darn. I was really hoping to be able to move sooner," I explained, my voice quivering as I spoke.

"Well, the freshman volunteering to help with Orientation Weekend are moving in this weekend. Normally we're begging freshman to get involved. Interested?"

Volunteering at orientation? I'd rather gouge my eyes out than play the Name Game with a bunch of strangers while they grill me on where the cool bars are. I could teach them the proper way to shotgun a beer, but I didn't think that was what they had in mind. I needed to get out of Reynolds, though, and it was the only way.

"Should I put you on the list for move-in day?" she asked.

I took a deep breath. There'd be no turning back.

"Yes," I replied. "I'll be there. I'd love to help out."

Later that night after convincing my parents that volunteering for Freshman Orientation would hone my social skills, I sat down on my bed and called Danielle.

"Hey, Danielle."

"You mean Your Highness," she corrected.

"And *you're* high if you think I'm going to say that," I replied. She was not making this easy. "Listen, I talked to Student Life last night," I began.

"Oh, I already called and made sure we were in the same room," she interrupted. "You could have saved yourself the trouble."

199

"Oh…right…well, I just wanted to make sure all our ducks were in a row," I improvised. "And funny thing, when I was chatting with the girl on the phone, she mentioned that they were looking for some freshman to help out with orientation. So I kind of signed up."

"Wow, way to be a team player," she replied sounding surprised. "Didn't expect that one."

"So, I'm going to be leaving a little earlier than planned."

"When? On the 10th?" she asked.

"Not quite. Right after graduation," I confessed.

"What? Right after? Like that night?" she exclaimed.

"The next morning. I can get a flight out there at nine."

"And you just decided this today?" she asked suspiciously.

"Well, I was thinking that I'd try to live dangerously now that I'm college-bound," I replied forcing a nervous laugh.

"I wish I could go with you, but my mom would kill me. She has all of these day trips planned for us before I leave."

"I would never ask you to change your plans for me, but I wanted you to know. I'm going to give Meg a call in a bit."

"I'll fly out a few days early so you won't be alone for very long," she offered. I should have known. I was expecting a lecture on how I was going to miss all of the post graduation parties, but Danielle being Danielle knew just what I needed to hear.

"I appreciate it," I began, "but like I said, don't switch too much for me. It's my choice to go early."

"Oh, I'm going to miss you, Jillian! There'll be so much going on after graduation. I wish you could stick around a little longer, but I understand. At any rate, there is so much fun to be had in NYC."

"Danielle, don't call it that. We're trying to blend."

"See! That's what I'm going to miss when Val attempts the ice luge at Tyler's party. I know you'd have just the perfect comment," she added wistfully.

"Yeah, I suggest taking a blow torch to any area that comes in contact with her mouth," I replied.

"There you go!" she cheered.

"One more thing," I added. "I'm not going to tell many people I'm leaving. Then I'll just be stuck saying all my goodbyes tomorrow, and I just want to enjoy the day. Would you mind keeping it between us?"

"Oh. Sure," she replied, sounding confused by my request. "I can tell Josh, though, right?"

"That's fine," I replied. "I just don't want to focus on it. It's going to be hard enough."

"You have my word," she added.

After clearing my wardrobe with Danielle and hearing about the atrocious outfit she saw Sarah buy at the mall last week, we said our goodbyes, agreeing to discuss the move more tomorrow.

I went to bed afraid to fall asleep and dream about the boy on the bike.

The next morning when I woke up, I lay in my bed remembering how I felt the first time I graduated. I knew there were bigger and better things ahead of me, and I was so happy to put high school behind me. Now, on my second time around, the knot in my stomach had become crippling. I wished I had more time. If I wasn't enrolled in that summer program, he wouldn't have made such a rash decision, and I wouldn't be faced with leaving him. We would have had an opportunity to figure things out over the summer.

For the first time in three weeks, I wished this hadn't happened. Sure, I was able to bring Nate and Meg together and rid our lives of future Val torture, but in the process I'd spoiled my beautiful, blissful ignorance. How was I supposed to move on knowing what I was missing? Was I expected to go to frat parties, dance on tables and go to laser light shows with burnt-out losers? How could any of them ever compare to Luke?

I stared at the cracks in the ceiling for longer than I should have because when I looked at the clock, I realized I only had an hour to get ready. Pushing my tumultuous emotions aside, I hopped out of bed, glancing like I did everyday at my calendar. The Word of the Day was *ambiguous*.

Ambiguous: having more than one meaning

Kind of a weak Word of the Day, if you ask me.

I put on my shiny, happy sundress and a fabricated smile before heading downstairs leaving Joan on my desk. There really wasn't anything that could make me feel better and, unfortunately, Joan would have just made me feel worse.

My parents were putting their coats on in the living room when I reached the bottom of the stairs.

"Jillian, sweetie, you look beautiful," my mom sighed. She wasn't used to seeing me wear dresses, especially shiny, happy ones. It was already making her weepy.

"We're real proud of you, Jill," my father added, resting his hand on my shoulder.

"Thanks, Dad," I replied. If they didn't leave soon though, I was going to lose it. "Now, before Mom ruins her makeup, get going. I want you to get good seats so you don't miss any commencing."

"Are you sure you don't need a ride, honey?" my mom asked.

"No, Luke's coming to get me in a few minutes," I replied casually.

"Oh, is he?" my father interjected, showing sudden concern.

"It's not like that, Dad," I replied.

It's so like that. Well, at least it was.

"Then what is it like, Jillian?"

"Henry, settle down," my mom interrupted, grabbing him by the shirt sleeve. "He's giving her a ride to graduation. Hardly a cause for alarm." She turned to me smiling and placed her hands on my cheeks like she used to when I was small. "We're proud of you. We love you. Make sure you father's mace is in your purse. Let's go, Henry."

My father followed behind her grudgingly and once they were out the door, I was left by myself to wait for Luke's arrival. I grabbed the navy blue gown off the hanger in the hallway closet and slipped it on. My eyes began to sting again just as I heard a rumble outside. I closed my eyes, willing myself to keep it together and grabbed the cap from the coffee table.

I opened the door just as he was about to ring the bell, startling him in the process. He had his gown on as well. It wasn't zippered so I could see his clothes underneath. He was wearing a tie and he looked really, really good. It was so unfair.

"Didn't mean to scare you," I said nervously.

"You look beautiful," he replied softly, grasping my hand and drawing me towards him. I indulged myself yesterday, but I couldn't let it happen again today. When he leaned in to kiss me, I backed away.

"Settle down, big guy," I began, aiming for a light-hearted tone and failing miserably. "I don't want to walk into an event where there are hundreds of cameras with swollen lips. That just screams high school hussy."

"I don't know," he replied, wrapping his arms around my waist and holding me tighter. "I think I like that idea a lot. That's a graduation picture I'd definitely want copies of."

"Come on, you pervert. Let's go," I replied, wiggling out of his grasp.

It was then that I realized the Lexus was parked out front and not his bike.

"I thought we were going to graduation on your bike?"

"As much as I want you on the back of my bike, I don't think this is the appropriate attire," he mused darkly, motioning to my dress. "Plus Grace pretty much vetoed the idea." Truth be told, I was honestly relieved he brought the Lexus. It would be much easier to ride in a car with him today instead of pressed up against him as we straddled a motorcycle. Not to mention that I might as well just show up with swollen lips since my hair would end up looking like I had a pre-grad quickie.

I was so in my own head that the ride to school was very quiet. Luke attempted to engage me in a debate over his music selection and, at any other time I would have gladly argued that Third Eye Blind actually had a few good songs, but not today. I didn't want to be reminded of our easy banter or our silly barbs. Today wasn't commencement; it was the end.

I knew that there were speeches and clapping. People cried and laughed. Jokes were made and inspirational prose was recited. I didn't listen to any of it. When it was time to collect our diplomas, Danielle fluttered across the stage. Megan employed a fierce strut. Nate offered a fist pump, Josh a charming nod. Luke smiled at his aunt and uncle, then locating me in the crowd, winked before returning to his seat. When it was my turn, I walked in a daze to the stage, accepted my diploma and took a seat feeling nothing but pain and remorse.

When it came time to launch our caps into the air to celebrate, I ducked away from the crowd heading toward the bleachers to find my parents. I thought that I had been covert until I felt someone tugging on my sleeve.

Tracy Sweeney

Luke.

"I was thinking we could take that ride now. Maybe do something about those lips," he teased.

"Actually, my parents want to take me to dinner to celebrate, so I'm going to head back with them. Sorry," I replied uncomfortably.

"Can I see you later?" he asked softy, pushing the stray hairs away from my face.

"Well, I'm not sure how long we'll be gone for."

Please don't make this harder for me, Luke. I don't know if I'm doing the right thing.

"Call me then?" he offered, sounding disappointed. I hated myself. I didn't reply. I just smiled.

"Thank you," I added softly.

"For what?"

Everything.

"For the ride."

"Anytime," he said, staring at me strangely.

By the time I reached my parents, my eyes were glassy and my nose was running. I convinced them after a great deal of debating that it would be easier to have a celebratory brunch on the way to the airport the next day. I wanted to go home and wallow.

That night, as I lay in bed, congested, miserable and surrounded by Kleenex, I heard a pinging sound outside. I shot up in bed, listening for the sound. When it happened again, I knew exactly what it was.

Luke was throwing rocks at my window.

I sat on my bed in the dark, watching the window as I listened to the pebbles bounce off the glass. I wondered if it would shatter if he continued. It would be so appropriate. Each ping against the window caused so much of a fracture in me that by the time the sounds stopped, I was convinced I'd never be whole again.

My parents drove me to the airport the next day. I ate breakfast. I nodded when they spoke. I was sure they chalked it up to nerves. When we arrived at the gate, my mom cried. I did too, but sadly, not for her. I'd see her again.

I could barely breathe by the time we boarded the plane. I knew I was making a spectacle of myself, but I couldn't find the motivation to care. A kind flight attendant handed me a box of tissues. I wondered if people had breakdowns on planes often.

I was shaken from my thoughts when the older woman sitting next to me rested her hand on my arm.

"Everything is temporary, dear," she said with a sad smile. "It'll be okay."

I slept restlessly throughout most of the flight—strange, vivid dreams flashing in my mind. At times I felt like they were frighteningly real, but I didn't understand them.

When we landed, I was the last to disembark. For some reason, there was a finality to actually stepping off the plane into JFK. As I walked sleepily out of the tunnel, my eyes scanned the crowd at the gate. The plane was heading back to Seattle soon. The people waiting were heading back to Washington. My eye caught one girl wearing a U-Dub sweatshirt. I couldn't help but stare as I passed by.

It would be so easy. I could be right back in Seattle if I wanted. I could walk right to the ticket counter, purchase a ticket, and be back on the same plane, homebound. I could be heading back to Luke.

I stopped in front of the sign that directed travelers to go down the escalator to baggage claim or across the building to ticketing. It wouldn't be the craziest thing I'd ever done. But I couldn't.

As I turned to follow the sign to baggage claim, a wave of nausea rolled over me. Within seconds, I was sweaty and shivering. Panicking, I looked around for a place to sit down, but all I could think about was that I didn't want to hurl all over the floor in the middle of a busy airport.

The nausea intensified while tiny gray dots appeared in front of my eyes. By the time the fuzzy black cloud moved into my periphery, I knew what was happening.

Before I hit the ground, my last coherent thought would have made me laugh if I had been able. It was so calm and collected considering the gravity of the situation.

Everything is temporary.

CHAPTER 17

Luke

It wasn't going to go well. I knew this already. I wasn't fessing up to an F on a trig exam or trying to convince Grace I had an inner ear infection when I staggered home drunk. This was big. And it was going to be met with resistance. But even knowing that I was about to drop a bombshell on two of the people I loved most in this world, I couldn't wipe the grin from my face.

I knew Jillian was overwhelmed when I told her my plans to move to New York. She still looked skeptical at graduation. I expected that because, shit, I was surprised myself. But I knew it was the right decision. Although she'd be living in a dorm with her friends, all I could think about was Jillian wrapped up in a white sheet in my small bedroom. She'd be busy with school, but we'd find time to be together and I wouldn't have to wonder what it felt like to wake up with her in my arms anymore. I planned to wake up with her in my arms a lot.

As much as I wanted to continue thinking of Jillian in my bed, her hair against my pillow and her clothes on my floor, I needed to have the painful conversations I'd been avoiding. So I pushed the image of her out of my head temporarily with every intention of revisiting it later and picked up the telephone.

"Jonas," I heard the gruff voice answer on the other end.

"Jonas, hey, it's Luke," I replied tentatively.

"Well, I was wondering when you'd work up the berries to call me back," he said coldly. "I called last Sunday and again on Wednesday. Called Friday morning, too."

"Jonas, I'm sorry," I began, feeling tongue-tied.

"I don't need your apology, Luke. Are you calling to tell me that you aren't coming because I think that's what's going on. Am I right?"

"It's not like that. There's this girl—"

"Jesus Christ, Luke," he sighed, sounding exasperated. "So what? You're not gonna work? You're gonna screw around all day? Is that the plan? Carter must be thrilled."

"No, that's not the plan," I replied defensively. "She's going to NYU and I'm going with her."

"To NYU? Kind of late to enroll, isn't it?"

"I'm not going *to* NYU," I added. "Just to New York."

"Ah. I see. And Carter said…?"

"I wanted to call you first," I explained.

"Good idea because a corpse wouldn't be able to make this call."

"It's not going to be that bad, Jonas. I know he won't be thrilled but he likes Jillian—"

"It's going to be a goddamn bloodbath," he interrupted laughing darkly. "But I'm not here to hold your hand or change your mind. You're a big boy now. If this is what you want, then do it. I just hope you're making the right call."

"I really appreciate what you were going to do for me, Jonas. I do. I just need to do this," I replied. It sounded like I was pleading. Maybe I was.

"I can't say I'm not disappointed. But good luck, kid," he added.

I hung up, feeling like shit. I hadn't waivered in my decision, but it still sucked being told that I was a screw-up. I really hoped he was wrong and Carter would see that my life wouldn't be ruined if I went with Jillian to New York. It would be the opposite.

Grudgingly, I made my way downstairs to discuss the change of plans with Carter and Grace. Carter was in the living room reading the newspaper, reading glasses perched low on his nose. I'd miss him—probably more than I'd be able to express.

"Hey," I called out to get his attention.

"All packed?" he asked, looking up over his glasses and smiling.

"Can I talk to you?" I asked cautiously.

"Is everything alright? Should I get my keys?" He started to get up, ready to drive us out to the cliffs and work out our shit like we always did. The man knew me better than anyone.

"Actually, I'd like to talk to you *and* Grace."

"Oh, sure," he replied, confusion crossing his face. "Grace, could you come in here for a second?"

When she entered the living room smiling, I had a brief flash of remorse. I sucked in a deep breath before I began.

"I'm not going to Seattle tomorrow," I announced.

"When are you going then?" Carter asked, visibly confused.

"I'm not…going to Seattle."

"You're going to have to give me a little more than 'I'm not going to Seattle'. Is this about Jillian?" he asked, putting the paper down and moving towards the edge of the couch.

"Listen. I know you're upset and I understand that, but I know what I'm doing," I explained, trying not to sound petulant.

"Which is what, Luke? What is your plan now because I need to understand this," he implored. My stomach was already in knots because I truly hated doing this to them.

"Luke," Grace interjected. "Jillian is a lovely girl, but if you're changing your mind based on your relationship with her, I think we need to discuss this."

"I know how this sounds and I know what you're going to say. But my mind is made up. I'm not letting her go off to New York without me."

"You can't be serious," Carter replied, incredulously. "Luke, be reasonable."

"I already called Jonas."

He stared at me for a moment, his mouth gaping and his brows furrowed. He slowly began shaking his head before raking his hands over his face.

"I love you, Luke, but you're out of your mind. You're eighteen."

"I know," I replied not saying it outright, but I wasn't asking for permission.

He continued to glare at me, and I was reminded of the bloodbath Jonas predicted.

"Listen," I continued. "I have a lot to do if I'm going to make this work. I need to make calls tomorrow. Set up some interviews. Look into apartments near campus."

"Are you moving in together? How do her parents feel about this?" Grace interrupted.

"Jillian's already been assigned to a dorm room with her friends. I just need something small, but I'd prefer something near her campus," I explained. I hoped that I at least sounded like I had my shit together. I still had a lot of loose ends to tie up.

"This conversation isn't over, Luke," Carter added. "But I think we both need to cool down a bit."

"We can discuss it as much as you want," I replied with conviction. "But I need to do this."

I wasn't trying to act like a dick, but there was just so much I was willing to take. I wanted his blessing, but I didn't need it. And if that meant leaving against his wishes, I would.

I headed back upstairs, giving Carter the space and time he needed to calm down. I laid down in bed thinking about what I would be bringing with me to New York. I had planned to take my bike with me to Seattle, but I wasn't about to drive it across the country. Since I'd be flying, I would be packing lightly. I really didn't need much.

My thoughts quickly shifted back to the image of Jillian in my apartment, wearing one of my shirts, something quirky like wool socks and nothing else. My body began to react and I shifted uncomfortably in my bed with thoughts of the cliffs replaying in my mind.

I needed to see her.

It was almost eleven when I checked my watch. I knew I should just stay put and call her in the morning. I knew I should show a little restraint. Hell, I knew I should be worried that if Henry Cross caught me, I could screw everything up. But I wasn't thinking that way. I shouldn't need to see her, but I did. I shouldn't be thinking about touching her again, but I was. And I shouldn't be skulking around her house at night, but that was the plan. I couldn't bring myself to feel bad about it—not even when I was marching out the front door and over to the Lexus.

This time I'd know where to park so that the car wouldn't alert her parents that I was there. This time I'd know to avoid the house with the yappy dog. This time I'd know which window to throw the rocks at. And this time I'd coax her downstairs and back to my car. If I was lucky, she'd be wearing that tank top again. If I was really lucky, she wouldn't be wearing it for long.

Just as I had imagined, I navigated the course easier this time sending a silent 'screw you' over to that rat dog next to her house. I grabbed a few small rocks and sent them up to the purple window, waiting patiently for the shadow to appear in the dark.

I realized that I hadn't really planned out what I was going to say. 'Hey Jillian, it's been almost a week since we had sex and I kind of want to try that again' probably wasn't the most romantic proposition in the world, but it pretty much summed up my feelings. We hadn't had any time alone and I needed to touch her again. Things were intense at the prom and I wanted to ease her mind about the trip to New York…and maybe ease that tank top off.

When she didn't appear in the window, I grabbed a few more rocks and chucked them harder at the glass. I still had to be careful. A broken window would not work well with my plan to remove her top.

I contemplated throwing a bigger rock or even trying to call her name, but it was too risky. I was going to have to leave and wait until tomorrow to see her, but the vision of her tank top on the floor of my car had gotten me pretty worked up. I was not looking forward to going home and taking matters into my own hands.

I headed to my car, and like before, walked backwards, watching the window for some movement behind the curtain. This time there was no smirk, no wave, just the darkened room and silence.

I sped off into the night irritated that Jillian was such a deep sleeper. If we weren't leaving for New York soon, I'd insist she get a cellphone so this shit didn't happen again, but luckily I wouldn't have to worry about disturbing her parents for much longer. Once we were in New York, things would be much different because I didn't plan on spending many nights alone.

Back at home, when I stepped into the shower and closed my eyes, it was her hands lathering the soap along my chest. Her touch along on my arms and around my shoulders. It was her fingers moving along my stomach and further below.

It was her wet body I imagined in the shower with me. Sliding up against and along mine. Meshing together. Grinding and grabbing. Holding on and pulling up. It was her working me into a frenzy. Gasping, panting, groaning and finally freezing.

211

But as good as it felt, when I opened my eyes, my shower was empty, and Jillian was at home.

New York couldn't come soon enough.

The next morning, I woke early knowing I had a lot to do before I could swing by Jillian's and after my failed attempt the night before, I *really* wanted to swing by Jillian's.

I stumbled out of bed and shuffled over to my desk to boot up my Mac. Lying next to the mouse pad were the contents of my pant pockets. I grabbed the empty gum wrappers and dumped them in the trash then tossed my lighter into the top drawer. I had been so distracted lately that I was slipping up. If Grace had come in and seen the lighter on my desk, it would've set her off. Underneath all of the trash were our prom tickets. Picking one up, I stared absently at it, not really seeing the paper in front of me, but Jillian's pale skin against her dark dress, swaying with me in the dark.

I pulled a pin out of my bulletin board and tacked it there. It was sandwiched between a cardboard coaster from Jonas' and the New York City street map I'd printed out. Shaking off the urge to call myself a sentimental wuss, I turned on the computer.

I spent the next hour looking through ads online. The good news was that I could already serve alcohol in New York because I was eighteen, which meant I could apply for a bartending position. The bad news was that the ads online were far from impressive.

Planet Hollywood was looking for a bartender. I could only imagine how badly I'd need to gouge my eyes out surrounded by useless artifacts from ghosts of celebrities past. Because everybody is just dying to see Dustin Hoffman's *Tootsie* dress, right?

There were a number of ads for shirtless bartenders and one where pants were optional. And I was pretty sure a few of them may have been part-time escort services because their tipping policy sounded suspect.

Weeding through the online garbage, I was able to find a few prospects all in the Village. They weren't fancy, but I'd be able to keep my clothes on.

If I planned to fly to New York with Jillian for her orientation, I'd need a place to live. That would mean putting a deposit down on an apartment without seeing it first. Obviously, not an optimal situation. I printed out a few decent apartments and made a few calls, narrowing the list down to three small studios all within walking distance of campus.

I wanted to get Jillian's input before I made any decisions, so I figured it would be a good time to head over and run them by her. It was unfortunately a lot later in the day than I expected, but early enough that I wouldn't need to worry that she'd be asleep and oblivious again.

Armed with the apartment listings, I drove the short route to her house, happy that it was a good excuse to show up unannounced.

Jillian's car was is the driveway when I pulled up. I jogged up to the front door and nervously rang the bell. I was accused of plotting to have sex with Jillian in the backseat of my car the last time I saw Henry Cross. Now that it was something I was actually considering, I was a little anxious. Fortunately, it was her mom who opened the door, looking surprised to see me.

"Luke!" she exclaimed. "To what do I owe this pleasure?"

"I was just dropping by to see Jillian," I explained. She knitted her brows and looked at me curiously.

"Honey, Jillian left for school this morning."

It was my turn to knit my brows and stare strangely back at her, almost as if the words weren't registering. She wasn't making any sense. Jillian wasn't leaving for New York for almost two weeks. Maybe she had her days mixed up or she was a lot crazier than she let on. Maybe she was joking. Maybe she didn't realize that it really wasn't funny.

"But she's not supposed to leave until the 12th," I stammered, feeling stupid for explaining.

"Oh, honey, she had a change of plans."

Again I was reeling, going over possible explanations for what I was hearing.

Maybe Jillian wanted some time away from her parents and was staying with Danielle. Maybe there was an emergency and she tried to reach me, but couldn't. Maybe she went there to scope out apartments early. Maybe her mother was truly insane.

I needed to talk to Danielle.

"Thanks," I replied absently, my jog turning into a sprint as I approached the car.

This had to be a huge misunderstanding and there would be a really logical explanation. And later when it was all sorted out, we were going to laugh because it didn't make enough sense to be true in the first place.

On my way to Danielle's house, I gripped the wheel so tightly that my palms were beginning to ache. My stomach was in knots and my knee was bouncing. This *had* to be a mistake.

Naturally Josh's car was out front when I arrived. I rang the bell waiting for someone to answer and set all of this straight. When the door opened, it was Danielle, and I was once again met with a look of surprise and confusion.

"Hey, Luke! It's good to see you. What's going on?"

"Have you heard from Jillian?" I asked, cutting through the pleasantries and straight to the point.

"Jillian? Um, yeah," she replied, "I wasn't supposed to tell anybody because I guess she didn't want to make a big deal of it, but she left for school this morning."

"Hey, man," Josh said, walking up behind Danielle and placing his hands on her shoulders. "What're you up to later?"

Josh went on to say something about Tyler's party and Danielle's parents not being home. I didn't really know what he said because I'd stopped paying attention.

She left.

"I have to get going," I managed to mutter, turning around and heading back to my car before either could respond.

She freaking left.

It still didn't make any sense. I knew we hadn't solidified our plans, but we solidified *us*. Didn't I deserve an explanation?

I kept rehashing our conversation from the prom over and over again, searching for clues in what she said and how she said it.

I don't want to lose this.

I wish we had more time.

Did she know she was leaving when we were at the prom? Is that why she reacted the way she did? But then why would she tell me she felt the same way, too? It didn't make sense.

Unless she really didn't.

No. I could feel it when I touched her. I could see it when she looked at me. I hadn't imagined it. There was more to this, and I just needed to figure it out.

Maybe I scared her by moving too fast. Maybe she didn't believe me when I said that I only wanted her. Maybe I should've been honest and told her I loved her. Then maybe I could've stopped this from happening.

However, the fact remained that she was gone, and she hadn't said shit to me about it. I pulled over to the side of the road, cursing and pounding my palms against the wheel.

What the hell happened?

I sat there staring off into the woods by the side of the road. I don't know how long I sat there as I tried to figure out what to do. I could call her, but what would I say? *Hi Jillian, it's Luke. What the hell?* As stupid as it sounded, I really needed to know. I needed her to explain it to me—spell it out—because this was seriously messed up.

As it started to get dark, I headed home feeling numb. Pulling into the driveway, I looked up at the house. Everything seemed different to me somehow. I sat in the car, letting it idle, unable to make myself move and go to the door because when I did, I would need to make a call that would be far more difficult than the one to Jonas. She was going to tell me why she left, tell me some bullshit excuse as to why she moved across the country without telling me. I didn't *want* to hear it, but I *needed* to hear it. She owed me that much.

Finally turning off the car and stumbling out, I dragged myself into the house feeling beat up and drained. No one was home so I was able to avoid a continuation of our conversation from yesterday. I was lucky considering I had no answers to give.

My bedroom was dark except for the eerie light from the computer monitor. I sat at my desk and was immediately assaulted by memories of Jillian. The prom ticket I had just tacked to my bulletin board was right in front of me along with the street map that I apparently didn't need anymore. A stack of blank CDs was piled in the corner, left over from when I burned her The White Stripes disc. The Chili Peppers CD mocked me as it elicited the image of Jillian leaning back against the desk, wide-eyed and panting.

With a swipe of my arm, I knocked everything off the desk and onto the floor, cursing and reveling in the comforting crash. The mug that held random pens and pencils shattered into a dozen pieces. Jewel cases cracked and the stand on my keyboard broke off. I wanted this destruction. But as I looked at the carnage on my bedroom floor, it didn't cure the dull ache in my chest. It only pissed me off that I needed to clean it up.

After returning the keyboard to my desk, I pulled up the page for NYU, searching for a main number. When the operator picked up the phone, my whole body tensed.

"Hi, I'm looking for the extension of a student that just moved in," I explained. "Jillian Cross."

"One moment, please," she mumbled. It was insulting that she sounded so bored when my heart was practically hammering in my chest. "We have a Jillian Cross, but her telephone account isn't set up yet. Would you like to leave a message and we can have it sent to her dorm?"

"You're kidding me," I muttered. "No. No thanks," I said, hanging up.

It was probably better off. What was I going to say to keep myself from sounding like a lovesick idiot anyway? I'd get my shit together and call back in the morning. In the mean time, I couldn't stay in the same room I'd spent the last three weeks jacking off in. I needed to get out.

I grabbed my keys, ignoring the mess on the floor, leaving the house and any thoughts of her behind. Ironically, the only place I wanted to be was the place that reminded me of her the most.

I parked my car in the same spot I had a hundred times before, but it seemed strange and out of place. I walked through the same path through the trees, ducking under the low branches, but it was like I wasn't really there. Still dazed, I headed to the center of the clearing in what was once my spot, but it wasn't mine anymore. Everything was different and everything was wrong.

I pulled the flask out of my pocket, glaring at it ruefully. Damned if she ruined that for me, too. I tipped it back and resigned myself to a night of forgetting, of moving on, of drinking her away.

I looked up at the sky, thankful for our dismal weather for once because the cloud cover hid the night sky. My flask wasn't as full as I would have liked it. It wasn't as effective as I'd hoped. But it dulled the ache, warmed my chest and made me feel just for a little while that everything wasn't so screwed up.

When I drained the last drop, I still wasn't drunk enough or numb enough. I was still empty and pissed and disappointed in myself for allowing any of this shit to happen. There was a reason I didn't get involved. There was a reason I kept people at arm's length. It was the reason I managed to survive what I did. You can't depend on anyone but yourself. Despite what people may say, when it comes down to it, everyone is just out for themselves. I knew it then, but I chose to push past my cynical nature and allow myself to feel, to trust her. And it did me a lot of good. I ended up sitting alone with a flask ruined by a girl that didn't even have the decency to tell me to go to hell before she took off.

Screw her. Screw everyone.

I was getting ready to make a trip to the liquor store down the street when I heard a rustling in the bushes. For a moment, all logic left me and my heart began to race as I wondered if it could be her coming back to explain that it was all a big misunderstanding.

For once, when Carter walked across the clearing towards me, I felt nothing but disappointment. This wasn't something he could fix and I sure the hell didn't need a pep talk.

I stared straight ahead, only seeing his movement in my peripheral vision. I made no attempt to hide the flask or pretend that I was just hanging out. I was in no mood to pretend. I probably couldn't even if I tried.

He slowly lowered himself down onto the ground, arms wrapping around his bent knees. He stared off into the distance as if he were looking at the same thing I was. I wasn't looking at anything.

I couldn't just sit there and wait for him to say something. It was torture.

"Aren't you going to ask?"

"Why you're here?" he replied. "I think it's pretty obvious. You and Jillian have a fight? Did you break up?"

I couldn't help the laughing. It was full of all the bitterness and anger that had been stewing since I left her house.

"You can't break up with someone who isn't your boyfriend," I replied harshly. "As a matter of fact, turns out you don't owe them anything at all."

Carter didn't waver and continued to stare straight ahead, no doubt processing the information.

"What did she say to you?"

217

"She didn't," I replied, earning a curious look from him, "say anything. She just left."

"Did you try speaking to her? There must be some explanation."

"Yeah. I'm sure there is," I replied. A couple of hours ago, I wanted nothing more than to call her and force an explanation. Now, I wasn't so sure I wanted to hear it.

"So now what?" he asked cautiously.

"What do you mean?"

"Well, yesterday you were moving to New York."

I knew it was hard for Carter to step outside the parenting role, but I didn't want to think about career paths or lack-thereofs at the moment. I wanted to refill my flask and forget everything.

"I really don't want to discuss this right now, Carter," I replied.

"Come on. It's freezing. You've done enough damage out here," he said as he stood up and brushed himself off. "Besides, Grace made nutella and biscotti."

He reached his hand out to help me up, smiling down at me. I came close to telling him to screw and shove his biscotti up his ass. But I didn't. I grabbed his hand and dusted myself off. I followed him back to his car and slid into the passenger seat. We drove back home silently.

I knew what I was going to do before I even sat down at the table to try some of Grace's biscotti and nutella. I knew it was going to suck because I didn't like admitting I was wrong. I wasn't going to call Jillian. I was going to call Jonas.

I excused myself and returned upstairs. Ignoring the mess on the floor of my room, once again I called Jonas to discuss my future.

"Jonas," the familiar voice answered.

"Hey, man," I replied quietly.

"Luke, I thought you'd be halfway to New York by now," he responded coolly.

"Yeah, about that," I began. "I'm not going to New York."

"Ah. Trouble in paradise?"

"You could say that," I replied, not wanting to give him a play-by-play. "I can be there tomorrow around eleven, if that's okay."

"Listen, Luke, what did I explain to you when we first talked about you working for me?" he began. "I needed someone dependable. Someone who wasn't going to go running off to the first frat party they're invited to. Remember? What happens if your girl calls next week and wants to see you?"

I tried to respond, but I was stunned by his response. I figured he'd give me a hard time, but it didn't occur to me that he might say no.

"You'd go, right?" he pressed.

Would I? I didn't know. I guess it wasn't a no.

"That's what I thought," he replied when I didn't answer right away.

"Jonas, I'd never leave you in a lurch," I argued.

"I know you don't think you would, Luke. I told you I know you're a good kid, but things are just too complicated for you right now. I don't think it's a good idea."

"If you just give me a chance," I countered.

"Listen, we'll talk again next month. If I haven't found someone permanently, we can revisit," he offered with a sense of finality. There wasn't much else I could say.

"I'm sorry," I replied. I felt like a piece of shit.

"I'll talk to you soon, Luke," he added before I heard the harsh click of a dial tone.

I hung up the phone and bent down to start picking up the mess I made earlier. My anger at the situation, no, *at her,* intensified as the implications came crashing down around me. I wasn't going to college. I wasn't going to New York, and now I wasn't working with Jonas either. This wasn't okay. This was bullshit.

I slumped down onto the edge of my bed, raking my fingers over my face. I needed a game plan, but how could I make a plan when the only thing I wanted just wasn't an option anymore?

Exhausted from the events of the day, I cleaned up and crawled into bed. Tomorrow I'd drive to Seattle and convince Jonas that I made a mistake.

Nothing was what I thought it was. I needed a chance to make things right. To forget any of this ever happened. I needed that fresh start.

I could barely remember back to the time when I daydreamed of coeds and body shots and the start of a new life. But I'd make myself remember. It had been erased by perfume, white underwear and Green Day. But it was all a mistake, leaving me wide awake and empty trying to forget her red lips and shirt.

When I woke in the middle of the night, drenched and covered in sweat, I knew she'd haunt me even if I left. But I would do everything I could to leave it all behind.

Impulsively, I picked up the phone, knowing it was stupid as I dialed. The extra rings told me that I was waking him up. I should've felt bad, but I was desperate.

"Hello," the groggy voice answered.

"Jonas," I began.

"Jesus Christ, Luke, what time is it?"

"I don't know. Four-thirty?"

"Are you kidding me? You better have a good explanation, kid," he warned.

I hadn't planned what I wanted to say, but it all spilled out.

"I know you don't trust me. God, I don't trust me, but you have to give me another chance, Jonas. I messed up and I know it, but I thought…Jesus, I don't know what I thought. Just, please. I have nowhere else to go."

I hated that I was pleading. I hated that it wasn't even what I wanted to be doing. I hated that she did this.

I heard him take a deep breath and slowly expel it into the receiver. The silence was killing me.

"Get here before noon," he replied, and then the line went dead.

I'd get back on track. I'd head to Seattle tomorrow, leaving all of the memories of her behind. I'd make it work. I'd learn the job. I'd flirt with coeds. I'd make a life for myself. I didn't need her. I didn't need anyone. I wouldn't make the same mistake ever again.

CHAPTER 18

Jillian

I'm wearing what has become my uniform. Yoga pants, hooded sweatshirt and Uggs. My hair is in a high ponytail and my face is without makeup. I don't need makeup. I'm not planning on going anywhere. The radio is on and it's pretty loud. Danielle is listening to 'N SYNC again and I just want to tell Justin—no, it's not gonna be me. I had my chance. I made my choice.

I hear them moving around in the bathroom and again in their bedrooms.

"Is she coming with us?" I hear Megan ask Danielle. She never learned how to whisper.

"What do you think?" she replies, sarcastic, but sad. I can't feel bad. I can't feel anything.

"We can't keep leaving her here. This is getting ridiculous. Something happened," Megan argues.

Something happened. It almost makes me want to laugh. Almost.

"What do you want me to say? I've tried," Danielle replies. She has. I always say no.

"Well, I've had enough." Megan sounds determined. I don't take my eyes off of the television as she approaches. I know what's coming next. This time, she kneels down beside me. That's considerate. I won't have to look up at her towering figure when I tell her to leave me alone.

"Jill, listen, if something's going on with you and you don't want to talk about it, I'll respect that. But you can't stay in like this every weekend." She motions to my outfit, clearly not pleased with my uniform.

"The party is very low-key. Plus, I heard that Mark Jensen is going to be there. He's in your philosophy class, isn't he?"

Nice try.

"I have plans," I lie.

"With who? The Iron Chef?"

Megan's not funny often. I like to throw her a bone when she is.

"I have an outline due to Professor Parsons on Monday. I need to start it, but you're right. I should get out more."

I wouldn't have believed me.

"Can I meet you there in a bit?"

"Really?" she asks, the smile playing on her face. So full of hope. Because she still has hope.

"Really," I reply.

And when they leave for the party, I reiterate that I'll see them soon. But I won't. I pick up the remote control. I turn on The Food Network. The secret ingredient is chicken.

I was jarred awake from my strange dream by someone yelling and running toward me. I was on the floor. Not the cold tiles of the terminal, but next to a bed. And the comforter on the bed was not purple.

I sat up suddenly and was overcome by a wave of nausea. Grabbing my head, I moaned, biting back the feeling that I was about to throw up.

"Jillian! Oh God!" Danielle exclaimed, falling to my side on her knees.

As much as I should have been thrilled to see her, I couldn't focus on Danielle. I needed to look around the room. I needed to see if anything, anything at all, was different. Unfortunately, my head was throbbing and Danielle was blocking my view.

"Don't get up," she ordered, nudging me back down onto the carpet. "What the heck happened? I heard a crash and you yelled…"

I didn't even know how to answer that.

I traveled back in time and tried to give you all a new and improved life. No thanks necessary. I broke more than I fixed.

The pain in my head was making it hard to form a complete sentence and the fact that I didn't really know what was going on had me reeling. The question I wanted to ask more than anything in the world was the question that scared me the most. Was it all a dream?

I sat up again slowly, struggling against her grip on my shoulders.

"Danielle, I need to know," I began, my voice quivering. "How are things...at work?"

"Work? Why are you asking me this?" she asked, her tone panicked and confused.

"I just need to know what's going on with the business," I added.

"Jillian, you have me worried now. I just finished telling you that the last thing I want to talk about tonight is all the stress work has caused. Tonight was supposed to be about fun, not work. But now I don't think we should be going anywhere. Did you hit your head?"

My heart sank listening to her answer, and the fit of nausea intensified. I didn't know what I expected her to say. I guess I wanted to hear that business was good. That she was happy and all of the work I did meant something. But it occurred to me, as I sat there staring at her with my mouth gaping, that I didn't fail my mission in the trip to 1999. There *was* no trip to 1999.

I craned my neck, scanning the room. Everything was as I left it almost four weeks ago. The same desk and computer were in the corner, the same books in my bookshelf, and the same white comforter on the bed.

It had been a dream. Val was still screwing their clients. Danielle was still miserable. Luke was still a stranger.

My nose began to twitch and my eyes watered. I couldn't believe how something so vivid could have been a figment of my imagination. I couldn't believe I made him up. There was never a contentious meeting behind the gym. There was never a fire alarm or an awkward dinner with his family. No Tacoma. No soft lips. No rocks against my window. No cliffs. He never loved me and I never broke his heart.

The tears pooling in my eyes spilled over as Danielle watched helplessly. She was probably ready to call 911. I never cried.

The knock at the door startled me. I didn't want to see anyone. I wasn't ready to have a conversation that didn't revolve around the fact that I thought I had spent the better part of the last month as a teenager. How was I supposed to talk about going to a reunion when I could still see Val's face at Luke's locker so clearly? I could probably pick out the color lipgloss she wore. It probably had a stupid name, too.

Josh appeared in the doorway, looking nervous and out of breath.

"You didn't answer the door. What's going on!" he exclaimed once he noticed me sobbing on the floor.

Welcome to Jillian's Nervous Breakdown, Josh. Make some popcorn. Take a seat. It'll be quite a show.

"I fell," I answered lamely, as I tried to wipe my running nose.

He looked over to Danielle, alarmed by the scene before him. "Danielle?"

"Jillian's just a little shaken up, Josh," she replied. I wasn't sure if she believed what she was saying. Her brow was furrowed, and she was staring at me. "At any rate, I don't think it's a good idea that we go tonight."

"No, no. Absolutely," he replied.

"You can't cancel," I interjected, my voice thick from crying. "It's just a bump. I'll be fine. Just go and have fun."

"We've been through this before. That's not an option, Jill," Josh argued. "We're not leaving you here."

I tried to get up from the floor to prove that I was capable of taking care of myself, but Danielle wouldn't release the death grip on my shoulders.

"Josh, honey, could you make sure she doesn't get up while I go and get some water from the kitchen?"

Danielle gave me a warning glance and headed for the door. Josh squeezed her shoulder lightly as she passed by him. It was such a tender gesture. Beautiful, really. So beautiful that once again, I found myself doubled over and grief-stricken. Nothing I felt had been real.

Josh moved awkwardly across the room, settling down next to me on the floor.

"You wanna talk about it?"

"There's nothing to talk about," I replied, trying to pull myself together.

"You know we love you, Jill. You can tell us anything. You can tell *me* anything. You know that, right?" He looked so genuine and concerned, and damn it, I just wanted to start crying again. Instead, I launched myself at him, hugging him tightly, sobbing.

"Jesus Christ! What the hell have you two done to her?"

I looked up into the bewildered expressions of Nate and Megan.

"Honey, are they trying to get you to switch to wheat pasta again? Just tell them no," she added. I let out a watery laugh.

"Meg, have some sensitivity. Jillian...well...I'm not sure what's going on, but it's not about wheat pasta which is really good for you, by the way," Danielle argued, pushing her way into the room and handing me a glass of water.

"Whatever, it tastes like cardboard. What's wrong, then?" she asked, looking in my direction.

"Nothing. I fell and...my head...I just...it's nothing," I stammered.

"Maybe we should get her to a hospital," Nate suggested. "She's kind of freaking me out."

"If you two can't be helpful, just go into the living room and wait there," Danielle ordered.

"I have an idea. Why don't you all go out to the living room, get your coats and go to the reunion," I suggested. *Please leave*, I wanted to beg.

"No way, Jill," Danielle added. "I think you have a concussion. Someone needs to check if her pupils are different sizes," she announced, disregarding any need for personal space and staring into my eyes.

"That's not true, honey," Josh countered. "I think she's fine. She knows who she is. She knows she fell. She's just a little shaken up."

"I'm calling the bar to cancel," Megan announced. "Considering the circumstances," she added, looking pointedly at Danielle, "I think it's for the best."

I'd had enough. Grabbing the leg of the bed, I pulled myself onto my knees and then onto my feet.

"See. I'm fine. Now go," I said, moving over to my bed. I let my fingers glide over the soft comforter, remembering the Egyptian cotton I had missed so much. I took a deep breath. I wouldn't cry again.

"Megan, call that new place," Nate added. "We'll get Pad Thai."

"No, Pad Thai!" I exclaimed, finally losing my patience. I'd already lost my mind. "I'm going with you. I can't stand this anymore. Just give me a minute to pull myself together. I don't want these goddamn skinny jeans to go to waste, anyway."

"Jillian, I don't think that's the best idea," Danielle countered.

"Listen, if I start to feel weird, I promise we can leave. I'm just not letting you cancel this thing because I'm a train wreck. Let me have some dignity, please."

"Fine, but you promise. The minute you start feeling wonky, we leave," Danielle replied.

"Danielle, I'm not sure about this," Megan added warily, handing me a box of tissues.

"It'll be fine. Okay, everyone. Move out. Let's give her some space." Danielle corralled the group and drove them into the living room. I was finally alone.

The open space in my room suddenly felt off. It didn't feel like my room anymore. Everything was the same, but I wasn't. How do you explain that when nothing actually happened? I should be the same girl I was yesterday. I should be filling my pink, sparkly flask with Grey Goose. I should be getting ready to tell Sarah and her crooked boobs that she's annoying. I shouldn't feel so empty.

I crawled onto the bed, curling up and clutching a pillow. The comforter was littered with balled up tissues. Hearing a rustling in the doorway, I looked up to find Danielle watching me nervously. She slowly crossed the room and sat down on the bed, careful not to disturb the pile of tissues I'd accumulated.

"Do you want to talk about it?" she asked, brushing aside a dampened piece of hair.

I looked at her, wondering how I could possibly explain the gaping hole in my chest. I couldn't, so I said nothing.

"Let's get you cleaned up," she added, grabbing a waste basket and throwing the tissues inside. I took a deep breath, knowing I needed to get up, but I could barely move. I stared at the comforter and decided to lie back down. The Egyptian cotton mocked me, so I dragged myself into a sitting position, slinging my legs off the side of the bed.

I willed myself up and shuffled over to my bathroom, with Danielle following behind me. The reflection in the mirror was startling. I had been used to seeing my seventeen-year-old self. Now, I was staring at the old me. The one I left behind. The one whose face was now a red, splotchy mess.

"Why don't you splash some cold water on your face, honey," Danielle softly suggested. "Are you feeling any better?"

I filled the basin with cold water and watched my reflection. I nodded almost imperceptibly at both Danielle and at the reflection that was practically that of a stranger. Leaning over the sink, I submerged my face in the freezing water. The sting of the cold on my face sent a shiver through my body.

"Better," I replied as I stood up, sucking in a breath. Danielle handed me a towel and rubbed my back as I patted my face dry.

"You don't have to do this, you know. We're all fine staying here and ordering in. We have *Transformers 2* from Netflix."

The scene flashed before my eyes for a brief moment.

Megan, bent over the hood of a car, pointing out parts to Nate and the rest of the shop class. Our own version of Megan Fox. I remembered Luke, leaning casually at the back of the class with me. 'She's not my type, Cross', he had said.

I had to keep reminding myself that he was just a fabrication. How was I ever going to function without thinking of him?

"I'm good. Really," I lied. "Let me just put on some makeup and fix my hair. I'll be out in a second."

She didn't look very convinced, but agreed, returning to the living room with the others.

I looked into the mirror once again. My reflection wasn't as red, wasn't as puffy as it had been a few minutes ago, but it was still incredibly sad. Taking a deep breath, I told myself that I just needed to make it through an hour or so at the reunion. It shouldn't be that bad. Hell, on some subconscious level, I had been going to school with these people for the last month. It should be second nature to me. After an hour, I could come home, crawl into bed and sleep away this nightmare.

After fixing my hair and makeup, I gave myself a quick nod and headed to the living room. The lively conversation stopped as everyone stared at me like I was off to the firing squad.

"Oh God, please don't stare at the crazy girl. It's not polite," I whined, grabbing my jacket from the coat tree. "Are we ready?"

"Jillian…"

"Josh, please," I interrupted. "Can we just go?"

He nodded grimly as they all followed me out the door.

I drove with Danielle and Josh. Nate and Megan followed us in Meg's car. I didn't say much on the ride over. The upside of having this nervous breakdown occur when it did was that I wasn't the least bit anxious about the reunion.

We pulled into a parking lot packed with cars. It was in a part of town we didn't usually frequent. There was a restaurant a few streets over that we liked, but we had never really ventured this far over.

"Is this the place?" I asked, pointing to the sign above the door that said The Big Leap.

"Um...yeah," Danielle replied. "I hope you can relax and have a little fun tonight."

That was a new one. Usually this was the part where she told me not to throw up on her.

Once Josh pulled the large door open, we were able to get a better look at the place. The dark wood bar ran the length of the room. All of the deep, maroon-upholstered barstools were occupied by customers. Black and white photographs were dispersed along the wall. They were reminiscent of Ansel Adams, with shots of the night sky, rocky ledges and crashing waves. It made for a striking contrast with the dark paneling.

"There's Sarah," Megan groaned. "Hurry, slide into a booth. I need alcohol before I talk to her."

I ended up sandwiched between Danielle and Megan. At least I could hide behind Meg if someone came along that I didn't feel like talking to.

An attractive waiter came over to the booth just in time. Megan was getting anxious.

"Evening, folks. You here with the reunion?" he asked. His smile was wide and inviting. It made me want to smile back.

"That's right," Nate replied. "So we'll need you to keep sending pitchers over to keep these lushes satisfied."

"All right," he laughed. "Anything else?"

"I'll have a water, too," Nate added.

"Sounds good, folks. My name's Peter. Just give me a shout if you need anything else."

"Water tonight?" Josh asked Nate.

"Yeah, I have to report at—"

"Megan Dunn!" we heard a nasally voice squeal.

"Hey…Sarah," she replied, forced into a conversation sans beer.

"I have been dying to talk to you. Let me see it!" She reached her hand out towards Meg. I watched the exchange completely confused. Megan brought her left hand out from under the table and placed it in Sarah's. The glint coming from her ring finger nearly blinded me. But as my blurry eyes focused on the engagement ring my best friend was wearing, I suddenly saw in my mind a scene play out.

Megan, running into the apartment, squealing that she had news. Nate following sheepishly behind her as we hurry out into the living room.

"Who wants to be a bridesmaid?!" she yells, lifting up her hand much like she was doing now. We grab each other, jumping up and down, laughing and crying.

"Megan, I have to tell you," Danielle begins dramatically, wiping away her tears. "I look awful in yellow."

We all break into a fit of laughter.

I can smell the brownies I had been making in the kitchen. I can feel the tears on my face.

It doesn't feel like a dream.

"The girls and I are going dress shopping in the morning. Nate has practice tomorrow because the game's on Monday night this week," she added casually. "You're playing the Chargers, right, baby?"

For the second time in the same night, I felt the bile rise up into my mouth.

"I need to get out," I panted, pushing Megan aside to move.

"Are you okay?" Danielle asked.

"I just…bathroom…" I stammered.

The minute Megan stood, I took off.

Megan and Nate were engaged. Engaged. They weren't engaged before I hit my head. They were engaged now. As I walked briskly through the bar, another image played in my mind.

We're huddled in a crowded living room. Nate, his parents and his granddaddy, Megan and her mom, Danielle, Josh and me. We're watching the television nervously. The phone rings and we jump, listening as Nate answers it. Megan grabs one of my hands and one of Danielle's. She looks up at the ceiling, her lips are moving in a silent prayer.

"Thank you, Coach," he says into the phone, wiping at his eye. He hangs up, pauses for a second and grabs Megan, spinning her around.

"Seahawks, baby," he exclaims. "Seahawks."

I slammed into a wall, not really paying attention to where I was going. I could still feel how tightly she held onto my hand. Stumbling into the bathroom, I backed myself up against the wall as I was assaulted by a flood of images.

Weekends at home in college, crying myself to sleep. Being forced to accompany the girls on their outings. Agreeing grudgingly. Helping Danielle write her business plan. Encouraging her to open the business on her own. Her first small office in Seattle. How nervous she was when she landed her first client. Going with her as an "associate". Attending Nate's first game as a Seahawk, decked out in dark blue, cheering wildly in the stands.

Danielle and Josh cuddling on the couch, barely acknowledging anyone around them. Happy, content. Megan and Nate celebrating their engagement. Happy, content. Me, in my bedroom. Alone.

Inside the safety of the ladies' room, I did the only thing I could think to do. Slowly, I pulled down the corner of my ridiculous skinny jeans, exposing my hipbone. There on my pale skin, in all its glory, was a Celtic cross.

I flew into a stall, retching, as I fell to the floor.

It was real.

My new "memories" confirmed that everything was different, everything except me. I was trying desperately to hold it together, but the more I began to see how I had affected the past, the faster my heart began to race. I didn't have the luxury of being able to hang out in the bathroom all night, though. Plus, I just threw up there and it was really gross. I needed to pull myself together, go back to the table and try to act like I was fine—that I wasn't having a complete nervous breakdown.

I pulled myself up off the cold floor and walked unsteadily towards the door. Taking a deep breath, I pulled the door open and stepped back into the dark hallway, but once I was there, I couldn't get myself to move toward the table. I didn't even know how to talk to these people anymore. How could I keep track of what was real anymore?

I closed my eyes, attempting to gather up my courage. I took deep breaths. I counted to ten. When that didn't work, I tried counting higher, breathing deeper. I finally focused on one of the black and white photos in front of me. This one was of a constellation that looked like the Big Dipper. The small, gold plaque at the bottom of the frame confirmed it was Ursa Major. There was another similar picture of Orion a little further down the hallway in the same kind of frame with the same gold plaque. Walking further along, I stopped at the entryway to the bar where two framed shots hung high above the doorway side by side. Deep down, I knew what words I'd see on the gold plaque, but I craned my neck to get a closer look. My heart beat wildly in my chest as I saw "The Phoenix" and "The Northern Cross" engraved underneath.

Suddenly, I felt like I was underwater. I couldn't hear the chatter coming from the other room. I couldn't see anything, but the names at the bottom of the pictures. I couldn't think of anything but Luke. Staggering back against the wall, panting, I stared up at the frames again in abject horror.

This wasn't a random bar. This was Luke's bar.

I quickly abandoned any plan that involved going back to the table and trying to act normal. This was way more than I could possibly handle. I needed to leave—fast—and preferably without having to speak to anyone whose life I may or may not have permanently altered.

Turning back down the hallway, I raced towards the emergency exit. The door was slightly ajar, and the cool air was filtering in. My chest felt tight and I could barely breathe. I stumbled into the alley, panting and shaking. I wasn't ready for this. I wasn't ready to face Luke.

Pacing, I began plotting my escape, but kept running into road blocks. No matter how I looked at it, my ride home was inside the bar and my purse was still at the table with all my money. My only option, aside from begging a cab driver to accept an IOU, was to retrieve my purse and bolt out the door before anyone could stop me. It didn't seem likely.

I was still looking for an exit strategy when I heard the creaking of the door hinges behind me. Startled, I spun around and gasped at the figure in the doorway.

It was him.

231

He was older now, with the scruff of a five o'clock shadow on his jaw. Even his features appeared sharper, more angular. But the hair was the same, a little shorter on the sides, but the same wild mess I imagined running my fingers through that first day behind the gym.

There was no mistake. He was the man in the black and white Facebook photo. The man who caught my eye almost four weeks ago. The man with the smile that made my heart leap. For the briefest moment, he seemed frozen in place as we stared blankly at each other. The pain of leaving him was so fresh that I was unable to say or do anything. I missed him so much.

His eyes narrowed almost imperceptibly and his lips pressed into a hard line. I thought I saw his nostrils flare. The hostile expression faded so quickly though, that I questioned whether or not I had seen him look angry at all. He suddenly seemed passive, unaffected by my presence.

"Jillian," he greeted me formally. He pulled out a pack of cigarettes, lighting one and blowing a stream of smoke off to the side. I cursed myself for watching his lips. Those were the lips that touched mine just two days ago. At least it was two days for me.

"Luke, I—"

"Are Josh and Nate here, too? I really should swing by and say hey," he interrupted, stubbing out the cigarette he had just lit. "Good to see you." He barely looked my way as he turned and stepped back into the bar.

I stood there, chanting to myself that I wouldn't cry. I couldn't make matters worse with yet another breakdown. Not in public. Not in front of him. Especially now that he hated me.

I stared at the door where he had stood. He wasn't the boy I knew anymore. He wasn't the same because of me. I broke his heart. I deserved the anger. I deserved the indifference even though I had done what I thought was right. I might never be able to explain that to him and he might never forgive me, but I did it for him.

And now, standing outside his bar in the cold night, there was one thing I was certain of. Leaving him once nearly killed me; I wasn't going to be able to do it again. I needed him. And I hoped, deep down, he still needed me, too.

CHAPTER 19

Danielle

I was driving down the highway on my way back to Reynolds when I heard the Mariah Carey song on the radio. For the rest of my life, I swear I will never think of anything but punch and puke when I hear it. Things had been going so well on prom night until Jillian went all Courtney Love on us.

I had this dream back then. It was silly, really. Jillian, Megan and I all living on the same street. We'd be in this cozy little neighborhood with pastel-colored cottages and white picket fences lining each side. My house would naturally be a little bit cuter than the others. The grass would be emerald green and the sky, at least in my fantasy, would always be blue. Our kids would play together on the lawn. Megan's kid would spend most of the day in time-out because you just know she would be mouthy. We would sit on one of our porches, laughing, gossiping and talking about our husbands. It would be perfect.

I blame the daydreaming on Luke. We hadn't been in the limo for more than five minutes when I caught him staring at Jillian as she teased Megan and Nate about their pre-prom hook-up. It was just a look. If I'd glanced over a second later, I probably would have missed it. But I didn't. There was something in his eyes when he watched her. I was so sure about them. Everyone had been laughing and having a great time. We all just seemed to fit together. Sure, it may have been a bit premature to envision the house, picket fence, and two-point-five kids. It had only been the first time Jillian had gone out with Luke…and what ended up being the *only* time she ever went out with Luke. So, as much as I was sure at the time that they had been a perfect match, I guess I was wrong.

I had always fancied myself a bit of a matchmaker. I did it with Rebecca and Paul back in middle school and then again with Maria and Kirk in ninth grade. Of course, Kirk cheated on Maria with Val, but they were really cute when he wasn't sleeping with other people.

When we got to New York, I launched my search for her Mr. Right Now. I scoured the student directory, canvassed the frat houses and searched the campus for that love connection Jillian had helped Megan find with Nate. It wasn't that there weren't viable candidates. There were tons. Jillian just shot me down after every attempt. She flat-out refused to even discuss getting fixed up. When I would ask her to come with me to Fordham when I visited Josh, she would insist on staying at the apartment, always claiming that she had an article to write for the newspaper or a paper that needed research. She would socialize when forced. She would laugh at something funny. She would listen when I needed to talk. But something was different about Jillian despite her protests to the contrary. I was just never able to figure out what it was.

By the time spring semester ended, she hadn't gone on one date our entire freshman year.

The next year brought only a slight improvement. She went through the motions and went out occasionally. She never dated anyone regularly—no one I would have called a boyfriend. I even asked her carefully one night if I should be expanding my search to the ...um...fairer sex. She punched my arm. Hard. I just wanted her to know that I supported any of her decisions completely. She didn't need to resort to violence.

By junior year, I started writing the business plan for my design company. Jillian spent a lot of her time in the library, and I...well, I usually didn't, so I was pretty lost. I think that's why she was so insistent about helping me write my business plan, and I wasn't above accepting her pity. Honestly, I wouldn't have been able to get through the process without her. I wouldn't have been able to do *any* of it without her. When I would get frustrated, it was Jillian who would tell me to buck up.

"Listen, Mona Whiner, you are going to do amazing things," she said one Saturday night while we were buried in textbooks. "Stop complaining and check this book for population statistics so we can estimate your target market."

"You are unbelievable," I replied, shaking my head. "It's Saturday night and you're here, cheering me on instead of doing something fun like running through the quad naked. There must be something you'd rather be doing!"

"Not really," she sighed sadly. "At any rate, I'm the president of the Danielle Powers Fan Club. I'll throw down with Josh for that distinction, and I'm going to hold your hand every step of the way because I know you were born to do this. You're so talented, Danielle," she added. "Now, let's get to work."

By senior year, Jillian knew almost as much about the design industry as I did. She even disagreed with the design for my final exam, telling me that I wasn't *maximizing the natural light* in the loft I decorated. I disagreed, but I had to appreciate her gumption. I had created a monster, but at least the monster spoke my language.

When it came time for me to go on my first client meeting, I dragged her with me. The client naturally loved us because we're adorable and we make a fantastic team. When I showed him the plans I worked up for his remodel, he was blown away. Jillian asked if she could take a series of photographs once I finished, and ended up writing an amazing article about the evolution of Craftsman decor. *Better Homes* picked it up, Jillian landed a steady gig freelancing, and my phone never stopped ringing.

That was what led me to my trip back to our alma mater, Reynolds High School. I got a call from the secretary at the school asking if I'd like to participate in Career Day.

Me.

Sometimes I still find it hard to believe that it was my name on the sign hanging outside of the office. Or that it was my name on the business cards. Jillian always said that I would've been able to do it without her, but I wasn't so sure.

As I passed through the familiar streets, I glanced at the clock on the dash, realizing that I had yet to eat anything all day. I had some time to kill, so I decided to zip over to the supermarket to grab a salad. The last thing I needed was for my stomach to start growling as I talked to these kids. I'm short. My stomach would be really close to the microphone.

Heading towards the salad bar, I stopped short when I saw a familiar face. Luke Chambers. Hanging out in the baking aisle? And man, did he look confused.

"Luke?" He turned around tentatively. "God, Luke, it's been years!"

He looked good, maybe a little bit uncomfortable.

"How've you been, kid?" he asked with a tight smile. It wasn't exactly the warmest reception in the world.

"I'm good," I replied. "You'll never guess why I'm in town. They asked me to speak at Reynolds High Career Day! Isn't that a riot?"

"Looks like you've done well for yourself," he said, folding his arms in front of his chest awkwardly.

"Well, it's a lot of work, but yeah, the business is doing well. I have some great people around me helping out, too. I mean, I would never have been able to do it without Jillian."

The tight smile that was barely welcoming, fell. He just stared at me, blinking for a minute, looking as if he were a hundred miles away.

"Luke? Are you okay?"

"Huh? Yeah. Sorry. That's good...that you have support and friends helping," he stammered. "I...um...I own a bar in Seattle."

"You're kidding? How did I not know this? What's it called?"

It seemed like a perfectly acceptable question to me, but Luke seemed reluctant to answer. What kind of bar *was* this?

"It's called...um...The Big Leap...but it's mostly a college bar. Probably not your scene," he explained, cautiously.

I was about to press him for the address when an older, attractive man with blond hair and sharp features came up behind us with his hands full of spice jars.

"You can never be too careful with a culinary genius," he joked, holding up the jars.

"Danielle, this is my uncle, Carter Chambers. Carter, this is Danielle Powers."

"Fletcher, actually," I corrected. "Josh and I were married three years ago."

While I hadn't expected epic fanfare, I wasn't expecting Luke to scowl either. I always thought he liked Josh.

"Nice to meet you, Danielle," his uncle added, nodding because of the items in his hands.

"Well, I don't want to keep you, but I'd love to come by with the gang and see the bar. Can I get your email address?" I dug into my purse, looking for my phone.

"I don't check my email very often," he added, shaking his head warily.

"Are you on Facebook? Twitter? LinkedIn?"

I mean, really, this is the Information Age. Was he always this difficult?

"Um, I'm on Facebook, but I never log in so..."

"Oh, great! Just change your settings so that you get an alert when someone posts on your page. Then you'll know when I message you. Yay! We'll set

236

something up soon," I added. "Nice meeting you, Mr. Chambers. Talk to you soon, Luke!"

A life without Facebook. I just can't imagine. Poor, uninformed Luke.

I waved a quick goodbye, relieved to be away from such a tense meeting. I knew some people hate running into old friends from high school, but that had been more painful than it needed to be. I had no idea Luke was so socially awkward.

When I arrived at the school, I checked in at the office. Everything seemed so much smaller. It was strange seeing the young school secretary behind Mrs. Jankowski's desk. She wasn't much younger than me.

"Hi, I'm Danielle Fletcher," I said to the girl behind the desk. She looked vaguely familiar.

"Danielle Powers?" she asked, looking at me inquisitively.

"Yes," I replied, searching her face. "I thought you looked familiar, but I'm sorry, I can't place how I know you."

"Anne-Marie Matthews. Well, I *was* Anne-Marie Matthews. I was a junior when you were a senior," she explained with an easy smile.

"Oh, I remember you! You dated Jon Nolan," I replied, suddenly remembering how they played tonsil-hockey in the cafeteria every day. So gross.

"That's me," she said, raising the back of her hand up to show me her ring. "I'm Anne-Marie Nolan now. And you married Josh Fletcher?"

"Yes, actually, we had a lot of people from high school in the wedding—Megan Dunn, Nate Barrett, Jillian Cross."

"Oh, Jillian! Is she still with Luke Chambers?" she asked with a gleam in her eyes.

"Oh no, no, they weren't together. She just went with him to the prom," I explained. It was such a strange thing to ask.

"Oh, you don't have to keep it a secret from me," she giggled. "I used to see them behind the gym together all the time. People complained about me and Jon, but those two gave us a run for our money." She laughed heartily while I just stared blankly at her. I knew I was just opening my mouth and closing it—not actually making any sound—but I couldn't stop. I didn't exactly know what to do with this information.

"Right...yeah...are you sure you meant Jillian Cross?" I asked, not entirely convinced that this wasn't just a big misunderstanding. I mean, what if Anne-Marie was crazy? She sucked her boyfriend's face off in public every day. For all I knew, that could have caused severe brain damage.

"You should have seen Luke the last day of school when we interrupted them. He seemed to have laid claim to the area behind the gym, and apparently we invaded their turf," she explained, laughing.

I was absolutely reeling. What do you say when you learn your best friend has been hiding something from you for over a decade? I thought back to Luke's reaction at the supermarket—how uncomfortable he was, how he looked physically ill when I mentioned Jillian. Then there was Jillian's surprise departure from Reynolds, just two days after the prom. In New York, she acted like she was a different person. Was it because of him?

I needed to test my theory. I needed to be sure, and there was only one way to do it.

"Excuse me a moment, Anne-Marie," I stammered, grabbing my iPhone as I walked into the hallway.

I shot Megan a quick message asking her to meet me for drinks at eight. I planned to fill her in and if she already knew, I'd have two asses to kick.

Opening my browser, I launched Facebook and searched for Luke's profile. He wasn't kidding when he said he didn't use it much. He didn't even have a decent profile picture. It was just a shot of what I assumed was his bar. Without a second thought, I sent him a Friend Request.

Dazed, I headed back into the office, attempting to make polite conversation with Anne-Marie until it was my time to speak.

I was told that I gave a good speech at Career Day, but I couldn't tell you what was said. My mind was focused on my best friend and Luke Chambers. Why didn't she think she could trust us? What happened, and why did it end?

By the time I got to O'Malley's, Megan was already in the booth waiting for me. I had spent the entire drive putting together a plan. I just needed to get Meg onboard.

"Let me get this straight," she said, placing her beer down on the table. "Jillian and Luke were getting it on in high school without telling anyone?" she asked incredulously. "I don't believe it."

"Classy. I didn't say they were 'getting it on'. I just know something was going on with them. Then she decides to leave for New York early and suddenly becomes all Winona in *Beetlejuice*. These are the facts."

"But why would she keep it a secret? Sure, we'd make fun of her because, Jesus, he was so broody and shit, but that's not a reason to sneak around."

"Well, she obviously had her reasons. Now the question is—what do we do about it?"

"What do you mean? It was over ten years ago."

"Yes, and has she moved on? And if you were in the supermarket with me today, you'd be pretty convinced that Luke hadn't either."

"You're basing all of this off something a girl we hardly knew said to you."

She had a point, but Anne-Marie referenced more than one occasion. Something told me that this wasn't a fluke.

"If I'm wrong, no harm done," I shrugged.

"So, what're you proposing?"

"A class reunion. At Luke's bar." I winced, knowing Meg wouldn't be a big fan of the idea.

"Oh, Christ. So you need to subject me to Sarah Spellman just to get the two of them in the same room? Why, Danielle? Why so mean?"

"Buck up. I won't stop you if you want to make fun of her boobs," I offered.

"Yes!" she hissed, pumping both fists. "So how do we do this?"

"We hop on Facebook and start sending out invitations."

I knew the plan could backfire. It could be an utter disaster. I couldn't even be sure that this would make her happy, but I had to find out. I had to try and pay Jillian back for all of the things that she had done for me over the years. I owed her so much.

It took a few days to receive the notification that Luke had accepted my Friend Request. I was getting pretty nervous, and honestly, a little annoyed that he hadn't paid attention to my directions. You see a notification. You accept it. Facebook isn't rocket science.

I poured over all of the details in his profile. It didn't take long. He was single, as I suspected. There were no photos, and only a few people posted on his wall. Most of them mentioned how great the bar was—nothing personal. The boy really needed a lesson in Facebooking 101. His profile was boring as hell.

"What's got you looking so serious?" Josh asked, looking up from his brief.

"I'm looking at Luke's Facebook page and it's dismal. I'm sending him a message about the reunion."

"Tell him he still hasn't accepted my Friend Request, and he owes me twenty bucks. Jillian was the first to puke on prom night, not you."

"You bet that I would puke on prom night?!"

"No, I bet you *wouldn't* puke on prom night. He thought you'd be excited about the Prom Queen thing and would drink too much. You *are* excitable, honey," he hedged.

"Not speaking to you, Josh," I retorted, turning back to type on my iPhone.

Luke – It was so good to see you last week. It got me thinking about high school, and before I knew it I was planning a reunion. Your bar seemed like the logical choice. I hope you don't mind. Did you get Josh's Friend Request? He says you still owe him $20. See you soon! Danielle

I pressed send and waited.

Reunion Night didn't start off very well. I was at Jillian and Megan's apartment helping Jillian get ready when I heard a gasp and a loud thump. When I went running into her bedroom, I found Jillian in a lump on the floor.

I was ready to scrap the entire plan. Megan was giving me dirty looks, pleading with me to keep her home, but Jillian insisted she'd be all right. I kept a close eye on her, but things got hectic once we were inside the bar. Sarah pounced on Megan as soon as we sat down, distracting me with the asymmetrical tube dress that wasn't supposed to be asymmetrical. Before I knew it, Jillian was pushing her way out of the booth to run to the bathroom.

As I turned to move out of the booth, I noticed Luke heading towards us.

"There he is!" Nate cheered, standing up and clapping him on the back.

"Nate, man, good to see you," he replied. "And I think I owe you few drinks, Fletcher."

"And I'll be collecting," Josh laughed. "We need to get together without these high school bozos and grab a few beers, man. It's been too long."

"That sounds good," he replied happily.

"Hey, are you working on Wednesday night?" Nate asked. I shot Megan a look. I hadn't even thought about inviting him.

"I usually take Tuesday and Wednesday off," he replied. "It's slower."

Nate was better at this than we were, and he had no idea that we were even scheming.

"Excellent! Danielle's opening her design showroom and she's having a cocktail thing. Don't worry. She isn't making us wear tuxes this time," Nate explained, giving me a dirty look. Was it so much to ask them to dress up for my Holiday Open House? I didn't think so.

The panic was evident on Luke's face, but he had already admitted to having no plans. I think he knew he was stuck.

"Um...sure...yeah...that'd be fun," he said half-heartedly.

Megan better give Nate a big reward.

"Well, I have a few things to handle out back. I'll see you before you leave?"

"Absolutely," I added. Luke nodded, heading down the hall and disappearing into a door near the restrooms.

"Do you know what, Nate?" Megan asked, slyly. "I am so doing that thing you like tonight."

"*The* thing?" he said with wide eyes.

"Oh, yes. *The* thing."

"Can we leave now?" he asked, straight-faced.

"Settle down, Big Boy. Just know that you did good," she added with a wink.

"What are you two up to?" Josh asked, eyeing us suspiciously.

"Just sit and look pretty, Josh. Let me handle the tough stuff."

241

This was perfect. Luke. Jillian. My Grand Opening. This I could work with. I might need to do some questionable things, and I would most likely piss her off, but if I could make this right for her, it would be worth it. Because it was never really about pastel houses and white picket fences. It was about being happy. And if I needed to jump through hoops to make this happen for her, I would. I just hoped she didn't kill me in the process.

It was time for the members of Operation Nate to join forces. Operation Luke had commenced. Jillian just didn't know it yet.

CHAPTER 20

Lake

I wasn't a pacer. I couldn't even say I had any nervous habits, but at the rate I was going, I would burn a path into my office carpet before last call.

No matter how prepared I'd been, no matter how many times I imagined the conversation, no matter how hard I convinced myself that none of it ever mattered, I was still completely unprepared to see her again. It took less than five minutes to feel like I was eighteen.

I wasn't stupid. I obviously knew I'd run into her at some point during the night. I was just expecting some warning first. But it was even more awkward than the day we met all those years ago. It felt like a lifetime ago when I stared at her red lips and wondered what it would be like to kiss her. Now that I knew, I wished I could forget.

More than ten years had passed. Her lips weren't as red, and her hair wasn't as long. Her body was much curvier than it used to be, but her eyes were just as big, just as brown. When she looked at me, I could tell that she was about to say something—make some excuse—about how it wasn't me, how she was doing me a favor, how she wanted to be friends. I couldn't just stand there while she spewed that bullshit. I wouldn't.

So I left to find Nate and Josh, but mostly to maintain some dignity. I was mad at Danielle for having this stupid thing at my bar. I was mad at Peter for thinking it was funny. I was mad at Jillian for looking at me the way she did. But mostly, I was mad at how much it all still bothered me. I hated myself for that the most.

So I paced, listening to my former classmates laughing and joking, knowing she was out there on the other side of that door. But even though I would have sold my soul for a chance to skip the rest of the night altogether, I knew I couldn't hide out in my office forever. It was almost last call, and Peter would need my help closing down. I had to man up.

Cursing the fact that I never finished my cigarette, I begrudgingly headed directly to the bar, not looking around—definitely not looking for her. When I took my place next to Peter, he was already giving me the side-eye.

"Thanks for stopping by, Romeo," he said. "Don't mind me. I'm just trying to run your bar here."

I rolled my eyes, brushing past him to grab a clean rack of glasses from underneath the bar.

"So, I take it from your chipper mood that things didn't go so well with Juliet," he added.

"You don't know what you're talking about," I muttered. Because he didn't.

Out of habit, I looked up and scanned the room, finding aged versions of people I used to know scattered throughout the bar. Val Cooper looked pretty spent, rubbing the shoulders of some guy I recognized from my shop class. Her dress was too tight and her face was pulled back. It looked like she may have purchased a new nose at some point, but the guy didn't seem to mind.

Karen Larson was definitely getting shut off. She was trying to start some kind of sing-a-long, but she was the only one actually singing. It was almost as bad as that song she sang at the prom. And that was saying a lot.

Everywhere I looked, I saw people I used to know doing the same things they were doing back when I knew them. Mike Wakefield still looked like a massive tool, and I still wanted to kick his ass. Maybe we never really leave high school. Or maybe high school never leaves us.

I was looking for some mundane task that would help me forget what an idiot I was when I saw everyone at her table stand up, pull on their coats and get ready to leave. Nate made his way over to me first.

"Hey, man, we're taking off. It was good to see you," he said, slapping me on the back again.

"We'll see you on Wednesday, though. First round's on me," Josh added, throwing his arm over my shoulder.

"It's an open bar, Josh," Danielle interrupted.

"Then they're all on me, aren't they?" he countered.

"The man has a point, Danielle," Megan chimed in.

I was trying to avoid Jillian, but it was impossible to ignore how uncomfortable she looked. Standing—practically hiding—behind Megan with her head tipped down, she barely took part in the conversation at all. If she was expecting me to make her feel more comfortable, she was crazy. The only comfort I had was that the bar was about to close and this night was almost over. When Peter flipped the lights on signaling last call, I jumped at the opportunity to make an exit.

"That's my cue," I added, shaking Nate's hand and then grabbing Josh's. "I guess I'll see you all on Wednesday."

Jillian finally lifted her head up slowly—and maybe I was wrong—but it looked like she was about to cry. I needed to get out of there. What right did she have to play the victim here? Why was she acting like this wasn't all her own fault? I had already spent far too much time trying to figure out what the hell went on in that girl's mind and I wasn't going to do it anymore. I turned away, struggling to control the anger brewing inside. With a wave and a tight smile, I returned to the bar before I did anything I'd regret. I didn't even look up when I heard the door close.

Later on, when the bar was empty and the floors were swept, I sat slumped over the counter, staring at a beer I didn't even want. Hours had passed, and the tightening in my chest was still as intense as it was when I first saw her because it really wasn't over. I'd have to do it all over again at Danielle's opening on Wednesday. I'd have to pretend it wasn't uncomfortable. I'd have to plaster a smile on my face. I'd have to stop myself from asking her what the hell happened. I'd have to risk saying too much because it all still seemed so raw. And I hated feeling that way.

The next few days passed in a blur. Sundays were always hectic during football season, and there was a Mariners game on Monday. I had a loyal clientele on game days so that kept me and the bar busy. I was distracted, though, forgetting to fax paperwork to one of the liquor distributors, and missing a business lunch I had scheduled with my attorney. By Tuesday, I was so tense and frustrated, I could barely sit still. For the first time in months, I took my bike out of storage and rode the coast. It gave me a chance to clear my head—get some perspective. I was acting like an idiot. And over a girl I never technically dated. As angry as I was at how things turned out, I had to cut the shit and move on.

That night, it didn't take long to reach Danielle's showroom in Magnolia Village. From the outside, the building looked small, but once I was inside, I was surprised at how much room she had. The old warehouse had been converted into a giant, open space, broken off into small segments with each area set up like rooms in a house. There were areas mocked up to look like living rooms, bedrooms, home offices. While I probably wasn't picking up on the nuances in each design, I knew that everything looked nice. She'd done well for herself.

I wandered through the "rooms" until I reached the bar that was set up at the back of the building. The place was packed with people, but most everyone seemed to gravitate toward the cocktail reception in the back. As I made my way through the crowd, I spotted Danielle talking to a small group of people and gesturing wildly. Once she saw me, she practically ran over any party-goers in her way to reach me.

"Luke!" she exclaimed. "You're here!" She was wearing a short, red dress, and looking every bit the spitfire I remembered. She was practically bouncing. "My, my. Don't you look nice," she remarked, sounding surprised. Maybe she expected me to show up on my bike, wearing a leather jacket. I couldn't expect her to know how much of my time lately has been spent in meetings with developers, lawyers and bankers. I was well-stocked in the suit department.

"Nice place you have here, kid. I'm impressed."

"Why, thank you!" she beamed. "I'm pretty proud of it myself. Can I get you a drink?"

"I was just heading over to the bar."

"No, no," she replied. "I'll grab Josh. Let him do it since he claims to have financed it."

I started to laugh, surprised that she wasn't the uptight mess I remembered. Maybe the Poor Bastard had gotten her to lighten up a bit.

She raised her hand up, signaling across the room to Josh who was wearing a black suit that resembled the tux he wore to the prom. At least this time there was no top hat or cane. When he looked up, the person he had been speaking to did as well. It was only then that I noticed he had been talking to Jillian. It was hard to recognize her at first with her head down and her hair shielding her face. I stared a little longer than I should have. I tried not to focus on the fitted, black dress she wore, but that only caused me to focus on it even more. Focusing was bad on all levels. I watched as she whispered something to Josh then disappeared into the crowd. I was still watching the empty space where she had been standing when Josh reached us.

"Josh, can you get Luke a drink and then show him around a bit?" she asked, flashing her dimples.

"You've got it, babe," he replied, pecking her on the cheek. "Follow me."

We made a beeline for the bar, passing through the crowds of people. I had never wanted a beer so badly in my whole life.

"What'll it be?" the young kid behind the bar asked.

"Whatever you have on draft is fine," I replied.

"Wow, you're a cheap date, Chambers. Is this the same guy that smuggled Jack into school?"

"That wasn't for me," I answered quickly. "That was for—"

I stopped myself before I began explaining that it had been for Jillian. I had no idea how much, if anything, he knew about what went on with us in high school. Maybe he thought we went to the prom together and it wasn't a big deal. Maybe he knew more. Maybe her disappearance had been a big joke for years.

"That was for something else," I muttered, in no mood to find out which it was.

"Something else, my ass," he replied. "You've gone soft. This makes me sad."

The young bartender handed me my glass and I watched as he poured Josh's scotch. I could tell right away that he was new at the job. He didn't quite have the confidence that comes from knowing your way around a bar. He reminded me of myself many years ago. Digging in my pocket, I pulled out a ten and jammed it into the glass jar on the counter.

"Mr. Fletcher." A young girl approached us, her voice in a hushed, urgent tone. "There's a problem out front. Someone parked in the fire lane and Mrs. Fletcher is convinced she's going to be shut down if we don't find the owner."

"My glamorous life," he said looking over at me. "A glorified valet."

"Don't worry about it, man," I replied, laughing. "Go do your thing."

"Danielle will kill me if you don't get the VIP tour. Maybe…" He craned his neck, looking out over the crowd. "Hey, Jill," he called, looking over the heads of the people standing in front of us. She whipped around at the sound of her name, hair everywhere, her face blank and unreadable. She walked towards us tentatively, forcing a tight smile on her face as she approached.

"Can you show your old prom date around? Danielle wanted me to do it, but there's an issue with the parking. Plus, you're much better at this stuff than I am."

Jillian's body language was a dead giveaway. She was as stiff as a board and her face was like stone. I think she may have stopped breathing.

"Um…sure," she replied, not sounding very convincing. I knew that it was shitty, but some part of me wanted her to be uncomfortable. Some part of me

247

wanted her to feel regret. It was stupid and immature, and obviously "some part of me" was twelve, but it was true. I wanted her to know what she gave up.

"After you," I insisted, motioning for her to lead the way.

"I'm sure you're not interested in a tour of her design room," she began, once Josh had left. She was fidgeting with the rings on her fingers, barely looking my way. "I'll tell them you loved it and let you off the hook."

But I didn't want to be let off the hook. I guess that didn't really jibe with that whole "letting it go" philosophy. Regardless, I wasn't going to bail on the tour.

"I was actually looking forward to it, but if there's some place else you need to be…"

"No, no, that's not what I meant," she stammered, shaking her head. "So…follow me."

If it had been another place and time, I would have enjoyed walking behind her. The black dress hugged her body and moved fluidly along with her. The fabric grazed the top of her knee, accentuating her long legs. It cinched a little at her waist, showing off her curves. In another place and time, I'd want to place my hands on the slight flare of her hips, and feel the smooth skin of her upper thigh. But that time was long gone.

We walked through mock-ups of kitchens and living rooms while Jillian prattled on awkwardly about Danielle's clients. Every now and then, I glanced over and had to remind myself not to look at the way her hair was swept over her shoulder and how her dress moved when she walked.

"So, these are the home office models."

She nervously motioned to a section of leather couches and dark wood desks as if she were on a game show. "Danielle works with a lot of smaller companies, setting up workspaces that help make employees feel more comfortable. They say it makes workers more productive."

"Very nice," I remarked, taking in the different styles. "I took a class on that."

She whipped around, caught off-guard. I should have been ashamed at how brazen I sounded. With anyone else I would have been.

"What?"

"The Hawthorne Studies. Frederick Taylor tried to prove that harsh lighting negatively affects worker productivity," I replied, even thought I knew that wasn't what she meant.

"Did you...was this in college?"

"U-Dub."

"But you said...you said college wasn't for you."

"Well, we all change our minds from time to time, right?" I replied.

She looked stricken and I knew I looked like the biggest dick. This wasn't how I wanted it to be. I hadn't meant for it to sound so cold. The words just seemed to fly out of my mouth. I wanted her to know that I wasn't the loser she knew in high school. I wanted her to know that I busted my ass and made something of myself. I wanted her to know that she didn't know anything about me anymore. But, listening to myself, I felt like I didn't know myself either. I sounded like an asshole.

"It was actually Nate who convinced me to enroll," I began, switching gears, thinking back to the day I ran into him. He was back from South Bend for the weekend, jogging down by the high school when I happened to drive by. I may have initially stopped because I wondered if he was still dating Megan, and if Megan was still in New York. I may also have been too much of an idiot to ask.

He was so happy to be playing football, and I was just so goddamn miserable. He called me on the change in my attitude right away, but I blamed it on work and the girl I was dating. I didn't mention that the girl had just asked me to take her to a Green Day concert and I almost lost my shit.

Thank you, Jillian, for ruining Green Day for me.

The girl ended up thinking I was a jerk, and I really didn't care enough to convince her otherwise. Being with Jillian seemed to have been the gift that kept on giving.

When the conversation switched to how much Nate loved Notre Dame, he thanked me for convincing him to talk to his dad about going there instead of FSU. I really hadn't done anything but tell him not to let other people make decisions for him. Then he turned the tables on me, asking why I decided not to enroll myself. He started talking about a business class he had to take as a requirement, suggesting that I should look into what they have available at U-Dub. What started off as a Saturday class on small business management, turned into a Bachelors Degree. I owed Nate for that.

"Wow, he never said anything...that's...that's great, Luke. Really."

And as if I needed something to make myself feel worse, she seemed so genuinely happy for me. How was it—even after all this time—I still said all the wrong things around her?

"We should probably get back," I added, as the guilt continued to wash over me.

"Yeah," she agreed softly. We walked quietly back to where the bar and refreshments were set up. The tour with Jillian had taken a lot longer than I had realized and the crowd had already thinned out. Danielle and Josh were standing by the bar with Megan and Nate. I had never been so grateful for the distraction.

"So, what did you think?" Danielle asked enthusiastically. "Did Jillian dazzle you with her knowledge of colors and textures?"

"You've got a great place here," I replied, dodging the question. I didn't want to dwell on what an ass I was. I wanted to change the subject. "Tell me. Have you ever worked on any restaurants or bars?"

"Well, last year I was hired by this small Irish pub that we go to because they wanted to bring in some authentic pieces directly from Ireland. I have some contacts over there and they made some calls. Long story short, the bar, the seating, even the wood flooring were all made in Killkenney and sent over to Seattle in pieces. We had everything reassembled and installed—one-hundred percent authentic. You should swing by and check it out. It's called O'Malley's."

I almost choked when she mentioned the name. What were the odds?

"I know it well," I replied. "I actually just bought the bar next door."

The group erupted with gasps and congratulatory pats on the back. My eyes were trained on Jillian, though, who looked shocked. At least shock, I'd learned, was better than pity.

"Excuse me for a moment. I need to run to the ladies room," she muttered, walking briskly through the crowd and out of sight.

"You bought The Rusted Nail?" Nate laughed, drawing my attention away from Jillian's sudden retreat. "Dude, that place is a mess. Meg's friend got food poisoning there a few months ago."

"Yeah, that's why it was up for sale," I replied. "The health department closed them down, and the owner couldn't afford to make the necessary

250

improvements. Which is why I asked," I added, looking to Danielle. "I could use some help with the remodel."

"Oh my goodness!" she gasped. "Really? Do you have any ideas about style or theme?"

"The deal just finalized, but I have some rough sketches," I added, leaving out that my sketches looked like a five-year old drew them.

"Oh!" she squealed, clasping her hands together. "We could head back to your place when we're done here and I'll show you some samples. Can I take some measurements this week? What's your schedule like?"

My head began to spin with the barrage of questions. It was definitely reminiscent of the Danielle I remembered from high school, which made me wonder if I had made a big mistake.

"Slow down, baby, you don't want Luke to change his mind before he actually hires you," Josh interjected, rubbing her shoulders and calming her down.

"Oh, right," she laughed nervously. "I'm just excited. Would you mind, though, if we stopped back at the bar? I just want to get some preliminary information from you so I can draw up a proposal."

While I would have preferred to meet with her another time, I wanted to leave the party, and it was a good excuse. Instead of proving to Jillian that she passed up a good thing, I succeeded in proving I was a major dick. Not my finest hour.

"That's fine," I replied. "Are you cutting out of here soon?"

She looked down at her watch and scanned the dwindling crowd.

"Well, the clean-up crew is coming in at eleven-thirty. I can be by before last call."

I agreed to meet her at the bar, saying goodnight collectively to the group. While I was relieved that Jillian hadn't returned, I still felt strange taking off without saying anything. It was probably better that way. Nothing I said to her came out right.

On the drive back to the bar, I found myself feeling even worse about the way I'd acted. I let the way she looked at me turn me into someone I hardly recognized. I was proud of what I'd done—proud that I got my degree. Without it, I wouldn't be where I was. It wasn't something I should have hidden from them, but it wasn't something I should have bragged about either. When it came down to it, it shouldn't matter if I got my degree or if I was

251

successful. I would've wanted her to stay even if I never accomplished any of those things. I would have wanted her to stay in spite of it.

"Hey boss," Peter greeted me as I walked through the door. "What brings you in this fine evening?"

"Meeting a friend," I replied, sitting down on one of the stools.

"Well, we had a pretty decent night. Dying down now," he added. "Your lawyer dropped off some papers for you."

I groaned, thinking about the packet of information he had left for me to sign. The paper-trail was never-ending. Danielle wouldn't be arriving for another half-hour so I decided to look over the paperwork in my office while I waited.

Walking through the hall, I stopped to stare at the framed photos on the wall—photos put up by the guy who claimed he wasn't pining. *Sure he wasn't.* I hadn't seen the cliffs in over ten years—not after the night Carter found me there, brooding about the girl that had left without saying goodbye. I had no desire to go there because all I'd see is her. So, the place Carter had taken me so many times to work out my anger only fueled my frustration.

We adopted a new routine. He'd call my cell or I'd call his and we'd meet midway between Reynolds and Seattle at a small diner past Tacoma called The Last Resort. The food was decent, the coffee was passable, but more importantly, no one paid attention to anything we did or said. It was as good as being alone.

And then there were the times I'd look up to find Carter sliding into a side booth in the corner of the bar. He'd drink his coffee and read the newspaper until I had some time to sit down and talk. Sometimes he'd stay all afternoon. Seeing him kept me grounded. Unfortunately, I was feeling anything but grounded after the evening I just had.

Once I sat down at my desk, I couldn't concentrate on the paperwork the lawyer left for me. I organized some invoices and checked on a shipment that was due at the end of the week. When I still had some time to spare, I logged into Facebook since Danielle had been so adamant about me checking it regularly. I froze when I saw the alert—a Friend Request from Jillian.

I stared at the screen in disbelief. I honestly didn't know what to make of that. I didn't even know if it was rude to ignore one of these things. I only created a profile because Peter convinced me it would be good for the bar. But I barely checked my email. I really wasn't interested in posting updates online for random people I never saw. The whole thing seemed weird to me.

I sat with my finger hovering above the enter key, debating whether or not to click accept. I was thinking about what pictures she might have posted and who could be in them when my office phone rang. I logged out of my email as I picked up the call coming from out front.

"What's up, Pete?"

"Hey man, your friends are here," he informed me. I could hear Danielle's chatter in the background. As long as I kept Josh around, working with Danielle would be fine. He seemed to have a way of reeling her in and, truly, the girl *needed* to be reeled in. Poor Bastard must have learned some survival skills over the years.

I grabbed the plans for The Rusted Nail along with some of the rough sketches I had pulled together to remodel it into a restaurant. I was by no means an artist, but I had an idea of how I wanted the new place to look. As I passed by the pictures in the hall once again, I thought that maybe I should ask Danielle to do a little redecorating here as well. Maybe I didn't need closure. Maybe I just needed a change.

Walking out of the hallway and into the bar, it wasn't just Josh and Danielle I saw speaking to Peter, but Megan, Nate and Jillian, as well. I may not have wanted closure, but it seemed to keep looking for me.

"Hey, guys," I said, pressing my lips into a smile. My face felt tight and contorted. I wondered if I looked as uncomfortable as Jillian had looked earlier. I probably looked worse.

"Luke, can I just tell you how very honored I am that you're trusting me with this job. I'm so proud of you, and I want this new venture of yours to be the talk of the town," Danielle said.

It was sweet of her to say. I knew her feelings were genuine, and if I weren't so aware of the fact that Jillian was in the room, I might have been able to return the compliment without fumbling over my words. Instead I thanked her and motioned for them to follow me to a booth along the wall.

"Oh darn, I forgot my design book," she exclaimed. "Jillian, sweetie, I think I may have left it in your car."

"Why would it be in my car?" Jillian asked, sounding tired and confused.

"Remember I threw it in there when we were moving stuff over to the warehouse earlier today?"

She scrunched up her nose while she appeared to be thinking back to earlier in the day.

"I don't remember seeing it. Maybe you took it out already."

"Just to be sure, can I just grab your keys and take a quick peek? I may have shoved it under the seat."

"I'll go look," Jillian offered, pulling her keys from her purse. I couldn't blame her for wanting to go. If I could've gotten away with offering to look for it, I probably would have, too.

"No, no. I don't want you walking across the street to the lot alone. Josh will come with me. Right, honey?" she replied, grinning up at the Poor Bastard.

Jillian handed her keys to Danielle, then looked over to Megan and shrugged. When she looked away, I watched as Nate and Megan exchanged curious looks. Megan leaned in to whisper something into his ear.

"I'll be right back, Luke," Danielle announced, as she and Josh breezed by me.

"I get the feeling Danielle still gets her way a lot," I said to Nate.

"Dude, you have no idea," he laughed. "But don't let it fool you. Josh is the one calling the shots in that relationship. He's probably the only one who she'll listen to when she gets an idea in her head."

"You're telling me," Meg muttered, shaking her head. Jillian looked at her questioningly, but Megan shrugged her off.

When Danielle and Josh came barreling back in, Danielle had a large leather portfolio in her hands and Josh had a number of smaller binders.

"I'm such a spaz," she began, shaking her head.

"That's old news," Megan interjected.

"Stuff it, Meg," she shot back. "What I meant was that it was in my car all along."

"As interesting as fabric swatches and paint chips may be, Luke, we're going to take off," Megan began. "We just figured we'd pop in since the bar was on the way to Nate's place. He has an early practice in the morning. See you girls for lunch tomorrow," she added, giving them each quick hugs goodbye. "I'll be at Nate's tonight."

"You, me and Fletcher are going out soon, hear me?" Nate said pointing at me as he headed to the door.

"As long as he keeps the top hat at home," I replied. Josh shoved my shoulder as Danielle protested in the background.

"You looked good, baby," she added, rubbing his arm. "Don't listen to him."

"He's just jealous because Jillian didn't pick out a tux with any flair."

Jillian's eyes widened at the mention of the prom, and she openly glared at Josh. Danielle smiled triumphantly, pleased with his response, before turning back to me.

"So, I want to leave these books with you, Luke. There are paint colors and swatches. I realize that it's a little overwhelming, but I'd just like to get an idea of your style before I go forward."

She thrust the heavy portfolio at me along with a number of glossy binders, and I handed her my sketches and the preliminary plans for the remodel.

"I know that a lot of guys aren't into choosing color palates, but if you have a young lady in your life that you'd like to run these by..." she sang with a smirk.

I was about to tell her that I was perfectly capable of looking at some books about colors when Jillian abruptly bolted for the bathroom. This was becoming a recurring theme with her.

"God, look at the time, baby," Danielle said suddenly, raising her wrist and checking her watch. "And I still need to head back to the showroom and make sure everything looks all right."

"Why are you going there?" Josh replied, shaking his head. "I thought you said—"

"Honey, have you seen the work these so-called clean-up crews do? I have," she said, answering her own question. "Luke, can you tell Jill that I'll see her tomorrow for lunch? I really think we should go before it gets any later."

I was momentarily seized with panic knowing that I'd be left alone with Jillian again. It occurred to me that she would probably be equally as horrified. After the way I had behaved, she probably didn't want to speak to me very much either.

"I'll call you tomorrow," Danielle stated, grabbing me for a hug.

"You hang in there," Josh added, chuckling, which was kind of strange.

When they were both out the door, I walked through the room, helping Peter by turning the chairs over onto the tables. I had only managed a few when Jillian walked back in. She looked flustered.

"Where's Danielle?" she asked, addressing me for the first time since she had arrived.

"She and Josh needed to go back to the showroom to check on something," I replied, coolly. "She said she'd see you at lunch."

"Great," she sighed.

She looked down at her feet, fidgeting with the purse in her hands. When she looked back up, her eyes were glassy and then I truly began to panic.

"Can I...I mean, can we..." she trailed off, frustrated, and my pulse began to race. I didn't want to have this conversation. "Luke, I know that there's nothing I can say to explain..."

I felt my whole body react—vibrating from her verbal left hook. My defensives went up immediately.

Don't tell me "It wasn't you, it was me", Jillian because I can't handle hearing that shit.

"Listen, Jillian, honestly, you don't need to do this," I interrupted. Which was a lie. I wanted her to be upset. I wanted her to *want* to explain. I think I even wanted her to cry. I just didn't want to hear it. "It's late. Let me walk you to your car."

She breathed in a ragged breath, finally nodding before following me to the door. Wordlessly, I waved to Pete over my shoulder and led her outside. The bastard actually winked at me.

We crossed the street in silence until we reached the public lot where most of our patrons parked. There were only a few cars left since it was so late. I think I expected to see the crap car she drove in high school, but I didn't.

"This is me," she said, signaling to a black Jetta.

"No more Red Baron," I remarked almost wistfully. I hadn't thought about what I was saying before I spoke. The last thing I wanted to do was bring up the car and any memories attached.

"Um...no," she replied absently, as she rifled through her purse. I heard her curse under her breath before she brought the pocketbook up onto the hood of the car and resumed her search, frantically grabbing at the items inside. She stopped abruptly, covering her mouth with her hands.

"Danielle has my keys," she announced, as if she were saying it to herself and not to me. She dug back in her bag, pulling out a phone and began dialing. Her whole body seemed to be humming with nervous energy. She shifted slightly from one foot to the other, playing with the buttons on the sleeve of her wool coat as she waited for the person to pick up.

"God damn it, Danielle, where are you?" she shouted into the phone. "You never returned my keys. Call me back as soon as you get this message."

She gripped the phone tightly, closing her eyes and taking a deep breath.

"Luke," she began calmly. "Would you mind if I waited inside so I can call a cab to take me to Danielle's house?"

"But they're going to the showroom," I reminded her, already panicking myself.

"Well, until she calls me back," she explained, throwing her phone into her pocketbook in frustration.

"I can drive you to Danielle's house. You don't need to get a cab," I offered awkwardly. "There isn't anyone who has a spare key to your car?"

Boyfriend, maybe?

"I live with Megan, but she turns her ringer off when she stays with Nate because he usually has to wake up so early. Danielle has my spare, but she's not answering her cell," she explained uncomfortably. At least we had that in common. Nothing would be more uncomfortable than driving Jillian home.

After trying Josh's cellphone and their house phone, Jillian finally conceded and tried dialing Nate's number, but it was sent directly into his voicemail.

"Why don't we swing back to the showroom? They're probably still there and Danielle's wreaking havoc," I suggested because imagining being stuck in a car with her was making me crazy.

"Are you sure?" she asked uncertainly.

"Yeah, that's fine," I answered coolly, showing her over to my car. I opened the passenger side door for her and walked over to my side. When I stepped into the seat, I was immediately assaulted by the smell of her perfume.

I flipped on the radio to avoid any forced conversation. I couldn't decide which was worse—a conversation about Seattle weather or a half-assed apology for taking off on me years ago. Both sounded pretty depressing so I avoided it altogether.

She sat rigid in the seat beside me, occasionally looking out the window. She was clutching her purse, and if I gripped the steering wheel any tighter, I might have broken it in two.

"Do you have any neighbors that might have spare keys?" I asked, causing her to jump.

"I don't think so. I was going to call Suzanne, but it's almost two in the morning," she added, shaking her head. "I just don't know."

"Relax. We're almost there. We'll figure it out." I wanted to sound confident, but I truthfully didn't want to talk about our options because none of them appealed to me.

As we turned the corner onto the side-street where Danielle's showroom was located, Jillian craned her neck, looking over me and out my driver's side window to scan the parking lot. The shift in her position caused her to move slightly closer, the scent of her perfume more concentrated.

"I don't see any cars," she sighed, leaning over further. Even though I knew it was empty, I pulled into the lot so she'd have a better view and move back into her own seat. My body was already reacting to how close she was. Apparently my dick didn't get the memo that we were pissed at her.

I drove the length of the building and everything was dark.

"I'm calling them again," she announced, plucking her phone from her bag. I watched her dial and could hear the tinny sound of the voice mail picking up.

"Do you want me to drive you by their house?"

She began shaking her head again, and I worried she was about to cry. This night had rapidly gone from bad to worse.

"Luke, I just—"

"Let's just go," I interrupted, before she had a chance to continue. "Where do they live?"

When I turned to look at her, she had her eyes squeezed shut and was leaning all the way back against the headrest.

"They're over near Magnolia Park," she sighed, keeping her eyes closed. While it was in the opposite direction of my condo, it wasn't going to take long to get there. She gave me directions, and we rode in silence without the comfort of the radio. I wished I hadn't turned it off. The silence was deafening. It was Jillian who spoke first.

"You still don't smoke in your car."

"Um, no. Habit, I guess," I replied, her comment seeming random to me.

"Your Lexus used to smell like lemons."

My chest constricted again, not as much with the longing I had been feeling, but with pure anger. I couldn't understand how she could think a walk down memory lane would be a good idea.

"Jillian, what are you doing?" I sighed, gripping the steering wheel, trying to keep my temper in check.

Her eyes widened once she noticed my reaction as she opened and closed her mouth, wordlessly.

"I just...I was just remembering," she stammered.

She didn't speak again until it was time to point out the street where Danielle and the Poor Bastard lived.

"I don't believe this," she moaned, as we pulled up to a large pacific lodge off the main street. The house was dark, but there was a silver sedan in the driveway. "They're not home. Where the hell did they go?"

"What do you mean?" I asked, confused. "Whose car is that?" I said motioning to the driveway.

"That's Josh's car. They were in Danielle's SUV. I don't even know what to say, Luke. None of this makes sense."

She drew in a deep breath, and it was clear that she was biting back tears. I didn't want to feel bad for her. I was so sick of feeling bad. I knew I had acted like a dick. I knew I was harsh, but this wasn't my doing. I didn't create this situation. *She* left *me*. I was frustrated and angry, and I just wanted to go home and forget that any of it ever happened. Instead, I was being forced to do something that might very well break me.

I couldn't believe what I was about to offer, but I wasn't left a choice. I was going to bring her back to my condo. Even though I spent every day at the bar surrounded by reminders of her, this was different. This was where I lived.

Would I ever be able to walk into my living room again without seeing her sitting on my couch? Would I continue to smell her perfume long after she left? And if Danielle didn't call, would I need to give her some of my clothes to wear to bed? It was a bad idea, but I was going to do it anyway.

"I'm going to drive you back to my place." Her head jerked in my direction, and while she still looked very upset, now she also looked completely incredulous. "You can crash there and when Danielle calls, she can come and get you."

"I can't ask you to do that, Luke," she replied, shaking her head rapidly in response. "Just drop me off at one of the hotels downtown. I'll have Meg pick me up in the morning."

"I'm not dropping you off at a hotel," I argued, frustrated. I was pissed at the situation and she wasn't doing anything to make it easier. I didn't want to argue with her so I flipped the radio back on. It may have been rude, but dropping her off at a hotel would be even worse.

So I drove silently in my car that didn't smell like lemons with the girl who didn't say goodbye, so that I could take her to my house and pretend that seeing her, talking to her, looking at her didn't bother me at all.

I don't know when I became such a liar.

CHAPTER 21

Jillian

When I was fifteen, the dentist told my mother that I would probably need to have my wisdom teeth removed sometime within the next few years. I knew people who had the procedure done. I had heard the horror stories, so this news did not sit well with me.

On each subsequent visit, I got more and more nervous waiting for the day that he would finally tell me he was going to yank them out. My heart would race, my hands would shake, and I would want to vomit. By the time he finally told me that we couldn't hold off any longer—nearly two years later—I was almost relieved. I wouldn't have to wait for the other shoe to drop anymore. I wouldn't have to feel like throwing up every time I went to the dentist. I could just get it over with. Ironically, in the end, the procedure hadn't been that big of a deal. It was the waiting and the wondering that had been torture.

As I sat in a car, next to the boy I loved—who wasn't a boy anymore—I was reminded of that feeling. I was going to apologize to Luke, but waiting for the right moment and wondering how he would react was slowly killing me. It was going to be painful. It was going to be uncomfortable. But unlike the wretched experience with my wisdom teeth, there wouldn't be any painkillers to dull the ache.

Luke, however, wasn't making it easy. I wanted to tell him that I had only done what I thought was right, but he cut me off. I wanted to tell him how happy I was to see him, and how hard it was not to touch him, but he wouldn't even look at me. Even though I was terrified of the conversation, I knew that we needed to have it, and he needed to hear the words. An apology might not mean much to him, but it was all I had to give. I was beginning to believe that my impending conversation with him might honestly be more painful than the oral surgery.

Complicating matters was the fact that I had no idea what I was going to say if he asked me why I left. It wasn't as if I could be honest.

Sorry Luke, I fell hopelessly in love with you and couldn't bear the thought of you compromising your happiness for me. Please forgive me. I know your future and I didn't want to screw it up.

Not likely.

I had no explanation. There wasn't any miscommunication. My parents didn't force me to leave. I didn't run away because I was afraid of my feelings. I was from another time and I was changing his life. I was blindly responsible for his future and I was in love with him. How could I ever explain the burden that type of responsibility bore?

What haunted me the most was that I wasn't sure I had made the right decision anymore. As my new memories flooded my consciousness, I was forced to experience the pain of leaving him all over again. The loss had stayed with me all throughout college—the heartbreak never quite healing. If he had behaved differently when I ran into him, I would have known I made the right choice, but his anger was palpable. Only a week had passed for me; I expected everything to feel raw and new, but over ten years had gone by for him, and he was still furious. I knew that could either mean he still cared for me, or it could mean he just really hated my guts. I was hoping for the former, because hating my guts would really put a wrench in my plans.

I stole a glance in his direction even though I had tried all night to avoid looking at him for too long. When I first saw him walking through the crowd at the party, I was shaken to my core by how striking he looked. Luke the boy disarmed me with his quiet confidence. Luke the man drew all the air out of the room without even realizing it.

I spotted him immediately as he walked toward Danielle, wearing a charcoal suit with his shirt open at the collar. When I saw him at the reunion, he was dressed casually—an oxford shirt rolled to his elbows and jeans. Tonight, though, he looked entirely different. I felt like I was watching someone who had just walked off the cover of GQ, not the boy who rode around Reynolds on a beat-up motorcycle. I loved that boy, but the man who took his place left me breathless.

While I didn't want to stare, I couldn't help but notice the tension in his jaw, and the way he gripped the steering wheel. We hadn't exactly been sitting in a comfortable silence, but as we made our way through Lower Queen Anne, his discomfort seemed to have grown exponentially. I figured we must have been getting closer to where he lived.

My suspicion was confirmed when he pulled onto a side street in a residential neighborhood. Midway down the street at a cluster of stone buildings, he pulled into a small, adjacent parking lot. Wordlessly, he threw the car into park and slipped out the door. Exiting the car, I was suddenly aware that I wasn't the only one feeling tense and uncomfortable.

He walked in step with me, hands shoved into his pants pockets, head down. The silence was unsettling, and I wanted so badly to find something interesting to say that would break the tension. I came close to mentioning how mild the evening was and how quiet his neighborhood appeared. Even in my head it sounded lame. Fortunately, I had the good sense to remain quiet instead.

"This one's me," he said motioning to the building on the end. I followed him up the cement steps and into the lobby of the building. Luke nodded over at the man on security detail, who tipped his head back at us in return. I could only imagine what it looked like to him and how far from the truth it really was.

Walking into the elevator, he pressed the number twenty-seven and for a moment I felt a flash of recognition. Brushing it aside, I stood uncomfortably, clutching my purse and looking everywhere but directly at him. I think I may have even looked convincing as I studied the etchings around the elevator door. Turning right, we walked along the carpeted hallway until we stood in front of number 2702. He pulled his keys from his pocket and opened the front door.

My heart began hammering again and my throat felt dry. I was suddenly terrified to see where Luke lived, but it was obviously too late. I followed him through the doorway into a large living-room with cream walls and dark wood floors. He hung his coat on a wrought-iron coat rack next to the door then reached out to hang mine up as well. I stared as he hung them side-by-side.

"Can I…um…get you something to drink?" he asked, rubbing the back of his neck awkwardly. I wanted to say no. I didn't want to be a bother, but my throat felt like sandpaper.

"Could I have some water?"

As he retreated into the small kitchen off the living room, I looked around, taking in the things that surrounded him in his everyday life. While it looked very much like a place where a single guy lived, it was uncluttered and tasteful. From the brown leather of the living room furniture, to the stone fireplace and the framed photos on the wall—everything was warm and comfortable. The back window of the living room looked out over the water. Against the night sky, it looked like black ink. I could see the lights from Bainbridge Island faintly off in the distance, and wondered if the ferry was visible by day.

"Here's your water," he said, returning from the kitchen with a small glass. I thanked him and took a gulp, happy to give my hands a task to perform. When he said nothing further, I felt compelled once again to break the silence.

"It doesn't surprise me that everything is so neat," I said, off-handedly. "Your bedroom back home used to be, too."

When I turned around, he was shaking his head and scrubbing his face with his hands.

"Have you checked to see if Danielle called you back?" he asked suddenly in a strained, tired voice. I fumbled for the phone in my bag, glancing at it and seeing that there were no missed calls. I wasn't surprised. She really had a lot of explaining to do.

"No," I added. "No calls."

"Okay, then. Well, you can sleep in my room," he began. "I'll just put on some new sheets or something, and I'll crash out here."

He sounded so defeated, and I wanted this all to go away. I wanted to fast-forward to a time when I had made everything better. I wanted there to be a painkiller.

"I can't take your bed," I shot back. "I've done enou—"

"I'm not arguing with you about this, Jillian," he warned. "It's been a long night."

He walked towards a door down the hall. I wasn't sure if he expected me to follow him, or if he was just going to pick underwear up off the floor or something. I stared out the window anxiously as I waited for him to return. My body stiffened as I heard him walking behind me.

"Here are some things for you to wear," he said, handing me a stack of clothes. "The bathroom is through there." He pointed to another door before returning to his bedroom, where I assumed he was changing his sheets. I didn't protest this time. I complied and headed off to change.

The amount of white in his bathroom was almost blinding, and the room was spotless. Luke either had a cleaning company or Grace had trained him well. It occurred to me that I could break the ice and ask about her. She was so sweet to me. I hoped that she and Carter were doing well. I smiled, pleased that I had some common ground I could speak about without causing him to look like he wanted to gouge his eyes out.

Unfolding the clothes from the stack, I found a pair of blue sweatpants and a gray t-shirt with the bar's name across the back. The pants were huge and hung off me like I was a circus clown. I tried rolling them at the waistband and the ankles, so that I didn't trip over myself as I walked. It didn't help much. The shirt, while smelling like detergent, also held a faint scent of something that may have been his deodorant. It felt strange to be wearing something of his, and wrong to be that close. It was all just a reminder of an intimacy we no longer had.

Looking in the mirror, I frowned at how pale I looked under the fluorescent lights. I smoothed out my hair and tried to make myself look presentable. I didn't know why I was bothering. It wasn't as if he had showed any interest in my appearance.

I folded my dress, carrying it along with my heels back into the living room. Luke was laying a blanket down on the couch. He was bending over and because he'd discarded his jacket, I was treated to a pretty spectacular view from behind. All that view did, though, was taunt me.

I cleared my throat and he regarded me hesitantly. It didn't escape my notice, though, that he allowed his gaze to drop slightly, taking in how I looked in his clothes. Unfortunately, I thought I looked a lot like Bozo the Clown.

"Thank you for the clothes," I began.

"Not a problem," he replied, throwing the pillows down on the couch. Looking past him towards the fireplace, I saw a number of pictures along the mantle. In the collection was a large photo of Grace autographing her cookbook.

"Is that picture from Grace's book-signing?" I asked, motioning to the mantle.

"Um...yeah," he replied, not looking up and still messing around with the couch cushions. "Her first one."

"Oh, she's had more than one?" I asked, thrilled that we may have opened up a line of communication. If I was able to get him to relax a little, he might allow me a chance to apologize. "That's wonderful."

I gave him a few moments to respond, but when he didn't, I attempted to engage him again.

"I'm not surprised she's done well for herself. She made a mean veal saltimbocca. It's not—"

"Jillian, what are you doing?" he asked, spinning around at me suddenly. His body was rigid, his elbows were bent, and his fingers were splayed out in front of him stiffly. It was as if he was trying to ward me off.

Caught off guard, I didn't know how to respond. I hadn't expected him to be so upset, so soon.

"I'm trying, Jillian. God, I'm trying so hard to get through this, but I can't do this with you," he exclaimed. "Not now."

"I was just trying to talk to you, Luke," I tried to explain.

"I can't *just talk* to you," he ground out.

"Well, what am I supposed to say? You won't listen to me!"

"And have you say what? It wasn't you, it was me? You had fun, but it was time to move on? I don't want to hear any of that."

"You haven't even given me a chance," I protested, my voice louder than I knew it should be.

"Fine. I accept your apology," he replied, harshly. "You can relax. Your conscience is clear."

"That's not what I'm looking for, Luke," I responded, moving closer to him, trying to connect like we used to. I took a deep breath because I knew this was it. Everything hinged on what I was going to say.

"I should have talked to you. I should have tried harder to convince you that following me to New York was a bad idea. I just wish you knew how hard it was for me. I wish you knew that I was doing what I thought was best."

"Best for who, Jillian?" he replied, wildly. "Don't tell me what was best for me. You leaving was *not* best for me."

"But it was," I argued. "Look at you! Look at what you've done. You're successful. You're happy."

"Don't patronize me. If you wanted a clean break, you should have just said so," he sneered, visibly attempting to control his anger and volume.

I had been trying to rein in my own anger and frustration, but his inability to hear me out was wearing thin. I wanted to shake him, hold him down, and force him to hear what I was telling him. But I'd had it.

"I wasn't looking for a clean break! I was in love with you!"

I let out a rush of air through my nose, shocking myself with my outburst. We stared at each other, chests rising and falling as we gasped for breath. It felt like a lifetime went by in those few minutes of strained silence.

"Go to sleep, Jillian," he finally said tersely. Turning away, he walked toward the window and ran both hands through his hair.

I stood frozen, unable to move toward him or the bedroom. I felt more than ever that I was living my life in limbo.

"Jillian," he added, his voice sounding tired. "Please…just go to sleep."

I could only see the faint reflection of his face in the glass. His eyes seemed to be shut and his head was tilted slightly back. Quietly, I walked to the bedroom, leaving him alone to stare into the black night.

Walking slowly to his room, I clutched my clothes to my chest, steeling my nerves. The last thing I needed was to break down and cry in front of him. I had done enough.

When I closed the door behind me, I didn't look around his room much. The walls were the same cream color as the rest of the house and the bedding was dark blue. I barely glanced at the prints on the wall. I fought the impulse to stare at the picture frames on his bureau.

I curled up underneath the covers on his large bed, trying not to inhale the scent on his sheets, his clothes—on everything around me. I focused instead on the words that we said, and how nothing seemed to come out right.

Before I fell asleep, what bothered me the most wasn't the embarrassment I felt over declaring myself to him during a fit of anger. What bothered me most was that I was a liar. When I told him I was in love with him, I had used the past tense.

I had the good sense to set the alarm on my phone before falling asleep. I couldn't think of anything more awkward than needing Luke to wake me up. Things had been tense enough; I didn't want to make it worse. So when the alarm went off at six-thirty, only four hours after I had fallen asleep, I scrolled through the messages on my phone, hoping to find some sort of explanation from my so-called friends. There was a text message sent at three-thirty in the morning from Danielle. My blood began to boil as I read it.

So sorry. Josh & I went out for 2nd dinner & cell died. Assuming ur w Luke. Pls forgive me! Can come & pick u up in the AM.

I read the text again, shaking my head because Danielle and Josh were not the midnight snack kind of people. It didn't make sense.

There were also two missed calls from Megan, as well as a text sent around five in the morning.

Talked to the crazy one. Call if you need a ride.

It didn't surprise me that Megan would be awake. Nate worked out every morning and rarely slept past six. She had adopted his sleep schedule so that even on days when she slept at home, I heard her puttering around in the kitchen before sunrise.

After selecting the message and highlighting the reply option, my fingers moved furiously, asking her to pick me up on Bolton Street in half an hour.

I dragged myself out of his bed and into his adjoining bathroom, thankful that I didn't need to leave the room to get cleaned up. I was sure after going to sleep without removing my make-up, I looked a whole lot more like Bozo than I had the prior night.

Groaning as I looked in the mirror, it occurred to me that I didn't have any toiletries, and I never carried much make-up with me. I didn't have much of a choice, though, so I took a quick shower anyway, piling my hair on top of my head. Dressing in my clothes from the party, I left his shirt and sweatpants folded on the edge of his bed, and like a child, put my ear to the door, listening for any sound outside. When it sounded relatively quiet, I carefully opened the door, tip-toeing out with my shoes in my hand.

I was about to search for a piece of paper so that I could leave a note when I heard a door open behind me. Luke stood in the doorway of the room across the hall, a large sweat stain in the shape of a V at the collar of his gray t-shirt and a towel draped over his shoulders. God hated me.

"Megan is picking me up. I was just about to leave you a note," I fumbled, wanting him to know I wasn't about to cut-and-run.

When he didn't answer, I threw on my shoes and grabbed my coat. In my haste to get my coat on swiftly, my arm got caught in the sleeve as I struggled to push it through. To my surprise, I heard his voice directly behind me.

"Let me…your sleeve is all…"

His hands hovered over my arm for a moment as I froze in place, utterly humiliated. This may have been just as bad as needing Luke to wake me up. He carefully held up the fabric of my collar, loosening the material that had bunched up around my shoulder. My arm slid through without any further hindrance, but my ego remained bruised.

"Thank you," I said, looking down nervously. "For everything."

"You're welcome," he replied, stiffly. After a moment of uncomfortable silence, I looked up just as he seemed to draw in a breath to begin speaking.

However, before any words were said, the sound of my phone vibrating distracted us. Megan's name was flashing on the illuminated screen.

"That's her," I began, reaching for the doorknob. "She's probably out front."

When I stepped into the hall, I swung around, staring back at him in the doorway. I hated leaving this way. I hated that I had failed so miserably at pleading my case. I hated that Danielle had put me in this position. I hated that I put myself in this position. I hated everything…but him.

"See you around," I said, sadly, before turning and walking back down the hall.

I pressed the button for the elevator as my over-active imagination caused me to envision a sweaty post-workout Luke running down the hall after me. When the elevator door opened, I had to face the facts that although everything that had happened to me sounded like fiction, this was not a movie.

As I stepped into the elevator, my nose began to twitch, the telltale sign that I was about to cry. I drew in deep breaths, attempting to control my emotions, but it was difficult. I didn't have a Plan B. I had his undivided attention. I apologized. I even told him that I had been in love with him, and none of it made any difference.

As I walked into the lobby past the security officer, wearing the same dress I had on the evening before, it occurred to me that I was doing the Walk of Shame without getting to do any of the fun parts. I noticed him surreptitiously glance at my clothes and cringed. I never thought that my first time sleeping in Luke's bed would have ended quite like this. I was mortified.

Swinging the front door open, I saw Megan's car parked in front of the first of the three buildings. I hobbled to the car on shaky legs, wrenching the door open when I got there. While I had prepared to yell and curse and vow to murder Danielle, I took one look at Megan, buried my head in my hands and burst into tears.

"Oh, sweetie," she exclaimed. "What the hell happened?"

I wanted to explain everything to her, but the words wouldn't come out. I kept trying to think of a place to start, but would find myself breaking down instead.

"Let's get out of here," she muttered more to herself, I think, than to me.

I was so unprepared. I had never intended to tell anyone that I had a history with Luke. Once I did, I was sure that Megan would want to know why I kept it from her and why he was so angry. I didn't have good answers for either question. The further away from his condo we got, though, the easier it became for me to calm myself down. As she navigated her way back downtown, I composed myself, ready to come clean.

"Luke hates me."

"Jillian," she began cautiously, "was there ever anything going on with you and Luke?"

I wasn't surprised by her question. If she ever had any suspicions, I had most likely confirmed them. Instead of launching into an elaborate explanation, I just looked up at her through sore, bloodshot eyes and nodded slowly. While I expected a litany of questions, Megan pulled out her cellphone instead.

"Change of plans, Danielle," she began. I glared over at her, still angry that Danielle's battery had conveniently run low. I wasn't stupid. I had been the target of her matchmaking compulsion many times before. She just messed with the wrong people this time around. "Meet us at the apartment in fifteen. This can't wait until lunch."

She ended the call, placing the phone back in her purse.

"She was trying to set me up with Luke, wasn't she?" I asked, bitterly.

"Honey, try to remember that she only wanted to do something for you because you do so much for her," she explained.

"So she stranded me with him?!" I exclaimed. "And you were okay with this? I can't believe—"

"Jillian, Danielle ran into Ann-Marie Matthews last month."

It only took a moment to place the name. It wasn't like it had been very long for me. I remembered the look on her face when she and her boyfriend stumbled upon me and Luke grinding against each other behind the gym. I also remembered thinking that she was a whore, as my own leg sat perched upon Luke's hip. We should've formed a club.

"And you knew?" I asked, suddenly feeling angry. "Why didn't either of you say anything?"

"Danielle also ran into Luke, and she thought he acted strange when she mentioned your name," she replied, uncomfortably. "She thought if we just forced you two together, you'd work out whatever went wrong."

"You realize that's like the plot of a bad Lifetime movie, right?" I sneered, incredulous.

"Jillian, I'm sorry, really," she replied, seeming genuinely upset. "I would never have agreed to it if I knew you'd be this upset."

"If you had asked me, I would have told you yesterday that I thought he hated my guts. Thanks to you guys, I now have confirmation on that."

"In our defense," she replied. "We had no idea how involved you were in high school."

"I understand that," I said, frustrated by the conversation. "But that's why you don't go around making decisions for people without consulting them!"

The words came tumbling out of my mouth before I even realized what I had said. Just like the decision I had made for Luke. I was a hypocrite, and suddenly, I was sobbing again.

"Oh sweetie, what the hell went on with you two?" she asked sympathetically. I was in no shape to give her the gory details though.

"Can we wait until Danielle's with us?" I managed to reply. "I promise I'll tell you everything." *Except the parts that can get me committed.*

When we rounded the bend heading to our building, I wasn't the least bit surprised to see Danielle, sitting on our front steps, wearing a purple track suit and baseball cap. She never left the house with a hair out of place, but in times of crisis, she dropped everything. I already found myself feeling marginally less angry with her.

I wiped at the tears along my cheeks and ran my fingertips along my bottom lashes. I shuffled out of the car, unsure as to how this conversation would go. I wasn't proud of what I had done, even though I felt it was for the best. I only hoped they'd see that.

As soon as Danielle caught sight of my red, splotchy face, she gasped, cupping her hands over her mouth. She launched herself off of the steps, embracing me tightly.

"I'm so sorry, Jillian," she said sadly. "I never would have...if I had known...shit," she muttered, frustrated.

"Why don't we all go inside so we can talk?" Megan suggested, motioning to the door.

"Good idea," I replied, as Danielle weaved her arm through mine and walked with me up the stairs.

271

When we got to the apartment, I crashed onto the couch, closing my eyes and trying to decide where to start.

"How did I not know this?" Danielle began, sitting in the chair across from me. "How did we," she added, motioning with her finger between herself and Meg, "not know about this?"

I was slow to respond, still trying to form the right way to explain that I fell in love with a boy in less than three weeks.

"We hung out a lot," I said, making it sound more casual than it was.

"Jillian, this," Meg replied, pointing at me, "does not happen when two people *hang out*."

"He's the reason you left early for New York, isn't he?" Danielle asked pointedly.

My eyes shot up, surprised that she made that connection so quickly. For someone who hadn't caught on before, she was piecing the puzzle together rather well. I groaned, knowing that the conversation was about to take a turn.

"Luke wanted to come with me to New York," I said, focusing on a discoloration on the carpet. I didn't want to see their faces when they realized how serious things had been. "I left without telling him."

When no one responded, I glanced up in their direction. Danielle was shaking her head slowly in disbelief.

"I couldn't let him give up a life here to follow me across the country," I explained, my voice sounding hoarse. "He wouldn't have had anything. No education. No job."

"He would've had you." I looked over to Danielle, her expression grave and disapproving.

"He would've resented me," I countered. "Maybe more than he does now."

"Jesus Christ, you were in love with him," Megan gasped softly, her eyes wide with shock. I didn't say anything at first. I didn't need to. When I looked up at her, she knew.

"And now he hates me."

I didn't want to elaborate anymore. I didn't want to plead my case. I just wanted to go back to staring at that spot on the carpet. Instead, I relayed the entire story of my night with Luke—from the car ride over to the showroom, to our showdown in his condo. Every bit was as painful as the first time around, although I conveniently left out the part where I told him I had been in love with him. When I was done, I wanted the ground to swallow me up—anything to escape the inevitable inquisition.

"So, we need a plan," Danielle announced.

"What?" I asked, confused by her change in tone.

"To fix this," she explained, as if it were obvious.

"Were you even listening? He. Hates. Me," I replied, punctuating my words for effect.

"No, he doesn't," she replied.

"He doesn't?" Meg asked, looking at Danielle with as much shock as I was.

"No. Were *you* even listening?" she asked, looking between Meg and me.

"Apparently not," she replied, sarcastically.

"Guys don't get angry like that, Jillian, if they don't care anymore," Danielle explained. "And they sure the hell don't invite the ones they hate to their houses for sleepovers."

"He was being nice, Danielle, when my *friend* stranded me," I countered, feeling annoyed.

"If Mike Wakefield was locked out of his car at the reunion, would you have brought him back to your apartment to sleep on the couch?" she asked, smugly. I threw up a little in my mouth. Hell no.

"Yeah, I didn't think so," she replied. "But he took you to his house, let you sleep in his clothes, in his bed. And instead of saying 'Don't worry about it, Jillian, it was a long time ago', he says that you leaving wasn't what was best for him. That's huge."

"She's got a point," Meg replied thoughtfully. "I dated Sean Myers for a year before he broke up with me for some slutty sophomore with big boobs. I would have dumped his ass at the nearest HoJo faster than he could say 'push-up bra'."

"That's all well and good," I complained. "But I still had a chance to say my peace and he wouldn't listen. There's nothing I can do."

"You're probably right," Danielle began somberly. "But there's something *we* can do."

"Oh Jesus," Meg muttered. "Theatrical much?"

"Can it, Meg," she retorted, not even looking in her direction. Instead, she focused on me, smiling with a glimmer in her eye. "Saturday night, we're going to his bar."

I stifled a groan. "If I go with you, there needs to be some ground rules," I warned her. "I dress myself. My keys stay in my bag. There will be no body shots or dropping anything like it's hot. Understood?"

"Done and done," she answered happily. "We don't need any of that, although I'd dress you cuter."

"I dress myself fine," I growled, thinking back to the skinny jean incident.

"Whatever," she sighed, dramatically.

Meg sat down next to me, giving me a one-armed squeeze.

"We'll fix this," she added, "and if Luke is still too Brooding-Leather-Jacket-Boy to get it, he's not worth it."

"Yeah," I replied, with a half-smile.

I just wish I believed that.

Later, after Megan had returned to Nate's, and Danielle had gone off to work, I puttered around my room, attempting to clear my mind of all the drama. I was about to sit down at my computer and begin research on an article when I decided to log onto Facebook. Then it all happened at once. My heart began to race, my hands started to shake, and I was positive that I was going to vomit. I reread the alert five, ten, maybe a dozen times. I still didn't believe what it said.

Luke Chambers accepted your friend request.

CHAPTER 22

Luke

When Grace would feel stressed out, she'd bake cookies—dozens and dozens of cookies. I wondered if the neighbors ever caught on or noticed that when a deadline loomed or a book was about to hit the shelves, they received a plate of snickerdoodles from her for no apparent reason.

Carter played chess. He liked to lose himself in a game, shutting out any outside variables plaguing him. He claimed that it centered him, giving him the focus he needed to tackle the problem. Well, unless he was losing to me. That usually made it worse.

Jonas was the polar opposite. After a tough week, Jonas would hit the gym, choose a particularly intimidating sparring partner and proceed to beat the crap out of him. He took me with him once—years ago—and I'd left with a black eye. I didn't find that very relaxing.

There was some merit to Jonas' approach, though. While I didn't feel like getting the shit kicked out of me, jumping on a treadmill—letting the aggression out during a run—worked wonders.

Less than a week ago, Jillian stood in my living room, shouting at me, saying things—things I just didn't want to hear. I didn't know what she expected me to say. I didn't know how she expected me to react. I wasn't even sure I believed her because if it were true, why would she have left? Wouldn't she have tried to contact me sooner? You don't treat the people that you allegedly love that way. At least, I didn't.

I was so worked up that I barely functioned the entire day. There was a part of me that wanted to tell her to go to hell so I'd never have to deal with her bullshit again. Then there was another part that wanted to touch her, and wouldn't stop thinking about that Friend Request. In the end, the part that was a pushover won out when I logged onto Facebook and accepted it.

I managed to resist looking at her profile for a day. I knew that if there were pictures of her with some guy, I'd be pissed. I knew I had no right to be, and that pissed me off even more. Then I'd inevitably get mad at myself for

275

wanting to kill the fictional guy. No good was going to come of looking at Jillian's Facebook page.

My sound reasoning was shot to shit when I logged onto Facebook the very next day and saw something Jillian wrote to Danielle pop up. She asked Danielle what time "everyone" would be getting together on Saturday night. It felt so wrong to pry—like I was eavesdropping on a conversation that I shouldn't. This was exactly the reason why I was against joining Facebook in the first place. Inevitably, my curiosity got the better of me. I wanted to know where they were going, and if the "everybody" Jillian mentioned involved another guy because clearly I was brain damaged. Apparently, running into Jillian had turned me into a creepy stalker.

Clicking on her profile, the small picture of Jillian sitting between Danielle and Megan was enlarged so that I could see the little details that were unnoticeable from the main page. Her hair was draped over one side and her head was tilted, resting slightly on Megan's shoulder. She was wearing red and she was beautiful.

Feeling conflicted, but obviously not enough to stop, I scrolled down, reading a message from Suzanne Santin Hentschel asking Jillian to have drinks with her. When I started wondering where they'd be going, I logged off abruptly and jumped on the treadmill instead. I wish I could have pinpointed the moment I decided it was okay to spy on people.

The next day, as if she knew I had been looking at her profile, Jillian sent me a private message. I hesitated just a moment before opening it up, nervous about what I'd find. I couldn't imagine what she wanted, worrying that she could tell I had been lurking. Facebook was complicated—you never knew. My whole body tensed as I started to read.

Luke,

I hate the way we left things on Sunday. It was never my intention to upset you. I just want you to know that I meant everything I said. While I know it wasn't the best way to handle the situation, I truly felt I was doing what was right. I loved you too much to watch you throw away your future.

Leaving you was the hardest thing I've ever done, and it was the most painful thing I've ever done.

I regret that I've caused you pain, and I regret that I didn't handle it better. I regret that I don't know you now, and I want to know you again. But what I regret most of all is that I never told you how I felt when I had the chance. For that, I have the most regret...and probably always will.

Jillian

I must have read her message three times before storming over to the treadmill and running until my body practically gave out. I had clocked more hours on that machine in the past week than I had in all the time I'd owned it. My body ached, my head hurt and my chest felt tight. I had literally spent the entire week running from her, and my legs felt like Jell-O.

By Friday, I was barely functioning. Even though I had spent my entire week thinking of her, I had yet to respond to her email. Never in my life had I ever felt so conflicted. No matter how much I thought it through, I'd always come back to the same thing.

I would never have left *her*.

Frustrated, I sent a text to Carter, asking if he could meet me at the diner for lunch the following day. I didn't want to explain everything that had happened with Jillian, but needed some perspective. I'd seem to have lost mine, and he always had a way of setting me straight.

Although I was expected at the bar, I took a quick detour and drove to The Rusted Nail instead. I knew Danielle would be there, tearing the place up. She had blown in on Monday and begun her renovation. Fixtures were ripped from the wall, countertops were demolished, and tables were thrown in the trash. It was a disaster, but Danielle seemed to be in control of the situation so I tried to relax and let her do her job.

I decided on a new name for the restaurant, and I wanted to speak to Danielle about the marquee. As I moved past the carpenters installing the new front door, I heard her voice from inside.

"You need to stop worrying about it so much," she said. "Trust me. I know what I'm doing."

I could only image the poor person she was terrorizing. As I scanned the room full of workers installing lights and painting the walls, I didn't find Danielle lecturing one of the contractors. She was lecturing Jillian.

"That's what you always say and look at what happened last time," she shot back.

Danielle looked as though she was about to respond when she noticed me approaching. Jillian followed her gaze, staring at me with wide eyes.

"Luke!" Danielle exclaimed. "To what do we owe this pleasure?"

"I didn't mean to interrupt," I added, glancing briefly over at Jillian.

277

"Oh, no, no. I was just telling Jillian that she needed to trust me. This…article she's writing about the renovation…it's going to be fantastic."

"Article?" I asked, because this was the first I had heard about Jillian writing anything.

"Of course, silly. That's how we work. I do a fantastic remodel. Jillian takes pretty pictures and then writes an amazing piece about it. The magazine picks it up and my phone starts to ring. It's a beautiful thing," she explained. "And you dropped by at such a good time. The fabric for the upholstery is on its way. I asked for a rush delivery and the kid at the fabric store kind of has a thing for me, so I think it should be here any minute."

"That's great," I replied, a little overwhelmed by all of the information. I didn't really care about looking at the rolls of fabric. She had given me some swatches. I picked a few I liked. After Danielle vetoed the majority of them, we decided on a striped print with oranges, tans and browns. Danielle claimed the dark wood would make it "pop". Who was I to argue?

"Jillian's going to take some photos of the rolls of fabric leaning against the old leather booths in the corner. It'll be a great 'before' shot."

"Sounds like it."

I was beginning to feel uncomfortable, having nothing of value to add to the conversation. Jillian hadn't spoken either, making the tension I was feeling seem that much worse.

"Excuse me," one of the workers interrupted. "Some guy is out front with a delivery for you."

Danielle hopped in place, clapping her hands. "Yay! It's fabric time. If you'll excuse me."

"I'll…won't you need help?" Jillian asked.

"That's what delivery people are for," she replied, shaking her head. "I'll be right back."

After a week of thinking of nothing but this girl, I found myself wishing that I had gone directly to the bar. I wasn't ready for this conversation. I was too aware of what I was doing with my hands. I ran one along the back of my neck, tucking the other in my coat pocket.

While I was still trying to think of a safe topic to broach, Jillian broke the silence.

"I sent you a message," she said softly. "On Facebook." This was exactly the conversation I wanted to avoid.

"I've been really busy," I lied. "I haven't been on my computer in awhile."

"Oh," she replied, looking down at her shoes. "Well...I did."

"Jillian! Luke!" Danielle called, walking through the doorway. It was a relief that our awkward exchange was over and we could focus on something else. "Wait until you see how beautiful the colors are against the grain."

Jillian walked over to Danielle, who was holding a roll of the material up against the wall.

"Nice, right?" she asked, beaming.

"It's great," I replied. "Listen, I need to get to the bar, but I stopped by to talk to you about the marquee."

"Oh yes!" she exclaimed. "Have you decided on a name?"

"Um...yeah," I replied, suddenly self-conscious. "Grace's Fire."

"Aw, Luke," Danielle sighed. "That's so sweet. Don't you think that's sweet, Jill?"

"That's a lovely idea, Luke," she said, gazing at me. Embarrassed that I had stared a little longer than I should have, I decided to make a quick exit.

"Well, I need to get going. I'll probably stop by tomorrow and check in."

"Actually, that won't be necessary," Danielle replied, happily. "We're coming to the bar tomorrow night."

"We?" I asked, even though I knew who she meant.

"All of us. Me, Josh, Nate, Meg, Jillian," she explained, looking at me like I was crazy. I suddenly felt like there was a lump in my throat.

"That's...great. Um, I'll see you tomorrow night, then."

"Bye, Luke," Danielle replied, with a cheerful wave.

I glanced at Jillian just as she was looking up at me.

"Bye," she added, with a tight smile.

Once I got into my car, I grabbed my phone, praying that Carter had responded. Fortunately, he replied that he'd meet me at the diner around eleven. I needed that talk with him now more than ever.

By ten forty-five the following day, I was settled into a corner booth, waiting for Carter to arrive. I fidgeted with the salt shaker, spinning it in place absently as I watched the door for him to arrive.

At eleven on the dot, Carter breezed in, heading straight to the booth we always occupied. He slid into the seat, watching as I rolled the salt shaker between my hands.

"So, are we going to exchange pleasantries, or should I just ask now why you look like hell?" he asked, nonchalantly.

"I was going to say hello first," I replied. "But that'll do. Thanks for that, by the way."

The waitress made her way over to us, filling the empty cups in front of us with coffee. Carter looked up at her and smiled, pausing to speak until she'd walked away.

"Seriously. Are you even sleeping?" he asked, searching my eyes. There were dark circles underneath them when I looked in the mirror that morning. That tends to happen when you wake up at five o'clock every day to run on a treadmill like a lunatic. "What's her name?"

Startled by his assumption, I knocked over the shaker, spilling salt all over the table.

"Why would you assume—"

"So you're saying this," he began, motioning to my face, "is not about a girl?"

I suddenly felt very uncomfortable—embarrassed to be falling apart over a girl from so long ago. I should be over this by now. I shouldn't be acting this way, and I sure as hell shouldn't be feeling this way. Biting back my nerves, I drew a deep breath, closing my eyes and resting my head against the back of the booth.

"Do you remember Jillian Cross?"

"Of course I remember Jillian Cross," he replied, as if the answer were obvious.

"Well, the girl we ran into at the grocery store last month is a friend of hers."

"I see."

"So I've seen her a few times during the past month...not a date. Just...casually."

I knew I was probably driving him crazy drawing this out but I sounded like such an idiot already. Telling him that I was screwed-up over a girl I knew in high school was going to take some time.

"How'd that go?"

"Not great," I replied. "We left things...there were a lot of unresolved issues."

"She didn't want you to go to New York with her," he said flatly. "She was right, you know. I know you don't want to hear that."

"Carter...I can't...how can you even say that? She just left. Who does that?"

Taken aback by my outburst, he raised his eyebrows which I was sure was a signal for me to get a grip. I wished it was that easy.

"I'm not saying that she went about it the right way. Not everyone reacts well to stress, Luke," he replied, with a pointed stare. "I'm just saying that it would have been a mistake to give up the opportunity Jonas was offering. Clearly, it was a good decision."

I groaned, burying my head in my hands and raking them through my hair.

"So, I'm assuming you still have feelings for Jillian," he hedged.

"I don't know what the hell I'm feeling anymore."

"I think you know exactly how you feel," he countered. "What about her? How does she feel?"

The words she said and the way she said them played over again in my head. I thought about the email, and how she claimed that she meant everything she said. Even though I had thought of nothing but that declaration all week, repeating it out loud was something else entirely. I closed my eyes, drawing a breath before continuing.

"She said she left because she was in love with me. She wants to get to know me again."

Carter stared at his coffee mug and for a moment I thought he wasn't going to say anything at all.

"Do you remember that first time I took you to the cliffs?" he asked, looking up at me cautiously.

"Of course."

"We talked about your dad."

He stopped, lost for a moment in his thoughts. "Forgiveness is a tricky thing. You can really want to forgive a person. You can really not even be all that angry anymore. But as much as you want to move on, you just can't. It's just a natural instinct we have to protect ourselves.

"Jillian didn't set out to hurt you. She actually thought she was helping you. You may not be ready to see that now, but I think in time you'll see things differently."

While it felt good to talk to Carter about Jillian, I didn't feel any less confused. I was still pissed off that she left, but at the same time, she was all I could think about.

We spent the remainder of the time discussing the plans for the restaurant. I told Carter that I was going to name it after Grace and ask her to plan the menu. He agreed that she would probably cry throughout the rest of the conversation, but once she recovered, she'd dive right into planning the restaurant's signature taste.

After we said our goodbyes, I drove back to my condo, deciding to freshen up a bit before heading to the bar for the night. I told myself that I was showering to wake myself up, but that really wasn't the only reason.

When I arrived at the bar, the place was already packed. Peter had his hands full so instead of going straight to my office, I headed behind the bar to help him out.

There were some nights that went by without incident. The patrons behaved. The crowd stayed under control. Then there were some nights when you knew right away that the amateurs had come out to play. An hour into the evening, I shut-off two drunken coeds and escorted a belligerent frat boy off the premises.

Not long after, I was forced to call a cab for one of our regulars who had decided he could match some kid celebrating his twenty-first birthday, beer-for-beer. He was pushing sixty, and his wife would not be pleased.

I helped Frank get into the cab out front, handing the driver some cash for his fare. Just as I was walking back to the bar, I heard someone shouting my name. Spinning around, I caught a glimpse of Josh through the crowd. The line at the bar was still two- and three-people deep. I waved, motioning for him to give me a second so I could help Peter out for a bit. As soon as I was back behind the bar, I glanced over to where I had seen Josh, finding Jillian instead. She was sitting with a wine glass in front of her, twisting it slowly as she listened to the others talk. Her hair was up, and because nothing in my life was fair, she was wearing a tight red shirt with lipstick that matched.

When we got the crowd at the bar under control, I made my way over to their table. Nate was in the middle of a story.

"So, I was like 'No, Olbermann, it's not cool for you to compare the game to Hannibal's trek across the Alps. This is football, man. We got rid of Dennis Miller for a reason.'"

I couldn't help but laugh when I caught the end of his diatribe.

"Hey, Luke," he said. "You agree with me, right? Olbermann needed to haul ass back to MSNBC."

"Yeah. I wasn't a big fan," I replied.

"Is it always like this in here?" Josh asked, nodding over at the crowded bar.

"Some nights, but I usually have a backup bartender. He's on vacation so I'm pulling double-duty."

"Well, I personally love when a place is jumping like this," Danielle began. "Jillian was just saying that she wanted to do some body shots."

God hates me.

"What!" Jillian exclaimed. "I never…Danielle, I swear to God…"

"We're not a body-shot type of place, Danielle," I replied, anxious to change the subject.

"I was just kidding. God, neither of you can take a joke."

Yes, Danielle, it's hysterical for me to think of Jillian laying on the bar, waiting for someone—me—to lick salt off her skin. So funny.

"And you pay to spend extra time with her," Megan interjected. "I thought you were smarter than that, Luke."

"Oh, can it, you," Danielle replied. "I'm wonderful and you know it."

"Well, I have to grab something from the supply room," I explained, looking for a clean exit. "I'll be back to check in on you in a bit. No body shots while I'm gone," I added, pointing at Danielle. She put her left hand over her heart and raised her right hand, swearing to behave.

When I reached the supply room, I took a moment to pull my shit together. If I could just make it through the evening, I would sit down and respond to her email. I'd be honest. I'd tell her I needed time.

After I grabbed a case of wine, I pushed awkwardly through the crowd to get back to Peter. Glancing over at the bar, I stopped dead in my tracks. Jillian was standing behind the bar—my bar—with Peter behind her. She had an empty martini glass in front of her and Peter held a silver shaker in his hands. He reached around her to bring the glass close, while Danielle leaned over the bar watching attentively. His face was practically in Jillian's hair.

I was going to kick his ass.

Incensed, I made it to the bar in a few quick strides. If anyone had been watching, it would have looked like I was about to kill Peter. It wasn't completely out of the question.

"Am I interrupting?" I asked, setting wine down and glaring at him.

"Oh, hey boss! I was just showing your friend here how to make a cosmo. We were just finishing and I was going to get her—"

"I think you need to get *those people* at the end of the bar some drinks. Right, Pete?" I suggested, lacking any obvious subtlety.

"Right, sure," he replied, looking at me like I was crazy. I honestly didn't care. I clearly *was* crazy. "You're the boss. Enjoy, ladies" he added, handing me the shaker.

"We didn't mean to get anyone in trouble, Luke," Jillian began nervously. "We were just joking about how hard it is to mix a good drink and Danielle practically begged him to show me."

She glared at Danielle, who just shrugged.

"Just having a little fun, Luke," Danielle added. "Don't blame Peter. I'm the sinner here."

"I'm not upset, Danielle," I replied. Because I wasn't anymore—at least now that Peter's face was out of Jillian's hair. I turned to Jillian, who was shifting uncomfortably in front of me.

"You wanted to learn how to make a cosmo?" I asked, changing my tone, attempting to sound like I wasn't ready to commit capital murder a minute ago.

"It's not a big deal, really," she stammered.

I held up the container and began shaking it.

"We keep the shakers chilled. When you pour the drink into a glass, you should notice small plates of ice forming across the top. Some bartenders don't take the time to chill both the glass and the shaker. You'll still get a good drink, but that's the difference between good and great."

I poured the red liquid into the glass and small flecks of ice rose to the top.

"Time," I added, looking at Jillian as I slid the drink to Danielle, "and a little patience. That's the key."

"Time," she replied, echoing my words. I hoped she understood what I meant. I hope she understood that I couldn't offer much more right now. I couldn't even coherently explain to Carter how I was feeling. Time was what I needed.

"Ooo-kay," Danielle drawled, grabbing the glass. "On that note, I'll meet you back at the table, Jill."

Before she could protest, Danielle was lost in the crowd, leaving us alone and me feeling self-conscious.

Did I really just make a martini metaphor? What the hell am I doing?

"What was he making you?" I asked, breaking the silence.

"Oh, just a glass of *pinot grigio*," she replied. "Please."

I showed her the brands we had in stock and she chose the one she wanted. She still seemed very uncomfortable, and I was sure I had only made it worse.

"I read your email," I said, pouring the wine, only able to mention it because I had something else to focus on.

"I figured," she replied, softly. "You seemed a little…tense."

"I meant to reply but it's been a crazy week."

"No, it's fine. Really," she said, focusing on her glass. "I just...I just wanted you to know."

When she looked up at me through her lashes, I felt as though my chest was caving in. It reminded me of the way she looked the first time I kissed her. It reminded me that I wanted to kiss her again. But as soon as the thought entered my mind, I was reminded that I still didn't trust her.

"Luke," she began. "I'll wait—"

"Um, boss," Peter shouted from the other side of the bar. I looked over to see two huge guys shoving each other right in front of him.

"Jesus. Stay here," I told her.

As a general rule, once a couple of guys started pummeling each other, the other yahoos in their vicinity usually took it as an open invitation to slug anyone they wanted. If a big fight broke out, I wanted Jillian to stay put.

Peter and I managed to pry the juiceheads apart, shoving them into opposite ends of the room. Their friends soundly decided to usher them out of the bar before any further damage could be done.

When I returned to the bar, Jillian was where I left her, but Danielle and the others were standing there as well.

"We're taking off," Josh announced, draping his arm over Danielle's shoulder. "Seems like you have your hands full tonight."

"Yes, and Luke, I'm planning a dinner in your honor this week," Danielle added. "We need to celebrate your new venture...and the amazing designer you hired. What works for you—Tuesday or Wednesday?"

Jillian was glaring at Danielle again, but Danielle seemed to be ignoring her.

"Um...either is fine," I stammered.

"Fantastic. Tuesday it is," she replied.

We said our goodbyes, Nate insisting on some fist-bump, and I was suddenly left alone with Jillian.

"Thank you...for the lesson," she said, looking at me that way again.

"Anytime."

And for a moment, neither of us said anything, but just stared at each other.

"Well, I'll see you on Tuesday," she added, finally breaking the tension. With a small smile, she turned and headed to the door.

I was left to obsess over ever word, every smile, every motion she made until Tuesday when I'd be subjected to another night of wanting her and hating myself for it. I guessed I'd be hitting the treadmill when I got home.

Everyone handles stressful situations in different ways. They bake. They focus. They fight. They run. They do whatever they can do to stop thinking about what she said.

They spend *all week* thinking about what she said.

They get by.

Then the really stupid ones do it all over again.

CHAPTER 23

Jillian

As we get older, our memories become less vivid—some get hazy, while others simply fade away. You may only remember parts of an event. You may forget some of the details. You may not know what you wore, or who said what. Sometimes, as we get older, it's just hard to sort through all of the names and dates and places. Everything gets jumbled.

I had a great memory during my first life. For some reason, I was able to retain the most useless details about the most random things. I would never forget where I parked my car and I never missed paying a bill. I remembered the birthdates of second cousins and the names of our mailman's kids. When someone told me a story, I remembered it—every detail. It was something I always felt came in handy.

Now, in my second life, the memory that had always worked to my advantage had become the bane of my existence. How was I supposed to keep two separate sets of memories straight when most people failed at remembering one?

Megan was angry at me. We had been eating salads for lunch because apparently in this life, I liked to deprive myself of real food. I was trying to focus on the conversation and not on the image of Luke's upper arms flexing when he grasped the martini shaker, but I obviously wasn't focusing hard enough because I slipped.

"We need to make plans to go dress shopping soon," she said, spearing a chunk of lettuce from her salad and popping it into her mouth.

"Dress shopping? Why are we going dress shopping? You know I hate shopping. Make Dani go," I complained, angry at shopping and his biceps and my salad.

When Megan let her fork drop with a clatter onto the table, I knew right away something was wrong.

"You know, Jillian, I know you're having a tough time, and I'm trying to be understanding, but Jesus Christ, could you pretend to be excited about my wedding for just a minute, please?"

And I officially felt like an asshole. In my defense, in my first life, Megan wasn't even engaged—nevermind planning a wedding. She mentioned shopping, and all I could think of was what happened the last time someone tried to dress me. It's what got me into this mess in the first place.

After throwing myself at her mercy and admitting that I was daydreaming about Luke, she calmed down, and stopped looking at me like I was the worst bridesmaid that ever existed. To further prove my loyalty and devotion, I agreed to go dress shopping with her the next day. It would actually be a welcomed distraction because thanks to Danielle, I needed to write a piece on Luke's renovation.

Contrary to what she said to him the prior week, there was never any article or any pictures that needed to be taken. Thanks to her "quick thinking", I was spending my Sunday night in front of a laptop, deciding how I'd like to approach Luke's story. I was pretty sure that the I-Fell-In-Love-With-the-Owner-When-I-Time-Traveled-Last-Month angle would be too much of a stretch.

Annoyed with my entire second existence and looking for something mindless to do, I launched Facebook. As I read through the timeline, I learned that Danielle was looking forward to a dinner party on Tuesday. I'm glad *she* was. Megan was sitting on the 50-yard line cheering on her future-husband—"the hottest show on turf". *Cue eyeroll.* And Josh just topped his high score in Words With Friends. *Nerd.*

Just as I was about to scroll down, a new alert flashed at the top of my page. Luke Chambers had become a fan of Farmville. *The hell?*

I wasn't sure which was more alarming—the fact that Luke was online at the same time I was, or that he was tending to an imaginary online farm. Clicking on the chat icon in the corner of the screen, the small box opened, revealing the friends who were currently online. There, between Suzanne and the boy who used to eat dirt in kindergarten, was Luke.

Impulsively, I clicked on his name, opening up a chat window. The Luke I knew would not be playing Farmville. I didn't think twice as my fingers pounded the keys, typing into the chat box.

Tell me this is a joke and you're not a Facebook Farmer.

It wasn't until after I had pressed enter that I thought about what I had done. My relationship with Luke was tenuous at best. I was in no position to judge his admittedly awful taste in Facebook games. Mortified, I was about to log off when his response popped up.

What is this thing? Nate sent me some link, now there are alerts everywhere and someone wants me to water something. How the hell do you get rid of it?

I read his response, laughing at his obvious frustration. I also made a mental note to ask Nate how long he'd been farming and if Megan watered his crops when he traveled. That information would come in handy next time he decided to make fun of my "epic dry spell".

Don't ask me. I'm not lame enough to join Farmville. Maybe you should take that up with Farmer Nate.

I was still smiling after I had pressed enter. Our conversations were so strained in person. It was refreshing to have some form of interaction with him that wasn't awkward and uncomfortable—even if it was about virtual livestock.

The strange thing about our visit to the bar on Saturday, though, was that suddenly there was a different kind of awkward between us. When I saw Luke at the reunion, he was so angry—barely able to look me in the eye. The expression on his face nearly shattered me. Then a few days later at Danielle's opening, he seemed detached—almost defensive. I didn't really know what to make of his behavior. Later that night when I was stranded at his house and forced to sleep in his bed, he was different—no longer aloof, but frustrated. It was the first time that I suspected that he was holding back. Then last night at the bar, I truly thought he was going to pummel that poor bartender. He could claim that he just wanted him to get back to work. He could claim that it had nothing to do with me. But something had changed. From the way he spoke to me about time being the key ingredient to the way he looked at me when we said goodbye, his resolve was slipping. Megan and Danielle were right. He didn't hate me, and honestly, I think that pissed him off a lot.

I had assumed he was done chatting with me until a response showed up on the screen.

This is why I hate Facebook. Nothing makes sense. People keep trying to play word games with me. What does that even mean?

Nate wasn't the only person doing ridiculous things on Facebook. I had probably thirty Words with Friends requests that I had been ignoring for months. I had no desire to play Scrabble in real life, nevermind in cyberspace. I just didn't understand the attraction. But it was too good of an opportunity to pass up. I downloaded the application and clicked on his name to challenge him to a game. And as I looked at the tiles available to me, I couldn't believe my luck. In a flash I had posted my first word: farm. Immediately after pressing enter, I logged off, giggling.

It didn't surprise me when I dreamed of the Luke I knew in high school that night. I reveled in the sight of him with a little less stubble on his face and a few less laugh lines in the creases of his eyes. He was my Luke. The Luke who followed me to the cliffs, beautiful and furious. The Luke who so eloquently told me that he wasn't going to wait for me to figure out my shit anymore. The Luke who knew I wanted him, too.

I could still see my Luke when I looked at him now. He scowled at me a little bit more than in the past, but he was still in there.

I woke the next morning to a thumping sound on my door and Megan's way-too-chipper voice.

"Wake up, Jillian. Time to find you an amazing pastel-colored dress you'll only wear once."

"I'm up," I groaned. "Now."

Rolling out of bed, I grabbed my phone from the nightstand. I was about to drag myself into the kitchen for some breakfast when I saw the Words with Friends alert. Luke was playing the game with me. I opened up the app and checked out his response, but ended up just staring at the screen. He had played the word "of" for five points. *Of? Really?* Out of all of the imaginative things to say, he picked that? I immediately clicked on the chat icon and began to type.

That's the best you can do? Are you in kindergarten? Seriously.

Using the M in "farm", I played the word "lame". When I pressed enter, I looked up into the angry eyes of Megan, standing in my doorway and glaring.

"Jillian! What're you doing? We have an appointment at ten o'clock," she exclaimed. "Let's move."

Powering down my laptop, I followed her into the kitchen for some breakfast before heading off to countless bridal shops in search of the "perfect" bridesmaid dress…that I'd only wear once.

Feeling guilty that I had been a less-than-attentive attendant, I chimed in when Danielle commented on color choices, and when Megan remarked about a certain style. I nixed a few dresses that would either make me feel wildly uncomfortable or paler than I already was.

When we had finished with our first appointment and were halfway through our next, I took a quick glance at my phone as Danielle and Megan debated acceptable colors for February weddings. Luke had responded to my chat message.

So "lame" is your A game? I think I can handle the challenge of your first grade vocabulary.

I couldn't stop the silly grin from spreading across my face. He had played "brat". Before I attracted too much attention, I played "flask" and put the phone away.

An hour later, I was standing in the dressing room of bridal shop number five when I heard my phone vibrate. He had made his next move, playing "red" which again, I thought was pretty lame. And it went on like this all afternoon. I had never played Words with Friends before and we had practically finished an entire game in an afternoon.

While I was preoccupied with beating Luke, Megan chose a dress. It was chocolate brown and looked decent on me. Danielle looked better, but Danielle looked good in everything. It took effort for her to look bad.

As we were driving home, I got another chat message from Luke.

Is there a white flag I can wave on this thing? How did I end up with a bunch of vowels? Is that normal? I'll willingly pronounce you winner of this round.

After reading his response, I immediately felt disappointed. I had been having such a good time sparring with him. I didn't want it to end. Any interaction with Luke where he wasn't scowling at me or ignoring me was a huge improvement. I also didn't want to push it, though. When I first emailed him, I never imagined that six hours later, it would have evolved into this. I was about to type a response, when Megan interrupted.

"Jillian, your eyes have been glued to that phone all day. What gives?"

I looked up from the screen to see her staring at me through the rearview mirror, eyeing the phone in my hands. Danielle spun around from her seat in the front, narrowing her eyes at me suspiciously.

"Yeah, Jillian," she added. "What's going on?"

For a moment, I considered deflecting and not telling them that I had been playing a game I had previously avoided like the plague all day with Luke. I couldn't think up anything believable in response though, so I decided to fess up.

"It's nothing. I've just...Luke and I are playing Words with Friends...but it's nothing, really," I replied, feeling the heat rise to my cheeks.

"Luke?" Danielle cried, bouncing in her seat. "Do you play this game with Luke every day?"

"No! NO," I exclaimed. "Just today. We're just messing around."

"Messing around?" Megan asked. "Did you hear that, Danielle? Jillian and Luke were messing around today."

"You two are ridiculous," I replied, rolling my eyes at their cackling.

"We're just teasing you, Jill," Danielle said, still fighting back the giggles. "Seriously, that's good that you're...playing games together."

"Or whatever it is that you want to call that," Megan muttered.

"I'm not speaking to either one of you anymore," I announced, crossing my arms over my chest and pouting.

"Oh, don't be that way, sweetie," Danielle replied. I could tell she still wanted to laugh, and it only fueled my annoyance.

"Have you thought at all about what you want to say to him on Tuesday night?" Megan asked, wisely changing the subject.

"He wants space. I'm not going to bring up anything that will make him uncomfortable."

"Well, don't worry too much," Danielle added. "We'll be there to help."

I smiled at her declaration, but knew that was part of the problem. I had enough of their help.

By the time Tuesday arrived, I was a wreck. I had messaged Luke back, accepting his forfeit and congratulating him on passing Words with Friends 101. Unfortunately, I hadn't heard from him since then. Like a crazy stalker, though, I logged onto Facebook a few times a day, first checking to see if he was online, and then reading the comments on his wall. Each time I did it, I felt stupid and ashamed.

I spent an embarrassingly long time staring at the clothes in my closet on Tuesday night. I needed something that looked good, but wasn't too obvious. Something that said "I'll give you time", but also said "Hurry up". I really wasn't a patient person, and I didn't want to waste any more time.

I tried on three different outfits, flinging the discarded options onto the floor as I switched to something new. Megan had left for Nate's earlier in the day so I had no one to tell me what looked good and what made me look like a hooker. I was pretty sure Luke was anti-hooker. I finally chose a sweater that was tight, but not salacious, and a pair of jeans that were fitted, but not obscene.

On the way to Danielle's, I stopped to pick up a bottle of wine. Aside from the glass I had at Luke's bar on Saturday night, I hadn't really been drinking at all. Poor Joan sat alone and untouched on my bureau at home. I think I had proven after the prom night fiasco that overindulgence wasn't particularly helpful in any situation.

As I made my way across the city to Danielle and Josh's house in Magnolia Park, my nerves began to get the better of me. Maybe I wasn't reading Luke right at all. I was so sure that he was holding back—sure that despite how cold he acted at first, that he still had feelings for me. After two days without any messages, I wasn't feeling as certain.

With the wine in hand, I started up the brick walkway, noticing the line of cars out front. It looked like I was probably the last to arrive. *Awesome.*

Taking a deep breath, I rang the doorbell. Josh must have been right near the door because it was opened moments later. As he stepped aside for me to enter, I was able to see right into the living room and hear the laughter filtering out. Directly in my line of sight, I saw Luke, lifting a bottle of beer to his lips and tipping it back. No one should be that sexy just drinking beer.

"Jillian!" Danielle exclaimed as I walked into the room. I chose to focus on her and not scan the room. I couldn't look up at him yet. I felt like I needed to get my bearings first. She enveloped me in a warm hug.

"Relax," she whispered in my ear. "He seems nervous, too."

"This was a bad idea," I muttered through clenched teeth.

"This was a fantastic idea," she said softly. "Jillian," she began, now in a louder voice, "Josh was just talking about the time he almost lit Luke's jacket on fire in chemistry."

"Do I have to start all over?" he complained, looking mortified.

295

"Oh, c'mon," she replied. "It's hysterical. I can't believe you never told us this!"

"Yeah, I wonder why," he pouted, glaring at Luke, who I assumed had spilled the beans.

Looking across the room, I was finally able to take in his appearance, and immediately wished I hadn't. When I saw him at the bar on Saturday, I thought I was unable to form proper sentences around him because I could see a hint of chest hair in the opening of his shirt. At Danielle's opening, I thought it was because the muscles strained underneath the fabric of his arm. But I was wrong. It was just him. Because tonight he was wearing a dark blue jacket with a light color shirt. There was no chest hair and no straining muscles, and I was still incoherent.

"So, I was a little uptight in school," Josh began.

"A little?" Luke asked, smirking and taking another scandalous sip of his beer. *Well, maybe it wasn't scandalous, but it felt that way.*

"I was nervous about this particular lab because it was going to account for a large portion of our grade," he explained, ignoring Luke's remark. "We were supposed to use certain chemical compounds to alter materials and report on the result. Despite his claims to the contrary, Luke was distracted and barely paying attention. When I asked him to pass me the rubbing alcohol, it spilled."

"Like…a drop," Luke countered, laughing as Josh scowled. "And Josh was so nervous that we'd get points deducted for wasting chemicals that he cups his hand and tries to sweep the alcohol back into the beaker—in the process, making a trail of rubbing alcohol all over the table."

"So, we get all of the chemicals prepped, and I'm about to light the burner. Just as I squeeze the spark lighter, I hear a pop. When I look down, the trail of alcohol is on fire and a blue flame is racing across the table. And this one," he added, pointing at Luke, "is staring off into space, leaning over onto the table completely unaware that the flame is about to reach the arm of his jacket."

"He lets out this yelp," Luke interjected, "and I stand up just as the flame would have hit the sleeve."

"Yeah, Pruitt comes running over to us with water, putting the fire out. Freaking out. I thought I was going to hyperventilate."

"When did this happen and why wasn't this story broadcasted to everyone in school?" Megan exclaimed, wiping the tears from the corners of her eyes.

"Like the last week of classes," Josh replied. "Luke was suffering from senioritis."

I looked up and for the first time met Luke's gaze—his cheeks slightly pink. It was the last week of school and Luke had been distracted. Maybe it was wishful thinking—maybe I was over-estimating what *we* were—but I wondered if I had played a role in their lab disaster. I wondered if maybe Luke had been thinking about us.

"All right, everyone," Danielle announced, carrying a dish of chicken, broccoli and ziti into the dining room. "Dinner is served! I hope you don't mind the carbs. We had a request from number fifty-three over here."

"What can I say," Nate replied, with a shrug. "I get hungry after games."

I hung back as Josh, Luke and Nate walked into the dining room, feeling that it would be easier to choose a seat once I knew where Luke would be sitting. I was still feeling uncomfortable and self-conscious. Plus, I didn't need him seeing pieces of broccoli stuck in between my teeth.

"Relax, Jill," Megan said as she passed by me. "You look amazing and he almost choked on his beer when you walked in."

"I'm not sure if that's a compliment," I replied, following her into the room.

As she took her place across from Nate, it left only two seats open—the one across from Luke and the one at the head of the table. While I would have liked to convince Danielle that she should sit across from Luke, I didn't think my reasoning would fly. Hesitantly, I sat down, but kept my eyes trained on the table.

"Well, fortunately, you both made it out of chemistry unscathed," Danielle said, laughing.

"I wasn't the one who usually got into a jam," Josh argued. "This is the kid who evacuated an entire school."

My heart began hammering in my chest, and I felt like my head was underwater. I blindly stabbed at a piece of broccoli, jamming it into my mouth so that I'd have an excuse not to chime in.

"Yes, for *Joan*," Nate added. "Whatever happened to poor Joan?"

"Retired," I deadpanned. "She has a place in Florida now. Weather's good. Booze is cheap."

"God, you never went anywhere without that thing," Megan added, rolling her eyes.

"Seriously, I thought you were going to lose your mind that day," Danielle said, unaware that I actually *had* lost my mind and had cried like an idiot in the middle of the hallway. Only Luke knew that. Embarrassed, I shot back quickly.

"I did a lot of stupid things back then."

I hadn't meant to send any messages to Luke. I honestly was just trying to explain away why I had acted so emotional and crazy that day. I couldn't tell them that I had time-traveled and fallen in love. Brushing it off was the next best thing, but when I looked up to see Luke studying me curiously, I wasn't sure I had chosen my words well.

Fortunately, Nate changed the subject, talking about shop class, Megan, and how he wanted to murder every last guy in the room that day.

"I only had eyes for you," she teased.

"And he certainly had eyes for you. At least part of you," I added, obviously bypassing my internal filter.

"Ohh!" Josh bellowed. "Are you saying Nate had wandering eyes?"

"Well, that *was* the general idea," I said casually.

"What do you mean?" Nate asked, looking at me suspiciously.

"I mean I told her to stick out her ass so you could look at it, and you did. Now you're getting married, and you're welcome."

"It was more complicated than that," Megan countered.

"I can vouch for that," Luke added, looking at Nate, not me. "*Everything* was complicated."

"You knew about this?" he asked.

Luke nodded, swallowing his food.

"You seduced me!" Nate gasped, looking at Megan. "That's so hot."

"Whore," Danielle shouted, laughing.

"Who, me?" he asked. "I was a boy scout before Jezebel here led me over to the dark side."

"You like the dark side," Megan replied, with a stupid, happy grin.

Their flirtatious banter led to wedding talk. While Megan filled Nate and Josh in on the bridesmaid dress search—something I'm sure they would have rather skipped—I looked surreptitiously at Luke. There was nothing covert about it, though, when I realized he was staring back. He held my gaze for a moment—not smiling, but searching my face for something. I just didn't know what.

A half-hour later, Nate had consumed a metric ton of pasta and most of our plates were empty. Josh had been reminiscing about how overbearing Danielle was in school.

"Do you remember the top hat?" he asked, glaring at Danielle.

"Dude, *everyone* remembers the top hat," Nate added.

"I don't care what you say," she replied defensively. "It was classy."

"*It* was stupid," Megan countered.

"No, stupid is spiking the punch," Danielle retorted, narrowing her eyes at Luke.

"No, stupid is *drinking* the punch," Nate added. That was obviously meant for me.

"Stupid is thinking that no one saw that your shirt was buttoned wrong when you got into the limo," I shot back.

"Then stupid is disappearing behind the gym with your date and coming back a half-hour later wearing her lipstick."

"I wasn't even wearing lipstick," I argued.

"Oh, snap! I can't believe you walked into that. I was totally guessing," he exclaimed, laughing. "Josh, gimme some," he added, raising his hand up for a high-five.

Again, with my face burning from embarrassment, I glanced over at Luke. This time he wasn't looking up at me. He was staring at his glass and swirling the liquid around inside. He was a million miles away.

While Danielle brought out pastries and coffee, Nate entertained everyone with his retelling of the Great Race of 1999 where Megan's sports bra beat him by a hair. Nate cried foul, stating that the sports bra used diversionary tactics to win. Megan felt that it was unfair to have the conversation when the sports bra wasn't present to defend itself. Josh suggested mediation.

The walk down memory lane was beginning to wear on me, though. It was difficult enough sitting across from Luke—nevermind listening to everyone recount the events that led to my breaking his heart.

"Remember when Wakefield threw up all over that freshman at the bonfire," Nate asked. He was laughing so hard he couldn't catch his breath. "Poor girl was traumatized."

I froze when he mentioned the bonfire—images of our night at the cliffs playing in my head. I wanted to look at Luke. I wanted to see that he was affected the same way I was, but I was terrified that he might not even think about it at all.

"I hated the bonfire," Danielle complained. "And poor Jillian was stuck at home, punished. I so wanted to bail and keep her company."

Luke let out a rueful laugh. "Yeah. Must have been hard missing out on all the fun," he added, meeting my gaze.

I doubted that anyone at the table would have noticed the silent exchange between us. I doubted anyone was paying close enough attention, but as he looked up at me through his crazy long lashes, the red tint in his cheeks and atop his ears spoke volumes. He was remembering everything.

"I remember Val was looking everywhere for you that night, Luke," Danielle added. "It was pretty pathetic."

"Did you hear what happened to her?" Megan asked, looking excited to share some gossip.

"No, what?" she asked.

"Sarah Spellman told me at the reunion. Well, Val started a consulting business with a girl she met at NYU. So, she starts sleeping with the husband of one of their clients—some socialite. The wife finds out—goes public, giving *Page Six* a full account of how she was wronged. When the news gets out, all of their clients fire them. None of the Upper Eastsiders trusted their husbands around her. The business folded last month. Sarah said she's moving back to Reynolds."

Speechless, I remembered the conversation I had with Danielle right before my big accident. Danielle, crying in our living room, saying that she was ready to walk away from the company she worked so hard to build, just to break free of Val. That poor girl who was Val's business partner—the one whose business was now closed—could have been Danielle.

"Wow," Danielle replied, dazed. "She mentioned something about going into business together once, but I never followed up with her. Good thing, huh?"

"Lucky break," I muttered.

"So many train wrecks in our class," Megan continued. "And there was way too much puke Senior Week. Wakefield at the bonfire. Jillian after the prom. And Karen at Tyler's party!"

"Oh man," Nate exclaimed. "The ice luge! You never should've left for school early, Jill. That was the best. Luke, man, you missed that, too. Karen had her mouth attached to that luge all night. Wakefield went to carry her to his car and wham! Pukes all over his shoes!"

"Yeah, where were you that night?" Josh asked. "You sort of disappeared after graduation."

"I was around," he replied, uncomfortably, suddenly looking at his watch. "Um, I actually think I need to get going."

"Already?" Danielle pouted. "You can't stick around a little longer? I promise I won't make you play Pictionary."

"Pictionary, wow. No, I mean I have to check in at the bar. Peter—"

"I thought Tuesday was your night off?" she asked, not letting him off the hook. Did she know why he wanted to leave? Did she know that we had hit upon almost every traumatic memory in our short time together? Did she even realize that he was probably dying to run as far away from me as he could get?

"Yeah, but I like to check in," he explained, never making eye contact.

Liar.

"Well, we'll have to do this again soon," she added, hopefully.

"Yes, absolutely. Thank you for having me," he replied, his voice sounding strained. He stood, giving her a quick hug.

"Maybe next week?" Danielle pressed.

"Um, maybe. I have a busy week with the restaurant, but yeah, maybe."

As he turned to leave, he waved, never making eye contact with me, and then he was gone.

301

"Well, Dan my man, it wasn't the food," Nate began, "because it was definitely your best batch."

"I'm sorry, sweetie," she said, ignoring Nate and covering my hand with hers.

"Why are we sorry?" Nate asked, looking between me and Danielle.

"He needed time, remember?" Megan chimed in, sympathetically.

"Time? What are we talking about?" he asked, exasperated.

"Jillian and Luke," Megan replied, with a glare that was clearly meant to tell him to stop talking.

"Wow, man, I'm lost," he said to Josh, shaking his head.

"Come on," Josh replied, signaling to the living room. "I'll fill you in."

I was so consumed with conflicting emotions that it was hard for me to focus on one. I felt numb. It was just too much—reliving the memories that were so recent and raw, and witnessing his reactions to them all at the same time.

I knew he was mad. I knew he didn't trust that I wouldn't hurt him again, but I also knew he hadn't let go. While I was the one resistant in high school— afraid to get attached and alter the course of time—this time it was Luke who was making things more difficult than they needed to be. I kept remembering his words from the cliffs—not so long ago.

I'm not letting you avoid this anymore.

"We knew it would take some time," Danielle began. "We'll go to the bar this weekend, or I'll plan a movie night. Or, maybe—"

"No," I interrupted.

"No?"

"No, he doesn't get to leave."

"Sweetie, he's already gone," she replied, looking at me like I had finally lost it.

It took me less than a minute to make up my mind. Pushing away from the table, I marched into the living room and grabbed my purse.

"Jillian, don't go home yet!" Megan pleaded.

"I'm not going home," I replied, matter-of-factly.

"Wait, are you…you're going after him?" Danielle exclaimed.

"Thank you for dinner," I said, hugging her quickly.

"Oh my God! I feel like I should stop you and wish you good luck all at the same time!"

"I'll call you," I said, rushing out the door.

I jogged to my car, unprepared for the rain that had begun to fall. In all honesty, I didn't really care. As soon as I shut the car door, though, the sky opened up and the rain fell harder, sweeping across the ground in sheets. I could practically feel it punishing the roof of my car. It didn't bring with it the type of sound that was calming, like the noise machines you buy at The Sharper Image. It was an angry downpour. *How fitting.*

As I drove frantically through the busy streets, the harsh lights of the city reflected off the giant puddles that the surprise storm had created. I focused on the clock on my dashboard and nervously laid on the horn when the car in front of me slowed to a crawl.

When I arrived in his neighborhood, I looked up at the street sign, blurred by the rain. I jerked the wheel roughly, pulling into the darkened parking lot. I didn't care that my umbrella was at home. I didn't care that there wasn't a hood on my jacket. I didn't care that the rain would turn my hair into a wet, frizzy mess.

I stumbled out of the car, running up the steps of the building behind a clearly smarter person holding an umbrella. I dashed into the elevator, and up to the twenty-seventh floor. Panting and shivering, I rang the doorbell then knocked impatiently.

When the door cracked open, I was blinded by the glare inside.

"Jesus, Jillian," he said, his shoulders sagging in defeat. "You're drenched."

"I'm not…I'm not waiting for you to get your shit together anymore," I stammered as drops of water trailed from my hair down my face.

As my words registered, he looked stricken. I don't know what came over me. I didn't have a plan. I hadn't prepared a speech, but he was standing in the doorway in a white t-shirt and jeans with no shoes, and I just snapped.

With every ounce of strength I had, I grasped his upper arms and pushed him back inside and up against the wall next to the door. Catching him completely off-guard, I launched myself at him, grabbing his face between my wet hands before my mouth descended on his. His hands tensed, suspended in the air at his sides. His lips tensed, unprepared for my attack. I tensed, afraid that he wouldn't respond and kiss me back.

Please, kiss me back.

Then, at the same time, he slowly tilted his head to the side, parting his lips and bringing his hands up to rest on my waist. God, I missed his lips.

Emboldened, I snaked my hand up into his hair, tugging roughly, eliciting a groan that sounded like I had tugged maybe a little too hard. Before I could ask if I had been embarrassingly overeager, he spun us around, pinning me up against the wall, touching his open lips against mine—breathing into my mouth and making me feel more alive than I had any right feeling.

"I'm not letting you avoid this," I whispered, echoing his words from years ago. "I know you want me, too."

He squeezed his eyes shut, leaning his forehead against mine, looking pained and conflicted. I needed him to focus. I needed him to come back to me.

"Luke, I swear to you, I could never hurt you again. I barely lived without you the first time. I just…I can't give you time. We've wasted—*I've* wasted—so much time. If you give me a chance, I'll prove what I already know. But if I'm wrong and you want me to leave, I will. And I promise I won't bother you again. I just have to know."

As he stared at me, his gazed unwavering, I thought of the moments in life when you know however the situation turns out, things will never be the same. I thought of how I wanted, for just a moment, to freeze time and stay here before he answered because if he told me I was wrong—if he told me he could never forgive me—I honestly didn't know what I'd do. I thought about how good it felt to be pressed against him, feeling the heat of his body and the warmth of his breath. I thought that this was right—*we* were right—and I hoped he saw that, too.

When Luke slowly backed away from me, my heart sank and I felt sick. I could hear my labored breaths and feel the tears begin to well up in my eyes.

Dragging his hands from the top of his head down his face, he turned and walked slowly toward the window facing the lights of Bainbridge Island as I stood frozen in place, unable to make a move or sound.

It seemed like forever—it probably wasn't—when he turned to face me, looking tired and young and more like my Luke than he ever had.

"I don't want you to go," he said.

And my heart started beating again.

CHAPTER 24

Luke

I was always a black and white type of guy. You're either right or wrong; a winner or a loser. You either want her, or you don't. You either forgive her, or you don't. Except nothing—*nothing*— was black and white with Jillian.

For over ten years, I wondered why she left without telling me. For over ten years, I thought that it was something I said, or something I did. I thought maybe she wanted a fresh start in a new school. I thought maybe she wanted a new life. Now suddenly, after years of wondering, I had answers, but the answers just seemed to complicate things more.

It took Jillian years to figure out that she wanted to know me again. It took me less than a month to turn back into the loser I was in high school, hanging on her every word. There was no way I could deny that I still wanted her—not after the way I had been acting. But wanting her wasn't the problem—it was *never* the problem…trusting her was.

So while I sat at Josh and Danielle's dining room table, I tried to forget that Jillian made a really big mistake a long time ago. I tried to forget that I almost chased her across the country. I tried to forget about all the time I spent wondering. I tried to just enjoy my goddamn dinner.

I listened to everyone recount all of their twisted high school memories. I joined in when it seemed appropriate, and ignored the pain in my chest when something hit a nerve. But the tension slowly began to build. When Jillian said she did a lot of stupid things in high school, I wondered if she was thinking about the nervous boy pawing her on a scratchy, old blanket. When she mentioned Nate's wandering eyes, I thought about how I watched her in shop class—never taking my eyes off her body. When she joked about the lipstick she wore to the prom, I thought about Dream Jillian and her red, red lips.

But it was when Josh mentioned Tyler Burroughs's party that I snapped. Instead of going to the party with Jillian, I was at home thinking about flying to New York and demanding an explanation.

It was too much. Almost instantly I was furious—not because of what happened in high school—but because I couldn't enjoy a simple dinner without being reminded of it. Forgive her or don't. It should be easy. But it just wasn't.

So I left, annoyed and frustrated, vowing that I would get my shit together. If I was going to keep seeing Jillian—if I ever wanted to be friends with Jillian—I needed to let this go.

I never would have expected the doorbell to ring. I never would have expected to see her at my door, wet from the rain and determined to come inside. I almost told her that it had been a long night and that we'd talk in the morning, but instead, I opened the door wider and let her inside.

Without any warning, her lips were on mine, my back was against the wall, and it was definitely not what I expected. The anger and the bitterness seemed to melt away because we were both here now, and here felt pretty damn good. But she pulled back and asked me the one question I wasn't fully ready to answer. It should have been easy—black or white, yes or no—but it wasn't.

No, I don't want you to go. Yes, you should because when you leave again, it'll destroy me.

So while she stood there, cold from the rain and still so beautiful, I did nothing but stare out the window like the loser I was once again, wishing that this wasn't so goddamn complicated. I wanted to tell her that I didn't need her— that I barely ever thought about her, and that she hadn't ruined me years ago. I wanted to tell her that I was fine. But I was tired of lying. So, I looked into her eyes and told her not to go. From the look on her face, I could tell it was obvious that she was surprised.

"I thought you were going to ask me to leave," she replied softly. I took some sick comfort in the fact that her voice was wavering.

"No, but I can't do this if…Jillian, if you leave like that again…"

"Luke, I know that this doesn't make any sense. I know it sounds crazy, but I remember everything so vividly—like it just happened. Not just big things like the prom and the fire alarm. I remember the little things. I remember how you used to look at me. I remember what it felt like to touch you. I remember the smell of your cigarettes and that crappy mint gum you always chewed right after. I even remember how I could taste it whenever you'd kissed me," she added, her voice sounding much lower. "So, I can't *go* anywhere, Luke, when all I want to do is feel that again. It's the *only* thing I want to feel. Tell me how to fix this. Please. I need to fix this."

As she spoke, her lips trembled and her hands seemed to shake, and suddenly, the whole situation just seemed ridiculous to me. You either want her, or you don't.

I didn't think about what happened in high school when I walked over to her. I didn't think about the years I spent wondering when I put my hands on her cheeks. And I didn't worry about how much she hurt me when I kissed her.

Walking her backwards across the room, I dragged my lips, my tongue and my teeth down her neck. Stopping just shy of the couch, I fell backwards, pulling her down onto the soft leather cushions with me. Just those few minutes away from her lips seemed too long.

As soon as I switched our positions—settling myself over her—she was grinding underneath me, and testing my paper-thin restraint. The flood gates opened, and I needed my lips everywhere—on her neck, along her jaw, against her ear. I couldn't even say that touching Jillian was familiar, or that my mind drifted back to when I was eighteen and kissing her behind the school gym. Nothing was the same. Nothing had ever felt this way.

"God, I forgot...," I muttered, dropping any pretense that I was in control. "I forgot how good you feel."

I had wanted her for so long, and she was here, and her hands were everywhere—gripping my arms, tugging my hair and pulling at my shirt.

I reached back, helping her pull the shirt over my head and pushing her further into the couch in the process. When she moaned and shifted, it felt so good that I didn't care that this was moving too fast. I didn't have the strength to slow it down. I didn't want to.

I ran my fingers slowly along the edge of her sweater, feeling the soft skin beneath—desperately wanting more. Sliding my hand under the fabric, I brushed my knuckles along her hip, remembering the hidden tattoo there and how I wanted to feel the raised skin against my tongue.

Just as Jillian's hands moved up from my back and into my hair, the telephone rang.

"Let the answering machine get it," she panted against my ear. As she swirled her tongue around my earlobe, my hips shifted forward and my eyes rolled back. I didn't give a shit who was on that phone.

"Yeah," I murmured, more in response to how she felt than to what she had said.

The phone continued ringing in vain because I refused to focus on anything else. When the machine picked up, I was greeted by a familiar voice.

"Hi sweetie, are you there?"

I groaned, not just because Jillian stopped running her lips and tongue along my ear, but because Grace's voice had suddenly filled the room. I was pretty sure that if you took a poll of things a guy does not want to hear when they're lying on top of a girl, their aunt's voice probably ranks up there with "Are you done yet?"

"I wanted to make sure you were still dropping by tomorrow. I have some things I want you to look over regarding the menu. Also, I can't believe I have to hear about this Jillian situation from your uncle."

Panicked, I pushed up off the couch, tripping over my feet and stumbling toward the phone on wall. I vaguely registered Jillian's laughter as I grabbed the receiver.

"Grace, hey, I'm here," I said, gasping for breath.

"Luke, sweetie, what's going on? Are you okay?"

I was okay, Grace. I was better than okay. Now, I'm definitely not.

"I'm fine. I was just in the shower," I lied, hearing the giggling behind me again.

"Luke, I hear giggling. Is Jillian there now? Oh my God, were you in the shower?" she gasped.

"Grace, no! *Please*, can we talk about this tomorrow," I pleaded, trying to keep my voice low and praying that she'd move on.

"Oh, I get it," she whispered. "Cough once if she's in the room with you or twice if she's just close by."

"Are you serious? I'm not...Jesus, Grace," I replied incredulously. "Listen, I'm coming by tomorrow to talk about the menu. You're welcome to ask me anything you like when I see you."

"All right, Luke," she huffed. "I'll see you tomorrow, but tell Jillian I said hello."

I felt a pang of guilt rushing her off the phone, but when I turned to face Jillian, no longer lying down but sitting on the couch, my guilt was replaced with disappointment.

"So...um...Grace says hi," I said awkwardly.

"How is she?" she asked, and I wanted to cringe because Grace was *not* what I wanted to be discussing.

"She's good—she's Grace. She wanted to make sure we were still going over the menu tomorrow."

"You're going to Reynolds?"

"It's my day off tomorrow. So...yeah..."

She shifted on the couch, glancing down at the floor uncomfortably. I knew I needed to say something—do something—to recapture that moment. I just didn't know what.

"Listen, Luke, I think that we should talk," she said, wringing her hands nervously.

Again, another of the things you don't want the girl you were just kissing to say. I thought that we had moved past all of the attempts at explaining what happened and were trying to move forward. I was sick of going in circles. I was sick of complication. Couldn't it just be black or white?

"Jillian, I don't want to talk about high school anymore. I feel like that's all we ever talk about, and I think we just need to not...talk about it."

"That's not what I mean," she replied. I could tell she was frustrated, and she was having a hard time looking me in the eye. "Um...would you mind putting your shirt back on?" she asked, sheepishly. "It's a little distracting."

While it was admittedly a boost to my ego, I still wasn't happy with the direction this was heading.

"Um...sure," I stammered, grabbing my discarded shirt from the edge of the couch.

"When I said we should talk," she began, focusing on her fingers again. "I kind of meant that I think *you* should talk. I've done a lot of talking—probably too much. I think you know where I stand, but I really need to know what's going on in your head."

As soon as she said it, I felt embarrassed and stupid because being with her again was all I had been thinking about. It wasn't something I took lightly, but she obviously didn't know that. She didn't know about the five o'clock treadmill marathons and the psycho Facebook-stalking. She didn't know because I was the asshole who hadn't told her.

I sat down next to her on the couch, turning to face her but giving her room. I hated that she thought I had just gotten carried away. It was never like that with her—not even when we were kids. It was time to tell her the truth.

"About six months after you left, a friend from the bar was talking about visiting his cousin in New York. He wanted to hit up some places out there, and asked me if I wanted to go along. I had barely taken a day off in six months and I needed a break. I wanted to go—*really* wanted to go—but I didn't trust myself. I didn't want to get that close to you again because if I was there, I knew I'd try to find you. I didn't even know how, but I knew I would. If I found you, I knew I would end up right back where I started, and six months after you left, I was doing all right. I liked my job. I liked Seattle. I didn't think about you every day. So, I didn't go because seeing you would mean going through all that shit again. And I just wanted to stop…feeling that."

When I looked up, Jillian's eyes were glassy and I felt terrible for making her sad, but it was the only way for her to truly understand.

"And it was a good decision because seeing you again *was* really hard and it was *years* later. And I'm not going to lie. I want to be mad. I don't want to still feel this…but I do. And it pisses me off," I said, with a small laugh. As she laughed along with me, a tear slid down her cheek, and I didn't care anymore about giving her space. I moved closer, wiping the tears from her eyes. "I'm sick of trying to convince myself that I'm not feeling this. I'm not going to risk losing you again. It's not what I want."

"And this," she asked, hesitantly. "This is what you want?"

I moved closer to her, leaning over slowly, and waiting until she looked in my eyes.

"This is what I want," I said, without dropping her gaze.

It was all I needed. This time, I wasn't caught up in the moment. This time, I wasn't rushed. This time when I kissed her, I took my time. I held her close, touched her skin and groaned when she wrapped her arms around me. When I finally pulled back, the shine in her eyes and look on her face nearly crippled me.

"I like seeing you smile," I said, brushing her hair back from her face. "You should do that more often."

"I think I'll be smiling all the time if we do *that* more often."

"I think I'd like to be doing *that* all the time." I grabbed her hand and ran my thumb across the soft skin.

"So, you're going to Reynolds tomorrow? You'll be gone all day?"

"Most likely. I was going to leave here around ten, so I can get there for lunch. Grace likes to cook when I'm there. And by cook, I mean prepare a mini-feast."

"I was actually hoping to talk to her about the article. Do you think she'd mind if I gave her a call?"

After the awkward conversation I just had on the phone with Grace, I wasn't sure if I trusted her to speak to Jillian unsupervised. I had what was either a brilliant or terrible idea.

"Well, if you don't have plans…you could come with me."

"Because taking me to dinner and a movie would be too normal of a first date for us, right?" she laughed.

"It's not a date," I countered.

"No, you're bringing me home to auntie," she exclaimed.

"I think you've already been subjected to meeting the family. And it's just Grace—not auntie. We've had this discussion already."

"I know, Luke. I'm just giving you a hard time. I forgot how much fun you are when you're frustrated."

"Oh, really, now? I was just remembering how much fun *you* are when *you're* frustrated," I said, liking the blush it brought to her cheeks.

"Yeah, you were frustrating," she said. She suddenly sounded very breathy. It was hard to suppress my smile. I liked having the tables turned.

"So? Tomorrow?"

"That sounds perfect," she replied. And it did.

311

"Well...I should probably get home. It's been a crazy night," she said, standing and grabbing her purse. "Plus, I'd like to get a good night's sleep before our big date."

"It's not a date. Trust me. You'd know if we were on a date."

"Really? Do you have some smooth moves you whip out for special occasions, Luke?"

"If I was whipping out anything, I can assure you that you wouldn't be going home."

I heard a faint hitch in her breath and her cheeks turned pink. Mine probably did too because I couldn't believe that I had blurted that out. It was good that she was heading home because I clearly couldn't be trusted.

"I'll just have to take your word for it," she replied. "So, I'll see you at ten?"

I held open the door, still wishing that she wasn't leaving, but knowing I probably wouldn't be able to control myself if she stayed. While I didn't actually have any smooth moves, I wasn't opposed to making some up.

"I wish you weren't going." I cupped her cheek in my hand and rubbed my thumb along the soft skin.

"Me either," she replied, closing her eyes. "Goodnight, Luke."

With both hands cradling her face, I pulled her forward and kissed her one more time. When she softly pulled on my bottom lip—barely touching, sweet and soft—I knew going slowly wasn't going to be easy. Maybe for other people, but not for us.

"Goodnight, Jillian."

I watched her walk down the hall to the elevator, glancing over her shoulder and giggling along the way. We looked like teenagers again, and it felt good.

The next morning, I woke up at seven-twenty feeling restless with hazy memories of Jillian still on my mind. On the bright side, it was the first time I'd slept past five in weeks.

Once I was showered and dressed, I hopped online to check my email. I had another one of those stupid farm notices, so I logged onto Facebook to try and stop them, or maybe kill Nate. Since you seemed to be able to do almost anything on Facebook, I assumed murder was an option as well.

As I scrolled through my admittedly short timeline, I scanned the list for the one person who interested me. Below Danielle, who was "feeling hopeful", was Jillian. I couldn't help but laugh when I saw her status.

Jillian Cross has some smooth moves, too.

Before leaving the house, I gave Grace a quick call to let her know I was bringing Jillian along with me. That quick call lasted twenty minutes while Grace grilled me about Jillian's likes and dislikes. When I wasn't able to tell her if Jillian had any allergies to shellfish, she obsessed over whether Jillian would prefer seafood salad or vegetable stir-fry instead. After a lengthy debate with herself, she settled on the stir-fry using veggies from the local farming co-op. Apparently these vegetables were by far superior to the run-of-the-mill veggies normal people buy at the supermarket. I knew this because Grace told me so, and I never questioned her—even if, to me, a vegetable was just a vegetable.

It didn't take very long to get to Jillian's apartment, and fortunately, Grace's phone call hadn't held me up. When I pulled up in front of her building, Jillian stepped outside and bounced down the stairs before I even threw the car into park. I wondered if that meant she was anxious or excited—or maybe a little bit of both.

I watched her walk to the car and tried not to gape at the sight of her. It was hard not to notice the curves on her body. The neckline of her blue sweater hung low, giving me a clear view of her neck, her collarbone and her bare shoulders. She might remind me of the Jillian I knew in high school, but she definitely wasn't that girl anymore. I was going to be faced with the most distracting drive of my life.

"Good morning," she sighed, settling into her seat.

"Morning," I replied. I had been so wrapped up in how she looked and how she felt that I missed my opportunity to lean over and greet her properly. I'd passed that comfortable window where it wouldn't seem awkward. So much for smooth moves.

"So, I logged into Facebook this morning," I began, as I pulled away from the curb.

"Oh, did you? Read anything good?" she asked. I could hear the grin in her voice.

313

"Are you going to showcase these moves?"

"I don't think so Luke—especially on the way to Auntie Grace's. You need to be on your A-game and these moves...they might blow your mind," she added, gravely.

"I think I can handle anything you throw my way."

"And *I* think we should be discussing the article for a bit instead," she countered.

She dug into her pocketbook and pulled out a mini tape recorder and steno pad. She pressed the record button and set it down on the center console. She was actually serious.

"And the conversation was just starting to get interesting," I muttered.

"Well, we can try to keep this one interesting, too. Tell me: why buy a restaurant when you seem to have your hands full with the bar?"

"That's hardly an interesting story."

"I'll be the judge of that," she replied, opening her notebook.

"Well, I told you already that I was taking classes at U-Dub and I had to take this Business Policy class as a prerequisite. Horrible class—professor was even worse. Anyway, one of the case studies involved a holding company that bought a number of neighborhood pubs. They targeted businesses that were floundering and refurbished them so they were able to buy them at a reasonable cost and help revitalize the neighborhood at the same time. It was something that really struck a chord with me. So, I started looking at some of the neighboring businesses. The Rusted Nail had been hemorrhaging capital for years. I don't know how they stayed afloat as long as they did. When I heard the owner was looking to sell, I had my lawyer make an offer. It was in such tough shape that I'm actually paying less than the value of the property. We're scouting out a couple properties now for a third acquisition."

I realized I was babbling, and suddenly felt embarrassed. Even once I had stopped to take a breath, Jillian hadn't said a word. I glanced over quickly to make sure I hadn't put her to sleep. She was staring at me—wide-eyed and honestly, freaking me out a little.

"You okay?"

"You're...you're buying a *third* property?" she stammered.

"Well, I imagined five—a couple bars, a couple restaurants, and I have my eye on this diner, but it's actually not in Seattle. But yeah, just the third for now."

"Jesus," she muttered. "So, wow...I...um...I actually forgot my follow-up question."

She flipped her pad over and ran her finger down the page.

"So, how does this normally work?" I asked, needing to break the awkward the silence. "The article, I mean."

"Oh, well, it's simple. We'll highlight the aspect of the renovation that will best attract business—both for you and for Danielle," she added absently.

Once I got her to talk about the areas she was planning to highlight, the conversation flowed comfortably. I explained how I wanted to combine the feeling of a neighborhood pub with that of a gourmet restaurant. Grace's Fire wouldn't be the type of place where you'd need a translator to read the menu. It would be good food for everyday people.

Before we knew it, we were driving into Tacoma.

"God, it's so weird being here," she said softly, staring out the window.

"You don't come back often?"

"No, I do. It's just...weird. I forget..." she said sadly.

We passed the site of the old Greasy Spoon where Jillian sat cross-legged on top of a picnic table and inhaled a cheeseburger.

"Oh my God! Ink Credible Art is still open!" she exclaimed.

"I thought you said you came back here?" It was like she was seeing Tacoma for the first time.

"I do, but I never paid attention...I guess I just missed it," she added. "Does Seth still run it?"

"I haven't been inside in years," I replied.

I was bombarded by images of her tattoo—the raised skin—how I wanted to feel it. Then suddenly I began wondering, in the time we'd been apart, who had seen that tattoo and touched her skin. It made me crazy.

"Have you ever gone back? Gotten more work done?" I asked.

"No," she replied. "I just have the one."

"You?"

"I had Seth do some work with the flames, but that was years ago."

When I asked him to add a few more.

It hadn't occurred to me that the ride to Reynolds was a veritable minefield of memories. It also hadn't occurred to me that our route was going to take us right past the cliffs. There was no way around it without tacking an extra half-hour onto the trip.

The conversation had lulled as we approached the area where I had parked my bike years ago. My whole body tensed as we passed the trees that lined the border. What was I supposed to say? *Over here on the left, you'll find the cliffs where you were deflowered?*

"Have you...do you ever go back there?" she asked, looking out toward the trees.

"To the cliffs? No. Well, once," I replied, remembering the day with Carter, and how he told me that I couldn't throw my life away. He kicked my ass in gear, and then made me eat a biscotti.

"Did you...bring someone?"

"There? What? No," I replied, outraged. "I went with Carter once after you were gone. I could never do that."

"I had no right to ask you that, Luke. I'm sorry. I was out of line—"

"Jillian, if we're going to do this, we can't tiptoe around each other anymore. I'm here because I want to be here. If you want to know who I dated, I'll tell you."

I'd obviously leave out how Vanessa broke up with me when I couldn't manage to take her to a Green Day concert.

"I don't think I want to know all of that," she said, shaking her head. "You're not dating anyone now, though, right?"

"No, I'm not dating anyone right now."

She smiled softly and fidgeted with the bracelet on her wrist.

"I have a hard time imagining you showing up at my door and taking me to a movie. It's so...conventional," she said, laughing.

316

"I can do convention. I can do a lot of things."

When I looked over at her, Jillian was opening and closing her mouth, but no sound was coming out. I had to admit that I liked knocking her off her game.

I finally pulled down the windy road to Grace and Carter's house. Once I parked the car, I met her on the other side, grabbing her hand and leading her up the walkway. Her fingers curled around mine as we climbed the stairs. Grace must have been watching from the window because I never had a chance to ring the doorbell. The door flew open and Grace came barreling out.

"Luke, sweetie!" she exclaimed, pulling me in for a bone-crushing hug. She turned to Jillian and smiled widely. "Jillian, it's so good to see you again. Come in, come in."

As soon as we walked through the doorway, I could smell something cooking in the kitchen. I thought I smelled sauce and fish and maybe even charcoal from the grill. It definitely didn't smell like vegetable stir-fry.

I led Jillian by the hand through the foyer and into the dining room, but stopped short at the sight before me.

Placed around the perimeter of the entire table were probably two dozen different dishes—pasta, fish, chicken, beef and salad. Each plate had what looked like a laminated tag in front of it. Dropping Jillian's hand, I moved toward the table and picked up a tag. It *was* laminated and had "Grandma LaBreque's Barbeque Meatloaf" in large letters at the top. The rest of the sheet listed ingredients and possible wine-pairings. I looked up at her, not really knowing what to say.

"I may have gone a bit overboard," she said, laughing nervously.

"Grace, is this the whole menu?"

"Oh gosh! Of course not!" she replied, laughing. "It's only the core entrees. We'll add seasonal dishes, obviously. Oh, and appetizers."

"I can't believe you cooked all this," I said, scanning the table. "I thought we were going to *talk* about the food. Not actually eat it."

"Well, how would you know if you liked the recipe or not?" she asked, as if it had been the silliest thing she'd ever heard. "So, I made a list of all the dishes," she continued, grabbing two clipboards from the table. "There's a space next to each for you to comment."

She handed me a clipboard and I glanced down the page—chicken milanese, white truffle macaroni and cheese, pistachio encrusted tuna—the list went on and on.

"I made a copy this morning for Jillian, too," she added, handing her a clipboard. "It'll be good to have a non-biased opinion."

So for the next hour, we sampled the dishes while Grace followed behind us asking how each one tasted and what type of sides we should offer. After an hour, the wine Grace had been plying us with seemed to be affecting Jillian.

"Grace, I'm not sure this coconut rice thing is going to fly," she said, scrunching up her nose. "Coconut belongs inside chocolate or in crappy mixed drinks."

Grace looked more amused than offended by her comment. I also noticed that in between tastings, Jillian's hand somehow found its way onto my arm. Whether she rested it casually on my forearm as she took a quick sip of wine or absently ran it along my shoulders, she was always touching me somewhere, and it was beginning to affect me...a lot. So much so, that when Grace asked me what I thought, my first reaction was that I thought it was time to leave so we could have some alone time. That wasn't what she was asking, though, and I had missed the actual question.

"I'm sorry, what?" I asked, embarrassed that I had been caught off guard.

"I asked if you thought the steak tips would taste better with more Worcestershire sauce," she repeated. "Nevermind. Let me just grab some," she added, hurrying off to the kitchen.

"Earth to Luke," Jillian said, waving her hand in front of my face. "Something on your mind? You seem a little...distracted," she teased, arching her eyebrow. She'd definitely loosened up a bit.

"Well, you're pretty distracting," I replied, leaning in close. "And you seem a little tipsy already. Surprising from the girl who once carried a flask."

"I'm older and wiser now. Joan and I don't party like rock stars anymore. I'm a cheap date," she laughed.

"This isn't a date. Remember?"

"True. It has some date-like elements," she said, looking up at me from underneath her lashes. "But it's definitely not a date."

"Date-like elements?" I asked, trying not to laugh.

"Yes, well, you picked me up at my place," she began, staring at her fingers as she ran them along the table cloth. "You held my hand. You fed me some fantastic food."

She stopped, looking up slowly, and I could tell she was struggling again with whatever it was that she wanted to say.

"But if this was a date, I think you would have kissed me already."

I grabbed the hand that was still tracing patterns on the tablecloth and pulled her closer, wrapping my free arm around her waist. Holding her still felt familiar and foreign all at once.

"It's a shame that this isn't a date because I really want to kiss you. But I imagine—since this isn't a date—that it would be inappropriate," I replied. My mouth was almost brushing against hers.

"I wouldn't want to do anything inappropriate…since this isn't a date," she replied. I could feel her breath against my lips. As much as I enjoyed teasing her, I wasn't sure how long I'd be able to hold out.

"Maybe we could make an exception—just this once—even though this isn't a date," I added, slowly, softly, barely touching her lips.

"Just this once."

When I moved closer, she sighed and I breathed her in. When she moaned in my arms, I held her tighter and kissed her harder. I couldn't get enough.

I had forgotten that Grace had only gone into the kitchen for a bottle of Worcestershire sauce until I heard a gasp. Startled, Jillian jumped back, almost knocking over a chair.

"Oh! I'm so sorry!" she exclaimed from the doorway, shielding her eyes with her hand. "Carry on. I'll be in the kitchen. Pretend I'm not here."

As embarrassing as it was having Grace walk in while I groped Jillian, I wasn't going to ask my aunt to hide in the kitchen just to avoid feeling awkward.

"Sorry about that," I laughed, nervously. "Let's try the Worcestershire," I added, desperate to change the subject.

"Still hungry?" I asked Jillian, smirking. Her eyes went wide, and her face flushed more. She wasn't thinking of steak tips and Worcestershire sauce. But with Grace in the room, there'd be no more time to discuss what was or was not appropriate for our non-date.

319

Jillian took her fork, dipped it in the sauce and took a bite of steak.

"Oh, Grace," she groaned. "This is amazing. Luke, you need to try this."

I went to reach for a plate, but Jillian grabbed another piece and raised it to my mouth.

"Here, taste mine," she said, matching my smirk. It was my turn to feel uncomfortable as her words played on-loop in my mind.

At three-thirty, Grace served the vegetable stir-fry, telling us that the food we had been gorging ourselves on couldn't be considered lunch. We were already stuffed, but she was so excited about her vegetables that we had to try it. When we were finished, Jillian pulled out her notebook and recorder, and asked questions about Grace's inspirations and favorite types of dishes. I listened to the two of them as they laughed and joked about some cook on the Food Network.

"You'd like her, Luke," Jillian laughed. "She's hot, but she'd force her *moots-a-rella* on you."

"I think you just made a food joke, but I'm not even sure," I replied, shaking my head.

Grace however was doubled over. "Or maybe her *pan-cheet-tah*," she added.

"Wow, you guys need to take this act on the road. There isn't enough food humor out there."

By the time Grace and Jillian finished gossiping about Food Network hosts, it was already getting dark, and it was time to head home.

"I hope I'll get to see you again soon, Jillian," Grace said, pulling her in for a hug.

"Well, with food like that, I think I'll be at the restaurant every night!" she exclaimed. "You're going to get so sick of me."

"Never," she replied, with a wink.

"Bye, Grace," I said, kissing her cheek. "Thanks for everything."

As soon as we headed back down the winding road, an uncomfortable silence fell over the car. I'd spent the last three hours waiting to be alone with Jillian. Now that we finally were, I didn't know what to say. Thankfully, she broke the silence.

"Well, I'm glad I brought my camera. The picture of the dining room tasting is priceless," she said, laughing. "She's too much."

"God, that wasn't even the half of it. You should've seen her when the first book came out. She held a book release party and was cooking for days."

"I'm sorry I missed that," she added, wistfully.

At times when I looked at her, I felt like she was still the girl I knew all those years ago—silly and frustrating, teasing and watching me squirm. Then there were times I looked at her and could barely see that girl. The most striking difference between Jillian as a teenager and Jillian now happened at times like this. She was so confident and ready to take me on when we were kids. There was never any fear or uncertainty. Now, even when she joked around, there was an underlying sadness. It would peek through when we were quiet. It showed on her face now.

"Me too," I replied.

"It was good to see her, though…as embarrassing as it was there for a little while. I felt like a teenager getting caught sneaking around."

"Better my aunt than your dad and his gun. Do I still need to worry about that?"

"Not unless you're skulking outside my window at three in the morning."

"Well, I was hoping that won't be necessary anymore." I was *hoping* for an invitation inside.

She shifted uncomfortably in the seat next to me, and I smiled. She understood exactly what I meant.

"I had a really good time today," she finally said.

I could see that she was looking at me, but I kept my attention on the dark road ahead.

"I'm glad. Grace was excited when I told her you were coming with me. She's…excitable."

"That's an understatement, but…I didn't mean that I had a good time with Grace today. I meant I had a good time with you."

"I had a good time with you, too," I replied, glancing over to her quickly.

If I wanted to survive the drive back, I couldn't dwell on how badly I wanted to be in Seattle already, and how much I wanted to touch her again. The tension would kill me. I knew I had to get her talking. So, I asked about Meg and Nate, and she filled me in on their wedding plans, including the ship they rented for the ceremony in February. Jillian suffered from motion sickness and was convinced she was going to be the first one to throw up. She asked about Carter and told some crazy stories about New York—some seemed to contradict others. I chalked it up to nerves. She made me nervous, too.

I found it hard listening to the things that happened while she was in college. Everything she mentioned—no matter how minor—reminded me that I wasn't there. I wasn't mad at her, though. I just hated that we wasted so much time.

When we began to approach the city, I had a decision to make. I would need to veer off in one direction to take Jillian to her apartment, and another if I didn't take her home, and I really, really didn't want to take her home. Well, I did…but to *my* home.

"So…I could drop you back at your apartment if you're tired. Or if you'd like, we can get a drink or something…maybe go to the bar or back to my place…" I winced because I knew I was stammering like an idiot.

"That sounds perfect, actually…but I don't think I'm up for going to the bar," she replied. "So, maybe your place? If that's okay?"

Yeah…it was okay. It was better than okay.

So instead of taking Jillian home, I drove to my place knowing full well that I wasn't doing it to get her a glass of wine. I was much more interested in the "or something".

The minute the car stopped, I reached over, sliding my hand behind her neck and pulling her closer. After spending the last three hours thinking about nothing but kissing her, I needed less thinking and more doing. I wasn't capable of waiting anymore.

It felt so good to just kiss her when I wanted to and not think about all the bullshit from the past. It felt so good when she kissed me back. It felt even better when she started to move out of her seat and lean over toward mine. And the best when she tried to crawl into my lap. Unfortunately, the space in my car wasn't conducive to that particular maneuver and we ended up wedged in the driver's seat.

Laughing, I opened the door, pulling her out of the car with me—still kissing her as I attempted to close the door and stand on my tired legs. We swayed back and forth until I leaned her against the car. She pulled away from me, panting, and smiled, and I just knew I was going to ask her to stay with me. I *needed* her to stay with me.

"I think you need to take me upstairs now, Luke," she said, breathlessly. And I thought so, too.

I grabbed her by the hand as we walked into the building, laughing like kids, and headed straight for the elevator.

"Hey, Luke," George said from behind his desk. George, the overnight security guard, clearly wanted to be introduced to Jillian. It would have to be some other time, though. I was sure he'd understand that I was in a bit of a rush.

"Hey, George, did you catch the Huskies game?" I asked as we waited for the elevator. "It's going to be a good year." Small talk was the key here. Don't engage.

"You can say that again. Have a good evening," he added with a smirk. George, a Boston native as well, had already not-so-subtly grilled me about Jillian after seeing her leave two weeks ago. I could practically sense his hand twitching to give me a high five.

When the elevator opened, I guided her inside and against the back wall—my hands on her hips and my lips on her neck. Just a tiny groan and sigh from Jillian set my hands in motion—moving along her body—exploring her curves and contours.

"I don't want you to go home tonight," I whispered into the crease of her neck. "I can't let you go again."

I felt her body sag against mine and I wrapped my arms tighter around her waist. I wanted her in my house—in my bed—now because unlike last night, once I started, I didn't think I'd be able to stop.

Once the elevator opened, I grudgingly pulled back, staring down the long hallway. My front door seemed to be miles away. Jillian moved behind me, wrapping her arms around my waist and pressing her chest against my back, while she nipped at the area below my ear with soft, wet lips. I let out a groan that probably woke the neighbors when she sucked my earlobe into her mouth.

"Move. Faster," I ordered, practically dragging her by the hand out of the elevator and to my front door. As I fumbled with the keys, Jillian's tongue was back on my neck, distracting me and making it almost impossible to find the right key for the lock.

We managed to get into the house without putting on a show for the neighbors, but once the door was closed, I couldn't hold back anymore.

"Jillian," I said, pulling her against me and pressing my forehead to hers. She was panting and beautiful. "Tell me we're moving too fast. Tell me to stop."

But instead of answering, she grabbed me by the sleeve, pulling me down the hall and stopping in front of my bedroom door. I didn't care that this was a reckless decision, and I didn't care how crazy the past two days had turned out. I didn't care about anything but her.

"I'm going to ask you again, Luke, because I need to hear it. Are you sure this is what you want?" she asked, gravely.

"You're the only thing I'll ever want," I replied because it was true. It was always her.

I pushed the door open behind her, and with my hands on her hips and my lips against her neck, I walked her backwards into my room.

Planting both of her hands on my chest, she twisted a fistful of fabric in each and pulled me forward, backing up again until she hit the foot of my bed.

"Can I take this off?" I asked, covering her hands with mine.

"That's usually how these things go," she replied, smirking.

"Really?" I asked, reaching behind me and pulling the jersey over my head. "I figured I'd ask since last time I had my shirt off, it was a little distracting for you."

"Maybe now I'm ready to be distracted," she said, with a wicked grin.

"Can I take this off, then?" I added, running my finger underneath the edge of her shirt.

"Luke, if you're going to ask permission to remove every article of my clothing, we need to have a talk. I'm not a patient girl."

Well, if that was how she wanted to play.

I didn't waste any time, ducking down and wrapping my arms around her waist. I quickly hoisted her up and over my shoulder, walking to the side of the bed and throwing her down onto it.

"What do you think you're doing?" she asked, flushed and breathless.

"I'm moving things along, per you request," I replied, crawling onto the bed next to her. "I aim to please, and furthermore, I'm not asking for your permission anymore. I'm taking off your shirt now."

I lifted up the fabric, exposing her stomach and dragged my mouth across the soft skin. I could hear the pace of her breathing increase and I smiled, enjoying how affected she was. Working my way up, I stopped when my lips reached the material of her bra.

When we were kids, I remember how I was nearly knocked on my ass when I saw her tiny white underwear. Now, I was almost incapacitated, staring at the black mesh material of her bra. It probably didn't help that the thin fabric hid nothing.

I tugged at the snap on her jeans and pulled on the zipper. Grabbing the material at her hips, I lowered them slowly as she squirmed, irritated by my pace. But I wanted to savor every moment. When the jeans finally gave way, her matching black underwear was displayed, and I was treated to a perfect view of the Celtic cross, peering out through the sheer fabric.

"I've thought about this for a long time," I said, pulling the edge of the sheer fabric down, fully exposing the tattoo. Looking up at her from below, I poked my tongue out and lightly traced the shape of the design, applying more pressure after each pass. Both of her hands had been resting alongside her ears, but as soon as I flattened my tongue, making wider strokes, she brought them down and into my hair, tugging and twisting strands between her fingers.

Sometimes, the things you want to savor the most seem to pass by the fastest. Sometimes there are moments you wish you could freeze and revisit whenever you wanted. As I looked at Jillian, lying on my bed—with her pale skin against the dark fabric—I knew this was one of those moments because everything would inevitably move by so fast.

Articles of clothing rained down on my bedroom floor as we pulled and yanked off the remainder of each other's clothes. Then it was just us. No bullshit. No pretenses.

The feeling was so intense and consuming and kept building and building—becoming everything I was and replacing everything I had. When I was finally able to let go and let the fire within me burn, I was never so happy to be reduced to ashes because I always felt at home in her flames.

And when we were both still and the room was quiet, I didn't mourn the fact that the moment had passed and it was over. I knew from the fire, there'd be rebirth—something stronger, something better and something to remind me why it was all right to burn.

CHAPTER 25

Jillian

On a cold day in November, I bumped my head and woke up feeling rough textures against my skin, wondering why my bed sheets were purple and not cream. I had no idea where I was until I saw that the calendar on my desk read April 29, 1999.

Four weeks later, I woke up on the floor of my bedroom—carpet against my cheek—next to a bed with a cream comforter. I didn't know if I had traveled back in time, or simply lost my mind. Turns out, it was both.

This time, as I slowly drifted back into consciousness, I didn't question what pillow I was sleeping on or whose arm was slung across my waist. I didn't wonder what made me so tired or why my body ached. I knew why. I knew exactly where I was, and it was exactly where I wanted to be.

I opened my eyes slowly, my lids fluttering against the light from the small window in the corner. In the daylight, his room looked so different. Or maybe it was just that I was seeing it differently. The last time I was here, I made a hasty exit, not bothering to look around very much.

I let the feeling of pure contentment wash over me. I was in Luke's bed—with Luke—our clothing on the floor and long forgotten. I'd like to believe that my second time in high school matured me a bit. So instead of grabbing my phone and taking a picture for posterity, I buried my face in his pillow, breathing in the scent of him to commit it to memory. Just the small movement of my head tilting caused him to stir.

"Why are you awake?" he asked, sounding groggy. I could feel the heat of his breath against the back of my neck, and I arched back into him shamelessly, craving his mouth on my skin again.

"I just woke up," I stammered, trying to control the impulse to grind against him. He hummed, moving his hand to my hip and brushing his lips softly against my shoulder blade. I tried to control my reaction, but a low groan escaped from my lips.

Way to play hard-to-get, Jillian. Although, I guess it was a little late for that.

"We didn't get to sleep until late," he complained, as if he had to remind me. "Or early, I should say."

I wanted to turn around and see his face and look in his eyes, but it felt so good to have his hand on my body and his mouth on my back. It was a decision no one should be forced to make. As I rolled over slowly, his hand moved with me, gliding across my stomach, until it rested on the opposite hip—gripping me tightly and pulling me closer. I felt like I was gasping for breath.

When I looked up into his eyes, squinting from the sun, but shining in the light, I wanted so badly to say something witty or endearing or sexy or cool. All I could do was breathe heavy.

"Good morning," he said, smirking at me.

"Yeah," I replied, proving that my parents didn't waste any money paying for my education. How was I supposed to talk to him? On an average day, Luke Chambers was stunning. After the evening (and subsequent morning) we had, he looked unreasonably beautiful. The hair that had been tamed a bit since high school now shot out into every conceivable direction. His neck and jaw were darkened by bristly whiskers. His bare chest was covered with a smattering of light brown hairs. And he was smiling at me with those bright eyes, clearly enjoying the fact that I was staring at his chest like it was my breakfast.

"It's a very good morning," I managed to add, ducking my head into his chest. His arms wrapped around my back in response, and I let out yet another painfully obvious groan. This time, I didn't care. I couldn't get close enough to him. I nestled into him, breathing him in. I could almost hear Suzanne asking me if I was smelling his smell.

Yes, Suzanne. I am. And it's ah-may-zing.

He rolled onto his back, pulling me with him so that I was able to curl up into his chest. I never wanted to leave his bed. There was nothing the outside world could offer that would convince me otherwise. I was sure we could have food delivered when we needed it.

"Sorry about the sunlight. Usually, I need a little help getting up in the morning after working at the bar all night. I would have liked to sleep in with you a bit," he said as his fingers trailed along my arm. "Next time, I promise I'll remember to close the shades…even if you're demanding that I take your clothes off."

"Next time? And I was not demanding that you take my clothes off!" I sat up to glare at him. In the process, the sheet that had been covering me dropped to the bed.

His eyes grew wide and he shot up, grabbing me by the elbows and rolling me under him. My legs clearly had a mind of their own, and parted so that he was able to settle above me. My legs were clearly very easy.

"I seem to remember someone telling me that I didn't need an invitation to take your clothes off. That's pretty demanding."

Holding his weight on one arm, he ran his other hand up and down my side. I was a squirming mess within seconds. "And yes, next time."

"Well, then. Does this mean we're going steady?" I asked, attempting once again to keep my cool and say something that didn't betray how much of an effect he had on me.

"I don't know about that," he replied. "I have a reputation to uphold, but I might make an exception."

"So, are you going to ask me to the movies and hold my hand when the lights go down?"

"Hold your hand? Clearly you aren't familiar with my reputation," he replied, burrowing his head into my neck and running his lips along the soft skin. My hands moved up into his hair, holding him against me as I tilted my head to give him better access. I'd have to let him know that he didn't need an invitation for that either.

"I'm well-acquainted with the myth," I replied, sounding breathy instead of snarky. "I just happened to know the facts behind the boy on the bike. I remember a lemony-fresh-Lexus-driving, osso bucco-eating softy."

"Softy? Softy!" he exclaimed, abandoning his spot on my neck. "I'll have you know, I'm hardcore."

"Mmmmm, yes, you are," I replied, craning my neck so that I could reach his lips.

He lowered himself onto me, and I relished the feeling of his weight pressing me into the bed. Every part his body touched mine, from our entangled legs to his soft, wet lips. Our first time together—since, well, our first time together—was rushed and frenzied, full of need and want. Then, later, in the early hours of the morning, there was a desperate desire to be as close as possible, as if we could make up for the time we spent apart if we just held onto each other tight enough. This time was different, though. While the desire and need and want remained, I stopped feeling like I had to hold onto him. I stopped worrying that if I let go, he'd disappear. Ironically, this time I didn't mind that he was taking his time. I wanted to revel in each moment because I'd travelled a long way for him—farther than he'd ever know.

When he finally brushed his lips softly against my neck, I had to fight to keep my mouth closed before I declared my undying love and devotion and suggested he marry me as soon as possible. I was pretty sure that post-coital proposals were tacky, so I kept it to myself.

"Yes, it *is* a very good morning," he said, his laugh muffled against my skin. He rolled slowly over, pulling me with him. "I should feed you, shouldn't I?"

"Would it require moving? Because if it does, eating isn't a priority." With my head on his chest and my arm slung across his waist, I had everything I needed right there.

"If you're considering staying in bed all day, I'm game. I don't need to be at the bar until later today. Your friend, however, will start blowing up my phone shortly with restaurant business. I'm okay with ignoring her for a while, though," he offered.

"Why do you have to work?" I whined. "You're spoiling all my plans."

I didn't think that I'd be able to leave now that I was with him. I'd turned into *that girl.*

"Oh? You have plans?"

I knew he was joking, but I also knew I sounded kind of clingy. I didn't want to send him running for the hills now that we had finally made some progress.

"I'm trying hard not to sound like a crazy person here, and it's not working."

"I know you like naming things. Are you naming my bed sheets? Because that's where I draw the line."

"I'm not naming your bed sheets," I shot back. "I'm just…happy to be here. I didn't think this would happen."

He didn't respond, but I could feel his fingers running through my hair. I wanted to keep the conversation light and not mention post-coital proposals, but he was making it so hard. Instead of thinking about inappropriate declarations, I focused on the things that needed to be said. We had talked so much about what had happened and why, but I still needed him to know how serious I was. I wasn't going to pledge my undying love, but I'd let him read between the lines.

"I agree with what you said last night," I began. "I don't think we need to keep going over what happened, but I don't want you to think that I'm here just because I saw you at the reunion. It wasn't like that."

Even though I wasn't facing him, I could hear him draw a deep breath. I knew he didn't want to talk anymore, but I really felt that he needed to hear this. I couldn't offer him a true explanation, but I could tell him what it was like for me. I twisted, turning my head so that he could see my face.

"There was never anyone else, Luke. Leaving like I did was stupid, but it was always you. I need you to know that."

"Jillian," he sighed. "I told you. We don't need to keep going over this."

"I know. I want to move past this, too, but I don't think I can if you don't understand what I'm saying. Despite how long it took me to be here with you, for me, I never really left."

"C'mere," he said, propping himself up against the headboard. The sad smile on his face made me anxious. He shifted slightly so that I could curl up against his chest again.

"I agree with you," he said, wrapping his arm around my shoulders and holding me close. "You were really stupid."

"Luke, I'm trying to be serious here," I exclaimed, pinching him in the side.

"Ouch! By wounding me?"

"God, you're still such a pain in the ass."

"And apparently, after all this time, that still turns you on."

"Ugh. Forget staying in bed with you all day," I replied, pulling away from him. This time, when I sat up, I remembered to take the sheet with me.

"Hey, hey. Settle down. You used to have a sense of humor," he teased.

I narrowed my eyes at him as I swung my legs over the side of the bed.

No more snuggling for him.

As my feet were about to touch the ground, I felt his arm wrap around my waist, pulling me back onto the bed beside him. I was irritated that he was still grinning at me, but at the same time, distracted by the adorable creases at the corners of his eyes. He smiled with his whole face.

331

"I told you last night," he said, trailing his fingers softly along my cheek. "You're the only thing I'll ever want."

Placing my hands on his face, I pulled him closer and attacked his lips. How was I supposed to keep my lips to myself when he said things like that? It was his own fault.

"So, we're okay?" he asked, and I could feel him smiling against my mouth.

"We're okay," I replied. It was actually better than okay. "So...the only thing you'll ever want, huh?"

"Yes," he said with the smirk that I love. "And maybe some cereal."

"Cereal? You sure know how to woo a girl, Luke."

"I think we're past the wooing stage, right? I hope so, because that's all I have."

"I figured that after living with Grace for so long, you'd only eat omelets and scones, maybe some crepes."

"Her scones were fantastic," he said wistfully. "But coming from a guy who couldn't eat Cheerios until adulthood, cereal is very under-rated."

"Then, fine," I sighed, stretching my arms above my head dramatically. "I guess I'll drag myself out of bed."

"Mmmm," he hummed, rolling and pinning me to the mattress again. "Not if you keep stretching like that. I can't believe I'm saying this, but I think you need to put on some clothes or breakfast isn't going to happen."

He leaned in, kissing me softly, but just as I was about to wrap my arms around him and make things less...soft, he pulled away, rolling over and pushing himself off the bed. While I really, *really* enjoyed watching Luke walk across the room to grab a pair of boxers from his dresser, the bed felt cold and empty without him. I was torn between wanting him back in bed with me and enjoying the view across the room.

After he made the unfortunate decision to put on the boxers and a t-shirt, he continued to dig through his drawers, pulling a few things out in the process.

"They'll be big, but they're better than nothing," he said, placing the clothes on the bed. "Well, maybe not better than nothing."

Looking so much like the boy I knew in high school with his crazy bed hair and devilish smile, he winked at me and walked out of the room, leaving me alone to change. While Brooding Luke gave me goosebumps in high school, and Sweet Luke made me swoon, Flirty Luke was definitely my new favorite.

I grabbed the navy blue t-shirt he left at the edge of the bed, and threw it on. Once I pulled on the shorts, I stopped in the bathroom quickly to freshen up. By the time I walked into the kitchen, he was pouring milk into two bowls of cereal on the counter.

"What you're cooking smells delicious," I teased.

"Have a seat, smart ass," he replied, motioning to one of the high stools at the counter. I hopped onto a stool, looking out the window as I settled in. I could see across the Sound toward Bainbridge from his living room window. He really had an amazing view...and not just the naked kind. I envied that he woke up to that every morning.

"My specialty," he said, coming up behind me and placing a bowl of Cheerios on the counter. He took the seat across from me, smiling as he sat down.

"I *really* like you in my shirts."

"Me too," I replied. "That's why I'm keeping it."

He dipped his spoon into the bowl, shaking his head and laughing. Maybe Happy Luke was my new favorite. Maybe I didn't need to pick a favorite.

While I wasn't a big cereal eater, I took a few bites, trying not to slurp like an animal. Luke seemed focused on his breakfast, not looking up much, and saying very little. For the first time since Danielle's dinner party on Tuesday, the conversation stalled. For the first time since Tuesday, I started to worry that we had run out of things to talk about. As he quietly poked around at his bowl, I couldn't help but wonder what had caused him to withdraw so suddenly. I had to know what he was thinking.

"Well, clearly, you never ate cereal at home because if you had, Grace would have told you not to play with your food," I said, attempting to draw him back.

"What?" he asked.

"You okay over there? You looked really distracted."

"Oh...yeah...um...I was wondering...are you free tonight?"

That was a surprise.

"Tonight? Yeah. Why?"

"I want to take you out. On a date," he replied, looking serious and determined—like this would involve some major negotiation. Did he really think I was going to say no?

"*That's* why you got so quiet?" I didn't want to laugh at him, but it seemed so silly.

"Well, I *have* monopolized a lot of your time. If you'd rather wait until the weekend..."

"No, I don't want to wait." We'd wasted too much time already.

"Good. I don't either," he said, and I melted because he looked so goddamn cute when he glanced down at his bowl and stirred the milk around before looking up at me again. The silly, shy smile never left his face. We were grinning at each other like a couple of fools, and anyone who walked into the kitchen at that moment would have thought there was something wrong with us. Maybe there was. Maybe time travel had done something to my brain because all I wanted to do was smile and stare at him.

"This is exciting," I added. "If this is a date, I was promised some smooth moves."

"I think you've seen *all* my moves," he replied, never missing a beat. I was probably blushing, but I wasn't going to let that stop me.

"I have a hard time believing that."

"Well, I may have a trick or two up my sleeve."

"That sounds promising. But wait, I thought you needed to be at the bar tonight." He may not have been monopolizing my time, but I was definitely monopolizing his.

"I need to check-in since I haven't been in since Monday, but I don't need to stick around. Peter's good. He has the place covered, and Carl's working with him tonight. I could pick you up at seven?"

"Seven sounds good. I have an article to write about a new restaurateur that I have to work on today."

"Yeah? Sounds really dull."

"No, it's a pretty interesting story. The owner rode a bike and wore a badass leather jacket in high school, even had a super hot tattoo, but he gave it all up to become the Donald Trump of Greater Seattle."

"Gave it up?" he asked, raising one brow and looking deliciously cocky. "Did I say I gave my bike up?"

"Wait. You still have it?"

"Play your cards right, and I may give you a ride."

My heart started racing and my stomach suddenly felt jumpy. I couldn't even explain why something so little would have such an effect. Just the idea of riding on his bike again gave me chills.

"Tonight?"

He nodded slowly, clearly aware of how affected I was. And I was really affected.

"So," he said, grabbing my bowl along with his and carrying them to the sink. "I should probably get you home so you can work on that article. Sounds like you have a really good handle on this guy."

Luke clearly enjoyed the upper hand a little too much. I followed him across the kitchen. When he turned around, I backed him up against the counter, trapping a hand on either side. It was obvious that he found this funny because he could barely contain his laughter. I'd show him funny.

"Not as good as the *handle* I had on him last night," I said, brushing my lips against his ear. And he liked that, or maybe he remembered exactly how much of a handle I had because when he kissed me, it wasn't soft or gentle. It was the kind of kiss you threw everything into. It was the kind of kiss you see in movies and think "that doesn't happen in real life". It was the kind of kiss I wanted from him every day.

When he drove me home, I wore the t-shirt from his bar and the oversized pair of sweats. He walked me up the stairs and I leaned against the door as he kissed me. He made it nearly impossible to behave rationally.

"See you at seven?" he asked against my lips, but I didn't respond. I could only nod so that my lips grazed his on each pass. He pulled back, laughing, and kissed my forehead before jogging down the stairs.

I needed to work on being more coherent.

When I opened the door to the apartment, I was surprised to see Megan sitting inside on the couch. She had her feet up on the coffee table and her cellphone against her ear.

"I'm seeing the florist in a half-hour," she said to the person on the other end. The sound of the door closing caused her to turn around. She narrowed her eyes at me, eying the t-shirt and sweats.

"That reminds me, Nate," she said, speaking in a much louder voice. "Jillian didn't even come home last night. I've barely seen the girl since she left Danielle's house. God knows what they've been up to. You know what they say—it's always the quiet ones."

I grabbed a magazine from the table by the door and launched it at her head. She ducked, narrowly missing a face full of *Entertainment Weekly*.

"Oh, what a coincidence! She just walked in...no, I'm not going to ask her that...I'm sure he did. Listen, I'll call you after the florist....love you more."

"Nice, Megan," I sneered, walking past her into my room.

"Not so fast, hot stuff. I need some information," she said, following behind me.

"I'm not giving you a play-by-play, Meg, so forget it."

"And I'm not asking. I'll wait until you have a few cocktails in you, and I'm sure you'll give it up willingly," she stated, matter-of-factly. "I just want to know if you're happy."

And as much as I wished that the magazine had actually made contact with her face, this was why Megan meant so much to me. I'm sure she had a hundred questions, but the one she chose to ask reminded me of why I loved her so much.

"Yeah, I'm happy. I didn't think you could get this happy. I think I've been cheated. You and Danielle have been experiencing a whole level of happy I didn't even know existed."

"Wow," she replied, staring at me with wide eyes. "Look at you."

"What?" I asked, looking in the mirror. She was staring at something, and I wondered if there was a gross hickey on my neck or something.

"You guys didn't even leave the house yesterday, did you?"

"Megan!" I exclaimed, growing impatient. "For your information, we drove to Reynolds as planned and had...well, *a lot* of food at his aunt and uncle's house."

"And you spent the night on his couch, I'm sure," she added, smirking.

"I thought you weren't asking for a play-by-play?"

"I'm not. This has been a decidedly G-rated conversation. I'm just trying to figure out *when* the rolling around on the floor took place."

"I'm hopping in the shower. Are we done here?"

"Shower. Good idea. Definitely needed after hot monkey sex."

When I grabbed the pillow off my bed, Megan lunged for the doorway. This time, when I launched it at her, I didn't miss.

I managed to spend some time fleshing out the article throughout the day, but I was obviously distracted. It was amazing how so many words led me to think about Luke—mouth-watering, succulent, meat—not to mention skewered. I never realized food could be so dirty. Every time I used one of those words, I'd think about Luke...and his bike...and Luke *on* his bike...and me on Luke on his bike. It was a vicious cycle that led to a very unproductive day.

By six-thirty, I was practically climbing the walls and full of nervous energy. While the prospect of riding on Luke's bike had filled my mind with lurid fantasies all day, it also made the process of choosing an outfit that much more complicated. I spent an hour obsessing over what to wear and whether to pull back my hair. Dressing for a first date with the love of your life was not easy.

When I heard the knock on my front door, I drew a deep breath before swinging it open. I almost had to clutch the edge of the door jamb to steady myself.

"Hey," he said, smiling brightly.

If he had come directly from the bar, you couldn't tell. Everything was just so very right—dark jeans, gray shirt and a vintage leather jacket. My plan to be more coherent was already in jeopardy.

"You look..."

"...beautiful," he interrupted. "That color..." As he stared at my red sweater, he licked his lips and laughed. "You know, you had this...I can't believe I'm telling you this. You had this red shirt in high school."

He ducked his head down, still smiling and laughing to himself. "I liked it a lot."

I could feel my face flame. While I remembered everything as though it had happened yesterday, more than ten years had passed for Luke. It didn't occur to me that he might remember details as clearly as I did.

"I think I know the shirt you're talking about. I wore it the day we went to..."

"...Tacoma," he added. "Yeah, that's the one."

Earlier in the day, I had mocked Megan for suggesting that we hadn't left Luke's bed in two days. It suddenly seemed like a great idea for a first date. I wondered if he'd agree.

"So, are you ready?" he asked. "We can go over our options."

"We have options?"

"This is me being smooth."

"Oh, I see. Don't let me interrupt, then. It's totally working."

"Wow, and I'm not even trying yet," he replied. "Come on. We'll walk and talk," he said, extending his hand. I threaded my fingers through his, and he squeezed my hand and drew me closer.

"So, we have reservations at a French restaurant in Belltown. I don't know how you feel about French food, but it's quiet there. We'll be able to talk...or not," he explained, rubbing his thumb along the back of my hand. "We also have reservations at an amazing seafood place by the Market, if you'd like that instead."

"Wait. You made reservations at two restaurants?" Most guys couldn't remember to make reservations at all.

"I'm covering all my bases. You're very opinionated."

"And you're adorable," I said, stopping short in the middle of the lobby and pulling him by the hand toward me. I raised my arms up and twisted my fingers into the hair at the back of his neck. He took the hint and leaned down, pressing his lips to mine. I couldn't believe he had done something so thoughtful and sweet, but then again, Luke had always been thoughtful and sweet. I shouldn't have been surprised.

When he pulled back, he held our embrace and we stood wrapped up in each other.

"If you're this impressed by the reservations, I'm dying to see your reaction once I actually feed you," he laughed. "But before you make your decision, there's a third option."

"There's more?"

"If you're not hungry, we don't need to go to the restaurant right away—"

"I like where this is going," I added, working my fingers back into his hair.

"It's not going where you think it's going," he said, giving me a look of disapproval. "At least not until later."

"Later sounds promising."

"Focus," he laughed, dipping his head down and widening his eyes. "Instead of going to the restaurant right away, we can take a ride on my bike first."

"Not what I thought you were going to say, but I think I like that idea."

"Don't worry," he said, speaking in a low voice directly against my ear. "I think you'll like what I have planned for dessert."

I'm sure he could feel my entire body go limp. I tried to cover it up by pretending to stumble. I'd rather he think I was a klutz than a fainter.

"Okay, then," he added. "Bike first, food second, dessert later." He really needed to stop that if he wanted to leave the building.

He pushed the lobby doors open and I walked out into the crisp air. It would be pretty cold on the bike, but I really didn't care. Luke came up behind me and I felt his warm hand on the small of my back. He guided me over to a bike that most definitely wasn't what he owned in high school.

"*That's* your bike?!"

I knew nothing about motorcycles other than the fact that Luke's old bike clearly looked like he had rebuilt it himself. This one certainly did not. It was really silver and really shiny and looked really, really expensive.

"Yeah. It's a great bike. My old bike was a far cry from a Harley...but I liked it," he replied. "This one's pretty fast."

"How fast?" I asked, getting nervous.

"Are you scared?" he asked, smirking again.

I shook my head and grabbed his hand. "No. No, I'm not."

He handed me a shiny black helmet, and I braced my hand on his shoulder as I climbed on. I guess it didn't really matter if I wore my hair up or not. When he slid into the seat in front of me, I wrapped my arms around his waist, breathing in the dull scent of smoke and leather.

"Don't let go," he said, lifting up to kick-start the bike. It wasn't something he'd need to tell me twice. Letting go wasn't an option now.

As we made our way through the congested city streets, we couldn't travel particularly fast, but the cold air was still biting at my skin. I pressed my cheek to his back and squeezed tighter, closing my eyes and knowing that there was nothing in the world better than this.

As soon as we passed through the city traffic and headed out toward the Sound, Luke shifted gears, and everything changed. Unlike my experience on his old bike, this time I would have sworn there was a rocket attached to the motor. We flew along the highway with the wind pulling at our bodies. I held on tight, loving the rush of adrenaline; I wasn't sure if it was from the speed or from Luke.

I couldn't stop the giggling and laughing and pure joy I was feeling. I loved the chill on my face and the smell of the salt in the air. I loved watching the terrain as it whipped by and the water as we approached. I loved trying to move just a little bit closer and holding on just a little tighter. I loved that I was here. And I loved that I was with him.

I had assumed that we were riding aimlessly along the coast until Luke pulled into a gravel parking lot. There were a few cars parked overlooking the Sound. Slowing down, he steered the bike onto a worn-down path, stopping when he reached the rocky edge of a cliff. From far away, it hadn't seemed so scary. Now that I was looking down into the Sound, I was intimidated by how high up we actually were.

Luke snapped the kick-stand down, and hopped off, turning to offer me a hand once he righted himself. Once I was off the bike, I was able to look clearly out at the water. The sky was full of bright stars—just like it had been so many years ago, and off in the distance, I could make out the snowy summit of Mount Rainier. It was breathtaking.

Grasping my hand, he led me over to the ledge, and I marveled at the water below. It was a really long way down.

"It's beautiful here," I sighed.

"It's just a place I come sometimes. I thought you'd like it."

I stared down at the water cascading along the rocks, only the white caps visible in the darkness. He pulled me into his chest and wrapped his arms around me as we listened to the waves crashing below. With my face pressed to his chest, I stared out at the dark, black water, and for the first time in a very, very long time, I felt like everything had fallen into place.

For us, it had always been about numbers—a month, ten years, three weeks. But to me the numbers didn't matter anymore. I knew the day I met him that my life had changed forever—everyone's lives changed forever.

So I would hold his hand and stand at the edge of the world, so ready to make that leap of faith. So sure that he was it for me. So grateful for a second chance.

I would hold his hand at the edge of the world, hoping that the month we spent together in high school meant as much to him as it meant to me. Hoping that the ten years we spent apart didn't spoil that. Hoping the three weeks we spent dancing around these feelings would lead us to something bigger and better and permanent.

I hoped that, like me, he was ready to close his eyes and jump because I'd do it in a second if he asked. When I was with him, I was never afraid.

CHAPTER 26

Lake

I never believed in fate. I believed in timing—good timing and bad timing. Everything boiled down to being at the right place at the right time…or not. Jillian walked into my life a month before school ended, six weeks before she was scheduled to move across the country. Even if things between us hadn't gotten so screwed up, the timing was bad. Maybe we'd have made it work. But maybe not.

When we met again, more than ten years later, everything just fell into place. *We* fell into place—living in the same city, at the same time, surrounded by the same group of friends. Timing was everything.

But suddenly, bad timing was keeping me up at night.

Megan was about to marry Nate and officially move out of the apartment she shared with Jillian. In less than two weeks, Jillian would have no one to split the rent with and no one occupying the other rooms. Keeping the apartment obviously didn't make any sense unless she looked for a roommate, but who really wanted to go through that hassle? She needed a new place to live.

I wanted that place to be with me.

While we had only been back together for two months, it had been a pretty amazing two months. We spent Thanksgiving in Reynolds with Carter and Grace. Although Jillian was a little hesitant, I insisted she stay with us. She could have easily stayed with her parents, but I convinced her that it would be easier to help Grace prepare if she was staying with us instead. I couldn't tell her I had ulterior motives. Every time I thought about going back to Reynolds, I would think about her, in my room, teasing me. I would think about how I never got to see her in my bed, and would ultimately get myself pretty damn worked up. So even though Grace wasn't exactly thrilled—despite my reminder that we were adults—I got my wish. And it was worth finally seeing Dream Jillian asleep in my bed.

By Thanksgiving morning, Grace was on such a food high, nothing fazed her. She informed me, in no uncertain terms, that the cranberry sauce Jillian made needed to be added to the restaurant menu immediately. She was coming up with new dishes every day, continually adding to our already lengthy menu. It made her happy and it *was* her namesake, but I knew if she didn't settle down, I'd need to intervene, and I really didn't want to intervene.

We spent Christmas again in Reynolds, but with Jillian's parents. Her dad made it very clear that I'd be staying with my own family in their house and not in a bed with his daughter. Apparently, the argument about being adults wasn't convincing enough for Henry. So I did the only logical thing I could think of. I jogged down the stairs at midnight, passing Carter who was drinking his milk and reading the newspaper at the kitchen table, just like when I was a kid. I grabbed my coat as he gave me the side-eye and left before he could dispense any advice.

I drove to her parent's house and parked down the street, walking past the yard that once had the yippy dog which was now, fortunately, gone. Unlike years ago, this time I wasn't filled with uncertainty. I found some small pebbles and began launching them at her window. I learned two things that night. One: I was a much better shot when I was eighteen—the pebbles careened off the roof, the siding, one even landed on her dad's car. Two: Cellphones are more effective than rocks.

After I called her and told her I was outside, she came out—all bedhead and beautiful. And I hadn't planned it. I hadn't even been thinking it consciously. But as I held her in my arms underneath the window I had pelted with rocks, both as a kid and now as an adult, it just hit me. So it wasn't over a candlelit dinner or some romantically-orchestrated date. I told Jillian I loved her as we froze in the driveway of her parent's house two days before Christmas. She told me she loved me too while wearing flannel pajamas and fuzzy slippers.

New Year's was spent with our friends in Seattle. There was dinner and dancing, a swing band and some champagne, but no countdown. Not for us. We slipped out before midnight to ring in the year together—alone—and it was the best New Year's celebration of my life.

Now, we were approaching Megan and Nate's wedding extravaganza, and her exodus from the apartment she shared with Jillian. Unfortunately, this coincided with the opening of my restaurant. Not the best timing.

So, while I wanted to plead my case and ask Jillian to move in with me, it felt all wrong. I was distracted. There was still so much to do before the opening. Grace and the kitchen staff were at odds because of her menu changes, and the final menu had yet to be...finalized. Overall, it was a hectic time.

I was impatient, though. I wanted this. It made sense. Maybe I was rushing things, but hell, she spent almost every night in my bed already. And I liked her there. I wanted her there. Her pans were in my kitchen because apparently mine sucked. Her Pop-Tarts were in my cabinet, and her disgusting vegetable juice was in my fridge. She belonged with me.

Despite my certainty, I decided it was best to wait until after the opening. I figured that once we settled in, I could sit down with her, and I'd do whatever it took to convince her to see things my way. Turning me down wasn't an option. It seemed like a good plan...until Jillian mentioned calling a realtor the day before the restaurant opened.

I managed to stall—just for a day, but I had run out of time. I couldn't wait until after the opening. I couldn't let her call a realtor. I had to ask her now. So instead of getting a good night's sleep the night before the restaurant opened, I was lying awake, staring at the ceiling, wondering if *it* would crash and *I* would burn. It wasn't an optimal situation. The timing...wasn't so good, but I was going to do it. I was going to open a restaurant, try to keep Grace from giving my staff a nervous breakdown, and ask Jillian to move in with me.

I wasn't going to get any sleep.

I remembered watching the numbers on the clock change from one to two and then from three to four. Somewhere between four and five, I drifted off. So when my alarm went off at six, I felt beat-up and hungover without ever having experienced the fun that usually preceded it. Definitely not the way to start this day.

"Luke, turn off the alarm. Don't get up," Jillian sighed, rolling over and throwing her arm across my chest. "It's so early."

I wanted to. God, I wanted to, but not today.

"I wish I could, but we have deliveries this morning. Grace has probably changed the menu ten times already, and both the fire department and the health inspector are coming by. It's going to be brutal."

"Tell them you had some inspecting to do at home," she added, running her fingers through the hairs on my chest.

"Baby, you're killing me," I groaned, lifting her hand and placing it back onto the bed.

"Fine," she pouted, rolling over and pulling the covers up over her shoulder. "I'm going back to sleep if you're not going to entertain me."

One thing was for sure, Jillian still knew how to goad me. I leaned over onto my side, pulling her against me, and she rolled her hips, pushing back.

345

"I can guarantee you'll be thoroughly entertained once I'm through with you this evening. So much so, you won't be complaining about the lack of entertainment again for quite some time."

"Promise?" she asked, stretching and arching her back. Unfortunately, my attempts to rattle her had done nothing but make me frustrated instead. She always seemed to gain the upper hand in our constant power-struggle. It might have had something to do with the fact that she was topless, but overall, she had me—topless or not.

"You can count on it," I replied, kissing her neck before rolling out of bed.

I fumbled around the room in the dark, blindly heading into the bathroom. Thanks to my bright idea and Jillian's subsequent grinding, I was already regretting my decision to get out of bed. Jerking off in the shower while my girlfriend was in the next room seemed to be a waste of a precious resource. If I wasn't sure that I was about to walk into a restaurant full of panicking new employees, I would have taken the time to "entertain" her before leaving for the day. But instead, I was faced with an unsatisfying, lonely shower.

When I stepped back into the bedroom with a towel slung around my waist, I expected to see Jillian sound asleep with her head hidden under a pile of pillows. She wasn't though. She was lying on her side watching me as I crossed the room.

"Are you just going to stare at me while I change, Cross?"

"That's the plan. Unless you need my help."

"You insist upon testing my willpower. Was I not good to you last night?"

"Too good. Maybe that's why," she replied, stretching again. I already felt my resistance weakening. "Maybe I want you again. Now drop the towel."

"On second thought," I shot back, trying to hide the grin on my face. "I may need your help after all."

Jillian rolled out of bed wearing one of my t-shirts. Everything about her looked good. She walked over to me slowly, a predatory look in her eyes.

"I think you have something I want, Chambers," she said, wrapping one hand around the back of my neck and dropping the other to the edge of the towel.

Maybe I could be a little late.

"And what's that?" I asked, officially waving a white flag.

"This." She pulled the towel roughly from my body and with a quick kiss on the lips, turned with it in her hand and waltzed into the bathroom, closing the door behind her. "Serves you right for turning me down."

"Come on," I whined, crossing the room toward the closed door. "Are you serious?" I tried the knob, but was only met with resistance. "You really locked the door?"

"I don't want you to be late, Luke," she sang from inside. I heard the unmistakable sound of my shower turning on. While it was my idea to get a head start without any distractions, I had changed my mind, or at least her boobs had changed my mind. At any rate, her punishment didn't fit the crime.

Groaning, I got dressed...uncomfortably, and made my way to the kitchen. I grabbed one of her Pop-Tarts, which were actually pretty decent, and was looking for my messenger bag when she came out of the bedroom, freshly showered, with her hair piled on top of her head.

"You don't fight fair, Cross," I said, glaring at her. Maybe I was glaring *and* checking out her legs.

"Poor Luke," she replied, with a pout. "Don't you have more important things to brood over today?

"I'm not brooding," I shot back. "You're a tease."

"Just a little," she countered, lifting herself up on her toes and brushing her lips across mine. "But you love me."

"I do," I replied, wrapping my arms around her waist.

I very nearly asked her right then, but I knew it was a bad idea—bad timing. If she said no—even if she wanted some time to think it over—I'd spend the rest of the day obsessing over her answer. I needed to be focused. I'd worked too hard to screw up the opening.

"You'll come at four?" I asked, changing the subject.

"I'll probably be there early. In case you need help with anything," she said, gazing up at me. I should have been thinking about the restaurant. I should have been thinking about all of the things that needed to be accomplished, but all I could think about was how I wanted to see that smile every morning.

When I arrived at the restaurant, as I had suspected, it was mayhem. Deena, the hostess I had just hired, was pacing in the lobby and chewing her nails.

"Mr. Chambers, Louis would like to see you in the kitchen," she said, nervously. "He's...upset."

Louis Bruneux had applied for the master chef position having only arrived in the US a few weeks prior. Our views on the bill of fare differed, but he brought a lot of experience and ideas to the table. I found that even when we disagreed, things turned out significantly better when we compromised. We worked well together, and I felt secure turning the kitchen over to him so that I could focus on managing the day-to-day tasks. If he was upset, I was upset.

Just as I was about to push through the swinging doors to the kitchen, I heard the clatter of pans as Louis marched into the dining room.

"Luke, you're here. Mon dieu! We have a situation," he said in a tone that made me feel like he wanted to pat me on the back and kick my ass at the same time. "Your aunt. She is...lovely. But I cannot prepare for the opening with these changes. Five today already. The menu, Luke. It must be final."

"I'm so sorry, Louis. Grace is just...excited. I'll speak with her as soon as she arrives."

"Arrives? Luke. She has been in my kitchen since daylight."

Letting out a slow breath, I pushed through the doors into the kitchen to find Grace bent over a large pot, surrounded by the entire kitchen staff.

"Next, you'll add in the garlic, ginger, sugar, and pineapple juice. Stir it up and let it simmer over medium heat. You have to keep a close eye, though. No walking away," she instructed, stirring the contents.

"Grace, hey. What's...going on?"

"Oh, Luke!" She started toward me but stopped, handing the spoon to my sous chef. "Continue stirring, dear," she said before making her way over and pulling me into an embarrassingly parental hug.

"I'm making the most amazing pineapple curry sauce to drizzle over the pistachio encrusted tuna."

"Grace," I began, leading her away from the crowd and back into the dining room. "There isn't any pistachio encrusted tuna on the menu."

"Oh, there is now. I spoke to Louis this morning. We already have the tuna steaks and I think it would fill that gap we have in the seafood offerings."

"There is no gap in the seafood menu. We have plenty of seafood to offer. I have a distributor arriving with a car full of fresh fish to prove it."

"I know, but wait until you try the sauce."

"Grace. The menu is final."

"But—"

"Grace, please," I pleaded. "If one of the menu items we're offering isn't a hit, we'll re-evaluate and make some substitutions. But for now, let Louis focus on the dishes we've already discussed."

"I'm sorry, Luke," she replied, shaking her head. "I just want everything to be perfect. You've worked so hard—"

"I know you're just trying to help, and believe me, I appreciate it. I just need to keep complications to a minimum tonight. I need everything to go smoothly."

And that included my talk with Jillian—whenever that took place. Added conflict was not welcome.

"All right, then. What can I do to help?"

"You can make sure that Deena understands the layout of the floor while I check the delivery schedule," I suggested.

Content with an actual task to accomplish, she smiled widely, patting me on the shoulder before heading to the hostess station to find Deena.

With Louis free to prepare the kitchen and Grace occupied with the front of the house, I was able to focus on the food deliveries and last minute prep. While the fire department and the health inspector did their final walk-throughs, I headed to the office in the back to finish up some paperwork.

Everything was running pretty smoothly...until it wasn't. And when it went to hell, it happened all at once. It started when the seafood distributor shorted us on our crab shipment, leaving not nearly enough for a dinner service. While I argued with him about rectifying the issue, time was ticking away and I finally had to pull it from the menu before it was too late. Then new menus needed to be printed and swapped out with the old. The whole process sucked up a huge amount of time.

Just as I was about to head back to the office, the fire alarm sounded. I assumed it was part of the fire department's test, but when it didn't stop, I rushed to see what was going on.

"You got some old wiring here, son," the officer yelled, pointing at the ceiling.

"What does this mean?" I asked, attempting to focus despite the deafening sound.

"Well, this switch here," he replied, pointing to a button on the control panel, "should turn off the alarm after a test. It doesn't."

Clearly.

"You're going to need to get your alarm company out here," he said.

I rushed out to the front of the restaurant, far away from the shrill sound, to make the call. I barely acknowledged Jillian, who was sitting at one of the tables helping Grace with the menus. I hated that I didn't have time to talk to her.

Once I got our alarm service company on the phone, I needed to speak to two associates and a manager before I was told a technician would be dispatched right away. So much for customer service.

When I walked back inside, Jillian rushed over to me with her hands covering her ears.

"What'd they say?"

"They're sending someone out now," I replied, feeling my chest constrict. The day was not going well, and definitely not as planned.

"It'll be fine, you know," she said. And it *would* be fine if she gave up her apartment and turned *my* place into *our* place. I could have easily forgotten everything—Louis, the menu, the blaring siren—and lost myself in her. She made everything better. I couldn't, however, forget that Grace was in the room, and we had subjected her to enough PDA during our menu-testing non-date.

A half-hour later, the alarm was off, but they were still working on the wiring. Instead of the constant siren, we were subjected to the occasional shrill spinning of a power drill. Neither were particularly conducive to a relaxing meal.

But the alarm technician finally finished, and soft music filtered into the dining room instead of a blaring siren. The doors opened, and patrons arrived. Mistakes happened. The valet I hired didn't show up, and one of the waiters tripped. But overall, once the night began, the service went off without a hitch. The place was packed, and I was sure that Jillian's article had a lot to do with that. There were also rumblings that a food critic was in the dining room, and I prayed that the waitress who dropped the risotto wasn't assigned to that section.

When I had a minute to stop and think and finally take a breath, it was late, and my body ached. The last patrons were finishing their meals and the kitchen was closing. Disappointment set in as I realized I would probably have to wait until tomorrow to talk to Jillian. I was tired and cranky, and the day had just been long and draining. With most of the kinks worked out, I knew tomorrow would be better, but I hated that I'd have to spend another day wondering how she'd answer.

"Luke, we're taking off," Carter announced, his arm wrapped tightly around Grace's waist. I don't know why I even noticed where his arm was. It wasn't out of the ordinary for him to hold her that way. Maybe it was how she leaned slightly against him. Maybe it was the way they seemed to meld together. It struck me suddenly, but so clearly, how much I envied them. I wanted what they had. And now that I had found it, I didn't want to waste time.

While a minute before I had decided to put off talking to her, I was suddenly convinced that it needed to happen now.

"Drive safe," I said, pulling him in for a one-armed hug and kissing Grace on the cheek.

"We're proud of you," he said before turning. "They would have been, too." With a tight smile, no doubt thinking of his big brother, my father, who should have been here to see this, he led Grace outside.

When I walked back out front, the wait staff was mopping, cleaning and clearing tables. I scanned the room and saw Jillian sitting in the corner laughing with Danielle, Megan, Josh and Nate. It reminded me of the first time I looked across the room and saw them all together at my bar. So much had changed, so much was different. One thing was the same.

"Luke, man, excellent night," Nate said, standing and shaking my hand. "Scallops were amazing. Meg didn't like the truffle salt on her fries, but personally I thought it was great."

"Jesus, Nate. Do you have a filter?" she sneered. "Ignore him, Luke. I loved my meal. I just apparently only like the kind of truffles that are chocolate-covered."

"No worries, Megan. They're not my thing, either," I replied.

351

When I finally looked over at Jillian, her eyes were shining and she was beaming. I wondered if she'd been drinking too much wine. She stood up and walked to me, her arms encircling my waist.

"You did it," she said, pressing her head against my chest.

And something shifted. Good timing. Bad timing. It was all bullshit. We spent so much of our time together worrying about whether our timing was good. No more. When it was right and good, you didn't need to plan the perfect time or place or way to tell someone how you felt. Timing didn't matter—not for us.

"Let's get out of here," I whispered to her.

"Okay," she said, searching my eyes. Maybe she could tell something had shifted, too.

We said our hurried goodbyes, and I left Louis to lock-up for the night. Our hands rested, joined together on the center console of my car, as I sped through the city back to my condo. All of the uncertainty and nervousness I had been feeling seemed to have been released. I had never been so sure of anything in my life.

Laughing and smiling like a fool, I pulled her across the parking lot, past George the security guard and into the elevator. Once inside, I held her face in my hands, kissing her lips—wet, firm, rough, and perfect. I wasn't holding back.

"I love you," I said, not taking the time to move away, speaking the words into her lips, pressing them into her skin. My own tattoo.

"So much," she replied, silencing me, pushing me against the wall like she had after Danielle's party, the night that changed everything. Now it was time to change everything again.

When the door opened, I led her by the hand over to the couch that faced the distant lights she had come to love so much.

"Today was crazy. You really have no idea." I was pacing and I couldn't stop.

"I know," she replied, chuckling.

"No, I don't think you do." I wanted to laugh at how absurd and perfect this was. "I made a decision the other day. I decided that I didn't care that we've only been together for a short time. Time doesn't matter because it's different with us, right?"

I needed her to tell me 'yes'. I needed to know she felt the same way. When we agreed to be together, we knew that going into this lightly could break us. With that knowledge came a certain understanding—we were in this for keeps. I needed to know she felt that, too.

"I'm not exactly following."

"Jillian, I don't want to pretend like we're a normal couple who just started dating. We're not. We're more than that." I looked over to her, suddenly feeling sheepish, only to see her nod slowly that she understood.

"So, I spent all day dealing with one problem after another, but through it all, what kept me going was the fact that I was going to ask you to move in with me—here—when it was all over." She gasped, but I didn't let it stop me. I couldn't stop now.

"But that's not what I want."

"Wait. You were going to ask me to move in with you, but you changed your mind, so now you're not?"

"No. I mean, no, that's not what I meant," I laughed, feeling crazy, delirious.

"I don't want you just to live with me. I want this. Us. All the time. Forever." I dropped down on my knees in front of her and grabbed both her hands. "I don't have a ring, but I'll buy you the biggest, the best...whatever you want...anything. Just marry me."

"What?" she gasped, stiffening. I knew I caught her off-guard; hell, I caught *myself* off-guard, but I was determined.

"Marry me," I repeated, softer, pleading. I had no shame when it came to this girl. I never had.

She stared at me silently, smiling, her eyes glassy and wet.

"Yes," she said.

Screw timing.

EPILOGUE

Jillian

B ehind the dark wooden counter stood a man—not just any man. Mine. I watched his back muscles flex beneath his crisp oxford shirt as he twisted the towel around a glass, and then returned it to the drying rack. It didn't matter that he had people to do this for him—mostly college kids who, like him, had been looking to find their place in the world. He never said it, but I knew he wanted to be to them what Jonas was to him. He told me once that he would have been lost without the bar when he thought that he'd never see me again. It was everything to him, and he enjoyed the work—even more than the restaurant with its reviews and acclaim. The bar, after all, was his baby…at least his first one.

"What do I need to do to get some service around here?" I asked, settling down on one of the barstools. I crossed my legs, allowing my skirt to fall away from my upper thigh. He turned around, his brown hair messy up top and his smile crooked as his gaze rested on my legs.

"I'm fairly certain you've been served quite well," he replied with an evil smirk.

"That may be true."

"But since today is a special day," he added, coming out from behind the bar, "I might be able to help you."

"Today's a special day? Remind me again?" I teased.

"I think I reminded you last night," he replied, whispering in my ear, "and this morning before work and again in the shower."

Yes, yes he did. I could still see the look in his eyes when he had tackled me in our bedroom. I had been rundown and exhausted, but he transformed my fatigue from the wrong type of tired into the kind that was so very right.

"I think I may need you to refresh my memory," I murmured, arching as his lips swept across my shoulder. I grabbed the back of his head as he trailed his tongue along my neck, nipping and teasing before descending on my lips, leaving me breathless and unsteady.

355

"Happy Anniversary, baby" he said softly, grabbing my hand and spinning the rings on my finger.

"Happy Anniversary," I replied. "So, where're you taking me?"

"Where am I taking you?"

Furrowing his brow, looking as if this was a question he needed to contemplate, he turned toward the bar and placed his palms flat on the hard surface. Pressing down so that the muscles in his arm tensed, he bounced on the balls of his feet, testing its sturdiness.

"Here's good," he said, smirking. "And don't even pretend you haven't thought about it," he added just as I raised my hand to smack his arm.

"I may have thought about it," I replied, feeling my face heat up. "That doesn't mean I'd do it."

"Um, yes, you would."

"What? No way. Do you know me at all?"

"I know everything about you, which makes me even more certain that yes—if you were worked up enough—you'd have sex with me...right here," he said, running his hand along the wood.

"You're delusional. You know that, right? Now, I'll ask you again. Where are you taking me...for our anniversary dinner?"

"You used to be fun," he pouted. "Is this what happens after you've been married for a year? The thrill is gone? It's all business? If you're going to be that way, I don't think I'll tell you."

"Oh, really?" I shot back. "Then I guess you won't be getting your present either."

"Present? Jillian, I told you I didn't want you buying me a present," he replied, pulling me back into his arms. "I have everything I want."

"Trust me. You don't have this. But if you're going to be a brat, I'll just give it to you some other time."

I pushed off his chest, attempting to wriggle away, but his grip around my waist only tightened.

"I can be very persuasive," he said lowly. My body was suddenly heavy in his arms as I felt his warm breath against my ear. He still had that affect on me.

"If you don't stop that, we'll never get to...wherever we're going," I replied, not sounding particularly convincing. "And I'm hungry."

"Mmmm," he groaned, dragging his lips along my jaw. "Me too."

"Luke," I panted, torn between wanting him and knowing that an anniversary celebration where we didn't leave the bar was lame. "Dinner."

I felt him laugh against my skin, shaking his head and pressing his lips one more time against my throat.

"We'll finish this later," he muttered, issuing a threat that wasn't very threatening.

When he looked up at me and smiled, I thought back to the black and white picture on the Facebook profile that now never happened. I remembered wanting so badly to be the one that made him happy. I wanted to be the one that made him smile with his eyes. Now though, his smile—the one I saw every day—was even better. It wasn't black and white, but real and mine.

The night he proposed to me, Luke told me that time didn't mean anything to us. Little did he know, the laws of physics didn't mean anything to us either. I would never understand how I ended up where I was or why, but I believed everything happened for a reason. I believed that I was always supposed to be here—in his arms—gazing at the creases in the corner of his eyes. I would never grow tired of that place.

"Do you know when I first realized I had fallen in love with you?" he asked, suddenly serious. "That day in Tacoma. I wanted to break Dice's hands every time he touched you, and don't think I didn't notice how he looked at you."

"If I remember correctly," I replied. "He was the first one to call me out about my feelings for *you*. He didn't think he could compete."

"I'd have liked to see him try. I was pretty determined," he said, laughing to himself. He looked up at me, long lashes and deep green eyes. "I wouldn't have given him a chance, Jillian. I always knew."

One of the things I loved about Luke the most was that he said exactly what he felt, exactly when he was feeling it. He never held back with me so I didn't with him. I reached for him, pulling him toward me, kissing him until I was breathless. After all this time and all we'd been through, something so little still meant so much.

"I love you," I said, holding him close and smiling against his soft lips as my hands began to wander.

"Jillian," he said, backing away and holding me at arm's length. "I'm going to have to ask you to settle down." He was fighting to keep a straight face, but it wasn't working. "There's no time for groping. Is it always about sex with you? Try to get a hold of yourself."

Mr. Sex-on-the-Bar was mocking me, and *that* was the last straw. Pouncing, I dug my fingers into the skin on either side of his ribs until he doubled over, trying desperately to beg for mercy. Luke, I had learned, was ridiculously ticklish. I found the sensitive spots along his sides in the dark when I would run my fingers along his back, memorizing the dips and curves of his muscles. While I had hoped to make him moan, he would twist and giggle instead. It took a little time to discover that Luke was ticklish everywhere. I didn't use his weakness against him often—only when I really needed to get my way, or if he really pissed me off. Like now.

I stepped away, satisfied that I had enacted my revenge. "We'll finish this later," I added, mimicking him.

"Come on. Let's get you something to eat," he laughed, grabbing my hand and walking us out the door and over to the adjacent lot.

"I know you said you're starving," he began, climbing into his car, "but dinner isn't until seven."

"Seven? Luke. It's only four."

"Yeah, we have some time to kill."

I didn't ask a lot of questions as we passed through the city. We had decided earlier in the week that we wouldn't do anything really extravagant. We were breaking ground soon, building what Luke called our Little Love Shack. The "Little" Love Shack was going to be over three thousand square feet and perched upon a cliff. Now was not the time to blow a ton of cash on a flashy dinner. I didn't need that. I never needed that. I just wanted to be together.

Instead of pulling into one of the hundreds of restaurants in the city, we quickly passed the city limits and headed toward the highway which really confused me. Just because I didn't want him splurging on a five-course tasting menu at the Ritz didn't mean we needed to leave the area altogether. I was pretty certain that Seattle had quite a few romantic, yet practical, places to eat. We owned one of them, for God's sake.

When Luke began taking the route towards the 101, I knew where we were headed. I just didn't understand why.

"We're going to Reynolds?" I asked. "Are you making Grace cook for us?"

"I'm offended that you would think I'd stoop to something so pedestrian," he replied, theatrically bringing his palm to his chest.

"Grace's cooking is not pedestrian."

"Jillian, we eat at the restaurant all the time. I think you have your fair share of Grace's food. What type of anniversary dinner would that be?"

He had a point, but still, heading to Reynolds was surprising. While he didn't know this yet, I figured we'd be making a trip there tomorrow to see our families—they'd want to hear the news in person. We'd obviously be spending a great deal of time in the car this weekend.

Despite being a little hungry when we set out, time seemed to fly and we were suddenly on the familiar stretch of road leading into Tacoma.

"I'm thinking of getting another tattoo," Luke announced as we passed Ink Credible Art.

"Oh, really? Is it a tramp stamp? Oh, oh! A rose? Maybe a butterfly. No! Tinkerbell."

"Are you done?"

"Maybe. No."

"I like your Celtic cross design."

"Luke, it's totally weird if you get a cross, too. I'm just saying."

"I'm not getting a cross," he replied, losing patience. "I like the *design*. Something Celtic," he added. "Maybe our initials in a knot."

I was really overwhelmed that he had been considering something so permanent. I wasn't naive enough to believe that a tattoo solidified a relationship. I mean, everyone remembers Johnny Depp's Winona Forever and how that worked out for him. But I already knew we were solid. I knew we were permanent. He *was* my Forever, and I didn't need the ink to prove that. I just liked that he wanted it anyway.

"I love that," I replied, although I wondered how that design would change once he heard the news.

We passed through Tacoma without stopping. I was convinced that he was going to take me to The Greasy Spoon or somewhere we had gone back in the day. There was really no place to eat in Reynolds unless he wanted to eat at a strip mall, and despite having warned him about overdoing this first anniversary thing, a strip mall was not where I wanted to spend it—especially in light of the conversation we were about to have.

"Luke, where are we—"

"You, my beautiful, sexy wife, need to relax. And in approximately five minutes, you'll know exactly where we're going."

Sure enough, when we passed the overgrown entrance to the cliffs, he pulled over, parking along the road when his car wasn't able to make it through the brush.

Walking around to the trunk, he pulled an insulated tote out of the back and slung it over his shoulder.

"Can you grab the blanket for me?"

Grinning from ear to ear, I grabbed the soft, plaid blanket from the trunk and followed Luke as he ducked under branches and boughs until he reached the clearing.

We had never come back here. There was always a reason not to, and truth be told, I felt somewhat guilty. Luke told me that once I left, he couldn't drive past this place without thinking of me, the car, and that night. It was too painful. I hated that I ruined it for him.

As we walked through the tall grass, I could hear waves crashing below. The moon was high and full, casting a pale glow across the water. Finding a spot in along the rocky edge, I spread the blanket out as Luke unzipped the cooler and began to unload the contents.

He set down plates and glasses, a salad and some wine. *What a waste!* When he popped the lid off of a large, steaming container, I threw my head back, laughing at the contents inside.

"Veal saltimbocca? I thought you said Grace wasn't cooking for us tonight!"

"She didn't," he said, proudly. "She gave me the recipe."

"You made this?" I asked, fighting back tears because of the damn hormones. "When?"

"At the restaurant. Go ahead. Try it."

I settled down on the blanket, drawing my legs up underneath me. He watched anxiously as I grabbed a fork and knife and dove in. It was so rich and sweet that I moaned as soon as it hit my tongue.

"Luke, this is amazing. What did you do? It's better than Grace's," I whispered, feeling like it was wrong to admit that out loud.

"I'm glad you like it," he replied, dropping down onto the blanket next to me. "I was thinking about the night you invited yourself over to my going away dinner. I didn't eat very much. You were too distracting."

"I was *invited* by your gracious uncle, and you and your strawberries were far more distracting than I could ever be."

"Don't be so sure," he countered. "It's never been easy for me to focus when you're around. But I like that you distract me."

"And I like when we distract each other. Especially when we're distracting each other multiple times in the same day."

"See what I mean? It's always about sex with you."

"Oh, and that's not why we're here, Luke?"

"No, Jillian, that's not why we're here," he mimicked, sighing dramatically. "If I were recreating our last trip here, you'd be making smartass comments to a flask."

"Joan was epic but I didn't have her with me then," I countered.

"I like how you argue that it wasn't with you, not that you wouldn't have been talking to it. Embracing the crazy, I see."

"It doesn't matter. I don't need a talking flask anymore," I said, pulling myself up onto my knees, scooting closer and wrapping my arms around his neck. "Just you. You're all the crazy I need."

"I just need you, too," he replied, dragging me onto his lap. "And I love you and your crazy. It almost seems worth all the bullshit we've been through to be here. It's been the best year of my life."

If I didn't love my husband enough already, his words shot right through me, confirming what I knew all along. He was it for me, and luckily, I was it for him.

"And there's so much to look forward to. Next year on our anniversary, we'll be in the new house, looking out at the ocean—maybe getting ready to start a family."

My eyes had already begun to water listening to him talk so openly about how he felt. It was still overwhelming to hear him talk this way—to hear him mention kids and our future. I had only gone off birth control the prior month. For some people, it took years. For others, it didn't.

"Maybe I should tell you about your present. Well, it's not really a present for you. It's more of a present for us."

"What did you do?" he asked, and I laughed because I had definitely not done anything alone.

"Well, we won't have to wait until next year," I began, the tears in my eyes spilling over.

"What do you mean? What's wrong?"

"We have an appointment on Monday with Dr. Simonsen," I said slowly, making sure he was taking in everything I was saying. "I took a test this afternoon—"

Before I could finish the sentence, he was on me, wrapping his arms around my shoulders, pulling me into his chest and pressing his lips against my face.

"Oh my God. How? But it's only been…are you sure?"

"The nurse I spoke to said that it's easy to get a false negative, not a false positive. It's…yeah…I am."

"Oh God, what do we…should you be sitting on the ground? And Jesus, it's cold out and you're in a skirt. Let's get home and you can—"

"Luke," I yelled, interrupted his manic raving. "I'm fine. We're all fine. I want to be here. With you. Alone under the stars," I explained. "Because next year, Baby Chambers will be joining us."

"Baby Chambers," he said, echoing my words. "I don't believe it. I wonder what he'll look like."

"He? It's a he? You know this already?"

"It takes a man to make a man, Jillian."

"Oh, God. Is this what it's going to be like?"

"No," he said, pulling me into his side, curling up next to me. "It's going to be so much better."

We stared up at the sky watching the late summer meteor shower, as stars traveled from one end of the night to the other, wishing upon each of them.

"I wish for him to be smart."

"I wish for her to be a good person. And funny, I think she'll be funny."

"I wish for him or her to have a house full of brothers and sisters."

"I wish for him or her to have one. My uterus finds fault with your wish."

"I wish you weren't such a pain in the ass."

"I wish you'd kiss me."

And when we were wished out and almost ready to leave, Luke rolled over, staring, smiling, bursting with happiness.

"Do you ever wish that you could go back in time? Fix the crap we messed up?" he asked, so sweet, so innocent, so unaware of what he was asking. I loved him with every fiber of my being.

I stared back at him, eyes brimming and wide and full of so much love for me and the baby we hadn't met yet. I knew my answer.

"No," I replied. "Never."

·

CPSIA information can be obtained at www.ICGtesting.com
Printed in the USA
BVOW05s1607160415

396488BV00001B/68/P